Company Confidential

Company Confidential

TOM McCRORY

Writers Club Press
San Jose New York Lincoln Shanghai

Company Confidential

Writers Club Press
an imprint of iUniverse.com, Inc.

For information address:
iUniverse.com, Inc.
620 North 48th Street, Suite 201
Lincoln, NE 68504-3467
www.iuniverse.com

ISBN: 0-595-13740-7

This book is lovingly dedicated to the memory of
my grandmother, Glenna Wrather Turner

It was at her side that I first observed
the art of storytelling

ACKNOWLEDGEMENTS

Special thanks to my brother, John Patrick McCrory, for his able assistance and professional insights on all matters related to the U.S. Army. Any mistakes are mine.

Heartfelt thanks to Chris Patrick, the big brother I never had and my Bishop, California trout fishing guide. Thanks for never laughing at my dreams.

To Scott MacKnight, for letting me pick his black-belt brain regarding the martial arts, and helping me through various computer-induced headaches.

I wish to express my appreciation to Larry Sandlin—the best songwriter in Nashville—and his wife Lou Anne, for their encouragement and taking the time to proofread the first draft of my manuscript.

Thanks to Mark Van Hoomissen for all his patience and 24/7 assistance explaining programming applications to a caveman. Your friendship & enthusiastic reaction to "CC" is greatly appreciated.

I am indebted to my cousin, Bob Turner, Jr., for his time and technical expertise in developing my website, computer troubleshooting and avid support of this project.

To Terry Kay, for sharing his "Tips and Tricks of Writing." Your generosity, expertise and answering my myriad questions will always be remembered.

To Tom Bird, for giving me the map.

To Eli Rill, for all you taught me about character development and sense-memory.

I'd like to thank the following friends, who have been there since the inception of this idea all those years ago, for their support, encouragement and morale boosts: John Curlin; Dan Finn; Charles Haston, Jr.; Mychelle Henyon; Kathy Kepfer MacKnight; Nick Maxin and Louie (Shakespeare) Zambrano.

To my friends and colleagues of the Products Group at Siemens Building Technologies—thanks for making SBT a much more enjoyable and professional place to work than the fictional cesspool of "Campbell Industries."

Thanks to Dad and Marlene for your support.

I am grateful to my sister, Kristin O'Kelley, for her love, support and always appreciated warped sense of humor. Thanks also to my brother-in-law, Anthony Lockhart, whose conservative outlook always makes for great conversation.

I appreciate the love and encouragement of my mother, Karen and my stepfather, Jim Williams. Special thanks to my Mom for her skillful line editing, and for teaching me—by example—that goals can be accomplished through hard work and persistence.

I owe a debt of gratitude to my children, Ryan and Caitlin. Your unconditional love, beauty and indomitable spirit are my greatest source of strength and inspiration.

Finally, to my best friend and beautiful wife, Cyndy. Thank you so much for allowing me the time to struggle through this challenging endeavor. This would not have been possible if not for your love, faith, understanding and superb editorial assistance. I greatly appreciate the patience and tolerance you exhibit while being married to a dreamer.

CHAPTER I

REGINA ROGERS TRIED to block out the loud moaning coming from the office at the end of the mahogany paneled hallway. It was already 6:45 PM, and she had to finish up her data entry assignment and get home before the baby-sitter quit. Having skipped lunch wasn't making her task any easier. Her head pounded from hunger, stress and the obnoxious orgasmic choir permeating the office building. She tried to focus on her task, but couldn't prevent her thoughts from drifting to a time, not so long ago, when she was part of the struggle on the other side of Glenn's closed door. She thought to herself how time changes everything.

Re-focused, Regina keyed in the last of the report on her white Compaq PC, punched save, and shut off the power. Turning off her desk light, she reached for her purse in the now darkened cubicle. Fumbling for her keys as she walked down the dimly lit hallway to the front door, she quickly passed the last office door, and tried not to look at the gleaming brass letters spelling: GLENN STEVENS, REGIONAL VICE-PRESIDENT. Regina unlocked the twin glass front doors, stepped through and re-locked them behind her. She couldn't believe the sounds were still audible outside. She wondered if she was ever that loud. She knew she was that stupid. Catching a glimpse of her reflection in the door, Regina checked her appearance. It hurt to think how much she had let herself go. Her present job status and Glenn's unkind scrutiny were constant reminders.

Walking through the nearly deserted parking lot, her mind wandered to what the remainder of her evening had in store for her. After taking the sitter home, the homework counseling, and the *"How was your day?"* sessions with the kids, she hoped to unwind in silence. Thank God it was Thursday. After tomorrow, she would have the entire weekend to relax. Although she was not sure how much relaxation would be achieved between shuttling the kids back and forth to their commitments. It was sad to acknowledge she had nothing else to look forward to. Getting into her faded '87 Nissan Sentra, she couldn't help thinking that it wasn't supposed to turn out this way. As she sped from the empty parking lot, she rolled down her window and let the cool Southern California night air ensconce her.

Minutes later, a tall figure appeared behind the double glass doors. Through the gold lettering stating: CAMPBELL INDUSTRIES, INC., the red glow of a cigarette could be seen. The man peered out at the dusky parking lot, not really focused on anything. Breathing heavily, he continued to drag on the cigarette. His shirt was unbuttoned, and his face and chest glistened with perspiration. He was wearing black and white houndstooth dress slacks and polished black lace up dress shoes. He laughed to himself about the corporate office's no smoking policy, as he finished his cigarette. Fuck corporate, he thought.

His thoughts turned to his just completed encounter with a petite Latino half his age. Maria Lopez was the best "personal assistant" he had screwed around with in a long time. She was a raven-haired beauty with dark smoldering eyes. The bitch was certainly limber. She had an unbelievable body, and the sweetest disposition of anyone who had ever put up with his physical and mental abuse. It seemed nothing he could do or suggest was beneath her. She was very proficient at taking care of his needs, no matter how twisted. What money and power can get you. He smiled, amused at his thoughts.

Maria finished buttoning her blouse and held her breath. Standing alone in the center of his huge office, lit only by a desk lamp, she felt tiny. She was hoping to exit the building without running into Mr. Stevens again. As always, she felt so ashamed, and couldn't believe she had let herself get in so deep. She found it hard to believe that she endured this treatment for six months. The salary and perks made it hard to walk away, but she had reached her tolerance level. She often tried to justify this degrading existence by letting herself think it was her best financial option as a single mother. Maria had never made this kind of money before—and might not ever again—but it didn't matter. She was embarrassed by what she had become—a personal whore—and dreaded what her three-year old daughter would think of her if she ever found out. She would never let that happen. After listening to Dr. Laura's radio show for the past three months, she had gained the courage to walk away from her past and get a fresh start. No one, she thought, would blame her for quitting. She would just call Regina in the morning and it would be over. Looking around the dim, opulent office for what would be the last time; Maria breathed a deep sigh of relief.

Glenn walked in, looked at Maria with contempt, and closed the door. He made a big production out of removing his keys and locking it behind him. He turned quickly, and threw his keys against the wall. "Did I tell you to get dressed?" he asked her tersely.

"Mr. Stevens, I have to get home for my daughter," said Maria.

"Like I give a rat's ass about your family life," he snapped. "Now take your fucking clothes back off, bitch! I'll let you know when I'm through with you." Maria started sobbing softly. Glenn grabbed her roughly by the shoulder, pulled her by the hair and pressed his face up to hers. She always thought his eyes were dark, hollow, and sinister, like those of the sharks she had seen at SeaWorld. Now, they were only a couple of inches from her eyes. She felt his nose touch hers. "Do you want this job, or not?" he hissed at her. The large man slapped her across the face, sending one of her large, gold-plated, clip-on earrings airborne across the room, hitting the back corner and falling to the floor. Maria was now crying uncontrollably.

Shaking, she screamed back at him "No! I don't want this job no more!" She tried to regain her composure. "I'm serious, you bastard! I quit!"

Glenn let go of Maria's long hair and deliberately walked around his large desk. He eased himself into his overstuffed black leather chair, and propped his feet on the desk. "Typical Mexican bitch. Too fucking stupid to know what's in your best interest. Nobody on the face of God's green earth would pay you this kind of money! Most streetwalkers in TJ don't pull in this kind of coin, senorita," he said mockingly.

"I'm not a streetwalker!" Maria shouted, as she wiped tears and mascara from her high cheekbones. "I don't have to take this crap from you!" she said. "You have always treated me like trash! I can take you to court for sexual harassment!"

"Sexual harassment?" Glenn replied. "Grow up. We're two consenting adults. They'll laugh your ass out of court."

Maria bolted for the door, turned the knob, only to find it locked. Glenn removed his feet from his desk and sat up in his chair. He buttoned his shirt, never taking his eyes off Maria. He leaned forward, and in his most syrupy delivery he said, "Maria, let's stop talking crazy. I would hate for this to get out of hand and for you to subject yourself to that kind of public humiliation. I'm sorry if I upset you, sweetheart. I guess I'm just a little stressed out about work and the company right now. I shouldn't have barked at you when I came back in. What we had earlier was beautiful…and so are you, baby. You're still my girl, OK? So let's put this behind us, and I'll see you here at nine o'clock tomorrow morning." Maria was silent. He thought to himself, did she buy that line of crap? The last thing I need is some dime a dozen bimbo fucking with my career. I've never let it happen before, and I'm not about to start now.

Glenn stood up and walked to Maria. She was shaking and tears and mascara were running down her face. In her hurry, Maria had not buttoned her blouse correctly. Glenn looked down at her, smiling warmly.

He gently unbuttoned her blouse, and re-buttoned it correctly, over her large, heaving breasts. It always amazed him that they were real. He admired the fact that her little frame could support such a huge pair. Using the palm of his hand, Glenn brushed the tears from Maria's cheeks. He slowly put his arms around her.

She looked up at him with fearful eyes. Maria felt so violently repulsed she thought she was going to throw up.

Releasing her still shaking shoulders, Glenn turned toward her and said, "We've got a good thing going here," and smiled at her.

Maria stared at his perfect teeth, and looked away. She took a step towards the door, when she caught a glimpse of his wife's picture out of the corner of her eye. She thought the woman was attractive, but looked very sad. The picture's presence had always made her feel guilty. She had tried to turn it over, or put it in a drawer on several occasions. Glenn would always put it back in its place, as if he wanted his wife to witness his indiscretions.

"Come on, sweetheart. I'll walk you to your car," Glenn said in a voice barely louder than a whisper.

Maria pulled her purse strap over her left shoulder, and took a couple more steps toward Glenn, and said in the most serious tone she could muster, "That won't be necessary, I know the way."

"C'mon baby, I don't want you to think I'm not a gentleman," Glenn said in a soothing voice. Maria smiled nervously at him, and continued walking out of the office. Glenn smiled back, turned and slowly began walking. He reached back with his left hand, a gesture for Maria to hold his hand.

She had no assurance that an escort to her car was all Glenn had in mind. The thought of him forcing her to participate in another round of his sexual follies was more than she could stomach. At that moment, Maria picked up a large, metal three-hole punch that was sitting on Glenn's credenza. She quickly lifted the hole-punch over her head, and brought it down as fast and hard as her diminutive body would allow.

The corner of the rectangular hole-punch hit Glenn squarely in the back of his head. The force of the blow knocked him to his knees.

Maria threw down the hole-punch and screamed defiantly, "Go to hell, Diablo! I quit! See you in court, asshole!" She could see blood oozing from the hole torn in his scalp. Maria quickly ran to the far side of the office and picked up Glenn's keys. Stepping around the disoriented, groaning man on the floor, she unlocked the door and made her way to the front double glass doors. She threw down his brass key ring, and grabbed at her shoulder, fumbling for her purse. Reaching in the imitation Louis Vuitton bag with trembling hands, Maria found her keys. Locating the key to the office door, she inserted the key, heard the gratifying sound of the tumblers engage, and pushed the door open.

Maria hurdled the entrance steps, and started running toward her car. As she passed Glenn's black Mercedes S600, she ran the office key down the side of the automobile in a jagged line. She felt proud of herself for making a stand. Smashing Glenn's skull and scratching his car were strangely empowering and liberating experiences. She reached her car, a red '92 Toyota Celica, and began fumbling with her keys to locate the key with the black plastic end piece bearing the Toyota logo. Holding the key between her fingers, she inserted it effortlessly into the door lock. As Maria opened the car door, she felt her knees go weak. Maria had never fainted before in her life, but guessed what she was feeling was pretty close to what it must be like. She slowly looked over her shoulder, only to confirm the reflection she saw in her car window was indeed Glenn Stevens, towering behind her.

"What? Leaving so soon?" Glenn sneered. The sound of his voice, and the look in his rage filled eyes snapped Maria back into action. She slid quickly behind the wheel of her car. Glenn reached in and squeezed her left shoulder tightly, trying to pull her out of the car. Maria stabbed at his hand with her car key. Glenn recoiled, shrieking loudly in pain. Maria put the key in the ignition, and started the engine. Glenn screamed, "You stupid bitch!" as he grasped at her throat. Maria tried to slam the car door on Glenn's arm, but he was holding it ajar with his left hand. Glenn wound his right hand through Maria's long hair and pulled it violently. "You want to play rough, senorita? You don't know the meaning of rough!" he snarled. Maria's head jerked back in pain.

All the while, she was stepping on the accelerator, revving the engine—desperately trying to reach the automatic stick shift on the floor between the front seats. Glenn was using all his considerable strength to pry her from the car's cockpit. Maria's right hand brushed across the dashboard as she was being violently tugged by Glenn. As she held firmly to the steering wheel with her left hand, she felt the cigarette lighter with her right, and pushed it in. Glenn was gaining leverage, and now had his right foot propped against the running board as he continued pulling Maria by the hair. Glenn's left hand now grasped Maria's slender throat, and began to cut off her air supply. Maria let go of the steering wheel, and tried to pry Glenn's hand off her neck. Now he had her firmly by the throat and hair, and began to extract the choking woman from the car.

Just then, Maria heard a click, and grasped for the cigarette lighter with her right hand. She pulled it from its receptacle just as Glenn jerked her out of her car and onto the pavement on top of him. Glenn did not relinquish his iron grip on her throat or hair, as he struggled to right himself. Forced on her left side, Maria looked up and caught a glimpse of Glenn's face. With her free right hand, she plunged the glowing cigarette lighter at Glenn's face. The smell of burning flesh engulfed them as the lighter burned into Glenn's neck. Maria was disappointed with the lighter's target, because she had hoped to put it in one of his eyes. He let go of her, knocking the lighter from her hand. She struggled to her feet, breathing deeply and lurched for the still running car.

Before she could get inside the car, Glenn grabbed her around the waist with both arms, lifting her off the ground, like a rag doll. "Okay, bitch…it's party time!" he said maniacally. Carrying her behind the car, he smashed her chest first onto the small trunk of the Toyota. The blow knocked the wind out of her. As she gasped for air, Maria struggled, but could not break free. Glenn's 6-foot-4 inch, 265-pound muscular frame had no trouble manipulating the 5-foot, 100-pound woman. He grabbed her by the hair, and pushed her face down on the trunk lid with a quick jerk. With one arm still around her waist, he repeatedly smashed her head on the trunk while pulling her hair. Maria screamed for help, not knowing if anyone could hear her. Tugging roughly on her hair with his right hand, Glenn reached under Maria's skirt, groping for her panties. He ripped them off, and pushed her mini-skirt up over her perfectly heart-shaped ass. Not relinquishing his hold on her hair, Glenn pressed Maria down against the car with his elbow and forearm. Using his left hand, Glenn unbuckled his belt, undid his slacks and pulled his briefs down over his erection with practiced dexterity. He forced himself into her from behind, violently thrusting in and out.

Maria's screams turned to crying, as Glenn began laughing like a man possessed. Maria yelped, "Rape! Rape!" The large man was still brutally pounding away. Maria could taste her own tears as they streamed down her face into her mouth.

Glenn started shouting at her, continuing his depraved ride, "After all I did for you! You ungrateful little bitch! This is how you thank me? That's bullshit! I want you to say thank you! I want you to say gracias, Mr. Stevens! Gracias, Mr. Stevens! Do you hear me? Say it! Say it loud where I can hear you!" His words reverberated across the empty parking lot. Maria was crying so hard, she couldn't form the words. Glenn pulled her hair so hard she thought her eyes were going to pop out. "Say it, bitch! Gracias, Mr. Stevens!"

Maria sobbed the words, "Gracias, Mr. Stevens, gracias, Mr. Stevens."

Glenn let go of Maria's hair and grabbed her buttocks firmly with both hands. He suddenly stopped his piston-like thrusting, and snapped his head back. His eyes rolled back in his head as a demented smile spread across his face. With a sickly groan, he eased himself out of her, not relinquishing his hold on her hips.

Maria was still sobbing, and hurt in too many places to count. She steadied herself against the trunk of the Celica, trying to formulate an escape strategy. Maybe he would let her go now. What else could he possibly want from her, she thought.

Glenn eased Maria over on her back, and pressed her bruised body against the left tail light with his body. Maria looked away, not wanting her eyes to meet his. The large man gripped her hair with his hand, and ripped her blouse open with his right, causing her purse to fall to the asphalt. He caressed her breasts, snickering softly. Maria opened her tear-filled eyes and glanced up at the disheveled man. Summoning her remaining reserve, she stomped her heel into his right foot. Glenn's laughter became louder. Maria began hitting him in the chest and kicking his lower extremities with a wild, convulsive display of anger. Glenn's right hand moved from Maria's breasts up below her chin. Maria tried to scream, but no sound came. He let go of her hair, and now had both hands around her delicate neck. Her heavy breathing changed to a raspy, gurgling sound. As Maria felt her windpipe being forced shut, her brutalized body went limp. She tried to focus, but the form above her was nowhere to be found. Bright, vivid colors flashed before her: Black, then completely red. Black. Red. She caught one last glimpse of his black shark eyes. Red. Black. The taste of bile filled her mouth. Red. Black. She could still hear his laughter, but it now echoed as if it was coming from inside a cavern. Red. Black. As her eyes rolled back in her head, Maria could no longer inhale. Red. Black. With a voiceless whisper, she mouthed the words, "Hail Mary, full of grace, the Lord is with Thee..." Red. Black. Red. Black.

CHAPTER 2

THE LARGE MAN released his grip on the motionless, petite body beneath him, no longer feeling the pulse of life. He stepped around her, and fell against the back of the Toyota. Breathing hard, he unconsciously bent over and pulled up his underwear and slacks, buckled his belt, and zipped his fly. He reached up, and rubbed the back of his throbbing head. Bringing his hand back, he looked at the blood on his hand. He wiped the blood on his sweat-soaked and mascara stained white pinpoint oxford dress shirt. A quick glance around the parking lot confirmed that they were alone.

Glenn staggered around the car, reached inside the open door, turned the keys, shutting off the engine. Silence filled the darkened parking lot. As he put her keys in his pocket, he stared at the lifeless body still propped on the trunk. He thought she looked especially sickly under the yellow hue of the low-pressure sodium lamps now illuminating the area from their round twenty-five foot aluminum poles. Brushing his sweaty hair off his forehead, he walked back to the woman. Crouching down, he picked up her ripped panties and put them in his pocket. He then lifted the warm, damp body over his shoulder. He walked across the parking lot, and up the front entrance steps. Opening the glass door with his free hand, he turned left and proceeded down a dark hallway. He pushed through a large brown door illuminated by an overhead red exit sign, and brushed the wall to his right, searching for the light switch. He flipped the plastic toggle switch upward, illuminating the warehouse. Adjusting his shoulder under her body for maximum leverage, he continued walking. His path was marked with bright yellow painted lines on the concrete floor. His destination loomed ahead, against the back wall of the warehouse. As he reached the large, metal, battleship gray container, he eased her body to the floor. He thought it ironic that this was probably the gentlest treatment he had given her all night.

Glenn took the first three steps up the attached metal ladder on the side of the container, and pushed open the heavy plastic lid. Stepping back down to the floor, he again lifted the limp body over his shoulder. His slick dress shoes did not afford much traction on the metal steps. Reaching the middle of the ladder, he launched the body over the side of the metal container with a quick, military press-like motion. The hollow thud sound echoed in the large warehouse. He climbed to the top of the ladder, and looked over the edge at her body sprawled in the garbage. With a fluid motion, he hurdled himself into the container, taking caution not to land on the woman. It took him three difficult steps in the chest deep refuse to reach the corner. Grasping a four-foot long, two-by-four sized metal bar he found resting on the surface of the debris, Glenn began digging out the corner. Once he cleared it to about a three-foot depth, he climbed out of the hole he created. As he crawled toward the woman, he snagged and ripped his trousers on a rough piece of metal. "Damn it!" These slacks are Hugo Boss, he thought. Glenn grabbed her body under the shoulder blades, gripping her armpits and pulled her on her back towards him. He gently eased her slender body into the corner hole of garbage. Maria's perfume filled his nostrils, as he looked at her admiringly. "What a waste," he said out loud. "You were one hell of a fuck." Gripping the metal bar again, he moved garbage over her with his makeshift shovel.

Now drenched in sweat, he climbed out of the container, down to the concrete floor. He broke into a half jog across the warehouse. Reaching the utility closet, he opened the door and turned on the light. He scanned the metal shelves until he found a bottle of Windex. He took the Windex, a cotton towel, turned off the light, and shut the door behind him. Jogging back across the warehouse to the behemoth container, he stopped outside the corner where he had left the body inside. He took the trigger-grip nozzle off the Windex. Pulling himself up to the edge of the metal wall, he emptied half the bottle's contents over the garbage covering the woman, hoping to mask her perfume's fragrance with the ammonia. Reaching over, he then grabbed a large piece of cardboard, and dragged it over the corner area to further ensure she was not accidentally seen. Jumping down to the concrete floor, he briskly walked around to the ladder, climbed three steps, and pulled down the heavy plastic lid. The booming sound resonated in the stillness of the warehouse.

Glenn jogged out of the warehouse, and hit the light switch, returning it to its original state of darkness. Closing the door behind him, he walked briskly down the office hallway, turned sharply to his right, and burst through the twin glass doors. Clearing the steps, he trotted across the parking lot, and retrieved Maria's purse from the pavement beside her car. Securing the nozzle to the Windex bottle, he sprayed the trunk, bumper, taillights, driver's side door, steering wheel and dashboard. He wiped off the cleaning fluid with the cotton towel, stopping occasionally to examine his work. Finished, he walked around the Toyota, inspecting it in the dark parking lot. Seeing a metallic glimmer out of the corner of his eye, he noticed the car's cigarette lighter on the pavement. Retrieving it, he wiped it off, and placed it back in its receptacle. Satisfied, he walked back into the office, gaining confidence in his still forming game plan.

Locking the front office doors behind him, he scanned the dimly lit marble floor. In the corner he spotted his brass key ring, quickly retrieved it, and walked past the receptionist desk, turning right into his office. He closed the heavy wooden door, pulled out his keys, and locked it. Throwing his keys on his large mahogany desk, he pulled her keys out of his pocket and tossed them next his. Beside the keys, he set the Windex, cotton towel and the purse. He quickly stripped off his shirt, slacks and underwear, leaving them in a crumpled pile on the floor. Walking naked across the thick wool carpet, he opened the door in the back of his office. He flicked on a fluorescent light revealing his executive bathroom. Stepping into the shower, he turned on the water. He flinched in pain as the stream of water produced by the showerhead came in contact with his neck. "Son of a bitch!" he growled as he placed his hand over the tender flesh burned by the cigarette lighter. As the water ran over his torn scalp and through his hair, he noticed the bloody water beneath him, swirling down the drain.

His body was throbbing with pain, as he stepped out of the shower. He quickly toweled off, and proceeded to his closet. He pulled a clean pair of briefs out of the built-in dresser drawer. He quickly buttoned a fresh dress shirt, and pulled on a patterned pair of cotton dress socks. Walking back into his office, he picked up the Windex and towel, and methodically began cleaning the three-hole punch, and returned it to its' spot on his credenza. He then wiped down his desk, telephone, and every hard surface he could find. Grabbing his keys, he walked into the lobby, still in his underwear and socks, and began cleaning the floor and glass doors. He opened the glass entry doors, and cleaned their exterior. He unconsciously ran his fingers through his hair as he stared at his reflection.

Back inside his executive bathroom, Glenn pulled a navy pinstripe suit from the closet. He stepped into the trousers, buttoning them at the waist and pulling up the fly. He reached down to the ripped slacks on the floor, and pulled the alligator belt out with a snapping motion. He inserted the belt through the loops of the slacks he was now wearing, buckled it, and slipped back into his shoes on the floor. He then retrieved his wallet, pocket change, and handkerchief from the still damp black and white houndstooth slacks. Sitting in his leather desk chair, he wiped the soles of his shoes clean with the Windex soaked towel. Taking one last look around, he gathered his soiled clothes from the floor of his office, picked up Maria's keys from the desk, along with the Windex and cotton towel, hit the light and shut the door behind him.

Rapidly walking down the dark hallway, he burst through the warehouse door flipping the lights back on. As they flickered, and the metalhalide lamps grew to full strength, he walked toward the container. He threw the clothing he was carrying into a cardboard box sitting on a staging table, and sealed the box with packing tape. He then climbed three steps of the metal container's attached ladder, lifted the lid and tossed the box in, dropping the lid as he jumped down to the floor. He no longer noticed Maria's perfume. He returned the Windex to its' original place, and stuck the cotton towel in his back pocket.

Glenn exited the warehouse, and walked back into his office to retrieve his suit jacket and her purse. Walking into the lobby, he entered the security code on the illuminated keypad mounted to the right of the glass doors. He stepped outside, found the key, and locked the door well within the allotted thirty seconds of the security system. He walked down the steps and over to his Mercedes. He unlocked the door, reached in and picked up his small, hand held cell phone. Putting the phone in his jacket pocket, he locked the door and began walking toward the Celica. He instinctively looked at his watch. The luminous jewel encrusted face of his Rolex read 10:45 PM. He located Maria's car keys in his pocket, and folded his long legs into the driver's seat. Pulling out his handkerchief, he removed Maria's wallet from her purse. Finding her driver's license, he read her address using the illumination of the car's dome light. "Where in the fucking barrio is this place?" he asked out loud. Opening the glove compartment, he found her LA County Thomas street guide. Perusing the index, and turning to the noted page, he got his bearings and closed the door. Starting the car, he shifted into drive and flicked the A/C on full blast.

*   *   *

TWENTY MINUTES LATER, the Celica pulled into the parking lot of the Harbor Breeze apartments in El Segundo. What a dump, he thought to himself. He slowly cruised around the complex until he found her unit clearly marked with a backlit number 12. Parking the car, he removed the still moist cotton towel from his back pocket, and wiped off the steering wheel, stick, dashboard and inside door handle. Exiting the Toyota, he closed the door using the towel. After wiping down the handle and the side of the car, he approached the ominous, prison-like structure. All the windows had wrought iron bars protecting them. He noticed a stray cat walking near the garbage dumpster. The faint sounds of salsa music drifted through the compound. The lower units were marked A and B. He figured 12-C must be upstairs. At the top of the stairs his theory was confirmed when he spotted the door marked "C." Glenn knocked and waited a couple of minutes. He then tried several keys on her ring before he found the right one. The place was dark, and he was hoping that Maria lived alone. He found a light switch, and flicked on the overhead light.

The apartment was sparsely furnished. A large picture of Maria and her daughter was framed and hanging over a worn couch in the den. Next to it hung a framed diploma from Los Angeles City College. The old, harvest gold refrigerator in the tiny kitchen was covered with pictures of the little girl, and artwork that was probably created by her. The light flashing on the answering machine caught his eye. Using his handkerchief, he pressed the PLAY button. After rewinding, the sound of a woman's voice with a heavy Mexican accent filled the air. "Maria, this is

Madre. Rosie, she misses you, but is ready for sleep. I will keep her tonight, and we will call you manyana. I love you, my angel."

Glenn quickly inspected the cramped two-room apartment. A small bathroom was off the bedroom, and the den and kitchen were one room. The entire flooring was cheap linoleum, with a few throw rugs here and there. A 13-inch television sat on a plastic milk carton crate in the far corner. Next to it was a boom-box with a stack of CDs on the floor. He noticed several items of purple and yellow Lakers' paraphernalia: blanket, coffee mug, plush basketball pillow and a miniature plastic rim and backboard hanging over the closet door. He thought to himself, what in the hell did she do with all the money I gave her? He searched under her mattress, and through the drawers of the wobbly dresser, hoping not to find a diary. After investigating the small quarters to his satisfaction, Glenn placed Maria's purse on the counter, next to the sink. He left her keys beside the purse.

Opening the front door with his handkerchief, he twisted the lock on the doorknob, and closed it behind him. Looking both ways, he quickly bounded down the stairs and out into the parking lot. Glenn pulled the cell phone out of his jacket, and began to dial. He pressed the END key when he realized what he was doing. No way was he going to leave a traceable record of this phone call. Pleased his mind was still sharp, he walked across the street to an AM/PM convenience store he spotted when he first arrived. As he walked to the pay phone, he noticed some young thugs standing to the side of the store. He knew being a white guy in a suit in this neighborhood, he practically glowed in the dark. He caught their glance, and looked away. Reaching the phone, he plucked a quarter from his pocket change, and dialed the Coastal Cab Company. Their number wasn't hard to remember since he had seen all their numerous ads stating: Dial C-O-A-S-T-A-L for quick, dependable cab service. After giving the dispatcher his coordinates, he hung up the phone and quickly went inside the store. It had to be safer inside, and besides, he was dying of thirst.

Glenn walked in between the narrow, grimy aisles to the back of the small store. Opening a refrigerated cooler, he pulled out a bottle of lemon-lime Gatorade. He walked to the counter where a short, Asian woman with a dark complexion greeted him with a rotten-toothed smile. "One-ninety-nine," she told him in measured English. He threw a five on the counter, collected his change and walked to the glass door. Peering into the darkness for the cab, he felt the as if all eyes of the assembled low-lifes were staring at him. Deciding to wait inside, he cracked open the Gatorade, took a long swig, and held the cold plastic bottle against the back of his throbbing head.

The Coastal cab pulled into the parking lot. Glenn pushed the door open, strode briskly to the cab, careful not to make eye contact with the punks, opened the door and eased his large frame into the back seat. The driver, a large black man chewing an unlit cigar, turned to look at him through the scratched Plexiglas and asked, "Where to?"

"City of Commerce Business Park. Off Garfield," his well-dressed passenger replied. As the cab merged into traffic, Glenn turned around to look out the rear window. The group of young thugs seemed to still be staring at him.

CHAPTER 3

REGINA NOTICED Glenn's office door open for the first time that morning. She knew by monitoring the switchboard that he had been on the phone for quite a while. Regina got up from her desk and walked to the end of the hallway. She simultaneously knocked on the massive door as she stuck her head inside. Glenn did not look up from what he was writing, but motioned her to come in. Regina sat in one of the leather chairs facing his desk. As Glenn slumped over the papers in front of him, Regina noticed what appeared to be a cut on his head.

Glenn looked up, smirked at Regina, raised his eyebrows and gestured as if it was time for her to state the intentions of invading his space. She said, "It's 9:45 AM and Maria Lopez has not shown up for work yet."

Glenn looked puzzled, "Isn't this some sort of 'admin' problem?" He wondered to himself if Regina knew Maria was in his office after hours last night.

"She hasn't called in, and there is no answer at her home," Regina continued. "I thought you would like to know."

Glenn stared at her for a moment, trying to decide the appropriate response. "Hell, its Friday…maybe she's trying to make it a three day weekend, or something. I'll tell you one thing, this will be her first and last time to pull a stunt like this here. If you need help today, just call the temp agency and have them send someone over," he said.

"OK, Glenn." Regina was mildly surprised by his cavalier attitude. After all, they were speaking of his latest office dalliance.

As she got up to leave, Glenn asked, "Oh, and can you bring me a refill on my coffee? Thanks." Regina thought about making a smart aleck reply, but before she could think of a comeback, Glenn said, "You look nice today. Have you done something different with your hair?" knowing full well this would disarm her.

Regina was taken aback by his comment. Glenn had not said anything even mildly flattering about her appearance in several years. "No," she said. "I barely had time to fix it this morning."

"Well, maybe you've lost weight then."

Regina mumbled a "thanks," managed a weak smile, and left his office. As she proceeded down the hall towards the break room, she thought to herself, what was that all about?

Not waiting on Regina to return with his coffee, Glenn got up and headed left out of his office. Pushing through the large warehouse doors he made his way over to Jose Castro's office. His office was located up one flight of wooden stairs, with a panoramic view of the warehouse operations. Jose had been the warehouse supervisor for 22 years, long before Glenn took the reigns of the Western Region office. After climbing the stairs, Glenn walked in to find Jose's office vacant. He looked at the various Campbell training certificates, proudly framed on the walls. On the wall behind his desk was his framed Associates Degree from Santa Ana Junior College. The desk was covered with shipping/receiving reports, paperwork and the obligatory array of family pictures. The A/C wall unit in his office grumbled ominously as it tried to cool the space.

Glenn stared out the main window, trying not to look at the gray metal container against the back wall, or think about its contents. He watched the warehouse employees moving about the cavernous space. Had any of them opened the container this morning? If they had, did they notice anything? Was the ammonia still masking her perfume? Perfume? Hell, could it mask the scent of rotting flesh? Had rigor mortis set in? He tried to clear his mind, unconsciously pulling at his starched collar to relieve the pressure on his burned neck. Just then he noticed Jose coming across the floor riding on the back of a forklift.

Jose was about six foot-two. Glenn thought that was unusually tall for a Mexican. Jose was lean, with graying hair, and a well-trimmed mustache. He clambered up the wooden stairs, entered the office with a broad smile, and said cheerfully, "Good morning, Mr. Stevens!" Jose stuck out his hand and shook Glenn's hand firmly. "What brings you to our part of the world?"

"Oh, just wanting to get a pulse check on warehouse operations," Glenn replied. "You gotta minute?"

"Yes sir, Mr. Stevens. What can I do to help you?"

Glenn pulled up a chair and motioned for Jose to take his seat. Glenn couldn't help noticing that the padded armrests were covered with duct tape. Glenn cleared his throat, and asked, "How are we doing on the inventory levels for wire-nuts?"

"We haven't had any shipping problems since we switched vendors," Jose replied enthusiastically.

"Who are we using now?" Glenn asked, trying to feign interest.

"Buchanan, sir. They're a real good company."

"How about resistors and transmitters?" Glenn continued, trying to speak over the noise from the air conditioner.

"No problems at all. Our fill rates are above projections with both product lines. Would you like to see the figures?" Jose asked anxiously as he fumbled through stacks of green-bar printouts on his desk.

"That won't be necessary," Glenn replied. "Sounds like everything's running smoothly in your department."

"I have a very good group of people to work with, sir," Jose said with a hint of pride.

Glenn nodded his approval, and shifted in his chair. Its metal frame was unforgiving to someone of his stature. "Any OSHA red flags?"

"No, sir" Jose said. "We do everything by the book."

"How about our recycling effort? How's that going?"

"We're doing very well. All used paper and computer printouts are kept in that bin over there," Jose said as he motioned at a green storage bin in the warehouse. "The employees have done a good job with aluminum cans, too," he added.

"What about the large trash containers—are we still sending them to the incinerator?" Glenn asked, trying to appear nonchalant.

"Yes, sir Mr. Stevens. You told us to stop using the regular garbage collection because it was better for us financially."

"True. And besides, this way we're not contributing to any landfills, huh?" Glenn replied with a knowing grin.

No, just polluting the atmosphere, you arrogant schmuck, Jose thought to himself. "How often do they make pick-ups?" asked Glenn.

"Every Friday, sir. As a matter of fact, they should be here before noon today."   Glenn felt a gnawing pain in his stomach, as he looked past Jose and out the window at the large gray container in the corner. Glenn collected himself and asked, "Would twice a week pick ups be helpful to you, Jose?"

"I don't think so. Once works pretty good, most of the time. I'm sure there are better things we can spend our money on."

Not wanting it to appear as if his total focus was the container going to the incinerator, Glenn thought he better shift gears. "From a personal standpoint, Jose, are there any problems you would like to bring to my attention?" Glenn asked in a composed manner.

"No sir. I've been here over twenty years, and I must say that your work over the past five years really has things running better than ever, Mr. Stevens."

What a suck-up, Glenn thought.

"Personally, I am very happy here at Campbell. Is there anything I can do to improve my performance or that of my team?"

Is this guy for real? Glenn thought. "No, Jose…I'm really pleased with all the progress the warehouse department has made. You are a tremendous asset to the Campbell organization. You and I are cut from the same piece of cloth. We both look at problems as opportunities. Thanks for the update and keep up the good work. If I can ever be of any assistance, you know where to find me."

"Yes, sir. And you are welcome. And thank you for your time," Jose was positively beaming with his newfound approval. Glenn rose from his chair, shook hands with Jose again, and opened the door. It was then a piecing beep–beep—beep—beep sound filled the air.

*   *   *

REGINA HURRIED down the hallway trying not to spill Glenn's coffee. She entered his office, and noticed he was out. His absence was actually a relief considering his closing comments at their previous encounter. She set his coffee mug, emblazoned with *UC-Berkeley Alumni* in script, down on the cork and wooden coaster on his desk. She checked his out-box, confirmed it was empty, and was turning to leave when she noticed the light reflecting off something metallic in the corner.

*   *   *

GLENN AND JOSE stood on the wooden platform outside Jose's office and watched as the navy blue garbage truck backed through the warehouse door. It parked just in front of the large gray container, and the "beeping" stopped. A hydraulic lift was lowered to the warehouse floor. Uniformed men with PACIFIC SANITATION logos on the backs of their shirts stepped down out of truck's cab, and walked back to the container. "Do you need me for anything else, Mr. Stevens?" Jose asked.

"No…uh, Pacific Sanitation…this is our incinerator company?" Glenn asked tentatively.

"Yes, sir. Before noon on Friday, just like I said." Jose started down the steps, but noticed he wasn't being followed. He looked back to see Mr. Stevens staring at the garbage truck. *Son-of-a-bitch is probably thinking* of a way to fuck with my job, Jose thought as he walked between the yellow lines across the warehouse floor.

Glenn watched as the two men stepped on the wheel brakes of the container with their steel-toed boots. Brakes released, they rolled the container onto the lift. Could they smell anything? Would they see anything? Hell, is anybody watching me watch the fucking garbagemen? Glenn pondered. He decided to start walking down the wooden steps, and heard the hydraulic lift begin to whine as he reached the concrete floor.

Glenn noticed a couple of warehouse workers walk past him, trying not to make eye contact. He stooped as if to tie his shoe, glancing cautiously up at the truck lifting the container. He tied and untied his shoe by the time the lift stopped. Re-tying his shoe he watched as the two Pacific Sanitation workers, who had ridden up the lift with the container, push the container to the edge of the lift. They simultaneously attached two bungee cord straps to the lower outside edge of the container. Glenn felt sweat trickling down his chest. They pushed the container's contents into the back opening of the truck with a fluid motion. Glenn observed that the container obstructed their view of the contents falling into the truck—or at least he hoped so. The man on the left side of the lift hit a couple of switches on the side of the truck, as the other pulled the container back onto the lift. The opening at the back of the truck slowly closed as the lift returned to the floor. The men detached the bungee cords, and slid the container off the lift and back to its original position. As the man on the right walked back to the passenger seat of the truck cab, his partner pushed two more switches at the base of the truck. As the driver returned to the cab, a grinding, metallic sound could be heard coming from the back of the truck, as its contents were compacted. The lift returned to its original position, as the driver started the engine. Glenn and the Pacific Sanitation truck exited the warehouse simultaneously.

Glenn ducked into the men's room. Jon Cassler, his District sales manager for Orange County, was at the sink basin washing his hands. Cassler was shorter than Glenn, about 5'-10" and Glenn liked that. Cassler was in his late 30's, had dark hair, large, thick glasses, and was an overweight, nervous, sweaty type. He was also the most amoral son-of-bitch Glenn could find to ride herd over the OC sales reps. His sales team despised him, but that didn't bother Glenn as long as Cassler had the stomach to execute some of Campbell Industries more devious, sometimes borderline illegal, action plans. Cassler was a Grade A asshole—something he seemed to take a personal, deviant pride in. "Hi, Glenn. How's it going?" Cassler asked.

"Fine, Jon," Glenn said abruptly as he rolled up his sleeves.

"You know, I was thinking that maybe we should charge our distributors for our product catalogs," Cassler said. "I mean, these are valuable sales tools for them, right? Why should we give these away?" Cassler asked, trying to engage Glenn in conversation. Glenn, not looking at Cassler, turned on the faucet, leaned over and splashed water on his face. Cassler handed him a paper towel, waiting for a positive response.

Drying his face and hands Glenn said, "Put it in a memo to me, and maybe I'll consider bringing it up at the next sales meeting."

"Thanks, Glenn. I think you'll see the logic in my proposal. I'll get right on it." With a haughty, self-serving smirk, Cassler left the men's room. Glenn shook his head as the World Champion ass-kisser made his exit. As he stared at himself in the mirror, his thoughts were of the incineration plant at Pacific Sanitation. He just might pull this off.

＊   ＊   ＊

GLENN STRODE into his office to find Regina kneeling in the back corner, behind his desk. "Lose something?" asked Glenn.

Regina, visibly startled, rose and said, "No, just picking up some lint off the carpet."

"Uh, okay…Thanks," Glenn replied, eyeing her cautiously.

As Regina made her way around the desk, consciously choosing the opposite direction he was taking, she said, "I brought your coffee."

"Thanks, again." Regina left the office as Glenn settled back into his chair. His confidence was returning as he thought to himself, I did it. I am golden!

*   *   *

RETURNING to her desk, Regina slipped Maria's gold-plated clip-on earring into the bottom drawer, and put on her headset.

CHAPTER 4

THE IRRITATING BUZZING sound from the alarm clock broke the early morning silence. Startled, Scott Murphy slammed the off button and tried to focus on the red, digital display reading 5:30 AM. Scott rolled out of bed and onto the floor. Completing his morning ritual of fifty push-ups and fifty sit-ups, he headed toward the bathroom. He lathered up his face and began shaving. Looking in the mirror, he hoped his eyes would not look too bloodshot on his first day at work. He barely slept at all the night before, unable to stop his mind from racing. This was the biggest step he had taken in his twenty-five years. Leaving home and starting a new job halfway across the country was a big change. But starting a career with a FORTUNE 100 company like Campbell Industries was certainly minimizing the risk.

Stepping into his small shower stall, Scott showered quickly, thinking of all he had been through over the past six weeks. He had left a secure sales job with Mid-American Electric Manufacturing Co., in Memphis; a job he had started immediately upon graduating from The University of Memphis. He had done well there over the past two years, hitting all his quotas. His former boss understood that the opportunity to work for Campbell Industries was one he couldn't pass up. He even wrote Scott a great letter of recommendation. Who could blame him? Doubling his base salary, a tremendous quarterly bonus plan, $500-a-month car allowance, 401K, stocks and a company-funded pension plan—vested after one year.

The call from the headhunter got the ball rolling. Her name was Kerry Balfour, and she worked for RecruitersWest. Anybody that was brought into work for Campbell from the outside went through Kerry and RecruitersWest. She told him they were looking for someone with a sales and marketing background, to take over an established territory in Los Angeles County; selling Campbell's electrical components to wholesale distributors. She said Campbell wanted someone with a Business degree, and only a few years of experience, because in her words, "They didn't want to have to break any established bad habits."

After interviewing three times, once at Campbell's training center in Memphis, once in Los Angeles at the Western Region office, and once in New Orleans, the company's headquarters; Ms. Balfour called him on the phone with, what was to him, an eye-popping offer. After a quick house-hunting trip, he had found a modest, but expensive by Memphis standards, 1-bedroom apartment in the Belmont Shore area of Long Beach. After tying up all his loose ends in Memphis, he rented a box truck from Budget rent-a-truck, and took the same advice as many before him, to "Go West, young man." Being twenty-five, with no strings, if he was ever going to take this kind of chance, he knew now was the time.

Stepping from the shower, Scott reached for a towel and dried off. Casting a quick glance to the alarm clock, he noted that the time was 6:15 AM. Wrapping his towel around him, he went into his small kitchen, prepared and quickly downed a bowl of cereal and a glass of orange juice. Returning to the bathroom, he brushed his teeth and blow-dried his hair. Getting dressed quickly, Scott pulled his best navy blue suit from the closet. Pairing this with a starched white pinpoint oxford shirt, and a burgundy foulard print tie that he thought would make a good "dress for success" impression. Lacing his black, wing-tipped shoes, he grabbed his wallet, car keys and brief case and headed out the apartment door. Locking the door behind him, Scott headed to the street where his new, white Nissan Maxima was parallel parked. He had purchased this car prior to moving, with the full intention of letting his new car-allowance cover his note.

Starting the car, Scott pulled onto 2nd Street heading for the 405-interstate on-ramp. Taking the 405 to the 710 North to the 5 North, a route he had pre-planned the night before using his Thomas Guide map, Scott looked for the Garfield exit. The Southern California traffic was definitely going to be a major adjustment for him. As he crawled along the interstate, he saw the exit sign ahead, and cautiously merged over to the right-hand lane. He felt as if his Tennessee car tags gave him away to the other motorists as a novice to the freeway system, or even worse, a tourist. Driving through the entrance to the Commerce Business Park, Scott took several deep breaths, trying to calm the butterflies in his stomach. Parking his car in the Campbell Industries parking lot, he noticed the L.E.D. dashboard clock read 7:25 AM. Always good to be on time your first day, he said to himself. Walking to the entrance, he passed a large, black Mercedes that had a long scratch down the side. He noted that the name: STEVENS was painted on the curb in front of the parking space.

Walking up five steps at the entrance, Scott pulled open one of the glass doors, reading the words CAMPBELL INDUSTRIES in gold-colored print on the doors. He felt a sense of pride and accomplishment as he approached the receptionist's desk in the lobby. The desk was a half circle of mahogany finished wood, with clear and frosted glass cubes as a backdrop. The Campbell Industries wordmark was attached to the glass in brass letters. "Good morning, Lori," Scott tried to say in a friendly manner.

"Good morning?" she answered back, quizzically.

Obviously, she either didn't remember him from his interview, or was pretending not to remember him, Scott thought. "I'm Scott Murphy. We met several weeks ago when I interviewed with Allen

Goldman. Today is my first day," Scott tried to say with confidence as she stared blankly at him.

"Oh, I guess you got the job," Lori said in a monotone reply. Her switchboard was ringing and she began to talk into her headset, not making eye contact with the man in front of her. Between calls, she looked up and said, "You can have a seat over there," motioning toward a row of maroon leather-clad chairs. Before he could say anything, she looked down and continued to answer calls. Scott walked over to the row of seats, unbuttoned his suit jacket, and sat down placing his briefcase beside him. He looked at Lori, and guessed her to be a few years older than him. She was attractive, with professionally cropped blond hair, blue eyes, minimal make-up, and business attire. He figured the reason he didn't think she was drop-dead stunning was because she oozed attitude with a capital A. He looked at his watch. It read 7:38 AM, but he knew he set it five minutes fast. Worried about appearing late, he shifted uneasily in his seat. Just when he thought he would get up and try another approach with her, he overheard her saying, "Allen, a Scott Murphy is here to see you."

Moments later, Allen Goldman walked into the office lobby. "Good morning, Scott. Welcome aboard," he said with a friendly smile.

"Morning, Allen, glad to get started," Scott said as the two men shook hands.

"Come in, and I'll get you set up," Allen said, motioning Scott to follow him. Allen was about five-nine, had graying red hair and a well-trimmed beard, with more gray than red. He wore thick, aviator-style gold-rimmed glasses. From their first meeting, Scott came away feeling that Allen was pretty laid back, and very knowledgeable about the electrical components industry.

As the two headed down the hallway, Scott followed Allen as he made a quick turn into the first office on the right. "Glenn…have you got a minute?" Allen asked tentatively. "Our new man, Scott Murphy is here."

Glenn looked up from his desk and muttered, "Oh, yeah. Come in."

Scott approached Glenn's desk and said with all the confidence he could muster, "Good to see you again, Mr. Stevens. I really appreciate the opportunity to be a member of your team."

Glenn stood, and offered his hand. Scott was prepared for the vice-grip after their last meeting. As he predicted, Glenn clamped down on the ends of his fingers before their thumbs locked, and crushed his hand. "Please Scott, call me Glenn," he said with a shit-eating grin on his face. Still squeezing Scott's hand, Glenn looked him up and down and said, "Isn't that the same suit you wore for your interview?"

Taken aback by his observation, Scott replied, "Could be, I'm not sure."

Still crushing Scott's right hand, Glenn's left hand reached up and flipped over Scott's tie. He squinted at the label as a sour expression came over his face. "James Davis? Never heard of it—what is this, some Sears brand?"

"No," Scott replied, clearly agitated. "James Davis is a men's store in Memphis. They've been rated one of the top ten in the country."

"Yeah, right," Glenn said bluntly. "Well, for what we're paying you, I'm sure you'll round out your wardrobe. This is LA—you're not in the sticks anymore," Glenn said smugly, as he released Scott's aching hand. Still standing, facing Scott, Glenn queried, "How tall are you Scott, six-foot, six-one?"

"No," Scott stammered, but still looking Glenn squarely in the eye. "Actually, I'm six-three."

"Hmph. Yeah, right. Maybe with your shoes on," Glenn snorted as he eased himself into a chair. What an asshole, Scott thought to himself. Why is this guy personally attacking me? I've never seen a guy his height with a Napoleon complex. Before he could think of something to change the subject, Glenn continued, "You look like a jock. Did you play ball in college?"

"Intramurals," Scott replied.

Glenn leaned over his desk, squinted his eyes and hissed, "Well, then you *didn't* play ball."

Trying to break the tension, Allen jumped in, "Glenn played water polo at Cal-Berkeley."

Scott wanted to say something smart-ass about water polo was not really *playing* ball, or take a shot at Cal-Berkeley. You mean the Kremlin's West coast office, haven for bleeding heart liberals…but all that came out was, "Oh. That's great."

"Well, Glenn…just wanted to bring Scott by to get reacquainted. I need to run him through a quick orientation," Allen continued, rising to his feet.

Following his cue, Scott got up and said, "Thanks for your time, Glenn."

"Allen will take care of you," Glenn said, his dark eyes still burning a hole through Scott, as a fake smile spread across his face. "Good luck and welcome to Campbell Industries." As the two men left his office, Glenn whispered deeply under his breath, "We will eat that son-of-a-bitch alive."

⋆   ⋆   ⋆

SCOTT FOLLOWED Allen down the hall to a large opening containing four cubicles. "Before we get started," Allen said, "would you like a cup of coffee?"

"No, thanks. I don't drink coffee."

Allen chuckled, "I wish I could function without it." He re-introduced Scott to Regina Rogers, who was typing away at her PC. "Scott—this is who *really* runs the office. Regina—you remember Scott Murphy?" Allen asked.

"Why certainly," Regina said as a smile spread across her face. She rose and offered her hand. "So nice to see you again. Welcome to California, and welcome to Campbell, Scott. We're so glad you decided to come to work here."

She seemed very sincere, Scott thought. "Thanks, Regina; and good to see you again, too." She seemed like a nice person, although she looked very tired to Scott.

The opening that housed the four cubes, including Regina's, was between two hallways, and had an office on each opposing wall. The office on the wall directly across from Regina belonged to Allen. All the offices and cubicles were tastefully decorated in shades of mauve, gray and teal. As he walked inside, a motion-sensor turned on the office lighting. Allen walked around his desk and sat in his chair. Scott eased into one of the two chairs facing Allen, placing his briefcase in the other. "Go ahead and take your jacket off," Allen said, motioning to a coat rack in the corner. Following instructions, Scott took his jacket off, and hung it on the rack.

As he did, he noticed a framed USC Football schedule poster on the wall. "Did you go to USC?"

Allen shrugged his shoulders, and said, "No, but I've always been a big fan. You'll find out I'm one of the few guys here who *didn't* go to college. I got married right out of high school, started having kids—and went to work for what is now one of our largest distributors, Alexander's Electric Supply in Long Beach—they'll be your account now. Anyway, working there was how I became acquainted with Campbell Industries. They were, and still are, one of Alexander's largest vendors. I came on board as a sales rep ten years ago, and have been a sales manager for the past four. And here we are…"

Scott felt a little uneasy about prompting Allen to explain himself and his background to the new guy. It didn't matter to Scott that Allen did not attend college. When he had interviewed with Allen, he felt as if this guy was a good person and he could learn a lot from him. He noticed a plaque on the wall that read: TO ERR IS HUMAN, TO FORGIVE IS NOT COMPANY POLICY.

"OK," Allen continued as he shuffled several papers on his desk. Handing one over to Scott, he said, "This list shows all your distributors, contractors and specifying engineers in the South Bay. It includes account numbers, addresses, phone and fax numbers, contacts, e-mails, et cetera. This next sheet shows your territory 3-year sales history, including this fiscal year-to-date numbers. You'll also note the column indicating gross margin—a major component in calculating commissions here. Have you purchased a Thomas Guide?" Scott nodded that he had, as Allen presented the next sheet. "This lists the LA County sales team members by territory, pagers and e-mail addresses. You'll notice that Regina has already included you on this list. You'll meet the guys at our Monday meeting, tonight at five. Oh, and as the rookie, you're now responsible for bringing the snacks every Monday."

"Snacks?"

"Yeah, it's a tradition around here that the new guy buys the snacks for the meeting. Some guys have picked up a fruit plate or a deli plate, some have done chips and m&m's, whatever—use your imagination. Oh, and be sure and pick up Cokes, Diet Cokes and bottled water."

Scott thought to himself, what a joke! I'm supposed to be a professional salesman, and they want me to be cruising the aisles of the local mini-mart? I guess this is part of paying your dues. Allen continued, "Of course, all this goes on your expense report, speaking of which, here is a copy of our expense report. I've already filled this one out for you as a template. You'll need to turn this in once a week at our Monday night sales meeting. This is your pager. Your number is on the back, and printed on your cards—which just arrived from the printer last Friday. Check it over, and if there is anything you need changed, just let Regina know. Here is your cell phone; its number is listed on the outside of the box. Try and keep your monthly usage below $200.00. This is your laptop. It's a Compaq—we have a national account with them—built-in modem, CD-ROM, the whole enchilada. Oh, and we're now running Office 2000—any problems with that?"

"None at all," Scott lied knowing full well that he had never used the 2000 format.

Picking up a large black binder from off the floor, Allen dropped it on the desk with a thud in front of Scott. "This is our HR manual. All sorts of information on benefits, insurance, et cetera. We have an HR rep in this office, her name is Sheila Bryant, and the rest of the HR group resides at corporate in New Orleans. After you've had a chance to review it, feel free to see Sheila with any questions you might have. That's it for now. Let me show you your cube and how to set up your voicemail."

Just then, Jon Cassler stuck his head inside Allen's office and said, "Allen—oh, sorry—I didn't know you were with anyone. There's a fucking cop here, asking everyone questions. Regina will let you know when you're in the box. I'm sure you'll want to make a full confession."

Allen, confused by Jon's ranting, introduced him to Scott, "Scott, this is Jon Cassler, my counterpart for Orange County."

"Nice to meet you," Scott said standing up and offering his hand.

"The new meat, huh?" Cassler smirked, ignoring Scott's hand.

"Scott has transferred from Memphis," Allen said.

"You don't *sound* like you're from *Memphis*," Cassler replied, all the while looking Scott up and down.

Scott felt very uncomfortable and thought to himself, what in the hell is he looking at? This little twerp really gave him the creeps. He asked the pudgy man, "What is someone from Memphis supposed to sound like, Jon?"

"You know, like a bumpkin. Like Jethro Bodine, like our very own Jimmy Brady from Alabama. But, hey…no offense."

"Yeah, none taken," Scott replied insincerely.

"Who did you work for in Memphis?"

"Mid-American Electric."

"Don't they make, like, low-voltage landscape lighting?"

"Yes, they do."

"Hmmph. Bet *that* was challenging work." Running his thumbs up and down the silk braces framing his protruding belly, Cassler said,

"Too bad we didn't have an opening on the Orange County team. Not saying that you would have made the cut—we *are* the best—but you would have had a chance to have me as your mentor," he said smugly. "Too bad, but I'll guess you'll have to fight the good fight under the tutelage of Mr. Goldman. Good luck, kid—you're gonna need it." Closing with a weasel-like laugh, Cassler departed.

"Now that you've met Little Lord Fauntleroy, let's go set up that voicemail," Allen said good-naturedly.

"This is the bullpen," Allen said as the two walked into an area with about twenty-five cubicles. "Don't forget to leave yourself a trail of breadcrumbs, so you can find your way out. This place is like a maze."

Scott said, "The place looks deserted."

"That's because, as Glenn Stevens likes to say, 'no one ever sold anything sitting in the office,'" Allen stated, leading Scott to his cube in the far corner. "But in all seriousness, you *don't* want to be noticed spending too much time in the office. Politically, and from a productivity stand-point, it's more important that the leather meet the pavement, and you're out in front of the customers." His cube consisted of a small desktop, a phone and two small drawers. A copy of the LA white pages and yellow pages sat on the work surface along with a yellow legal pad. Narrow half-walls divided his cube from the cubes on either side.

Regina approached them, followed by man wearing a tie, but obviously wasn't dressed for the corporate world. He was about six-foot, with red hair and a stocky, athletic build—a real All-American look. Scott guessed he was in his late 30's. Regina said, "Excuse me Allen. This is Sergeant Harris with the LAPD. If you have a minute, he'd like to ask you a few questions."

"OK, no problem. Uh, Scott, follow the instructions on this card and set up your voicemail. I'll be back in a minute." As Allen left with Sgt. Harris, Regina smiled nervously at Scott, and followed them out of the bullpen.

What in the hell have I gotten myself into? Scott thought. This is one hostile workplace. If this was the *big leagues,* he wasn't sure he wanted any part of it. As he perused the voicemail set-up instructions, he took a deep breath. Maybe he shouldn't judge the company by his first encounters with the VP and the OC sales manager. Maybe they were just having bad days…or maybe they were just pricks.

At least he would be working for Allen, who seemed like a real decent guy—not a shark in pinstripes. Regina also seemed pleasant. But what in the hell were the cops doing here? Great. I get a high profile job with a top-flight organization, and on my first day they get busted for insider trading or some other white-collar offense, he sighed. He wasn't going to let this get to him. Punching seven-seven he heard, "Please leave your outgoing message at the tone. Press pound when you are finished."

After the tone, he said in what he thought to be his most professional-sounding tone, "This is Scott Murphy. I am unavailable to take your call right now, but leave your name and number at the tone and I will return your call as soon as possible." He pressed the # key, and then punched in ** as instructed to playback his message. He guessed it sounded okay, when he felt a hand on his shoulder.

Turning, he found himself looking up at the cop who had left with Allen moments ago. "Mr. Murphy—I'm Sergeant Harris with the LAPD. Do you have a moment? I'd like to ask you a few questions?"

"Uh, sure, I guess. I should tell you that today is my first day here, so I'm not sure what I can tell you."

"Mr. Goldman told me that. Could you join me in the conference room where we can have a little privacy?"

Scott followed the police officer into the well-appointed conference room. He had been in here once before, during his interview. Sgt. Harris motioned Scott to take a seat at the head of the long, oval table, and then he took the seat to his right. On the walls surrounding the table were stylish, framed photographs of the Campbell facilities around the world, and several pictures of large commercial buildings that used

Campbell products in their construction. The Sergeant took a sip from a gleaming, purple coffee mug, with the words Campbell Industries embossed in gold. Judging from his stare, Scott quickly surmised this guy was all business. "So you just started today, Mr. Murphy?"

"That's right, and call me Scott."

"I understand you transferred from the South, Scott."

"That's correct. Memphis."

"That's a fun town—I've been to Beale Street. I've got a cousin there who works for FedEx. He lives in Collierville—you know where that is?"

"Yes, that's a nice suburb. It's a really booming area," Scott replied, wondering when he would get to the point.

"Have you ever heard of an employee here named Maria Lopez?"

"No, but I haven't had the chance to meet everyone yet."

"I don't know if you'll meet her anytime soon. Seems she was working here as a temp—a secretary—and her mother has reported her missing. Apparently no one has seen her since she left work here last Thursday."

"I haven't heard anything about her, Sergeant Harris."

Harris could tell that Murphy was a straight shooter. "If you do hear anything that strikes you as unusual Scott, please give me a call. It could be helpful to our investigation," Harris said as he pushed a business card across the table to Scott. "Oh, and call me Mike."

CHAPTER 5

SCOTT STEERED his car out of the City of Commerce Business Park, simultaneously loosening his tie and opening the sunroof. This had certainly been an auspicious beginning. It wasn't even noon, and he had been verbally screwed with by Stevens, insulted by Cassler, and interrogated by a cop. This was quite an outfit.

Driving back to Long Beach, he noticed that the freeway traffic was much lighter this time of day. Allen had told him to go home, review his territory sales history, look over the HR manual, fire-up his laptop, and shop for munchies to bring to the five o'clock sales meeting. No need to check in, if anything came up, they could page him. So far, a disappointing first day, but at least he was out of that seemingly hostile office.

Parallel his car on the now deserted street in front of his apartment complex, Scott gathered his briefcase, jacket and HR manual and walked to his unit. Once inside, he dumped his load on the small, round kitchen table, and opened the refrigerator. Taking out a bottled water, he went into his small living room and sat in his recliner. This was his first *big* purchase after graduation, and had quickly become his favorite chair. After further reflection on his morning, and a few sips of water, he was sound asleep.

*   *   *

STIRRING from what turned out to be a two-hour nap, Scott left the apartment and walked over the bridge connecting Belmont Shore to Naples Island. This street was one of the main factors in his decision to rent here. As much time as he would be spending in his car, to have your bank, dry-cleaners, convenience store and a multitude of restaurants within walking distance seemed to be a big plus. He entered the Mexacali restaurant and took a seat by the window. After ordering two chicken tacos and a coke from the waitress, he looked out the large window to 'people watch.' There were all types in California. He wondered how some of these people could hold down jobs—and if they couldn't, how in the hell could they support themselves with the high cost of living out here? Watching the parade of Rollerbladers, bimbos, surfer-dudes and burnouts, he finished his lunch and returned home.

Scott drove to the Lucky's supermarket on the corner of 2nd Street and Pacific Coast Highway—PCH to the locals—and walked inside. Grabbing a shopping cart, he proceeded to the deli counter. A group of people were standing to his right, as he tried to get the attention of the man working behind the glass case, "Hi, I'd like to order a…"

"Take a number!" barked the dark, mustached man in the paper hat and dirty white apron, as he motioned to a ticket dispenser with a digital display that said: Now Serving 28. He took his ticket, and shook his head when he read the 36 printed on it. The man behind the counter seemed to be deliberately working slowly. Scott couldn't help but to notice the man's indifference to the customers. He also noticed that he was the only guy in a tie waiting to make a purchase. Why in the world couldn't Regina or Lori or *somebody* in the office take care of this besides him? If this was the newest guy's responsibility, one of his next questions for Allen would have to do with when they planned to bring the *next* new guy on board.

"Thirty six!" snapped the counterman.

Scott stepped forward, and said, "That's me. I would like…"

"I must have your ticket!" the man growled at Scott.

He handed his paper ticket over and said, "*Now* can I order?" The dark man glared at him, nodding his approval. "OK, I would like to order a fruit plate that can feed twelve people."

"Can pick up tomorrow at 6 AM."

"6 AM? I need this now."

"No can do now. 6 AM only. Yes or No."

"No." Scott thought about asking to see a manager, but a quick glance at his watch showed the time to be ten 'til four. Steering the cart down the beverage aisle, he threw in a twelve-pack of Cokes, a twelve-pack of diet Cokes and at the end of the aisle grabbed two six-packs of Evian bottled water. Two aisles over he quickly added a bag of Tostitos, a bag of pretzels, a bag of plain and a bag of peanut m&m's—he remembered Allen saying something about m&m's—and a bag of cheddar popcorn. Hurrying through the checkout and across the parking lot, he quickly loaded the three bags into his trunk. This should be fine, he thought. What do these guys expect for a meeting—a four-course meal? Laughing at the absurdity of it all, he accelerated onto the 405 freeway.

*   *   *

THE FREEWAY TRAFFIC had picked up considerably as Scott weaved his way toward the office. Once there, he opted to leave the grocery bags in the car until he could locate Allen and ask where he wanted them. "Hello, Lori," he said smiling. She looked up from the magazine she was reading, nodded, and resumed her reading. The clock behind her read 4:50 PM. Turning left at the end of the corridor, he noticed that Regina was not at her desk.

He saw that Allen's door was open, and knocked as he stuck his head inside. "Scott! I was wondering if you were going to make it back," Allen said in a humorous tone.

"I have the *snacks* for the meeting. Where do you want me to put them?"

"In the main conference room." As Scott left Allen's office, he noticed that the bullpen was now buzzing with activity.

Ducking into the conference room, he dumped his briefcase on a chair. Passing Lori twice with no acknowledgment either time, he returned to the conference room with his three bags of groceries. By now several of his new colleagues were milling about the room. Scott spoke to the person closest to the door, "Hi, I'm Scott Murphy—the new guy. Where should I put these?"

"Oh, just put them in the center of the table so we can rip into them. I'm Kevin Forrester." The bags were set down in the center of the table, as instructed by Forrester. They were barely out of Scott's hands before the sales team started rummaging through them.

"What is this shit? Popcorn? Potato Chips? Give me a break!" said a blond, well-dressed, GQ-looking weasel. He shot Scott a look of disgust.

Before Scott could say anything, Allen walked in and said, "Let's get started gentlemen," as he closed the door behind him.

Scott went to the seat where he had left his briefcase only to find a nerdy-looking guy sitting in the chair. "Hi, I'm Scott Murphy. I left my briefcase in that chair."

"That's your problem, rookie. This has been my chair for the past ten years," he said without making eye contact. Scott briefly thought about pulling this guy out of his chair and slapping him across the room. What was wrong with these people? Apparently they all needed a good old-fashioned ass whipping.

Taking a more diplomatic course of action, he said, "No problem, but can you tell me *where* you put my briefcase?"

"In the corner, by the demo wall," he said motioning to the far left hand corner of the room. Scott felt as if all eyes were on him as he retrieved his case. Turning to the table, he noticed an open seat with a tent-card in front of it declaring: ROOKIE. There were other open seats, but trying to show them what he was made of, Scott took that seat, as several giggled like schoolgirls.

"Gentlemen, and I use that term *loosely*, I would like to introduce you to the newest member of our team, Scott Murphy," Allen said from the head of the table. As the group stared at him, Allen continued, "Scott has moved here from Memphis to join our team. He graduated from Memphis, and has two years of outside sales experience. Let's all do what we can to make him welcome. Scott, would you like to say anything?"

Scott felt cold sweat running down his sides as he faced the menacing stares from the assembled group. "I'm just really glad to be here…and I look forward to working with each of you."

"He doesn't sound like he's from Memphis," remarked the GQ twerp sarcastically.

Before Scott could deliver a witty comeback, Allen suggested, "Why don't we all introduce ourselves to Scott, tell him a little about yourself, the territory you cover, and how long you've been with Campbell. Let's start with you Janet," he said gesturing to the woman on his right.

"Hi, Scott. My name is Janet Carter. I was recently promoted from the customer service department. I've been at Campbell for four years. My territory is West LA." Janet was tall, thin, and very attractive with sharp distinctive facial features. Her brown hair was cut in a short, professional bob, and she was wearing a beige suit with a skirt so short her jacket almost covered it when she stood. Great legs, too, Scott noted.

Next to Janet was the GQ twerp. This guy, in Scott's estimation, probably spent fifty bucks on a haircut, and everything else he made on his clothes. His hair was probably bleached blond, and judging from his tan, he must spend a lot of time outdoors, or in a tanning bed. He was wearing a double-breasted black and gray houndstooth Italian suit, with a black tie that had a red and gold diamond-shaped print. He was staring intently at the small screen of his Palm Pilot.

Allen interrupted his trance, "Tim? Could you turn off your *brain* and join the meeting?"

Tim looked up, not amused at Allen's remark. "I'll have you know that this tool is the closest I've ever come to having a magic wand," he sniffed. "You have a sense when you hold a Palm Pilot that you're grasping some distillation of human knowledge that represents centuries of evolution..."

Allen cut him off, "Enough geekspeak about your gadget fetish, Tim. Just introduce yourself to Scott."

He stood up, all five-foot-nine of him, ever so cocky, "I'm Tim Newsom. I've been at Campbell for two years, since graduating from Cal-State Northridge..." His over-animated gestures revealed a gold link bracelet under his right shirt cuff, and flashed his gold cufflinks. Scott also noticed a wedding ring on his left hand and a signet ring on his right. "...my territory is what we call the "Wilshire Corridor. Within it are some of our most high profile accounts and facilities. I would be remiss if I didn't mention that as we begin a new fiscal year, I won Salesman of the Year last year, and have every intention of a repeat this year." A collective groan came from the group.

"Darrin Johnson is my name," a deep bass voice boomed as an athletic, black guy stood up. "I have been at Campbell since graduation from UCLA twelve years ago. I am married with two kids—both girls—and I cover the South Central LA—Compton—Carson territory." Darrin struck Scott as a real professional, no-nonsense kind of guy. He thought this was a guy he could trust.

The nerdy guy who moved Scott's briefcase spoke next. "Marvin Beadles, Cal-State Fullerton, I handle all the aerospace accounts, and have done so for fourteen years," he said in a nasal monotone, not bothering to stand or look in Scott's direction. This guy was wearing a transparent short sleeve, cotton-poly blend shirt, a tie that was too thin to be considered fashionable, and black, polyester Sansabelt slacks, topping a pair of brown Hushpuppies. He had thick unruly, dark hair that hung over a thin face framed by large, black horn-rimmed glasses. All that was missing was the pocket pencil protector.

Kevin Forrester, sitting next to Scott leaned over and whispered, "Marv has the aerospace accounts because his father-in-law is a big shot at Boeing. His wife works there, too." He then stood and said, "I'm Kevin Forrester—we met earlier. I went to Long Beach State—*Go 'Niners!*—and I've been at Campbell for five years. I now have the Smog-Belt territory—Ontario, Simi Valley and all that good stuff— because it's close to my new house in Upland. I used to have the South Bay territory, your *new* territory. I'll do all I can to help transition the customers to you. Welcome aboard, Scott!" This guy seemed OK to Scott. Forrester had light brown hair and mustache. He was slightly overweight, but seemed to be very laid back and easy going, in a frat-boy mentality sort of way.

Then, a short, thin Asian man stood, "I'm Jerry Fujisaka…UC-Irvine…I'm married with no children…have been at Campbell seven years…oh, and I cover the Glendale area, including Chinatown, Little Tokyo and Little Saigon…welcome, Scott." Jerry was very articulate and well dressed. He stood five-seven, had coal-black hair and a well-trimmed mustache.   ·

A slow, Southern drawl permeated the quiet, "I'm Jimmy Brady, I started with Campbell at the corprutt office in New Awlins. I transferred here two anna half years ago from the Memphis Trainin' Center—but I've been with Campbell for sixteen years—that's six longer than Allen. I graduated from the University of Alabama-Birmingham, and I'm glad to have a fella Conference USA member here in La-La land." He smiled broadly. "OK, what else…uh…I'm pursuin' my masters at USC. I'm married with three young-uns. I handle our national accounts in LA, and I'm also responsible for the western region's product trainin' efforts. Glad to have ya on the team, Scotty." Jimmy was about 6'0" tall with receding brown hair, honest brown eyes and an easy smile. Scott pictured Jimmy as a responsible family man.

As Brady seated himself, Allen said, "OK, thanks for the introductions. Everybody grab a drink and let's get started." He waited about ten seconds. "Guys—*and* Janet—as you all know we have committed to 15% growth this year. We must hit that threshold for yours truly to see any bonus money." The group snickered. "I also get a kicker if we beat the Orange County team in overall sales dollars. We all need to bust our tails to bring the 'Eagle Award' back to the LA team—where it belongs. By the end of the month I will have met with each of you to review your sales goals and personal goals…"

*   *   *

AS THE MEETING BROKE UP, Kevin walked Scott out to the parking lot. "Let's meet at Hof's Hut on Second for breakfast—say 7:30? Then we can schedule a quick pass through some of your larger accounts. It'll probably take us two to three days for me to hand over everything."

"I really appreciate your help with this."

"No problem, just remember, payback's a bitch!" Kevin said laughing. "See you tomorrow for phase one of operation brain dump." Kevin said as he slapped Scott on the back and walked over to get in his Ford Explorer. Scott couldn't help noticing that the majority of the vehicles in the parking lot were SUVs. Why would people in Southern California need SUVs? As he eased himself into his Maxima, he noticed Tim Newsom in his rear view mirror speed out of the parking lot. He was driving a white BMW convertible. At least somebody else drives a sedan, he thought.

KNOCK-KNOCK-KNOCK-KNOCK. Scott looked around to see Cassler knocking on his window. He pulled the toggle switch toward him to bring down his window. "How was the first day, champ?" Cassler asked, smirking.

Champ? Why is he calling me champ? Scott thought. "Fine. Thanks," he said.

"Glad to hear it. You're single, right?"

"Right."

"I'm married. Yep, married guy. It's not for everyone. Hey, is this your car?"

"Yes, I just bought it." Scott had an uneasy feeling about the way this guy was looking at him.

"My wife has one of these. They're great cars for women, you know?"

Scott briefly considered swinging his door open hard on Cassler's kneecaps, but refrained and said, "Yeah, I'm sure they are. See you later." Scott rolled up the window and put the car into reverse. Cassler walked away, disappointed that he couldn't rattle Scott. As he pulled away, Scott watched in his side view mirror as Cassler climbed—with some difficulty—into his Ford Expedition. He wanted to go back and ask Cassler if he needed a boost, or a ladder, but thought he would save it for another time. After all, this was just his first day.

CHAPTER 6

SCOTT WAS SEATED with his back to the wall, under what appeared to be a stuffed and mounted Great White Shark. He sipped his orange juice and perused the menu as he waited for Kevin. It was 7:50 when he noticed Kevin walk through the front door. Standing to get his attention, Scott motioned him over to the table.

"Traffic was a bitch, man!" Kevin said as he pulled out his chair. "One of the disadvantages of living inland." Kevin's hair was wet from hair gel, and his tie hung untied around his open shirt collar.

The waitress approached the table, "Would you gentlemen care to order?"

"Do you take orders to go?" Kevin asked, winking at Scott.

"Sure."

"Then grab your coat and purse, and let's go!" The waitress blushed, and smiled. Looking at her nametag, Kevin continued with a big, toothy smile, "Kristy with a 'K', my name is Kevin—also with a 'K'—and this is my partner Scott. I need coffee—black—and lots of it!" Kevin was approvingly looking the waitress over. She appeared to be in her early twenties, slim, light skin, red hair and soft green eyes.

"Anything to eat?"

"Yeah, how about a Denver omelet—extra cheese, Kristy."

Scott put down his menu and said, "I'd like the multi-grain pancakes."

"Thanks, guys," she said flirtatiously, leaving the table.

"Dude, she's *hot!*" Kevin exclaimed with a wide-eyed expression.

"Not bad," Scott added.

"Not bad? Please tell me you're not gay! I can't be cooped up in the car all day with a fag—that would be like riding with Cassler."

"Afraid you wouldn't trust yourself?" Scott said laughing.

"*Oh,* looks like we have ourselves a quick one! You're okay, man," Kevin said with a smile, approving the wit of his breakfast companion. "You're not having coffee?"

"No," Scott replied, "I've never picked up the habit."

"That's cool. I'm going to ask Kristy for her number—whaddaya think?"

"Hey, go for it."

"Cool—just making sure you didn't have dibs on her."

As their breakfast arrived, Scott pulled a legal pad from his briefcase as Kevin made goo-goo eyes with the waitress. "What can you tell me about the South Bay territory?" he asked, trying to get Kevin's thoughts on transitioning the accounts.

"Oh, you've got your typical wholesaler bullshit. Alexander's will take a *huge* amount of time. They can be a real pain in the ass. They'll suck the life out of you if you let them. Allen used to work there. Paramount is a small independent but loyal to Campbell. Signal Hill is another like that. Anchor Electric in Los Alamitos will jerk you around a lot. They buy a lot of that Powerlyte crap. You've got several branch locations of chains—Burke Electric, ESD, Saddleback, Graybar—most of these houses pull stock from their main warehouses, so you won't see any credit. But, as Allen says, 'it's the salary portion of your job to support these accounts,' so you'll have to do the PR thing, make sure their litera-ture and pricing is up to date, handle warranty returns, issue credits…that sort of thing." Kevin pushed away his empty plate and began to tie his tie, looking at his reflection in his spoon.

Kristy arrived with the check, and Scott said, "I'll get this."

"No way. You're the new guy."

"But, you're helping me out—I hate for you to pay for this."

"Dude, I'm expensing it," Kevin said as he handed Kristy his corporate American Express card. "Oh, and Kristy, I'd like you to give yourself a twenty-five percent tip for your courteous and professional service."

"Thank you, sir."

"Sir? It's Kevin."

"OK, Kevin, I'll be right back with this." Kristy smiled and walked away.

"Check out her ass, man," Kevin quietly drooled, staring at the departing waitress.

"I really do appreciate you taking the time to help me get acclimated," Scott said, trying to return the subject matter to business.

"No problem, man. Besides, Allen told me I *had* to," Kevin said laughing.

Kristy returned, handing the check and AMEX card to Kevin. "Thanks Kevin. I've enjoyed waiting on both of you. Is there *anything* else I can do for you?" she asked, in a manner that Scott observed as being very seductive.

"How about your phone number?" Kevin asked with a mischievous grin.

Kristy smiled, took back the check, and leaning over the table revealing a nice rack, she scribbled on the back with big, loopy strokes. Handing it back to Kevin, she said, "Call me—*if* you're single and have a steady job."

"Based on that criteria, I believe I've qualified!" Kevin said to Scott motioning for a high-five. Scott delivered the hand slap, they both got up, Kevin gave Kristy a half-hug, said good-bye and they left.

Walking to the parking lot down across the street, behind the Thrifty's Jr., Kevin said, "You're driving—I'll ride shotgun. I need to get my sunglasses out of my truck."

As they pulled out of the parking lot, Kevin slid on his Oakley Blades, and said, "Just go right on Second Street, and we'll avoid the freeways.

I'll take you to Alexander's first, to get it over with…my last time getting beat up there, *thank* God."

Scott following Kevin's instructions, looked out at the ocean to his left. "What are those structures out there?"

Kevin glanced over and replied, "I think they're oil derricks, or something like that. My understanding is that the houses across the street didn't like looking at them, so they put up those facades to make them look like some sort of buildings, I guess. Man, what a great start to my day—I got her number! Hopefully she won't flake on me. This one could have potential, bud."

"Hope it works out," Scott said.

Kevin pulled down his sunglasses, and looked at Scott. "You got a girlfriend?"

"No, I just moved out here, and haven't had a chance to meet anyone."

"Leave a girl back home—where was it—Nashville?"

"No, Memphis. No, no girlfriend. I dated a girl for a while in college, but we broke up shortly after graduation…different value systems."

"Value systems? Man, this is LA—you won't find any chicks with values out here!" Kevin said, amused at the thought. Kevin pulled the lever on the right-hand side of his seat, and eased into a reclined position. "OK, we've covered your accounts, let me fill you in on all the office gossip. Where to begin? Lori Johnson, the receptionist, single and a babe. I hear she's a dick-hound, but she won't give sales reps the time of day—*major* attitude—she wants someone to show her the money! Janet, well let's just say she got her promotion the old fashioned way—she earned it—on her back!"

"With *Allen*?"

"No! Allen's a good married guy—he doesn't screw around—which makes him a minority in that office. He didn't want her promoted, he knew she wasn't qualified, but he was shot down by Glenn—who was sticking it to her—Janet and anything else wearing a skirt in that office. Did you meet Maria Lopez—the chick that's missing—she was Glenn's secretary?"

"No, but a cop asked me about her yesterday."

"Yeah, that's strange. He talked to me, too. She probably just had enough and left—or met some guy, who knows? Anyway, it was well known that she and Stevens were pounding the Posturepedic. Man, she has a hot little body on her, too. I think she has a kid…oh, and speaking of the devil—Glenn Stevens—steer clear of him, he's cutthroat. A real corporate curtain-climber. I think he's actually upset that the economy has turned around…he enjoyed downsizing—gave him a chance to fuck with people's lives. Let's see…who else? Sheila Bryant in HR—another hot number. Some guys think Glenn breeds these chicks on a ranch someplace. Regina? She's a hard working single mom—divorced. She takes care of us. Rumor has it that she used to do Glenn, too—who knows?"

"What about Jon Cassler?"

"Cassler? What a fucking prick! If he were any more stupid, he'd have to be watered twice a week! That guy is the biggest ass-kisser I've ever seen in my life. *Completely* incompetent! Glenn likes having him around because they're a lot alike—neither has a conscience. Don't let him get on your nerves—he's married, but I think he's a closet homosexual. Tim Newsom, as you probably picked up on, thinks his shit doesn't stink. He's a sawed-off little pretty boy, who doesn't know jacksquat about our product line, but he plays the political game good. Watch your back around him…I'm sure when he was a kid, his report card said he doesn't play well with others. Darrin and Jerry are good guys. They were both hired to fill quotas, and handle the minority accounts. Darrin is a hard worker and keeps to himself. Fujisaka is a little frustrated with all the bullshit political games played at Campbell. You remember Jimmy from last night?"

"Yeah, the UAB grad."

"That's Jimmy. Son of the South. Another good guy. He has deep ties into home office, so nobody gives him a lot of shit. He'll also help you with any technical or product application questions you come up with. Solid guy. Have you met Jose in the warehouse?"

"No."

"I'll introduce you. Been there a long time. It's good to get on his good side, because he can be very helpful expediting orders for one of your customers in a crunch. Take him to lunch every now and then—he digs that. What else…uh…the Orange County sales team is pretty *aloof*. They've outsold us the past two years. Cassler acts as if it has something to do with him—which it doesn't. Customers *hate* that fat dweeb! I guess that's about it, oh, turn right up at the light."

"What about Beadles?"

"Good ol' Marv'—he's a major league dork. Let's just say, he brings a lot of joy whenever he leaves the room. I told you last night his father-in-law and wife both work for Boeing. I think daddy-in-law cut a deal with Glenn's predecessor to let that twerp handle our aerospace accounts. He's a classic engineering toad, who should be doing blue-print take-offs, and not be in front of customers. Even though he's knowledgeable, don't ask him to answer any technical questions—he'll just tell you what manual to look in—after he tells you the answer is something someone in your position should already know. But I wouldn't let him get to you. He has the social skills of your average computer geek. It's nothing personal. Uh, okay, turn right again up here, and right into the parking lot. Oh, and park over by the garbage dump-sters—they like the spaces up front to be used by customers. Plus I think they like the symbolism of having the reps park there. Welcome to your largest account…Alexander's."

Scott parked by the garbage dumpster, as instructed, as Kevin placed his chair in the upright position, and tossed his shades on the dash. Kevin buttoned his collar button and pulled up his tie. "FYI on dress code: Always wear a suit and tie at the office. If you're not going into the office, there are several accounts who don't mind, hell, actually prefer that you call on them in a golf shirt and khakis. I'll tell you who they are—and Alexander's isn't one of them. Are you ready?"

"I was born ready," Scott said self-assuredly.

"I like that," declared Kevin. The two got out of the car, pulled on their jackets and walked across the parking lot toward the building. A large sign reading—Alexander's Electric Supply Co., Inc—was spelled out in blue, cursive lettering, facing the street. At the bottom Scott noted that it read: Established 1966.

"See that green Lexus?" Kevin asked. "That belongs to Nick Lunsford. He owns all of the Alexander's chain. You'll never see him in a tie, but he insists that all his reps wear them. I guess it makes him feel important. He's a real hard-ass. But if follow-up and follow-through are your strong suites, you won't have too much of a problem with him. As with any account, just make his problems go away. Oh, and you'll meet quite a few guys here with the last name of Alexander. They don't own anything, they just work here. Apparently their old man was something of a gambler, got in over his head, and Lunsford took the company away in a leveraged buyout about ten years ago. He was the sales manager here before that. I know the company has grown under his direction, but I can't help but to feel sorry for the Alexander boys. They got screwed by their own dad. I also think them still working here strokes Lunsford's ego."

After several introductions, the two worked their way back to Nick Lunsford's office. Nick motioned them in, and said, "Well, look what the cat drug in." Lunsford stood up revealing an athletic build on a six-foot-two frame. He was tanned, with brown hair and piercing green eyes. He was wearing a royal blue golf shirt with the Alexander's logo on the left chest, and starched khakis. He appeared to be in his early fifties, and in great shape for his age. Scott noticed US Navy memorabilia scattered throughout his office. On the desk was an upright grenade, mounted on a piece of cherry wood, with a note attached to the pin that read: SALESMEN TAKE A NUMBER.

"Nick, this is my replacement, Scott Murphy. I know you probably think I can't be replaced…"

"It's about damn time. I never thought we would get rid of your worthless ass, Forrester," Lunsford said, unsmiling.

Scott couldn't tell if he was joking or not. "Nice to meet you."

"We'll see if you still feel that way after you leave here," Lunsford said firmly.

After shaking hands with Lunsford, Scott and Kevin seated themselves following Lunsford's lead. "OK, listen up," Lunsford snapped. "Here's what I expect from a rep. When I call, and I leave a message in your fucking voicemail, I want my call returned within an hour. If I page you, I want you to call me back within fifteen minutes. Learn your product line. Don't park in front of my building—that's reserved for customers. Call on *all* my branches. Make sure my staff has current catalogs and price sheets. I want you to make joint contractor calls with my outside sales reps on a weekly basis. We have a trade show twice a year. I expect you to participate by manning a booth, doing product demos, and contributing a door prize. I want you to conduct quarterly product training sessions for my staff—after hours. We have a desk set up for vendor salesmen—don't let me catch you making long distance or personal calls from my phone. If I have a problem with an invoice, I expect you to handle it. I have better things to do with my time than fuck around with your billing department. And finally, do not hit on or ask out any women that work here. I have two daughters that work for me, and I will not have them getting involved with sales scum. If I have any problems with you, I won't hesitate to call Allen Goldman—he used to work for me. Do I make myself clear?"

"Crystal clear," Scott replied nervously.

"Then we will have no problems," Lunsford said, squinting menacingly as he drummed his fingers on his desk.

Kevin seemed to enjoy watching Scott get reamed by Lunsford. "Scott here is new to our company," he interjected.

"Is that right? What did you do before?" Lunsford asked in an accusing tone.

"I worked as a sales rep for Mid-American Electric in Memphis."

"Memphis? Are you familiar with the Naval Air Station out in Millington?"

"Yes, sir."

"Well, I was stationed there for four years while I was in the Navy. I married a Memphis girl. All of my wife's family is there. We ended up out here when I finished my hitch in Long Beach. Did you attend The University of Memphis?"

"Yes sir, I graduated two and a half years ago."

"Good for you, son. I have a nephew who just started there—you probably wouldn't know him, since I would guess he started after you left. Your school usually has a helluva basketball team, too. What was that coach's name that took them to the Final Four in '85?"

"Dana Kirk."

"That's right, Coach Kirk—pretty crafty son-of-a-bitch. Hell, I remember back when the Larrys—Finch and Kenon—played UCLA in the championship game in the early seventies. And now Coach Cal seems to have them back on the national scene."

"He's doing a great job." Scott replied, as his confidence grew from this newfound common thread. He squared his shoulders and looked Nick straight in the eye. "Nick, I may be new to Campbell, but I want you to know that I take my job and my career very seriously. But you should also know that I don't work for Campbell. I don't work for Allen Goldman. I work for Nick Lunsford, and my other distributors. I know full well that in reality, it's you, not Campbell, that signs my paycheck. I may not always have all of the answers, but I can promise you that I will get the answers you need—and quickly. If you ever have a problem with the way I handle your account, I don't want you to hesitate to let me know."

"I think you and I will get along just fine," Nick said as a genuine smile spread across his face. Kevin thought he was going to fall out of his chair.

CHAPTER 7

THE NEXT DAY started much the same. Kevin met Scott for breakfast—and he was late again. No cute waitress this morning, just a guy who talked too much about how he really wasn't a waiter, but an actor. Scott thought it was pretty funny when Kevin told him to "Act like a waiter and get their food." Scott was again the designated driver, while Kevin continued to navigate. After calling on Alexander's, ESD and Saddleback yesterday, Kevin had told Scott that, if all went well, they would probably complete a first pass of his distributors today.

Kevin was still in shock about the way Scott and Nick Lunsford had hit it off yesterday. He was impressed, and frankly, a little jealous. After trying for years to develop some kind of rapport with that hard-ass, the rookie had done it in twenty minutes. Beginner's luck, Kevin rationalized to himself.

They had already hit two Graybar branches and a Burke branch that morning, when they parked in front of Paramount Electrical Distributor Co., Inc. The non-descript, light green, cinder-block building was situated in the back of a large parking lot. It had a prison-like appearance, due to the absence of any exterior windows. The city of Paramount, California also struck Scott as non-descript, as they made their way to their destination. Scott had assumed that *Paramount Pictures* was located in Paramount. This notion brought a hearty laugh from Kevin. A small, wooden sign hung over the door, with Paramount

Electrical Distributors—*WHOLESALE ONLY*—in crude, black, hand-painted lettering. Scott observed that there were no cars in the large parking lot, bordered by a chain-link fence.

The two men opened the weathered, wooden door and closed it behind them. The dimly lit counter area had two bar-type stools unoccupied in front of it. Behind the counter, a young guy with a scrappy goatee and a *Paramount* baseball cap was reading the sports page of the *Los Angeles Times.* Scott couldn't help but to notice the four rows of nearly empty shelving behind the counter. "Hey, Kenny! Is Charles in? Kevin asked.

"Yeah, in his office," Kenny said, looking up and stroking his chin whiskers.

"This is your new Campbell rep, Scott Murphy," Kevin said.

"Nice to meet you, Kenny," Scott said stepping forward to shake hands across the counter.

"Yeah. Same here. Do you have a card?"

"Sure," Scott said, pulling a business card from his shirt pocket and handing it to Kenny.

"Thanks…just in case I have to call about something, you know," Kenny said as he put the card down on the counter beside him, and resumed reading the paper.

"Scott here is a great guy! He'll take good care of you," Kevin said in a way so sincere that Scott found it almost flattering, until he remembered what a bullshit artist Kevin was. Leaving Kenny at the counter, they walked through a battered wooden door.

"Like I told you, Charles is Vietnamese, but a sharp guy. You don't have to worry about him crossing our product to a competitor. And, don't call Charles 'Chuck,' 'Charlie,' or 'Chas,' or anything like that. He wants to be called Charles and only Charles. And his last name is pronounced, 'Win,' although it's spelled with an 'N' or something," Kevin said as the two made their way down a narrow corridor.

"Charles," Scott repeated. "Got it."

At the end of the hall, the word MANAGER was printed on an open door with adhesive, black lettering. Sitting behind a desk, talking on the phone was a young Asian man. Scott guessed he couldn't be older than twenty. He acknowledged their presence and gestured them to be seated in two folding metal chairs, as he continued to speak on the phone. Scott noticed that the desk was spotless, along with the walls, except for a conspicuous *Makita Power Tools* pin-up girl calendar. This month featured a tanned, bikini-clad brunette, wearing a cowboy hat and boots, wielding two 12-volt cordless drills in a gunfighter pose. Over the past two days, Scott's pre-conceived glamour of his new job was quickly fading.

"OK, OK, OK, thank you. OK. Goodbye," the young man said as he completed his phone conversation. "Hello, Kevin! This must be your replacement. I'm Charles Nguyen," he said in a soft voice, placing the handset on the cradle.

"Replacement? You know I can't be replaced, Charles!" Kevin said in mock disappointment.

"Right, right," Charles said smiling.

"I'm Scott Murphy," he said as they shook hands. "Here's my card— It includes my pager number."

"Thank you," Charles replied, fumbling through his desk drawers. "I know I have a card in here somewhere...ahhh, here's one," he said, handing Scott a dog-eared card. Charles' business card looked like a Kinko's 500 for $9.95 special. Plain black block print on a white card. No logo. Charles' title read the same as his door: MANAGER.

"You'll notice Paramount doesn't stock a lot of product," Charles said as if an explanation was necessary. "We bid a lot of job-work. Bid and spec—you know, that sort of thing—not a lot of walk-in trade. What I buy is typically drop-shipped straight to the job site, often we never touch it. We have always enjoyed a good relationship with Kevin and Campbell Industries. I am looking forward to working with you, too, Scott," Charles said with an unwavering smile.

Kevin had told Scott that Paramount was loyal because he figured nobody else would set them up. Paramount was the new kid on the block; opening only five years ago. He said he probably would not have messed with them either, except that a few years ago, one of his goals was to sign a new distributor in the South Bay territory—a bonus that equaled 7% of his base salary was riding on it. So, he signed them up, and cashed his check. He also told Scott they could sometimes be slow pay, and to monitor this closely. He said he had told Charles before, that he expected Campbell to be paid first when the bills came due. He also said that by Paramount getting the Campbell line, it gave them instant credibility with other manufacturers, and opened the door to several new lines and additional business for Charles. Kevin mentioned that occasionally, Paramount would hit a big job, often some sort of minority-owned business, state government contract, so they were worth supporting from a revenue standpoint.

"I'm looking forward to working with you, too," Scott said enthusiastically. "I'll be by on a regular basis, but if something comes up, don't hesitate to contact me."

"I'm sure you will be as good to us as Kevin has been," Charles said warmly.

∗   ∗   ∗

LEAVING PARAMOUNT, Kevin had decided that their next stop would be Anchor in Los Alamitos, but lunch was next on the agenda. He had suggested that they check out an all-you-can-eat lunch buffet at Domenico's Pizza on Naples Island—just three blocks from Scott's apartment.

As the two entered the restaurant, it took a moment for their eyes to adjust to the dark interior. The host, wearing a white tuxedo shirt, but no bow tie, approached them. "Two for lunch? Excellent. Come this way." He led them to a round table with curved bench seat in the shape of a half-circle. The table was covered with a long, white tablecloth, topped with a circular piece of glass. As they slid onto the red, vinyl covered bench, the host asked, "Will you be ordering off the menu, or enjoying the lunch buffet?"

"Buffet," Kevin said, not waiting for an answer from Scott.

"Excellent. And to drink?"

"Michelob Light," replied Kevin, not looking at the host, but at the buffet spread.

"Iced tea," answered Scott.

"Excellent. Help yourselves to the buffet anytime, gentlemen," said the host, laying down two sets of silverware wrapped in maroon, cloth napkins, and walking away.

"Iced Tea?" Kevin sneered, "Light-weight." Before Scott could reply, Kevin blurted out, "Shit! Will you look at that?" Following the direction of Kevin's gaze, Scott noticed that across the restaurant sat Glenn Stevens. And he was all over their fellow sales rep, Janet. The tablecloth obscured their view, but the two were seated extremely close to one another, and their hands appeared to be working overtime under the table. Judging from the dewy-eyed, horny expression on Janet's face, this was a consensual act. Scott recalled Kevin's gossip about Janet's path to career advancement.

Kevin and Scott walked over to the buffet table, trying not to draw attention to themselves. Scott felt especially conspicuous. Their worries were unrealized, since Glenn and Janet never took their eyes off each other. Returning to their table, Scott tried to avert his eyes as he munched on a slice of pepperoni and pineapple pizza. Kevin chowed down on his calzone and slurped his beer, watching the entertaining show before them as if he was at a sporting event. He also felt it his place to narrate the activities for Scott. "Oh, man. It looks like his hand is completely up her dress! And she's obviously massaging his unit, if you know what I mean," he said gleefully.

Scott glanced over occasionally, still in disbelief of this public spectacle. Scott said, "For Christ sakes, he's a VP! He's married! Hell, *she's* married! Doesn't he care about anybody seeing them together?"

"Stevens?" Kevin questioned in disbelief. "That son-of-a-bitch has brass balls! He thinks he's bulletproof. Hey, it looks like they're taking a breather." Scott looked up and saw Janet, now seated not as close to Glenn, fishing through the contents of her purse. She took out a tube of lipstick. Taking off the cap, she drew a slow, sensual circle around her mouth with the lipstick, as Glenn looked on approvingly. Placing the cap back on the lipstick, she set it upright on the table. With a leering smirk on his face, Glenn knocked the tube of lipstick off the table. Janet covered her open mouth with both hands, feigning mock surprise. Smiling, she descended under the table to retrieve the lipstick.

Glenn leaned back, stretching his long arms across the back of the half-circle red vinyl bench. A sinister grin spread across his face, as he closed his eyes, and leaned his head back. Scott noticed Glenn had a Band-Aid on his neck. A good forty-five seconds had passed, when Kevin slapped his hand down on the table. "Oh my God! She's still under the table!" he said trying to suppress his excitement. "Janet's giving him a blow job! Right here, right in the open—or at least under the tablecloth." It had now become similar to a car wreck scene for Scott. He wanted to look away, but couldn't. "I bet that bitch could suck the chrome off a trailer-hitch!" Kevin squealed. He was so giddy, one might have thought he was getting the blow job. "I wonder if she'll come over to our table next! Man, when she was in customer service, she used to be just OK, but since her promotion, she's cut her hair, traded in her glasses for contacts, and started dressing really sharp, showing off her great gams. A real ugly duckling story," he continued, never taking his eyes off Glenn's table. Scott couldn't help noticing the patrons walking to and from the buffet, oblivious to what was taking place.

At that moment, Glenn lowered his head, snapping his eyes open quickly. Scott felt they were locked on him, even in the darkened restaurant. Glenn's eyes were unwavering, and Scott felt as if they were boring a hole through his head. Kicking Kevin under the table, Scott tensely whispered, "He sees us."

"No way. It's too dark in here. And even if he does, we're not doing anything wrong. Just a couple of sales guys, having a little lunch. Can we help it if our boss's boss ordered oral sex for desert? Hey, and maybe it's not what we think. Maybe Mrs. Carter is just having a real hard time finding her lipstick—although my money's on just a real *hard* time!"

Scott watched in disbelief as Janet emerged from under the table. Glenn looked at her admiringly, as she returned to her seat. With her lipstick tube in one hand, she picked up a maroon cloth napkin, and held it with both hands up to her mouth. "Oh, man! Kevin said, almost hysterically. Scott watched as Janet wiped her mouth with the napkin, took a sip of Glenn's martini, and reapplied her lipstick. Glenn leaned over and kissed her on the forehead, in the manner a father might kiss his daughter, Scott thought. Glenn then gestured to the waiter that he was ready for his check.

Scott slowly finished his pizza, as Kevin continued to recount what they thought they had witnessed. After signing his check, and returning his corporate card to his wallet, Glenn slid out of his booth, followed by Janet. Glenn retrieved his suit jacket from a nearby coat hook. Scott noticed Janet's tight, white silk blouse, and her short, navy, pleated skirt. No doubt about it, she had great legs.

Just when Scott convinced himself he was imagining things when he thought he had made eye contact with Glenn; he watched as Glenn, with Janet walking behind him, passed the exit and walked directly toward their table. "Uh, oh," Kevin said quietly, the situation no longer humorous from his perspective.

"Here's a couple of hard working Campbell sales reps. Boys, how are you?" Glenn said in a booming voice, smiling a fake looking smile.

"Good, Glenn," Kevin answered, not looking up from his plate.

"Yeah, just taking a lunch break," Scott said, trying to sound like what he thought someone who had not just witnessed a sex act in public, might sound like.

"Hi, guys!" Janet said, downright bubbly, Scott thought.

"Is Forrester showing you the ropes, Murphy?" Glenn asked.

"Yes, sir. We've covered a lot of ground the past two days."

Glenn's smile had vanished, and Scott couldn't help noticing the cold, dark eyes staring right through him. "Glad to hear it. You know, Domenico's is one of my favorite lunch spots. How was your food?"

"Very good. We had the buffet," Kevin said; casting a quick glance up at Glenn, before averting his eyes back to his plate.

"And yours, Murphy?"

"Very good, sir, I can see why you like this place," Scott replied, realizing the double meaning of his answer only after he blurted it out. Kevin coughed, as if he were choking on something, and took a swig from his beer mug.

"Well, I'll tell you fellas, I'm only a Vice-President, but my service here today was down right *Presidential*," Glenn said, grabbing his crotch and winking devilishly at Scott. "Gotta get back to the old grind. Good seeing you both," Glenn said in a self-righteous tone.

"Bye, guys!" Janet chirped, as she, and her shapely legs, followed Glenn out of the restaurant.

CHAPTER 8

SGT. MIKE HARRIS wheeled his white, unmarked Ford Crown Victoria into a parking slot designated for visitors. As he entered the building, he noticed the same attractive receptionist he had met before, stationed behind her large mahogany desk. "Good afternoon. I'm Sergeant Mike Harris—we met before. I have an appointment to see Ms. Rogers."

"I'll see if she's available," Lori said, flipping her hair without making eye contact. "Regina—a Sergeant Harris is in the lobby to see you. She'll be right out."

"Great. Thank you."

"You'll need to sign the visitor's log."

"OK, no problem." As he scribbled his name and time of appointment, Sgt. Harris thought about trying to engage in some small talk, but figured a cop was of little interest to this cold fish.

Regina walked into the lobby, smiling nervously. "Hello Sergeant. What can I do for you?"

"Nice to see you again, Ms. Rogers. Is there some place I could speak to you alone? It will only take a few minutes."

"Uh, sure...follow me." Regina led Sgt. Harris down the main hallway into the conference room. "Any word on Maria?"

"No, ma'am. We're still investigating."

"Would you care for a beverage?"

"No, ma'am, I'm good."

Regina cautiously eyed Sgt. Harris as he opened his notepad, and scanned his notes. "Please, have a seat."

"Thank you, ma'am…Ms. Rogers, you told me previously that the last day Ms. Lopez was seen at Campbell Industries was last Thursday. Is that still your recollection?"

"Yes. She never showed up for work on Friday. I called her and left two messages on her machine, but she never called back."

"Yes, ma'am. We've checked out her place, and heard your messages on the tape. What time did she leave work on Thursday?"

"As I told you before, I'm not sure. Maria did not report directly to me."

"Yes. Uh, do you recall where you last saw Ms. Lopez in the building?"

"*Saw* her?"

"Yes, ma'am."

"I think it was in the break-room…around four o'clock."

"Where was she working after that?"

"I'm not sure I know."

"Was it in her cubicle?"

"I don't recall."

"Was she working with anyone else in the building?"

"I don't recall."

Sgt. Harris looked up from his notes and gazed sternly at Regina. "Ms. Rogers, anything you might recall could be a tremendous help to our investigation." Regina didn't answer, turned to face the product demo case against the wall, and fidgeted with the hemline of her skirt.

Sgt. Harris stood up. "Would you mind if I looked at the contents of her desk, again?"

"Why no, certainly. And per your instructions, no one has moved any of her belongings, Sergeant."

"Good."

"Sergeant?"

"Yes?"

"Maybe I do remember something…" Sgt. Harris returned to his seat, and re-opened his notepad as he anticipated Regina's next comment. "It seems I recall that Maria had some work to do for Mr. Stevens that afternoon." Regina swallowed hard, before continuing. "As I told you before, she was acting as his personal secretary. I believe she was in his office late Thursday afternoon."

"According to my notes, you said you left the office to pick up your kids about a quarter 'til seven. Is that still your recollection?"

"Yes."

"And you left the building through the main entrance?"

"Yes."

"Did you see Ms. Lopez in Mr. Stevens' office as you were leaving?"

"No—the door was closed."

"Was Mrs. Lopez inside?"

"I don't know for sure."

"Do you think she could have been in his office at that time?"

"Yes, it's possible," Regina blurted. She suddenly felt very uneasy, knowing that her outpouring to Sgt. Harris could cause her to face the wrath of Glenn. She also felt a strange sense of relief. If that bastard was somehow involved with Maria's disappearance, she wanted him to be held accountable.

Regina led Sgt. Harris to Maria's desk, and stood by as Sgt. Harris entered the cube. "Will that be all you'll be needing me for Sergeant?"

"Yes, ma'am. For now. Thank you for your cooperation." Sgt. Harris pulled a pair of latex gloves from his back pocket. Carefully slipping them on, he re-examined the contents of Maria's office. After looking through the three drawers, several hanging files and the assorted items on her desktop, he removed the gloves and left the cube. He then left the building, returning to his car.

Sgt. Harris was in his car, using his cell phone to call the crime lab unit, as Glenn and Janet sped into the parking lot. As he completed his call, Sgt. Harris observed Glenn and Janet exit the black Mercedes, and make their way to the building's entrance. Sgt. Harris watched Janet's legs gracefully climb the steps, only reinforcing his initial impression of the caliber of women working at Campbell. He got out of his car to follow them inside. He stopped by the Mercedes, and noticed the long scratch down the side, as if someone had 'keyed' the car.

He entered the lobby, and couldn't help noticing that suddenly, it seemed that the receptionist found him interesting. Her eyes followed him as he walked past her and down the hallway. As he approached Regina's cube, he saw Glenn with his back to him, his arms waving wildly. Regina was seated, absorbing the brunt of his tirade. "What in the hell is going on here? I leave for lunch, and you're letting the fucking cops poke around my office?"

Sgt. Harris tapped Glenn on the shoulder. "Mr. Stevens?"

Stevens wheeled quickly around and glared down at the officer. "Who in the hell do you think you are?"

"Do I detect that you are upset?"

"Damn right I'm upset! You would think someone had been murdered! Isn't this a little extreme, Sherlock? All this production for one missing person? This is a place of business—you can't come in here and disrupt things like this. Do you have a warrant?"

"Do I need one?"

Glenn stared down at Sgt. Stevens, and took a deep breath. "Why don't you come into my office and tell me what this is all about."

"OK."

The veins on Glenn's neck were visible to Regina.

As the two men seated themselves in Glenn's office, Sgt. Harris took out his notepad. "Mr. Stevens, I'm still investigating the disappearance of Ms. Lopez."

"You haven't found her *yet?*"

"No, sir. When we first spoke, you told me that the last afternoon Ms. Lopez was seen at work was last Thursday."

"That's correct."

"You also told me that you had last seen her in the office around 3:00 PM."

"OK."

"Would it be possible that Ms. Lopez could have been in your office working as late as say, 6:30 or seven o'clock?"

"Anything's possible, I guess. What are you getting at?"

"Well, if that's the case, it could mean that you were the last person to have seen her here."

"OK, if that's the case, and I'm not saying it is, so what?"

"Well, sir, I was hoping you wouldn't mind if some of my colleagues from the crime lab inspected Ms. Lopez's cubicle and your office."

"My office?"

"Yes sir—she did work in there at times also—isn't that correct?"

"Yes, when needed."

"I would appreciate your cooperation so I can expedite this investigation. It's all pretty routine."

"Routine, huh?"

"But, if you prefer, I can call the judge for a search warrant, and trouble the detective squad. I could even go out to my car and get a roll of crime scene tape and seal off…"

"No, no, that won't be necessary. I would appreciate it if your men can work quickly, so we can have as little disruption as possible."

"Certainly, sir, I understand."

Glenn left the conference room as Regina was walking in. Sgt. Harris couldn't help noticing the menacing glare Glenn cast in Regina's direction. "The men from the crime lab are here to see you, Sgt. Harris."

"Thank you, Ms. Rogers. Could you direct them to the cubicle Ms. Lopez occupied? I'll meet them there."

The team from the crime lab dusted Maria's desk for prints and collected fiber samples. Sgt. Harris was posted outside the cube, taking notes and Polaroid's, as he catalogued the contents of her workstation.

Employees slowly walked by, observing the commotion. Regina stood and said, "There's nothing to see here. Move along and let these men do their work."

Sgt. Harris smiled at her approvingly. "You could've made a good cop."

"I doubt it…but I do enjoy police shows on TV." Regina returned his smile, but it quickly dissipated as Glenn approached, his scowl still intact.

"Regina—can I see you in the warehouse?"

"Certainly, Mr. Stevens." Sgt. Harris watched as the two walked away.

✶   ✶   ✶

SLAMMING OPEN the warehouse door, Glenn walked quickly to the wooden steps leading to Jose's office. With Regina in tow, he burst into the man's office, startling Jose as he was reading over a bill of lading. "Jose—can you let Regina and I borrow your office for a moment?" Glenn snarled threateningly.

"Yes, sir. Be my guest," Jose replied as he quickly left and scurried down the stairs.

Glenn slammed the door behind him. "What in the hell did you tell that cop?"

"Nothing, Glenn…I, I just answered some questions…"

"You stupid bitch! Did you tell him Maria was last seen with me?"

"No…I told him I had last seen her was around four o'clock…in the break-room." "Did you tell him that I used to fuck you?"

"No! That's not something I brag about."

"Did you tell him that I fucked Maria?"

"No. That's none of my business…"

"You're damn right it's none of your business! What time did you tell him you left the office that night?"

"Uh, 6:45."

"What were you doing working that late?"

"My job!"

"Did you tell him you saw Maria with me when you left?"

"No."

Glenn paced a few deliberate circles around Regina. Regina glanced out the window and noticed Jose and several warehouse employees who were trying not to notice the two of them. Before she realized it, Glenn had stopped his pacing in front of her. As he leaned over, he grabbed each one of her arms around the biceps, gripping firmly. He moved his face so close to hers she thought their noses would touch. Glenn hissed, "Regina…there is nothing I value more in my employees than loyalty. Can you appreciate that?"

"Yes, Glenn."

"I don't want some stupid cops nosing around this office on a wild goose chase. Can you understand that?"

"Yes…Glenn you're hurting me," Regina whispered as she tried to avert her eyes from his piercing stare.

"I'm hurting you? I give you a great job—paying you more than anyone else in their right mind would pay you, and I'm hurting you?"

"Glenn, my arms…"

"Next time some cops asks you questions concerning the whereabouts of some fucking Mexican secretary, you tell him to check with the INS! Understand?"

"Yes…"

"Good. I have a damn business to run here. You're either working for us or against us."

"Glenn, you know I value my job…"

"Fuck with me, and you'll regret it," he said as he released his vice-like grip and thundered down the wooden stairs.

"Believe me, I do," Regina mumbled, as she tried to compose herself, Jose slowly entered.

"Miss Regina? Is everything all right?"

"Yes, Jose. Thank you. I'm fine." Regina smiled weakly, and patted Jose on the arm as she left his office. Jose noticed her tear-filled eyes.

∗   ∗   ∗

THE CRIME LAB UNIT had now moved to Glenn's office, and was finishing up. Jeff Davis, the team leader, walked over to Sgt. Harris, who was taking notes in the doorway "I think we've got everything we need…see you back at the ranch."

"Hey, Jeff, before you go, there's one more sample I'd like to get."

"Where?"

"When you came in, did you notice the black Mercedes in the first parking place?"

"Sure, hard to miss."

"Well, there is a horizontal scratch that runs the length of the car, on the driver's side. Can you get me a paint chip from that scratch?"

"Sure, but do we have permission from the owner?"

"Yeah, it's no problem. Just part of the investigation."

"Cool. You got it."

Sgt. Harris watched through the front glass doors, as Davis secured the requested paint chip from the Mercedes. As he waved good-bye to them, he heard the receptionist say, "Hello, Mr. Stevens." Sgt. Harris turned around to see Stevens walking quickly toward him through the lobby. He did not return Lori's greeting.

"Well, Sergeant, about have things wrapped up?"

"Yes sir, Mr. Stevens. That'll be all…for today. You can resume using your office, and I'd appreciate it if you could have someone box up Ms. Lopez's personal belongings."

"Uh, sure."

"I'll let you know if and when we locate Ms. Lopez. Thank you for your cooperation."

"You bet, officer. Sorry if I seemed upset. Lot of pressure running an organization this size."

"I can only imagine, sir. Thanks, again."

"Thank you," Glenn said with a tight grin.

                    *   *   *

AFTER SHOWING Sgt. Harris the door, Glenn returned to his office and picked up the phone as he flipped through the phone directory in his personal organizer. Quickly punching the number, a voice on the other end answered, "LAPD, how may I direct your call?"

"Lieutenant Andy Cavanarro, please."

Moments later another voice came across the line, "Cavanarro speaking."

"Andy?"

"Yeah."

"Glenn Stevens here."

"How in the hell are you, Glenn?"

"Good, thanks."

"What's up? You're not on the committee for our 25th reunion are you?"

"No, but…"

"I didn't think so. A big-shot like you couldn't be bothered with something like that."

"Well, I am pretty busy, but I am looking forward to seeing everyone there."

"How's Pam?"

"Who?"

"Your *wife?*"

"Pamela? Oh, she's great."

"Why she ever puts up with you, I'll never know. I mean, she has so much money of her own—what in the hell does she need you for?"

"She inherited her money—she's never earned a dime in her life," Glenn snapped.

"Gee, touchy subject, I guess."

"Sorry, but she can be a real ball-buster. You know how married life is. Look, the reason I called, Andy, is that we've got a little police problem here at the office."

"What's going on?"

"Oh, it seems that the mother of some secretary we had working here has reported her missing, and a cop keeps poking around here, you know, disrupting things."

"Who's the cop?"

"Sergeant Mike Harris. Heard of him?"

"Oh, sure. I know him. Good kid. Model cop. A real eager beaver. What does he think happened to the girl?"

"I have no idea. He's pretty tight-lipped. My theory is that she had enough of LA, and went back to Mexico. But, who knows?"

"So what can I do for you, Glenn?"

"I wouldn't want you to get your ass in a sling or anything, but I would be personally grateful if you could pull some strings and take this case away from him."

"How grateful?"

"Say, five?"

"Sounds like enough gratitude. Consider it done, buddy."

"I really appreciate you taking care of this for me, Andy. Now maybe we can get back to business as usual around here."

CHAPTER 9

SCOTT'S FIRST WEEK with Campbell passed quickly. His days were spent meeting his new customer base; his nights were full of self-study at home, trying to get a handle on the Campbell product line. Not to mention learning how to use his laptop and filtering through what he thought was pretty voluminous e-mail for a new guy. Apparently, all irrelevant information was copied to everyone in the company. He had planned on more study over the weekend, but Kevin talked him into taking a break on Saturday night, promising him a good night out on the town.

Kevin met Scott at his apartment around 8:45 PM—fifteen minutes late—and directed him to an establishment called Yankee Doodles, at the corner of 2nd Street and PCH in Long Beach. The parking lot was about three-quarters full.

As they walked toward the entrance, Kevin said, "This place won't really start hopping until around ten or eleven." At the door, a crew-cut coifed, steroid-monster of a bouncer with a droopy-eyed expression, and a T-shirt that appeared to be three sizes too small, asked them both for ID's. Scott didn't think either one of them looked under twenty-one, but Kevin explained that they had been busted for serving minors about two months ago. Returning their driver's licenses, the bouncer collected five dollars cover from each, stamped the backs of their hands with the black letters YD, and told them to have a good time. Once inside, Scott was surprised at the cavernous space; the outside facade was deceptive. There was a large dance floor in the center, with a DJ in a booth, playing loud music. There were three drink-serving stations, one on each side, and one at the back of the floor-space.

To the right were clusters of tables and chairs, and to the left several rows of pool tables, two foosball tables, and half-a-dozen dartboards. "You want to shoot some stick, Murph?"

"Sure."

"I'll go get us a table, you go to the bar over there and get us a couple of beers."

Making his way to the bar, Scott couldn't help noticing what appeared to be a dozen waitresses flitting around the bar. They appeared to all be in similar attire: Bikini swimsuit tops, *very* short cut-off denim shorts, and white Keds; accented with overly dark, tanning bed tans, and mounds of cascading, flaxen, peroxide-bleached hair.

Scott had only been in line for a minute when he heard a high-pitched voice say, "Hi, there!" Turning around, he looked down at the unknown greeter. She was petite, blond and tanned, with large green eyes, surrounded with heavy eyeliner. She was wearing a short beige sundress with white sandals.

"Hi, yourself."

"I'm Barbie."

"Is that short for Barbara?"

"No, it's just Barbie. Why?"

"Nothing. That's a pretty name. I'm Scott."

"Hi, Scott, you're tall," she said, smiling the smile of the intoxicated. "What do you do, and what do you drive?"

"Excuse me?"

"I need to get some specifics out of the way before I know if we should continue or not."

"Continue what?"

"If I want to get to know you."

"OK, I'm a sales rep, and drive a Nissan, if you really want to know."

"Oh, I do. What year?"

"What year what?"

"What year Nissan?"

"It's new. A Maxima."

"Oh, that's good," she said smiling approvingly.

"What do *you* drive, Barbie?"

"*I'm* asking the questions, here. Where do you live?"

"Long Beach."

"What part of Long Beach?"

"Belmont Shore, not far from here."

"That's good…means you're not a gud."

"What's a *gud?*"

"G.U.D. Geographic Un-Desirable. Rent or own?"

"Rent."

"Oooh, not good. I'll have to deduct a point."

It was now Scott's turn to order. "Two Amstel Lights," he shouted above the music to the bartender.

"Four bucks, dude."

Scott placed a five on the bar, picked up the two bottles, and turned back around to face Barbie. "*Nice* meeting you."

"But I'm not done asking you questions!"

"I'm done answering, Barb." Scott walked over to the pool table where he saw Kevin racking the balls.

Barbie's girlfriend, a tipsy brunette staggered over and asked her, "So? Nothing there?"

Barbie rolled her eyes. "Who knows? He might be gay. Let's move on, girlfriend."

The two men stood by the pool table. "You break, Murph."

"Eight ball?"

"You got it." Scott selected a cue stick after rolling several across the table, trying to find one that wasn't warped. Realizing that they were all warped, he stuck with a black and tan model. Slamming the cue ball into the packed balls, Scott dropped two stripes.

"Whoa, no money on this game. You look like a hustler!"

"Just the results of a misspent youth," Scott said laughing as he dropped another stripe in the side pocket.

"Hey, Murph—dude, I saw you talking to that chick at the bar, man. She looked pretty hot."

"No big deal. A little superficial for my tastes."

"What do you mean, superficial?"

"She actually wanted to know what I did for a living, and what kind of car I have."

"All the girls here think like that. Man, they're all fucking gold-diggers. What planet are you from?"

"Oh, call me old fashioned, but I think it would be nice to meet a girl that I had common interests with…"

"Common interests? How about sex? Is that enough of a common interest for you?"

Scott dropped another stripe in the far corner pocket, and said, "I would rather meet a girl who could be relationship material. Look, I think I can do better than finding someone who's nothing more than an orifice or a receptacle."

"Dude, that's all these girls are! They don't go to college, or at least not for long. They take care of themselves, stay in shape, dress hot, and deliver all kinds of wild sex on demand. Best of all, they don't hassle you about marriage. In exchange, you have to spend your money on them— and lots of it! Hell, you don't even have to be rich, just have a high limit on your cards, man."

Scott missed his first shot, as Kevin circled the table, eyeing his best option.

"So you're telling me that you're not interested in a girl you can have an intelligent conversation with?" Scott asked.

"Murph, what I'm telling you is, when I go out with a girl, the only time I want to see her mouth open is when she's making like Janet on Glenn!" Kevin then dropped the eight ball in he side pocket. "Shit!"

"Rack 'em up, cowboy."

                  *   *   *

AFTER BEATING KEVIN three-to-one in a best of five eight ball challenge, and downing four beers, Scott was looking at his watch. Kevin noticed, and all but cried, "Oh, come on, man! Don't start wimping out on me now!"

"Well, it's already midnight, and I've got a lot to get done tomorrow…"

"Like what?"

"Oh, laundry, grocery shopping, and I was going to try and swing by this gym, The Sports Connection. When I moved in, my landlord gave me a free workout pass…"

"The Sports *Infection?* That's a mommy gym. Why waste your time there? Besides, what are you trying to be, Mr. America? Come on, it's still early. Let's go to a titty bar."

"I've never cared much for those places."

"Murph! You're really starting to worry me, dude!"

As Kevin was staring at Scott with mock amazement, Barbie's brunette friend sidled up to Kevin. "Am I interrupting?" she asked, flirtatiously.

"No, not at all. I'm Kevin, and you are?…"

"Amber."

"Nice to meet you, Amber. That's my bud, Scott."

"Oh, I know about him," she said eyeing Scott with a contemptuous look.

"Hey, he's new out here…just learning the ropes, you know."

"Yeah, whatever. Tell me about yourself, Kevin."

"Well, Amber. I'm a pilot for American Airlines. I'm single. Good looking. Great sense of humor. Own my own house in Newport Beach…"

"I thought your house was in *Upland*," Scott whispered.

"Would you shut the fuck up?" Kevin hissed under his breath. "*...and* I like to have a good time!" he said to Amber.

"Me, too!" Amber said enthusiastically, as she wrapped her free hand around Kevin's waist, balancing her frou-frou drink in the other.

Placing a firm hand on Scott's shoulder, Kevin looked at him and smiled. "Please collect the balls, and pay the man. I'm outta here. See you, Monday, choir boy."

"Is he a pilot, too?"

"No, no, no. He works for the airline, but in reservations." As they walked off, Scott could hear Kevin bullshitting away, "I love to travel, but I'm not home as much as I'd like. I do get to fly to Hawaii three times a month. Maybe you'd like to join me on my next layover there?"

"*Cool!*" Amber gushed.

                    ✳   ✳   ✳

THE RINGING TELEPHONE almost made Scott fall out of bed. As he groped for the handset, he noticed the clock displaying 4:18 AM. "Hello?"

"Murph, it's Kev," the voice on the other end whispered.

"Kevin? Do you know what time it is?"

"Yeah, that's why I called, I wanted to set my watch. Listen, bud, I need your help."

"What's up?"

"I'm at that chick Amber's apartment..."

"You mean you didn't take her back to your swinging bachelor pad in Newport Beach?"

"Funny. Now listen, I need you to pick me up outside her apartment. My car is still at your place. I want to get the fuck outta here before she wakes up."

"Where does she live?" Scott asked, getting out of bed.

"Not far from you. The WaterGrove apartments on Ocean Boulevard. I'll meet you out front."

"I think I know where that is…see you in a few minutes."

"Thanks, man. You're a bud!"

"Hey, what good's a choir boy if he can't help save the fornicators?" Scott said, using his best televangelist Southern accent.

Scott pulled on some khaki shorts, and reached for the golf shirt he had been wearing earlier in the evening. Realizing the shirt fairly reeked of bar stench, he opted for a clean T-shirt from his dresser. Driving through a deserted Long Beach, he turned right on Ocean Boulevard, and looked on both sides of the streets for the WaterGrove apartments. Right past a bus stop with a Rick Dees, Mornings on KISS-FM placard, he spotted a figure trying to flag him down, by the curb. As he rolled the car to a stop parallel to the entrance of the apartments, Kevin opened the door, flopping down in the bucket seat. "Whhheeeeewwww! You are a lifesaver, man! I thought she was going to wake up when I was talking to you on the phone."

Scott executed a quick U-turn, and accelerated. "So, is she *Mrs. Right?*"

"Mrs. Right for the night, bud!" It seemed to Scott that this was business as usual for Kevin. He noticed that Kevin was holding his socks in his left hand.

As they approached Scott's place, Kevin asked, "Are you hungry? How 'bout letting me take you to breakfast, man."

A quick glance at the dashboard clock revealed that it was now 4:45 AM. "Why not?"

"Cool. There's a Denny's further down PCH on the left. They're a lot like Amber…they serve *all* night, too!" Kevin laughed at his joke, as Scott, shaking his head back and forth in mild amusement, drove past his apartment and continued on to their breakfast destination. "That blonde you passed up, Barbie, she's Amber's roommate, and she brought this other dude home with her, pretty cool guy, too. We all had some drinks, and I thought for a while all four of us were going to get at it, but Barbie and the dude went to her room, leaving me alone with Amber. Amber pulled off her shirt—she wasn't wearing a bra—and man, we're talking brick house, baby! And then she started to do this little dance—I think she's worked as a stripper before, anyway she…"

Scott slid Eric Clapton's *Journeyman* into the CD player, and noticed the sun starting to peek out over the ocean, as he let Kevin revel in what was probably an embellished recollection of his encounter.

CHAPTER 10

AS HE PARKED HIS CROWN VIC in the precinct's crowded parking lot, Sgt. Harris opened his door, and tried to balance his coffee in one hand, and his briefcase in the other. Some coffee spilled down the edge of the cup, running down his arm. Why can't somebody invent a lid that works on a Styrofoam cup? he thought to himself. Setting the cup on the roof of the car, he removed his handkerchief from his back pocket, and wiped off his arm and the sides of the coffee cup.

Entering the police station, the desk sergeant said, "Hey, Mike— Lieutenant Cavanarro was here looking for you earlier."

"What did he want?"

"Beats me, but he said for you to call him at this number," the desk sergeant said, handing Sgt. Harris the hand written message. He walked to his desk, set down his coffee and briefcase, pulled off his sunglasses, and looked at the note.

His office was situated in the center of the station house, a large cubicle with glass windows on the top half of the cube walls. His desk was a big, metal, battleship gray behemoth that had probably been around since the '40's. His desktop was covered with papers, two black, acrylic in and out boxes, a black, multi-line telephone on the right, and a battered, rusty chrome desk lamp perched on the corner. Framed pictures of his wife, two kids, and the family dog sat clustered in a group to his left.

He picked up his handset, and entered Cavanarro's number, wondering what in the world the Lieutenant could possibly want with him. A gravely, smoker's voice on the other end said, "Cavanarro, here."

"Lieutenant Cavanarro?"

"Yes?"

"Sorry sir, I wasn't expecting you to answer the phone yourself…"

"Is this Mike Harris?"

"Yes, sir, it is."

"Good. I gave you my direct line. Thanks for getting back to me so quickly."

"No problem, Lieutenant. What can I do for you, sir?"

"I wanted to speak to you about a missing person investigation you've been working on—Maria Lopez."

"Yes sir, that's my case."

"Has she turned up yet?"

"No, sir."

"Do you have a minute to discuss your findings with me?"

"Yes, sir."

"Good, tell me everything you know, so far."

"Lieutenant, can you hold a moment? I have to get the case file from my briefcase."

"Sure, Mike; go ahead."

Pushing the hold button on his phone, Sgt. Harris opened his briefcase and retrieved the Lopez file. Over the weekend he had been studying the results of the tests conducted by the crime lab. He thought he was on to something, but was curious as to why the Lieutenant was interested in this case. "Sir, are you still there?"

"Yes, Mike; I'm here."

"OK, it seems Ms. Lopez was last seen at work eleven days ago. Her mother reported her missing a day later, when she didn't return to pick up her daughter. She was employed at Campbell Industries in Commerce. Are you familiar with that company?"

"No, can't say that I am."

"Anyway, Campbell is a large manufacturer of electrical components. Ms. Lopez was working there as a secretary. Her car was found parked in front of her apartment in El Segundo. With her mother's permission, I searched both the car and her apartment. No signs of a disturbance."

"Sounds like a dead end."

"Well, maybe not, sir."

"Whaddya mean?"

The Lieutenant's question had a strange tone to it. Mike couldn't put his finger on what it was that didn't sound right. "Well, sir, the company she worked for, Campbell Industries, well, I've interviewed her co-workers now twice, and had a crime lab unit out there last Wednesday."

"The crime lab? Who authorized that?"

"Captain Maxwell, sir."

"Oh, OK. So what made you want to bring the lab boys in?"

"Well sir, in the two rounds of interviews, I found some contradicting statements from a few of the employees, namely an administrative person, and the head guy."

"What kind of contradicting information did they give you?"

"Well the head guy, a VP, I think—contrary to what he's telling me— I believe he was the last person to see Ms. Lopez at the office that day."

"So?"

"I have a gut feeling that he knows more about her disappearance than he's letting on. The guy's a real hot-head."

"Last time I checked Mike, being a hot-head is not against the law." Once again, something about the Lieutenant's condescending tone of voice did not sound right to Sgt. Harris. Call it policeman's intuition. "OK, Mike, you've got a missing girl, no signs of a struggle or forced entry at her apartment, and a hot-head employer. Any evidence?"

"Yes, sir, I believe I'm starting to build a case against the VP, Mr. Glenn Stevens."

"*Glenn Stevens?*"

"Yes, sir. Do you know him?"

"Uh, no, no…uh, tell me about this *case* you're building, Sergeant."

"OK. The crime lab—it was Jeff Davis and his team—found carpet fiber samples that match the carpet in Mr. Stevens' office in both Ms. Lopez's car and apartment. There's no mistaking these, they tell me it's very expensive wool carpet."

"Well, Mike, the girl did work there."

"Yes, sir."

"Did she have occasion to be in this VP's office on a regular basis?"

"Yes, sir, I believe that's so."

"You don't have much there. Anything else?"

"The administrative employee I was telling you about, I think she believes the last place Ms. Lopez was known to be was in Mr. Stevens office."

"Hey, there's a shocker—like I said before, Mike, she *worked* there!"

There was no mistaking the sarcasm in the Lieutenant's voice. Why would this case be of such interest to him? And the way he blurted out the name Glenn Stevens, it would be hard to convince Sgt. Harris that this was the first time the Lieutenant had heard that name. Did he know Stevens? Or was he just busting balls? "Well then, Lieutenant, I'm sure you won't find it surprising that after checking the phone records over the past six months, we found what I would consider to be an inordinate amount of calls from Campbell Industries to Ms. Lopez's home phone, and vice-versa—many after normal business hours."

"That's nothing—the girl calling her employer and her employer calling her. Hhmmpphh! You're still shooting blanks, Mike. Anything else?"

"I noticed a scratch on the VP's Mercedes, looked like someone had keyed the car. The boys at the lab found paint on Ms. Lopez's ignition key that match the paint on the Mercedes."

"So a disgruntled employee, who left her job without notice, keyed her boss's car? Bet that's the first time that's ever happened!"

"I'm sure it's not, sir. But I do have some three eyewitnesses who say they saw a man matching the VP's description in late that same Thursday night, in the parking lot of an AM/PM store across the street from Ms. Lopez's apartment in El Segundo. That man left in a cab. After a few calls, I found out that Coastal had a pick-up at that AM/PM, and delivered its fare to the Commerce Business Park—home of Campbell Industries."

"Did he pay by credit card?"

"No, sir, cash."

There was a pause on the other end of the line. "I know you're trying to move up, and I encourage that attitude Mike, but to put it bluntly, you don't have dick."

"Well, sir…"

"No, hear me out. Not a bad stab, a little sloppy and amateurish, but you'll learn. You really went above and beyond the call of duty with all this effort on a missing persons case. Hell, she could turn up today. You just can't try and force your findings to fit your theory. The truth has a way of surfacing, Mike."

"Yes, sir. I'm sure it does," Sgt. Harris said through clenched teeth.

"I'm gonna do you a favor, Mike. As of right now, I'm officially taking over the Lopez missing person case. This way, you can get back to doing what you do best, and I'll wrap this one up, hopefully finding the girl in the process. Can you get the case file over to me by noon?"

"Yes, Lieutenant, not a problem."

"Good. Thanks for your cooperation, Mike. You've got potential. Keep plugging away, and I'm sure you'll get your Detective shield some-day. Just chalk this one up to a good learning experience."

"Yes, sir, I certainly will. I'll run this file by shortly."

"Thanks, Mike. Bye for now."

Sgt. Harris felt that Lt. Cavanarro had just talked to him as if he were right out of the academy. He also didn't quite feel right about turning the Lopez case over to the Lieutenant, but it was out of his control. Lt.

Cavanarro was pulling rank—but the guy always struck him as not being exactly squeaky clean. With that in mind he rummaged through the evidence box, removing a Ziploc bag, containing the Toyota's cigarette lighter. He then removed the last page of the crime lab's report from the Lopez folder. The last page of the report that found traces of burned, human flesh on the metal element of her car's cigarette lighter.

CHAPTER 11

ALLEN HAD PAGED SCOTT earlier in the day to remind him that on the second Monday of every month, they held a district meeting, from 4:00 to 5:00 PM. This would be held in the training room, and precede the 5:00 PM LA County sales team meeting. Allen also told him that he had scheduled a three o'clock meeting for him with Sheila Bryant, Human Resources. This meant Scott would have to complete his snack shopping earlier than planned.

*   *   *

ARRIVING AT THE OFFICE, Scott exchanged the usual *friendly* greetings with Lori, and headed for the conference room to unload his groceries. He had gone to Albertson's this time, and came away with a fruit plate, little finger sandwiches and a plate of chocolate chip cookies. This time, there should be no bitching from the peanut gallery.

After getting the food situation in order, he headed across the hall to Allen's office. As he walked over, he said hello to Regina. She smiled warmly, returned his greeting, and acted as if she were genuinely glad to see him. Allen's door was open, and Scott stuck his head inside. "Allen?"

"Scott! Come in, come in. Sit down." Scott thought that Allen too, seemed glad to see him. "How are things going?"

"Pretty good, I think."

"Good, good. Got the first week under your belt—it's all downhill from here!" Kevin chuckled. "Oh, by the way, I got a call from Nick Lunsford last Friday. I don't know how you did it, but you made a great impression on him."

"I think I can work with him."

"He's a tough character—I know first hand. But, based on the feedback I got, I think you're going to do well with Alexander's."

"I hope so. Uh, I put the food for our meeting in the conference room. You wanted me to see Sheila in HR at three?"

"Yeah," Allen said looking at his watch. "It's a little early, but I can walk you over there now."

The two men walked down the hallway adjacent to the bullpen, passing the two sets of double-doors leading to the training room, and walked into another large bullpen type area. Offices lined the perimeter, while the customer service cubicles filled the center of the room. The mauve, gray and teal decorating theme was consistent with the rest of the building. The closed office door in the right hand corner had gold lettering on the door stating: SHEILA R. BRYANT, HUMAN RESOURCES MANAGER. There was one long, rectangular exterior window facing the room, but the blinds covering it were closed. "Sheila?" Allen inquired as he knocked on the door. Rustling sounds could be heard inside the office.

"I'll be with you in just a minute," a female voice answered from within the office. More thumping, jostling sounds came from the office. As the sounds stopped, two faint voices could now be heard, the second belonging to a man. Another minute passed before the door opened. "Allen, you're a little early. And you must be Scott Murphy. I'm Sheila Bryant," she said, smiling and extending her hand in greeting. Sheila was another looker, about 5'6" with blond hair that appeared to be her natural color, fair skin and big, blue eyes. She was dressed very professionally, in a well-tailored black jacket and skirt, with a red scarf around her neck. Scott noticed she was not wearing a wedding ring. She appeared to be a little flustered as she showed the two into her office.

Once inside Scott noticed Glenn sitting in one of the chairs facing Sheila's desk. "Business or a social call, boys?" he asked them in a mocking tone. Glenn was one cool character.

Allen stammered, "Scott has a three o'clock with Sheila, you know, just covering some of the benefits package, training, the usual. If this is a bad time…" Scott noticed that Allen's demeanor had changed from friendly to tense.

"No, no. I just finished my two-thirty, with Sheila," Glenn said standing up, grinning broadly at Sheila. Both Scott and Allen noticed Sheila blushing. She appeared to be very uncomfortable. As he left the office, Glenn made a production out of zipping his unzipped fly, and winking at Scott.

"I'll let the two of you get started," Allen said in an embarrassed tone, following Glenn out of her office.

Sheila smiled at Scott as she tried to compose herself. What an awkward situation she had put herself in. Scott noticed that Sheila's blouse was buttoned incorrectly, apparently in her haste to get to the door. "Thanks for stopping by, Scott."

"Sure." Scott just wanted her to skip the formalities, and get on with whatever it was she wanted to discuss with him. He figured he was as uneasy as she was. This was some kind of workplace.

'I've received your personnel file from home office in New Orleans, and everything appears to be in order. Did Allen give you your Campbell HR manual?"

"Yes, he did."

"Have you had time to review it?"

"I have."

"Good. Any questions for me?"

"None at the moment," at least not about the book, Scott thought to himself.

"OK, good. If you need to see a doctor or dentist, you can see me for the forms to file with our insurance carrier. You should be receiving a Campbell group policy insurance card and a prescription drug card within the next few weeks. In the interim, this is your temporary card," she said, handing the paper card to him. "It's really a good plan. And I noticed in your file you're from Memphis?"

"Guilty."

"Uh, okay…well I've enrolled you in our new employee orientation class to be held in Memphis in November. Memphis is where our training center is."

"Yes, I know. Sounds great—a free trip home."

"Good. And have you had the opportunity to meet Tim Newsom?"

"I've had the pleasure."

"Uh, that's great. He'll be joining you for this class. Even though Tim has been with us for two years, his schedule has never worked out for a trip to Memphis to take this class—until now. So you'll know somebody in the class."

"Neat-O," Scott said sarcastically, not knowing why he felt animosity towards Sheila. She hadn't done anything to him. Tim being in the class was not her fault. Her encounter with Glenn was none of his business. He guessed he was just mad at the whole damn company for shattering his expectations of what a top company should be like. They said their goodbyes, and Scott left sticking his temporary insurance card in his shirt pocket.

Walking back down the hall, he encountered Kevin. "So, how was your Sunday, Kev?"

"Man, slept 'til 3:00 PM—then I tried to find the little man who took a shit in my mouth while I was asleep—major cotton-mouth—what a fucking hangover!"

"Looks like you've recovered."

"Yeah, almost. Thanks for coming through for me, big guy. I won't forget it."

"I won't let you. And don't tell your friends—I don't want to become some sort of cab service for the socially deviant."

Scott followed Kevin into the training room. It was a large room, with stadium seating. The seats had desktops that could be folded away into the armrests, sort of like the bulkhead seats on an airplane. This room was used for the monthly district meetings, and for distributor training classes. Scott guessed it seated seventy-five to a hundred people. Down on the stage-like floor, Glenn was standing next to Cassler and a heavy-set man Scott hadn't seen before.

As they were seated about midway down, Jimmy waved, and mouthed the word, "Howdy," from the same row. Janet acknowledged them with a smile from her seat two rows below. Lots of teeth and lots of leg, Scott thought. Darrin and Jerry said hello. Marvin was staring blankly into his laptop. Regina and Jose sat three rows behind them. Scott noticed that the LA team sat on the right hand side of the room, and the Orange County team sat on the left. The customer service reps and quotation department staff seemed to be scattered equally on both sides. Allen walked down the center aisle to join Glenn and the others on the floor. Scott turned around and saw that Sheila and Lori were seated in the very back row. He then noticed Tim was the only occupant of the front row.

Speaking into a hand-held microphone, Glenn asked, "Jon, are we ready to get started?" Jon's eyes scoured the room, and he turned to Glenn and nodded affirmative. "Can everyone hear me?" Glenn asked, still speaking into the microphone. "I'm glad everyone could join us for our monthly get-together. We have some year-to-date district sales numbers to go over, and a couple of awards I want to present, but first, I want to turn the meeting over to Lieutenant Andy Cavanarro, from the LAPD. He's going to give us an update on the Maria Lopez situation. Lieutenant…"

"Thank you, Mr. Stevens," the heavy-set man said gruffly, taking the microphone from Glenn, who continued to stand beside him, to his right. Cassler flanked him on his left. Allen had taken a seat next to Tim on the front row. Lt. Cavanarro was about 6'1" with black, slicked-back hair. He had a perpetual Nixonian five o'clock shadow, complete with the perspiration on his upper lip. He wore a navy, chalk-stripe suit, a blue shirt with contrasting white collar, and a bright yellow tie that had a navy zigzag pattern running through it. He had on gold cufflinks, a gold lapel pin, what appeared to be a large class ring on his right hand, a wedding band and pinkie ring with an onyx stone on his left hand. A gold, diamond-encrusted, Rolex Presidential watch with the gold Jubilee bracelet encircled his large, left wrist. He looked more Mafiosi than cop.

"I appreciate Mr. Stevens giving me the opportunity to address you all today. As Campbell employees and co-workers of Maria Lopez, I felt it my duty to inform you that we still have no leads concerning her disappearance. I have personally taken over this case from Sergeant Harris. Any statements you made to Sergeant Harris are in the case file, and now in my possession." Lt. Cavanarro nodded to Cassler, who began walking up the steps of the center aisle, holding a stack of cards. "Mr. Cassler is passing out my business cards, with all my contact information. If you think of anything else pertinent to this investigation, or if you happen to hear from Ms. Lopez, please contact me directly. There is no need to contact Sergeant Harris, as he is no longer involved with this investigation. If there are any new developments, I will contact Mr. Stevens, and I'm sure he'll pass that information onto you. Are there any questions you may have of me?" Faint murmurs filled the room, but generated no questions.

"Thank you, Lieutenant Cavanarro. We at Campbell Industries are truly grateful for the efforts of the LAPD on our behalf," Glenn said, after taking the microphone from Lt. Cavanarro. "Jon will go over some year-to-date numbers with you all, as I see the Lieutenant out. When I return we'll hand out 'Quotations Rep of the Month,' 'Customer Service

Rep of the Month,' 'Sales Rep of the Month' and 'Employee of the Month' awards."

Taking the microphone from Glenn, Jon began, "This month has shown tremendous growth, as usual, in the Orange County territory…"

∗   ∗   ∗

ONCE OUT OF THE BUILDING, Cavanarro pulled out a Lucky Strike cigarette and tapped one end against the face of his watch. Thinking the tobacco was packed sufficiently, he placed it in his mouth, lighting it with a chrome Zippo, and took a deep drag. The two men continued to walk to the police cruiser.

"So, you have the case file, Andy?"

"Yep."

"Anything jump out at you?"

"Well…I'll tell you, Glenn. Sergeant Harris is sharp. As a matter of fact, he had gathered enough circumstantial evidence to begin constructing a pretty good case." "Case for what?"

"Not for, against—against you, pal."

"Me?"

"That's what he was working on…"

The rage in Glenn spilled over. "That little prick! Who in the hell does…"

"Easy, easy Glenn. I'm not saying it would hold water, but some of his findings are interesting."

"How interesting?"

Lt. Cavanarro smiled knowingly at Glenn. "Have you taken any cab rides from El Segundo in the past couple of weeks?"

"Uh, I don't know what in the hell you're talking about, Andy," Glenn said unconvincingly as the blood drained from his face.

"Remember when we agreed on five to make this go away?"

"Yeah, I've got it right here."

"Good. I'll take that now, but to make all that he had compiled just go away, I'll need a little more for my trouble."

"How much more?"

"I was thinking another twenty would do the trick."

Glenn frowned at Lt. Cavanarro. The Lieutenant wondered if he had asked for too much. Maybe he should have settled for an extra five grand.

"OK, sure, you got it."

"By Friday?"

"That won't be a problem."

The Lieutenant was visibly pleased by the news of his latest windfall. "I didn't think so, knowing your wife's financial situation, and all. If anything turns up, I'll be in touch." He threw his cigarette butt on the ground, and crushed it under his black, wing-tipped shoe. Getting into his car he said, "Don't worry. Everything's under control. Now you take care, Glenn."

"Yeah, thanks. You too, Andy." As his car lurched out of the parking lot, Glenn returned to the office, trying to convince himself that everything was under control.

CHAPTER 12

FRIDAY AFTERNOON, at 4:25, Sheila knocked on Glenn's office door. "Come in, come in."

"Thanks for seeing me, Glenn."

"I've always got time for you, gorgeous," he said leering at her. "Close the door, and have a seat." As Sheila closed the door, she walked toward one of the chairs facing Glenn's desk. Glenn stood up, dropping his pants to reveal his blue, oxford cloth boxer shorts. "Actually, I was thinking, on my lap."

Sheila didn't smile, as she sat in the chair. "That's what I need to talk to you about. That behavior is now officially over," she said triumphantly, as she slid a piece of paper across his desk.

Glancing at the paper, Glenn shouted, "You're resigning? What in the hell is this supposed to mean?"

"Glenn, it's time for me to move on."

"Just where in the hell do you think you're moving on to?"

"I am going to work as Vice President of Human Resources—for Powerlyte."

"Powerlyte? You have got to be fucking kidding me!"

"This is no joke."

"Those rat-bastards can't possibly be paying you what I am!"

"Actually, it's a substantial raise…"

"You must have fucked ol' man Peterson's brains out!"

"Glenn, I'd like to keep this as professional as possible—and knowing who I'm having this conversation with—I know how difficult that…"

"Fuck you, you slut!"

"Thank you. My point exactly."

As Glenn sat there seething in his underwear, Sheila tried to keep her composure. "Glenn, I really do appreciate the opportunity you've given me here at Campbell. I have learned a lot. Let's not go out on a note like this," she said smiling.

"OK," Glenn said returning her smile. "If you're really grateful then how about bending over this desk and giving me one for the road?"

Sheila didn't bat an eye. "Glenn I know I haven't conducted myself as the consummate professional. With you as a mentor, how in the hell could I have been expected to?"

"Thanks for the compliment," Glenn said, standing and pulling up his pants. Flopping back in his chair, he stared at the ceiling. A few moments passed, and then he mumbled, "You were special to me."

Thinking this was just another angle to get her consent for adios-sex, Sheila refused to let herself think this pig across from her had any redeeming qualities. True, she was no angel, and did what she had to, in her mind, to get ahead. She was also relieved to see it finally come to an end. She was actually surprised that during the entire interview process with Powerlyte, she never once caught any guy looking down her blouse. She had become so jaded at the ripe old age of thirty-two, that she didn't believe such a workplace really existed. She wouldn't miss this place!

"You should know that I've already spoken to New Orleans. I offered two weeks notice, but since I'm going to work for a competitor, they told me I should leave today."

"Probably not a bad idea," Glenn said, not looking at her, but staring outside through the blinds on his window.

"You should also know that they have someone in mind for my replacement. She's been working at corporate HR for the past two years.

Of course, you'll have to interview her first. I have met her several times, and she seems very sharp, and very professional."

"What does she weigh?"

"She's a very attractive girl, Glenn."

"That's the first decent news you've had for me."

"Well…I've never been good at good-byes, so I guess I should just leave." Sheila stood, and offered Glenn her hand to shake.

Glenn smiled at her, and walked around his desk. "C'mon—after all we've been through, a handshake good-bye? I won't let you leave without a hug."

Sheila tried to determine if he was sincere or not, but couldn't tell from the shit-eating grin on his face. It really didn't matter, if it would expedite her exit from his office. "Sure, Glenn," she said, stepping forward to embrace the creep one last time. Glenn squeezed her tightly, for what seemed an inappropriate amount of time. "OK, Glenn—that's enough!"

Glenn loosened his embrace, lowered his hands and grabbed her butt, squeezing hard. Staring at her with a maniacal expression, he said, "That's Grade A, baby! If those Powerlyte boys don't appreciate it, you know somebody who does."

Pushing away, Sheila walked quickly to the office door. "Thanks for giving me all I needed to remember you in the proper light, asshole!" She slammed the door behind her.

Glenn watched Sheila through his window as she got into her car, and drove away. That's the second quality piece of ass I've lost this month, he thought to himself. He caught a glimpse of his wife's framed photo, and suddenly felt nauseous. Pam was the only woman he couldn't control, and the thought of Sheila joining that club made him sick. Rising from his chair, he walked over to his bar, and poured himself a glass of single-malt scotch. Downing the drink in one fluid motion, he walked out of his office. Turning left, he made a beeline for the receptionist's station.

"Hi, Mr. Stevens!" Lori said in a perky tone, seated in her chair.

"Good afternoon to you, sweetheart." Glenn walked around the desk, and stood behind her. Gripping her shoulders, he began to massage them firmly.

"Oooh, that feels good!" she purred. "But, Mr. Stevens, it's almost five, and the whole office will be passing by here in a few minutes, and…"

"And what?"

"And…I just don't think they should see us, out in the open, and…"

"Feeling shy, are we?"

"Well, it's just that…you, know…why don't we go in your office?"

Glenn picked up Lori's stapler off her desk, and threw it underneath. "Oops! Would you mind getting that?"

"Uh, sure. OK." Lori slid off her chair and knelt under the desktop to retrieve the stapler. Turning around, she noticed that Glenn had stepped forward, and was unbuckling his belt. His excitement was obvious. "Mr. Stevens! It's almost five, and…"

"Shhhhh! Nobody will see you under there. You just be a good girl, and take care of business." Lori looked up at him with uncertainty, as his pants dropped to the floor. "Sweetheart, since you're down there picking up the stapler, perhaps you can help me find the five hundred bucks I think I lost under there, too."

"Where?" Lori asked.

"Check the money-clip in my right front pocket. Finders-keepers, baby."

Stevens was right, Lori did find five hundred dollars in his money-clip. She removed the wad of bills from the clip and slipped them into her blouse. She resigned herself to the fact that this was going to take place, and found the prospect of getting caught with Glenn strangely exhilarating. As she was pulling down his boxer shorts, she heard foot-steps approaching. "Good-night, Mr. Stevens."

"You have a good evening too, Jose." Lori began working on Glenn, as she heard a group of footsteps enter the lobby.

"Glenn? What are you doing back there?" Regina queried.

"Just filling in for Lori—she had to leave early. You know what I always say, some jobs are worth staying late for. Have a great weekend, Regina."

"Thank you, Glenn." After he said good-bye to the others in the group, Lori felt his hands tightly grip both sides of her head, over her ears. He began violently forcing her head back and forth, with a quick, short, thrusting motion.

Scott and Allen walked into the lobby. They had just finished reviewing what Scott had accomplished this week, and his itinerary for the next week. As the two approached the receptionist's station, they were surprised to see Glenn standing rigidly behind the desk, his body jerking quickly back and forth, and breathing heavily. He looked as if he were operating a jackhammer. His eyes were closed, his jaws were grinding furiously, and the veins in his neck were bulging. The desk obscured his arms from the elbows down. Suddenly, they could hear a whimpering noise, sounding as if it was coming from a wounded animal. Glenn suddenly stopped his convulsive movements as his eyes popped open. "Aaaaauuuugggghhhhh," was the sound he made as he exhaled deeply.

As Glenn's eyes snapped open, Scott realized that he and Allen had stopped walking, and were staring across the desk at Glenn. With a piercing gaze, and through flared nostrils, Glenn said, "Have a good weekend, boys."

"Thanks, you too," Scott said. Allen didn't say a word as he headed for the exit. Scott followed, but for some reason, couldn't resist the urge to look back as he walked through the glass doors. He saw Lori jump to her feet, and walk quickly around the desk, and disappear into the hall-way. Judging from what appeared to be smeared mascara, she was crying. His eyes then caught Glenn's. Glenn smiled a wicked smile, snapping his hand to his head, in a quick mock salute gesture.

Scott caught up with Allen. "Hey, I just saw Lori—I think she was under her desk when we walked by Glenn. What in world was going on back there? Do you think she was performing oral sex on him? Right in the lobby?"

Placing his key into the door lock, Allen opened his car door and seated himself. Closing the door, he rolled down his window. Staring straight ahead, he said, "Don't tell anyone what you just saw…"

"But I didn't see anything!"

"Let's just say that poor, stupid girl was not a totally willing participant," Allen said, slamming his car into reverse, and then drive, his tires chirping as he grabbed a little rubber.

CHAPTER 13

IT HAD BEEN an extremely lazy Saturday. After sleeping in until 11:00 AM, it was all Scott could do to roll off the couch and make a run for the border—Taco Bell—to bring home a sack lunch. Consuming his fast food in front of the TV, he tried to focus on college football. He hadn't slept well the night before—or really, since he started working for Campbell. He found the amorality of his workplace very unsettling.

After watching the conclusion of the second game, neither of which was all that entertaining, Scott went to the refrigerator to get a beer. Looking at the clock on the microwave, he calculated that it was 3:30 PM in Memphis. He figured his parents would be home, and he felt like talking to somebody.

Scott's dad never really understood why he had left Memphis to work for Campbell, in the first place. He had worked for the railroad all his adult life, as had his father before him. Working there for two summers convinced Scott to put an end to the family tradition. His dad had never set foot on a college campus, and was never convinced as to why Scott wanted to attend. He also never understood his desire to major in business. Being a union man, he never trusted anyone who wore a suit. He always said, "No man ever got any real work done wearing a tie."

His mother was a homemaker, a real-life June Cleaver. She kept the house immaculate, and demanded that everyone else conform to her high standards. Good grammar and good grades were important to her, who, unlike his dad, wanted her kids to go to college. She was a great cook, too. And, in Scott's opinion, she was the glue that held the family together. In her regimented household, they always had dinner together, attended Church as a family, and spent holidays together. His mom was more supportive of his move to California than his dad, but informed him that she expected him home every Thanksgiving and Christmas.

Kathy, his kid sister, had graduated from UT-Martin this past spring, but was still living at home. Even though she was three years younger than him, they were close growing up—still were. Kathy was the only family member who was really excited about his opportunity in California. She told him that she would now have a free place to stay if she wanted to vacation there. She had started a marketing job with the triple A Memphis Redbirds baseball team; and was doing very well. She had been dating the same guy for three years, and would in all likelihood marry him in the not so distant future. Scott had no problem with this, because he thought Robert was a good guy.

"Hello?" A friendly, feminine voice on the other end said.

"Hi, Mom!"

"Scott—how are you, son?"

"Oh, I'm OK. Just wanted to see how you and Dad were doing?"

"We're fine. Kathy's not here, I'm sorry to say. She would've loved to talk to you. Robert's new company, Union Planters Bank—did I tell you he got a job with Union Planters?"

"Yes, Mom."

"Well, anyway, they sponsored the Tiger football game today, and gave their employees tickets. So, they went to the game, and were going out to dinner afterwards."

"I saw the game on TV today."

"Really? Out in California?"

"It was on SportSouth—I have cable."

"Well, I'm glad you got to see your team play. So how is work going, son?"

"It's different."

"Different, how?"

"I don't know, Mom…these people out here…they seem to be lacking a value system."

"Well, I'm sure once you get to know them—you can always find something good about anyone." His mom had obviously never met Glenn Stevens. "Are you eating well, dear?"

"Yes ma'am."

"Probably a lot of fast food, I bet."

"Sometimes, but I'm doing OK."

"Hold on dear, your father wants to talk to you."

"OK."

Scott knew his mom was forcing his dad to take the phone. His dad had never wanted to talk to him. He really didn't like to talk to anyone, except Kathy. They had a special father—daughter relationship. Scott had always felt he could never please his dad, no matter how hard he tried.

"Scott?"

"It's me, Dad." After a long pause, Scott broke the silence. "I watched Memphis play Southern Miss today—they lost—as usual."

"Kathy was at the game."

"Yeah, Mom told me." His dad was never much of a football fan, he preferred baseball, but Scott was looking for some subject to break the ice. "I also saw Tennessee beat Georgia."

"Sounds like you're watching a lot of television."

"Yes, sir…I guess…at least today…So what have you been up to, Dad?"

"Working hard, as usual. Kathy got me season tickets for the Redbirds—box seats. I've enjoyed going to their games. I'm so proud of that little girl—she's doing really well with them."

"That's great."

"How's the job, Scott?"

"The work itself isn't bad, but it's taking me a little while to get acclimated to the area, and the people."

"I never told you to move out there and live with all the fruit and nuts."

"No, sir, you didn't."

"That's right. But instead of learning a trade or finding a real job, you wanted to be another hot-shot in a tie." Scott didn't answer, and after what seemed like two minutes of silence, his dad blurted out, "Here's your mother."

Before Scott could bask too long in the warmth of their father-son Hallmark moment, his mother came back on the line. "Thanks for calling, son, but we really should be wrapping this up. We don't want to run up your long distance bill. Next time, you can call collect."

"It's not a problem, Mom…"

"Well, it was good hearing from you. Take care of yourself, son. I love you, honey."

"I love you too, Mom."

"Gee, that was worthwhile—I feel so much better!" Scott said out loud to himself. His parents wouldn't understand this environment, anyway. He was pretty sure neither of them had been west of Oklahoma their entire lives. It was just so damn unbelievable—the recklessness, the shamelessness, the self-absorbed, lust-driven, behavior he had been witness to over the past few weeks was mind-boggling.

Settling into his couch, contemplating ordering a pizza, he turned up the volume as he prepared to watch the UCLA Bruins take on the San Diego State Aztecs—being played right up the road from him at the scenic Pasadena Rose Bowl, according to announcer Keith Jackson. A knock at the door broke his trance.

He opened the door to find Kevin draining a can of Bud Light, holding the four remaining cans by their plastic six-ring holder. "Murph! What's going on?"

"Hey, Kevin, come on in…"

"Watching a little football, huh?"

"Yeah."

"Got a date tonight?"

"I've been so busy with work and getting situated, I haven't really had a chance to meet anyone."

"Man, I'd go help you look, but I've got a date with Kristy tonight. She lives a couple blocks from you, so I thought I'd stop by to bust your balls."

"Kristy?"

"Yeah, you remember, the red-headed goddess we met at Hof's Hut."

"Oh, yeah, the waitress."

"Yeah. Taking her to dinner and a movie, and if all goes well, a naked tour of 'Mount Kevin,' if you know what I mean. Wanna beer?"

"Sure, thanks." Kevin pulled a beer from its plastic ring, and tossed it to Scott, as he plopped down on the couch.

"Kev, can I talk to you—seriously?"

"*Seriously?* Why not, there's a first time for everything, I guess."

"It's about work."

"Work? Not on the weekend, dude."

"Does the lack of professionalism, or at least discretion, at the office bother you?"

"Nothing, and I mean *nothing* at that place surprises me anymore."

"The way Glenn conducts himself—like at the restaurant—it's unbelievable."

"Not really, Glenn is bulletproof. As long as the Western Region office keeps sending big fat checks to mother Campbell, nobody's gonna touch him."

"Yeah, but what about ethics, what about the legality of…"

"Ethics and legality? Here we go again—you're not in the boonies anymore, Lil' Abner! This is big business—the almighty dollar is king!"

"OK, I know, but Glenn is *so* blatant…"

"Because he can be! As long as the numbers are up, he can do what-ever the hell he wants to! Increase sales annually, and home office and the stockholders could care less how it gets done. You ever heard that expression: 'Absolute power corrupts absolutely?'"

"Yeah."

"That's Glenn! He's the man, and he knows it!"

"But what about the way he treats some of the women…"

"They're asking for it!"

"They could get him in deep shit with HR. In any other major cor-poration…"

"They would have to say something to get him in deep shit—and they're not going to say anything that would cut off their cash flow. He pays them extremely well. You saw Janet at the restaurant—you can't rape the willing. A lot of these chicks really dig Glenn. Money and power are magnets to them. And as far as big companies, don't be so fucking naive…"

"Look, I'm not. But if the women won't stand up for themselves, isn't it my place to say something…"

"Your place? Are you fucking nuts?"

"If I don't say anything, doesn't that make me an accomplice?"

"Man, I think you've lost your mind! The best advice I can give you is to keep your mouth shut, keep your head down, do your job and cash your check. Don't fuck with Glenn, Scott—he plays hardball."

"I'm not sure this is the kind of company I want to work for…"

"Don't take my advice, and you won't!"

The only sound to be heard for the next several minutes was that of Keith Jackson and Bob Griese giving the play-by-play commentary from the television. "Look, Murph, you're a decent guy and all, but this is the real world. You gotta adapt. And don't take it so seriously…"

"I take my career very seriously."

"That's gonna give you ulcers and make your hair fall out, man." Kevin stood, and handed one of the three remaining beers to Scott. "I gotta pick up Kristy. You should try and get out tonight. All work and no play makes Scotty a dull boy!"

"Yeah, I'll think about it."

"You're thinking too much. Just do it, bud."

"Okay, okay."

"See ya."

CHAPTER 14

THE LIMO came to a stop in front of the building. Looking out his window, Glenn figured this must be his four-thirty interview. The driver walked around the long, black Lincoln, and opened the door. Out stepped two of the finest looking legs Glenn was sure he had ever seen. As she stood and the rest of her came into view, he was pleased to see that she was a complete package. She was tall, about 5'10" in his estimation, with long, wavy, dark brown hair. Sunglasses were perched on a pert, upturned nose. She was wearing a conservative charcoal pinstripe suit with a white blouse. Her black attaché case matched her low-heeled pumps. The driver followed her after retrieving a suitcase from the trunk.

Walking into the lobby, Lori greeted her with the look one attractive woman gives another when she feels she has been upstaged. "Hello. My name is Lisa LeDoux. I have a four-thirty appointment to see Mr. Stevens."

"OK, let me see if he's available," Lori said with a hint of contempt. "Mr. Stevens, a Lisa LeDoux is here to see you. She says she has a four-thirty appointment." Lori listened to the voice in her headset, looked up and said, "He'll be right with you."

"Thank you so much for your trouble."

Glenn burst through the lobby door, practically beaming with a large smile on his tanned face. "Lisa…I'm Glenn Stevens. Welcome to the Western Region office!"

"Thank you Mr. Stevens."

"Please, call me Glenn. Was your flight all right?"

"Just fine, sir."

"Driver, could you bring her bag into my office?" The driver nodded affirmative as he followed the two down the hall to the first office on the right. "Just sit it over there. Thanks, pal," Glenn said as he tipped the driver a twenty. They didn't have to pay the fare since Campbell had a corporate account with Le Bas Limousine Services, and would be billed directly.

Now that her sunglasses were off, her large, brown eyes mesmerized Glenn. She was a looker, but extremely poised and confident. Nothing ditzy about this girl. "Have a seat, Lisa." Glenn walked slowly around his desk, so he would have a standing vantage point as she crossed her legs. After appreciating the view, he seated himself, and asked, "Would you like something to drink?"

"A diet Coke would be great," she said, returning his smile. Standing back up, Glenn walked over to his bar, filled a glass with ice cubes, and poured the requested soda. He handed her the glass and returned to his chair.

"So, you're a Tulane graduate?"

"That's correct."

"And you've worked at home office for the past two years?"

"Yes, sir."

"Well, after speaking with everyone at corporate, and reviewing your resume, I have to say everything looks great," he said in a way she felt was more talking at her and not to her. "Lisa, if I may be frank, I'd like to ask why would a young lady as attractive as yourself want to be bogged down with trivial HR matters in corporate America, when obviously, you could be working as a super-model?"

"Sir, I don't consider anything about Human Resources to be trivial. I have found that helping people achieve their full potential and navigate the intricacies of a corporation to be very rewarding. Ensuring safe employment practices, and writing and administering legally sound employment policies and procedures are vital to the success of an organization today. I take myself very seriously, and have very specific goals. In regards to your modeling statement, even if I could get into that line of work—which I doubt—I'm sure I would find it to be boring and unchallenging."

His leering gaze made her slightly uncomfortable. "OK, fair enough. So, what makes you want to leave the big brass in New Orleans and join our little outfit?"

"My goal is to move up in the Human Resources department at Campbell, and this position would be a logical progression in my career path. Southern California is attractive to me because I want to pursue my MBA, and I've been accepted to Pepperdine."

"Good school. I myself went to…"

"Cal-Berkeley," she interjected.

"How did you know that?"

"I've done my homework," she smiled. Glenn was impressed. Looks and brains. She would be just the kind of challenge he was looking for. Now if only she would take off her jacket and let him see what kind of rack she was packing.

Since Glenn seemed unfocused, she thought she should get this conversation on track. "Do you mind if I ask you a few questions?" Lisa queried, leaning forward.

"No, not at all."

"I understand the last person in this position, Ms. Bryant, went to work for one of our competitors…."

"That's correct."

"Last I checked a formal exit interview had not been filed. Do you know why she left Campbell?"

"My understanding was that this would be a promotion to a VP title for her."

"Okay. Well, what skills and qualities are you looking for in your next Human Resources Manager?"

Glenn reflected a moment. "Someone who is bright, articulate, a hard worker, good people skills, and someone who has a firm understanding of the Human Resources function within our organization."

"Glenn, based on that criteria, I feel very confident that the potential for a good fit between your needs and my abilities exists."

Taking he statement out of context, Glenn though to himself, does it ever, but aloud he concurred, "Yes, I believe you're right, Lisa. How 'bout I show you around the office?"

They left his office, and as they walked down the hall, Regina approached them. "Regina! I'd like you to meet Lisa LeDoux from New Orleans."

"Hi Lisa, we spoke on the phone."

"That's right. Nice to meet you, Regina." She shook Regina's hand firmly. Looking at her, Regina felt this one would not end up as one of Glenn's bimbos—not that she didn't meet the physical criteria—Lisa was absolutely beautiful. She just seemed too smart, too self-assured for his bullshit head games. "I hope everything works out for you," Regina said smiling.

"Thank you, I really appreciate it."

"Who's in the conference room?" Glenn inquired.

"The LA Sales team. It's their Monday night meeting," Regina answered as she continued walking.

"Well then, let me show you off to some of the sales guys!"

Opening the door as he knocked, Glenn said, "Gentlemen, I hope I'm not interrupting anything…"

"No, Glenn, come on in," Allen said with a hint of resentment.

Suddenly, Scott felt a sharp elbow in his ribs. He snapped around at Kevin, but he was looking at the door. "What was that for?" he muttered quietly.

"Check it out, man. Babe sighting at twelve-o'clock!" Scott followed his gaze to find himself looking at what had to be the most beautiful girl he had ever laid eyes on.

"Thanks, Allen, I'll make it quick. I just wanted to introduce Miss Lisa LeDoux to the guys, and gal, Janet." Janet smiled weakly, but her face took on a scowl as she sized up what she thought to be a potential rival. "Lisa works in HR out of home office, and she has graced us with her presence today, to see if we can convince her to replace Sheila."

"Hello," Lisa said with an angelic smile.

"*Hello, Lisa!*" several of the guys said in mocking fashion.

"OK, that'll be all. Carry on men," Glenn said, leading Lisa from the room.

After the door closed behind them, hoots, howls and catcalls filled the air. Their Pavlovian response was very upsetting to Janet. "Did you get a load of that?" Kevin asked, not expecting an answer. He didn't get one, as Scott sat lost in his thoughts of the vision that had just stood before him.

As they left the room, Lisa was aware of the juvenile response that followed her introduction. She was surprised that the sales team felt they could act in such a boisterous manner in front of management. Several people at home office had warned her that they played fast and loose with rules and protocol in the Western Region office. She would have to strongly consider whether or not she could function in such an environment.

Turning the corner, she encountered a dumpy, but well-dressed man leaving the men's room. His eyes were red, and he appeared to have a white, powdery substance on his upper lip. As he ambled toward them, Lisa couldn't help noticing that even in her low heels, she was taller than him.

"Eating those powdered doughnuts again, Jon?" Glenn asked, not sounding amused.

"Wha...oh, uh...yeah, I guess you caught me," Cassler said, wiping his mouth with his handkerchief and smiling nervously.

"Jon, I'd like you to meet Lisa LeDoux, from home office. She's interviewing for the HR position."

"Hi there, Lisa!" Cassler said, extending a sweaty, dead-fish hand for her to shake.

Trying to mask her repulsion, Lisa replied, "Nice to meet you, Jon."

Glenn placed his hands on Lisa's shoulders in a way she felt was inappropriate. Looking down at her he smiled and said, "Jon is our..."

"Orange County sales manager. Chapman College grad," Lisa blurted out.

"Very good...be careful, Jon, she knows her stuff. Anyway, I'd like you to talk with him for a few minutes. Jon, when you're wrapped up, you can bring her back to my office, OK?"

"Sure, Glenn. Follow me, Lisa." Following Jon, she pulled away from Glenn's grip. As she walked behind Cassler, she turned to see Glenn still standing in the hallway, smiling approvingly. He was tall and handsome, and acted as if he was cocksure of that fact. Several of the girls at home office had told her what a hunk they thought he was. Anyone in his position would have to be self-confident, but his demeanor had a creepy edge to it.

Cassler's office was not as lavish as Glenn's, but still surprisingly plush to Lisa. Back at home office, only the President of Campbell Industries had a nicer office than these two. A copy of Lisa's resume was on his desk. "Sit, sit," Cassler said, motioning to a leather chair in front of his desk. Falling into his seat, he made a big production out of propping his feet on his desk. Lisa noticed that there was a small hole worn in the sole of his left shoe. Cassler picked up her resume, and read to himself, occasionally making a grunting sound. Lisa eyed the assorted awards, plaques and certificates hanging on the walls. She found herself thinking that Cassler did not fit the stereotype of a sales manager.

Dropping his feet to the floor with a thud, Cassler lay the resume down and peered at her through his thick, coke-bottle lenses. "Are you married?"

"No."

"I am," he said in a tone she took to be defensive. "No kids though, we're dinks."

"*Dinks?*"

"Yeah, you know, double income, no kids, D.I.N.K—DINKs." His laugh was unnerving. "My wife is a court reporter—good money in that, I'll tell you."

"I'm sure there is."

"This is her picture," Cassler said, handing her a gold 8x10 frame.

"She's lovely," Lisa said, quickly returning the photograph of a very plain, obese woman who appeared to be about ten years older than Cassler.

"Do you plan to get married?" Cassler asked her in an oily voice.

"Well, I'm sure I will someday if I meet the right person…"

"If you were to get married, and say you had a kid, would you continue working, or stay at home?"

"This line of questioning is totally inappropriate, Jon. I would think someone with your management background would be well aware of that," Lisa said firmly.

"Uh, yeah…I guess…I, uh, I was just wanting to see if you really knew the legalities of the corporate interview process. Big part of HR, you know," he stammered, unconvincingly.

"Yes, I know."

Laughing nervously, Cassler stood and offered his sweaty handshake once again. "You passed! You've got my vote! I'll take you back to Glenn."

Walking down the corridor, Lisa's mind was racing as she tried to analyze her initial impression of the Western Region office. Could she thrive or even survive in this workplace for the three years it would take her to get her Master's? She reassured herself that she could do anything. Her parents had instilled that ideal in her. But did she want to do this? Following Jon, she couldn't help noticing his strange gait, or that from behind he was really pear-shaped. She scolded herself, knowing that rule one of her HR training was not to judge others by their appearance. But even trying to view Cassler through the eyes of a professional, she couldn't get past the thought of what an odd little man he was.

The conference room door opened as they passed, and Lisa could feel herself being ogled by the exiting salesmen. "Lisa! Lisa!" A voice called out from behind her. She turned to face a pleasant looking guy in his mid-30's, with light brown hair and a mustache. "Just wanted to introduce myself…I'm Kevin Forrester, I cover the Inland Empire territory. Welcome to California!"

His smile seemed sincere, and she noticed he wasn't wearing a wedding ring. "Nice to meet you, Kevin."

"And this is my partner in crime, Scott Murphy, new guy. Covers the South Bay."

"Hello, Scott. It's always challenging starting a new job."

Scott's mouth went dry, as he felt beads of sweat start to roll down his sides. "Hi," was all he could manage.

Lisa noticed Scott, also was not wearing a wedding band. She wasn't sure if he stood out from the group because she found him attractive, or because he was the tallest person leaving the room. He had warm brown eyes that peered out from under a full head of thick, brown hair. His athletic build did not escape her glance, either.

Scott felt as if he'd been struck by lightning, and wasn't sure if he could move. She was a dark-haired beauty. What a smile! And so poised and lady-like. Before he could find any other words to say, Tim interrupted him. "Lisa, I'm Tim Newsome, you've probably heard of me."

"Can't say that I have…"

Scott shuffled forward as the rest of the team made their way out of the conference room, and exchanged greetings with Lisa. Kevin caught up to him, put his arm around his shoulder, and said, "'Hi?' That's all the Top Gun—Mr. I was *born* ready—could come up with? Uh, oh…did little Scotty see something he liked? Is she your type, or what?"

Scott felt himself blush, as he replied, "I don't know what you're talking about."

"Hey, I'm not stupid…well, OK, maybe I am, but I do believe I recognize the dumfounded look of the infatuated when I see it."

"I'm sure you do."

"*So*…should I give you a chance with this one, or just move right in and claim her for myself?"

"You do whatever you want to, I mean, you don't even know if she'll take the job here…"

"Oh, she'll take the job, and since I saw the way she smiled at you, I'll lay low for a couple weeks and give you a shot, but if you fall on your face, she's fair game, bud!"

As the two walked out of the empty lobby and into the parking lot, Scott asked, "You think she smiled at me?" Kevin laughed at him.

*   *   *

BACK INSIDE, Cassler delivered Lisa to Glenn's office. "She's got my vote, big guy!" Cassler said as they walked in. Turning to Lisa, he offered his sweaty hand for the third, and what she hoped final time, and said, "Good luck!"

"Thanks for your time, Jon," she said in a tone so sweet it concealed her true feelings.

As she took a seat, Glenn asked, "So, whaddaya think?"

"I think this would be a great opportunity for me, Glenn."

"Looks and brains, I like that!"

As she tried to process the true meaning of what she thought to be an inappropriate comment, she asked, "Do I need to call the limo service to get a ride to my hotel?"

"Where did they put you up?"

"At the LAX Wyndham."

"That place is a dump! I'll see if Regina can get you a room at the Marriott."

"Well, I wouldn't want you to go to any trouble..."

"It's no trouble, Lisa. Then after I get you checked in, I hope you'll let me take you to dinner so I can talk you into joining my team."

"I don't think you'll have too tough a time talking me into it—this is what I really want to do."

"Good. Then I'll spend our evening together trying to see what else I can talk you into," he said with a lecherous smile.

CHAPTER 15

AFTER CHANGING PLANES at Memphis International Airport, Lisa's Northwest flight landed in New Orleans at 7:05 PM central time. Her two days in LA had been quite an experience. Glenn offered her the Human Resources Manager job for the Western Region office; and she accepted—without sleeping on it. She was really confident about her decision, and excited about entering this new phase of her life. The thought of moving to California, starting a new job—with better pay, and more responsibility, and studying for her Master's at Pepperdine had her adrenaline rushing.

Stepping off the Jetway, she spotted her mother standing against the wall across the corridor. They exchanged smiles as Lisa approached. Her mother was a very attractive, cultured Southern Belle. Many people thought they could pass as sisters. As Lisa stopped in front of her, she noticed the tears welling in her mother's eyes. "You're moving to California, aren't you?"

"How could you tell, Mother?"

"I could see it in your eyes, sweetheart," she said as she pulled Lisa toward her and embraced her warmly. "This is a big step, dear."

"But not a permanent one, Mother," Lisa tried to say reassuringly.

As the two women made their way to baggage claim, past the food vendors and souvenir stands stocked with Mardi Gras beads and masks, Lisa looked over and was glad to see that her mother had stopped crying.

"This will only be for three years. You know Campbell's headquarters are here—and here is where I'll be with my next promotion. They really have mapped out a career path for me, they're paying for me to go to school, and I'm really excited about the opportunity, Mother."

"Oh, I know you are, and I know three years will pass before you know it; but I'm still allowed to miss you."

"Now don't start going into that 'I'm your only baby' stuff."

"Don't worry, I'll save that for your father. I'll be fine, dear. And, you should know that your father and I are very proud of you."

*   *   *

AFTER COLLECTING her suitcase off the baggage carousel, Lisa and her mother headed to the parking garage. Her mother remembered parking on the G7 row, and she was correct. She loaded her suitcase into the trunk of her mother's Mercedes C320. Lisa opened the passenger side front door and eased into the buttery, tan leather seats. She was really exhausted from the rounds of interviews and completing two cross-country flights so close together.

Leaving the airport in Kenner, her mother smoothly merged the forest green sedan onto the interstate. They would be on I-10 for about fifteen minutes, before finding the North Broad Avenue exit. Taking a deep breath, she thought about how good it was to be home—and how much she would miss this place. Off in the distance, under the darkening sky, she could see the Louisiana Superdome.

The car's headlights lit their way through the exclusive Garden District. When she was a child, the Spanish moss hanging from the large oak trees seemed eerie. She recalled that feeling tonight. The car slowed as it entered the long driveway, which gave the driver the option of continuing in a half-circle back to the street, or driving straight to the detached garage beside the large house.

Once parked in the garage, the women could hear the sounds of footsteps crunching pine needles as they approached. Lisa saw her father's large frame fill the garage door. "How's my little girl?" he said as she stepped into his strong arms.

"I'm fine, Daddy," she said, squeezing him tightly.

Her father was still in his suit trousers and dress shirt from work. He typically did not wear a jacket, since it would be obscured by his judge's robe—that, and the heat and humidity of New Orleans. "Have you eaten yet, sweetheart?"

"Just airplane peanuts!"

"I took the liberty of ordering your favorite pizza from Bonano's! I'll get your bag and lock up. You and your mother go on in."

Lisa and her mother entered through the kitchen door. Her mother went to the refrigerator and removed a bottle of chardonnay. Taking three glasses from the cabinet, she turned to Lisa and asked, "Will you be having wine, dear?"

"Yes, please!"

Her father walked in carrying her suitcase, and said in passing, "I'll take this up to Lisa's room. The pizza's in the oven. You girls get started, and I'll be right back!" Her father was always so upbeat and positive. That was one of the many things she would miss, she thought.

Returning to the kitchen, Lisa's father asked, "Is this a celebration dinner we're having?"

"I guess so, Daddy—I took the job!"

"You should have called…I could have made reservations at the Commander's Palace."

"Oh, we still have a few weeks to do that, Daddy."

"Since I wasn't home in time to join your mother at the airport, tell me all about it, sweetheart."

"Well, I've been offered—and accepted—the Human Resources Manager position for the Western Region office of Campbell Industries in Los Angeles."

"Good for you!" he said with apparent pride.

"They're covering all my relocation expenses—along with my tuition at Pepperdine."

"That's important."

"I'll have a few weeks to tie up loose ends here, and then I'm off."

"Your mother and I would like to go out to LA and help you get settled. Have you found an apartment?"

"Yes, they showed me this place, Oakwood—it seemed nice enough—it's temporary housing for corporate transfers. I can stay there for the first six months, while I get acclimated to Southern California, and decide where exactly I want to live—hopefully someplace between the office and campus."

"Sounds smart."

Lisa's mother smiled at the sight of the two conversing. She interjected, "And Donald, Lisa has assured me that this will only be for three years."

"Is that all?" he said, winking at Lisa. "I was hoping to get some peace and quiet around here—three years? Hell, I won't even know she's gone."

Lisa laughed, and said, "That's right, Mother, I'll be home before you know it."

"I guess you're both right," she said, not sounding convinced.

"Mother, with Campbell's home office being here in New Orleans, I'll be coming home several times a year, for meetings and training classes. I even have to come back for a workshop in November. Throw in the holidays, and you'll probably see me as much as you do now!"

"I suppose," she said, but her mother's intuition was telling her that this decision was not in her daughter's best interest.

CHAPTER 16

ALLEN HAD PAGED him earlier in the day to let him know that there was no need to pick up munchies for tonight's meeting. He told Scott that the monthly meeting was being moved off-site for a little "team building exercise"—whatever that meant. Some restaurant called Calamity Jane's. They would be joined by Glenn Stevens and the Orange County sales team. After a sales call at Saddleback, he headed for the office, where Allen said everyone would meet and carpool to the meeting.

Lori was not at her desk as he entered the building. On his way to Allen's office he was greeted by Regina. "Hello, Scott! How are you today?"

"Great. Is Allen in?"

"Yes, go right in." Regina was always smiling and positive. He wondered how someone with her temperament thrived in this kind of workplace.

Allen looked up as he entered the office. "Hey, Scott—we'll be leaving in a few minutes."

"No problem. Do I need to bring anything special?"

"No, I think everything will be provided," Allen said in a sarcastic tone.

Walking back through the building he saw the sales team gathering in the lobby. Passing Glenn's office, he glanced through the slightly opened door and spied Lori seated facing Glenn's desk. She was smiling, as she seemed to be listening to Glenn pontificate on some unknown subject matter.

"You're a designated driver, rookie!" was the greeting blurted out by Tim. Scott noticed Cassler laughing, huddled to the side with the Orange County sales team.

"No problem, Timbo—you wanna ride with me?"

As Tim glared at Scott, Kevin interrupted, "I'll ride with you."

"Me, too," said Darrin.

"Got room for one more?" asked Jerry Fujisaka.

"Sure, as long as somebody knows how to get there."

"I could find it blindfolded!" said Kevin with a hint of glee in his voice.

As Kevin, Darrin and Jerry piled into Scott's car, he noticed Cassler and Janet getting into Glenn's Mercedes. Tim and Allen climbed into Marvin's SUV, as the Orange County guys split themselves into three carloads.

"Okay, you'll want to take the 5 Freeway South, to the 91 East—this place is in Anaheim," Kevin directed as they drove from the parking lot.

"I really wish we didn't have to have meetings at Calamity Jane's," sighed Jerry.

"Me, too. My wife is not very fond of the idea," added Darrin.

"What's wrong with Calamity Jane's?" inquired Scott.

"It's a titty-bar, and these guys don't know how to relax and have a good time," Kevin chimed in.

"A strip club?" Scott queried with dismay.

"Uh, oh—hey, you're not married like these guys—why would you object to having the meeting at a titty-bar—an all-expense paid meeting at a titty-bar, I might add."

"Well, I just don't think that's the most professional setting for us to conduct business," Scott said.

"I agree," said Darrin.

"He's right," added Jerry.

"Jesus Christ! You guys are p-whipped at home, and Scotty must be some kind of Southern Bible thumper!" Kevin said, sneering in disgust. "This is a classy joint. I mean, they serve good food—you can get a massage—and a hair-cut!"

"Look Kev, if that's where you want to go on your own time, fine with me, but I just don't think a high profile organization should have a meeting at a strip club."

"Scotty, Scotty, Scotty—all large companies have meetings at titty bars—it's the American way!"

"You're nothing if not a patriot, Kevin," Scott said, laughing, as they merged onto the 91 Freeway.

"Take the Orangethorpe exit—and this *is* a legitimate place to conduct business. Glenn has actually recruited employees there. Where do you think he found Lori?"

"At Calamity Jane's?" Scott asked incredulously.

"Hey, he heard the story of her life, and a few couch dances later, bingo—Glenn found his new receptionist."

"Unbelievable," Scott muttered.

*   *   *

AFTER PARKING, they joined the others congregating by the entrance. Cassler took a head count, then directed everyone to go inside. Walking in, Scott turned around to see Cassler handing a wad of bills to the doorman to pay the group's cover charge.

Once inside, Glenn, Janet, Cassler and Mike Brophy, one of the Orange County sales guys, all took a seat at a table by the runway stage. Scott, Darrin and Jerry took the table farthest from the stage. "Mind if I join you fellas?" drawled Jimmy.

"No, not at all," said Darrin. Kevin sat at a table with Allen, Tim and Marvin, who had brought in his briefcase. Unzipping the case, he removed his laptop, set it on the table and booted up the computer. The glow of the screen illuminated their table in the darkened bar.

"Can I ask you a question, Jimmy?"

"Sure, Scott."

"Does home office approve of us having business meetings at a place like this?"

"Well, let's just say that when times are good, activities such as these are not closely scrutinized. And besides, it would be hard for them to find out."

"How so?"

"Well, you see, everything we drink here is put on our corporate credit cards, and all the cash you boys tuck in these girls panties, well let's just say that, uh, Allen and Jon have been known to approve these cash expenditures on your expense reports."

"OK, I understand the cash, but what about the credit card receipts? Doesn't home office get suspicious when they see large amounts spent at a place called Calamity Jane's Topless Club?"

"You don't know much about the topless dancer profession, do ya son?"

"Can't say that I do."

"Well, when businessmen, uh, entertain their clients and so forth here, and charge their tabs, the receipts don't say 'Calamity Jane's,' they say 'Consolidated Restaurant Corporation,' what you might call a parent company. So to home office, this could have just been a big steak and lobster dinner meeting."

As Scott pondered the ethics of this, a buxom blonde in a white bikini appeared with a tray of bottled beers balancing on her left hand. "Hi, guys! I'm Monica, I'll be taking care of you tonight."

"Who ordered these?" inquired Jerry.

"That good-looking gentlemen over there," she said, nodding toward Glenn.

Cassler stood and said, "OK, OK, settle down you perverts! We have a few items to discuss before the festivities begin. I'll turn it over to Glenn."

"Thanks, Jon. First of all, this is a reward for a job well done. You guys have really gotten off to a fast start this fiscal year—not that I'm accusing anyone here of sandbagging." Laughter spread through the group's tables. "Both sales teams are ahead of last year, and ahead of plan year-to-date. I am very pleased. So before the girls come out and you start ignoring me, I would like to present one award here—the top salesperson for last month. Although he hasn't been with us long, this salesperson is ahead of plan, had a super month, gotten a couple of big jobs, and has made some tremendous inroads with a key distributor for us. Sorry Jon, even though the Orange County sales team was ahead of LA for the month and year-to-date, this month's winner comes from Allen's team."

Standing, Tim said, "This is getting to be old hat, guys…"

"Sit down, Tim," Allen interrupted.

"That's right, Tim, sit your ass down—this month's top performer is….Scott Murphy—the rookie!" Scott sat in disbelief as Jimmy, Darrin and Jerry were congratulating him and patting him on the back. He knew that he secured a decent sized job with Paramount, and that Alexander's was off to a fast start, but he had no idea he was ahead of everyone else. "Come up here Scott, I've got something for you," Glenn said, with a shit-eating grin on his face.

Standing, and walking to Glenn's table, Glenn shook Scott's hand firmly. Then Allen stood and shook his hand. He felt a hand patting him on the butt, and he turned to see Janet, seated and smiling. "Way to go—and nice ass," she said with a lusty smile.

"Scott, as our top salesperson this month, it's my privilege to present this plaque to you, along with this gift certificate to the Rusty Pelican restaurant."

"That's my boy! Taught him everything he knows—I'm his friggin' mentor!" Kevin shouted.

"Thanks, Glenn, I really appreciate this," Scott said.

"No, thank you, Scott. Thanks for jumping in with both feet and getting some quick results. I like someone who takes initiative." Scott couldn't help noticing that Tim was glaring at him. "Oh, and I have one more token of my appreciation…Miss Monica…" Loud music blared, as Glenn grabbed Scott by the shoulders, and forced him into his chair. He noticed Janet and Cassler laughing, and then saw that Monica, the same Monica who had delivered his beer moments before, but was now slithering toward him topless, wearing nothing but a white thong.

She walked a couple of seductive circles, then stopped in front of him with her back facing him. Spreading her long legs, she bent over, grabbed her ankles and peered out at him upside down from between her legs, her blonde hair touching the floor. She then shimmied backwards, until her ass was almost touching his face. As the group's catcalls mounted, Scott felt his face redden. Monica stood and turned, straddling herself across his lap. She cupped her enormous breasts in both hands, and pushed them in his face.

"Grab 'em, Scotty! See if they're real!" He heard Kevin screaming frantically.

Monica smiled and purred, "If you wanna touch 'em, it's okay. I hear you've been a *good* boy."

She practically glistened—her body was covered in what Scott guessed to be baby oil—and he couldn't help wondering if she was ruining his suit slacks as she sat undulating on his lap. "No, thanks, they're very nice…I don't need to touch them. But, thanks for the dance," he said firmly, indicating that her services were no longer needed.

Judging from his stern look, Monica decided he didn't want to play anymore. "OK, your loss, sweetie, but I've already been paid for," she said with a pout.

"You're right, my loss," Scott said as he got to his feet. He put his plaque and gift certificate on the table, and shook Monica's hand, "Thanks, again. You do nice work, ma'am."

"How would you know? I was just getting started. Why don't you sit back down, and let me give you the full treatment. I'm a *professional*, honey."

"Obviously, and I'm sure your parents must be proud," Scott said as he made a beeline for the men's room.

"She was too much for him! I bet he has to go jack-off!" Cassler shouted behind him. The laughter from some in the group followed him.

Glenn tried to console Monica, as her mascara-laden eyes began to run. "What did I do?" She implored. "Is he gay, or something?"

"There, there, honey; he's just a little shy, or *really* strange. But there's nothing wrong with you, sweetheart. You're gorgeous." Glenn handed her a hundred dollar bill. "This is to reserve a private couch dance later, baby."

"Thanks," she said, standing on her tiptoes to give Glenn a kiss on the cheek. "You'll see how good I am."

"I am looking forward to it!" Glenn said, as he looked her up and down. As Monica sashayed away, Janet frowned at Glenn.

✶   ✶   ✶

LEANING OVER THE SINK, Scott was splashing water on his face as Allen walked in the men's room.

"Just a little friendly advice…that wasn't the best way to handle that, Scott."

"What do you mean? I let her do her little dance, I thanked her, what more do you want?"

"Glenn likes his guys to appreciate his gestures. When he plans a meeting like this, he wants the guys to enjoy it, and let him know how much he's appreciated, you know, stroke him a little."

"OK, fine. I'll tell Glenn how much I appreciated his gesture on my behalf. But you could've given me a heads-up as to what to expect here."

"I didn't know you'd have a problem with it."

"Do you really like these kinds of places?"

"Well…"

"I mean it's kind of sad, don't you think? These girls, degrading themselves, probably to fund some drug problem, I mean it's just a step above prostitution."

"Well, I wouldn't go that far…look, these places make me a little uncomfortable, too, but sometimes you just have to go with the flow. Besides, you're single—no wife to give you a hard time about this."

"Single or not, I just don't think this is where a damn sales meeting should take place—whatever you guys want to do on your own time is fine, but this is just unprofessional," Scott fumed. He then walked around a half stall and stood in front of a urinal, unzipping his fly. "OK, I'll be a team player. I'll tell Glenn thanks, and apologize if there was any misunderstanding. OK?"

"Good. It's called playing the game, Scott. You're off to a good start with Campbell…sorry if I put you in an embarrassing situation."

Cassler burst through the door. "What's going on ladies? Hiding in here so those big, bad girls can't get you?"

"Knock it off, Jon," Allen said.

"Hey, I'm just glad he's not on my team," Cassler said as he approached Scott, and peered over the urinal stall.

"That's a good way to lose some teeth," Scott snapped, frowning at Cassler.

"I was just checking to see if you had a dick."

"If you're through enjoying the view, I'd appreciate it if you'd back off." Scott flushed and zipped his fly, and turned to find Cassler blocking his way.

"Back off? *Back off?* Who in the fuck do you think you're talking to? I'm a fucking District Sales Manager, and you're just some bumpkin prick from *Memphis!*"

Scott noticed the veins protruding from Cassler's neck, and his upper lip drenched in perspiration, as he said, "I don't work for you."

"Look, I'm the number two man, asshole. If I say jump, you say how high, got it? Never question my authority!"

"I'm gonna ask you one last time to step back," Scott said seriously, looking down at Cassler.

"OK guys, let's break it up," Allen interjected.

Cassler shouted at Scott, "Fuck you! You don't tell me to do anything—got it, prick?"

Cassler shoved Scott with both hands. "Don't do that again," Scott warned.

"Fuck you! What are you going to do, hit me?" Cassler said, shoving Scott again, this time harder. Before Allen could get between them, Scott coiled his right arm, and drove his fist fast and hard into Cassler's nose. Cassler was thrown back across the tiled floor, through a stall door, landing on a toilet.

Allen stepped in front of Scott, "That's enough! Get out of here Scott!"

Cassler looked down at the blood streaming from his nose onto his white shirt. "You're history, buddy! I'll sue! I'll have your fucking job for this!" Scott slammed the men's room door open, and stormed out. "You better leave. Before I kick your ass!" Cassler screamed behind him.

"Shut up, Jon," Allen said as he helped him off the toilet seat and to his feet.

"Would you look at this—he ruined my fucking tie! It's a Zegna, damn it!"

Scott weaved through the tables scattered throughout the dark room, making his way toward the exit. Glenn took his eyes off the topless girls pole dancing to the loud music, as he saw Scott walk past. Glenn stood and grabbed Scott firmly by the arm, and yelled, "Murphy! Where in the hell do you think you're going? The meeting's not over."

Scott wheeled around, and stared menacingly at Glenn. "Thanks for the wonderful time. Now I suggest you let go of my arm, sir."

"Listen to me boy, you have no idea who you're fucking with."

Scott replied coldly, "I think I have a pretty good idea." Glenn noticed Allen and Cassler walking across the room. Cassler was holding a handkerchief to his nose and his shirt was covered with blood. Glenn could feel Scott's bicep flex under his grip. Staring at the younger man, he noticed his eyes were unwavering. He also noticed that the eyes of the group were no longer on the bare breasts, but rather on the two of them. In measured words, Scott said tersely, "This is the last time I'm going to ask—let go of my arm."

Glenn prided himself on knowing when to pick his battles, and he quickly surmised that this was not a battle he wanted waged in this environment. "Your call, Murphy," he said, releasing his grip on Scott's arm. Scott proceeded to the exit, followed by Allen, Kevin and Jimmy.

As Scott opened his car door, the three men burst from the club into the daylight. "You all right, son?" Jimmy asked.

"Yeah, just swell."

Kevin asked, "Scott, what went on in there, man?"

"Oh, just a misunderstanding, I guess," Scott said, as he sat down in the driver's seat, and closed the door.

Allen knocked on the window, and Scott lowered the glass. "Listen to me, Scott. Just make your usual calls this week, and stay out of the office. Let me take care of everything. I'll call you and let you know what's going on."

"Okay, Allen…if you think that's best, but I don't want you sticking your neck out for me—you have a family to think about."

"Don't worry about me, I've been playing the game for a while," Allen said as Scott put his car in reverse.

"Is Scott going to lose his job?" Kevin asked.

"Not if I can help it," replied Allen as they watched Scott's car leave the parking lot in a hurry.

CHAPTER 17

SCOTT PARKED his car in front of the garbage dumpster. Walking back to the trunk, he removed a large cardboard box. Heading through the office entrance, he approached the receptionist. "Hi, Sheri, I have a ten o'clock with Mr. Lunsford."

"I'll let him know you're here, Scott." Scott looked at the framed pictures in Alexander's lobby. Mostly nautical themes, and some looked pretty old. "Scott, you can go on back, he's ready to see you," Sheri said with a smile.

Scott made his way to Lunsford's office in the far west corner of the building. "Scott—good to see you son. Have a seat," Nick Lunsford said smiling from behind his desk.

"Thanks. I wanted to drop off these Campbell golf shirts for your recessed light promotion—one shirt for every twenty-five C-9's purchased."

"Always on top of things, I like that, Scott. Oh, and I received the flyers you dropped off last week. They'll be going out in a mailing tomorrow."

"Great. If there's anything else I can do, as always, just let me know. I won't take up anymore of your time today, sir."

Scott stood to shake hands, but Nick remained seated and said, "I spoke with Allen this morning…I understand you got into a scuffle the other night." Scott returned to his seat, and let took a deep breath.

"Yes, sir, you could say that. To tell you the truth, I'm not sure how much longer I'll have a job with Campbell…"

"Bullshit! For smacking a punk like Cassler? They should give you an award."

"So I guess Allen gave you some of the details…"

"He told me that that dirt-bag Stevens was holding some sort of meeting at Calamity Jane's—he also told me you won salesman of the month, by the way—and that Cassler started something with you he couldn't finish."

"So they're admitting that Jon started it?"

"Absolutely. I'm only sorry that you didn't do more damage…"

"Well, it all happened so fast…."

"Look son, you don't have anything to worry about. I told Allen in no uncertain terms that if he lets Stevens railroad you out of a job to protect his queer sidekick, that he can give me an RMA for all the Campbell shit I have on the shelves, send over a truck and pick it all up this afternoon! I also told Allen not to take one iota of crap from Stevens about this, and that if he tried, to have Stevens give me a call—I'll put him in his place in short order, you can take that to the bank."

"Thanks, Mr. Lunsford. I really appreciate your support."

"Thank you son, you're doing a helluva job for me. And call me Nick."

*   *   *

AFTER LEAVING ALEXANDER'S, Scott was feeling pretty good about his meeting with Nick. Turning down Second Street, he parked in the lot behind Legend's. He walked around to the front of the restaurant, and went inside. It took a moment for his eyes to adjust to the dark interior. The long bar on the right was framed with the football helmets of PAC-10, Mountain West and WAC schools, and the defunct LA Rams and LA Raiders. Scanning the restaurant, he saw no sign of Kevin. "Party of one?" a smiling brunette hostess asked.

"Uh, no. I'm expecting someone to join me."

"Would you like to go ahead and get seated?"

"Sure, that would be great." Scott followed the waitress to a table, and chose a seat facing the door so he could see Kevin when he arrived. Mounted on the wall to his left, framed under glass were the football jerseys of the Ram's "Fearsome Foursome."

"You work for Campbell Industries, right?" a voice across from him inquired.

Scott turned and saw the cop who had interviewed him at the office. "Yeah, that's right. I'm…"

"Scott Murphy—I remember. "I'm Mike Harris, LAPD."

"Right. Nice to see you again," Scott said as the two men shook hands. "Any breaks on the case?"

"Not my case anymore, but to answer your question, no."

"That's too bad. I don't hear anything about it around the office anymore."

"That doesn't surprise me. You had just started at Campbell when we last met—how are things going for you?"

"Oh, could be better, but all in all I guess things are going OK."

"How's the head guy, Stevens?"

"Same as usual, I guess."

"How do you like working for a guy like that?"

"The jury's still out."

"Have you seen Lieutenant Cavanarro around your office lately?"

"No, can't say that I have. But I'm not there a whole lot…"

"That doesn't surprise me either."

"What? That I'm not at the office a lot?"

"No, that Cavanarro hasn't been around there a lot."

Sgt. Harris stood, pulled out his wallet, glanced at his check, and laid a ten-dollar bill on the table. "Well, I'm on the clock. See you around, Scott."

"Yeah, see ya." As Sgt. Harris walked out the door, he passed Kevin walking in. Scott waved to get Kevin's attention.

"Hey, man, sorry I'm late. Wasn't that the cop that was at the office after Maria Lopez was missing?"

"She still *is* missing, Kevin."

"I know…you're right. What did he want—is Cassler pressing assault charges, or something?"

"Not that I know of…Sergeant Harris was just having lunch."

"Did he recognize you?"

"Immediately. He told me that there were no new leads in Maria's case as far as he knew, but it's not his case anymore."

"Just a coincidence, huh?"

"Yeah, just a coincidence, I guess."

A blonde waitress in a tight Legends' T-shirt interrupted them. "Can I get you guys anything to drink?"

"Iced tea," said Scott.

"I'll take a Coke, and, uh, what's your name?" Kevin inquired.

"Cheryl."

"Hi, Cheryl. I'm Kevin, and this is my associate, Scott."

"I'll be back in a minute with your drinks," she said briskly walking away from them.

"Man, I don't think she's digging us at all…maybe she's married. Did you see if she was wearing a ring?"

"I didn't notice," Scott said perusing his menu.

"So how are you doing, man?" Kevin asked.

"Fine. Just doing what Allen tells me to do. I have an appointment with the new HR manager on Monday, and hopefully all this will just blow over."

"I don't know, man…nobody's ever stood up to Glenn the way you did—man, it was awesome! I thought the two of you were going to rumble."

"I guess I'm glad it didn't come to that…"

"Oh, dude, you should see Cassler—his nose is all swollen, and you gave him two black eyes—he looks like a fuckin' raccoon!"

"Maybe from now on he'll think twice before he starts something..."

"Oh, I know! That little prick is on such a power trip, man. You did us all a favor."

*   *   *

AS THE TWO MEN worked their way through lunch, Scott was lost in thought, as Kevin kept trying his luck, unsuccessfully, with Cheryl the waitress. Maybe this incident would blow over, and he could keep his job. He certainly felt he had the support of Allen, and Nick, which couldn't hurt. Money talks, and Alexander's was a major account for the Western Region office. Maybe the meeting would go well with the new HR manager, and nothing too damaging would go in his personnel file. After all, he had done nothing wrong, no matter how one looked at it. He had a right to defend himself from a pervert like Cassler. But did he hurt himself politically with Glenn? All this concern over a job he wasn't even sure he wanted anymore.

CHAPTER 18

"GOOD MORNING, SCOTT! Lori said, absolutely beaming.

"Good morning, Lori," Scott said, a bit startled by her friendly greeting.

"How was your weekend?" she asked smiling.

Stopping, Scott said, "Not bad…and yours?"

"Oh, it was nice. Thanks for asking."

Who was this? Lori had never even addressed him by his name before, much less asked any personal questions. "Well, I gotta see Allen."

"OK—it was good talking to you, Scott." As he walked away, he couldn't help thinking that if she'd been any sweeter to him, he would've gotten a cavity. What was that all about?

"Right on time, as usual," Allen said, looking at his watch.

"What can I say…"

"Had a nice conversation with Nick Lunsford the other day…"

"He told me that he had spoken to you…"

"You have a real ally in Nick."

"That's good to know."

"OK, Scott…let me fill you in on some things that have gone on here this morning. Have a seat."

"Thanks."

"Well…we really bombarded Lisa this morning on her first day. Oh, Lisa's our new HR manager…"

"Yes, I met her briefly when she was out for an interview."

"Good. Anyway, I met with her first thing, followed by both Jon and Glenn. She needs to get your version of what happened the other night, and hopefully we can put this incident behind us. Let me emphasize that in my opinion, you did nothing wrong—and I don't want you to think that you did."

"I don't."

"Good. Just answer her questions, and she'll write up a report with a recommendation for Glenn and home office."

"Any political minefields I should avoid?"

"No—just tell the truth. I'm behind you one-hundred percent."

"Thanks, Allen…I really appreciate it."

Opening a drawer on his credenza, Allen pulled out a box. Handing it to Scott, he said, "You forgot these—your plaque and gift certificate—you earned them."

Walking with Allen down the corridor to the HR manager's office, Scott dropped off his *Salesman of the Month* plaque and Rusty Pelican gift certificate at his workstation. For some reason, he felt strangely at ease. He guessed it was because he really didn't care what happened. If they gave him one ounce of crap, he was ready to walk. This wasn't the only place he could get a job. He could probably get his old job back with Mid-American—but that would mean having to live near his father again—not his first choice. Nothing against his family, but he kind of liked the idea of 1,800 miles separating them.

They already had replaced Sheila's name on the door. It now read: LISA LeDOUX, HUMAN RESOURCES MANAGER. Allen knocked on the door. "Come in…"

"Scott's here, as promised, Lisa."

"Great," she said with a genuine smile, and onyx eyes that sparkled. "Scott, I'm Lisa LeDoux. It's nice to see you again."

"Same here," Scott replied clearing his throat, as he felt the moisture leaving his mouth. The previous calmness he had felt was now replaced with butterflies in his stomach. She was absolutely radiant. This was the most beautiful woman he had ever seen in his life.

"Have a seat, Scott."

"Thanks."

"Stop by my office when you finish up here Scott, OK?" Allen stated as if he had an option to do otherwise.

"Sure, Allen."

"How has your first day at Campbell been, so far?" Scott asked, not sure if he sounded smooth or like a dork.

"Interesting, to say the least," Lisa said with a soft laugh. He couldn't believe how straight and white her teeth were—perfect. Her dark hair was full and shiny. She was dressed to the nines—obviously very career minded. Even her perfume was just right, pleasant and flowery. She struck him as being an unusual mix—a feminine woman who also seemed very strong. Picking up a maroon Mont Blanc fountain pen that matched her fingernail polish, she opened a manila folder in front of her. "Are you ready to get started?"

"I was born ready," Scott said, wishing he could have his programmed response back even before he uttered the words.

"Okay…" she said, arching an eyebrow. "Scott, as Human Resources manager, it's my job to mediate any disputes between employees. I've spoken with Jon, Allen and Glenn about an incident that occurred at a sales meeting a couple of weeks ago. Now I'd like to get your version of what happened. Any questions?"

"How do you want to start this?"

"Tell me about the sales meeting."

"I'd use the term 'sales meeting' very loosely to describe our little get-together."

Lisa looked confused, glanced at her notes, and said, "I understand that the meeting was held off-site…at a restaurant."

"It wasn't a restaurant."

"It says right here…Consolidated Restaurant…"

"It was a topless bar called Calamity Jane's—apparently, Consolidated is the parent company, or some kind of credit card clearinghouse so businessmen can expense their charges, without raising any eyebrows over at accounts payable."

"Hmmmm, a strip club," she mumbled as she made notes in the margin of the paper in front of her. While she was looking down, Scott took advantage of the opportunity to study her. She was absolutely stunning. Probably knew it too, he surmised. Way out of his league. Better focus on this interrogation, he thought.

"I understand that you were presented with the *Salesman of the Month* award…"

"That's correct."

"…and how did you feel about that, Scott?"

"I don't think my feelings have any bearing here. Sticking to the facts, I appreciated the plaque and gift certificate—the lap dance in front of all my colleagues—I could've done without."

"Lap dance?"

"Glenn insisted…his way of showing his special appreciation, I guess."

"It sounds like you were uncomfortable there…I thought all guys liked frequenting those kinds of establishments…"

"Well, I don't know what kind of crowd you run with…"

"That wasn't called for…"

"I'm sorry, you're right." As she made more notes, he felt really stupid for making such a smart-ass remark. She was not the enemy—at least not yet. But if he continued to be so defensive, it probably wouldn't take her long to determine what side she was on. Why was he acting like this? Was he intimidated by her appearance?

"OK, so you're saying that part of your recognition for being a top performer was an unwanted lap dance?"

"Yes…and I really am sorry for being a smart aleck…I guess I'm just a little uncomfortable discussing all this with you."

"Don't be—sorry or uncomfortable. This was not a professional environment to conduct a sales meeting, and I wasn't trying to make assumptions about you and all men…I must say I find your stance on topless bars refreshing. You're certainly not the average guy." She smiled warmly. Scott felt as if she could melt him with her piercing eyes. He hoped she didn't think he was staring at her. He hoped he didn't look as if he were hypnotized. For that matter, he hoped he wasn't sitting there slack-jawed and drooling.

"What happened next, Scott?"

"I excused myself from the festivities, and went to the men's room."

"Did anyone from Campbell follow you in there?"

"Yes, Allen and Jon. Jon made a few snide comments—that I'd prefer not to repeat to a lady—and then he shoved me. I told him to back off and not do that again."

"Then what happened?" she asked, leaning forward, her sculpted face nestled in her left hand, propped on her elbow.

"He shoved me again."

"At this time did you feel he was threatening you with bodily harm?"

"Let's just say I was ready to leave, and he was obstructing the exit…so I hit him."

"In self defense?"

"Yes."

"OK, so that's your story…"

"Does someone disagree with my recollection?"

"There are some interesting versions being recanted, but the story-line is basically the same. And, it helps that you have Allen to corroborate your version. I don't think any blame can be placed on you. Did you want to file a complaint against Jon?"

"Me? File something against Cassler, huh?"

"It's your prerogative…"

"No, I don't guess so…I really don't think I'll have anymore problems with him."

"I wouldn't think so…how about Glenn?" she inquired.

"Not sure I want to go there."

Scott was getting the impression that she was staring at him! Did he have a zit on the end of his nose? Was his fly open? What was she looking at? Standing, he said, "Well, if that's it, I need to get back to work."

"Sure. Sure…thanks *so* much for your time, Scott. I don't think you have anything to be worried about."

"That's good to know."

"It was nice seeing you again, and hopefully the next time we get a chance to talk, we'll have a lighter subject matter…"

"Let's hope."

"…and if I can ever be of any assistance, please don't hesitate to let me know."

"Thanks, I appreciate that," Scott said as he shook her hand. Releasing her hand, he hoped she hadn't noticed how sweaty his palms were.

*   *   *

AFTER HE LEFT, Lisa sat down and scribbled a few more notes on her report, but noticed the difficulty she had concentrating on the work at hand. She couldn't stop thinking about Scott. He had all the basic superficial requirements—tall, handsome, athletic build, a deep voice, conservative dresser—not as flashy as the other guys—and self-confident. She wasn't sure if he had a good sense of humor or not—she had learned that was a quality she also desired—but she was sure of one thing—this was a decent man.

Closing the folder and leaving her office, she made her way over to Glenn's office. Along the way she caught herself looking to see if she could catch a glimpse of Scott roaming the halls. Focusing on the task at hand, she told herself that she was going to be very straightforward and succinct with Glenn. She was not going to let this incident get blown out of proportion. Besides, she wasn't defending Scott—she was going by the book. This was cut and dried.

"Glenn? Got a minute?"

Glenn looked up at Lisa, smiled and said, "For you? You can have all the time you need. Sit." Glenn motioned toward a chair facing his desk.

"Thanks. I've spoken with Allen, Jon and Scott, as you requested…"

"So are we going to can Murphy?"

"*No*…I wouldn't recommend that…"

"What? You want me to approve some sort of probation for him?"

"Glenn, he did nothing wrong."

"He beats the crap out of one of my Sales Managers, and you call that doing nothing wrong?"

"It was self-defense."

"His word against Cassler's."

"Allen was a witness—both he and Scott say that Jon provoked it—Jon assaulted Scott first."

"Allen's a witness?"

"Yes, sir."

Glenn stood, walked around his desk and seated himself on the desktop, invading her personal space. Looming over her, he asked, "So just what is it you think we should do here?"

"First of all, I would recommend that future sales meetings not be held at topless bars…"

"It was a restaurant—I have the receipt to prove it!"

"…I don't think home office would approve of that kind of restaurant."

"Listen, Missy…as long as my numbers are up, home office doesn't give a fuck where I hold my meetings!"

"I wouldn't put that theory to the test if I were you…I also recommend that you put Jon Cassler on probation—three days unpaid leave—and a letter in his personnel file."

"Cassler?"

"That's what my recommendation is for you—a copy of which will be forwarded to the President of HR."

"Oh, come on! Is that necessary?"

"And finally, don't call me Missy—my name is Lisa," she said, staring at him firmly.

After reflecting for a moment, Glenn broke the silence and said, "OK, OK, this is your call. I'll follow your advice. I would hate to override you on your first day—I want you to be able to establish yourself here. And sorry about the Missy thing…I thought all you Southern girls liked to be called Missy," he said, grinning.

"You should really get to the South more often, Glenn."

Sliding off his desk, Glenn knelt directly in front of her, as if he were going to propose. Leaning very close to her, he smiled, placed his hand on hers, and said, "You're a strong woman Lisa—I like that."

"Thank you, Glenn. I take after my mother. Oh, and by the way, your hand seems to have been placed inadvertently on mine. I'm sure that won't happen again." Lisa stood, forcing Glenn to lean back. Looking down at him, crouched in a catcher's stance, she handed him the folder, and walked to the door. Turning, she generated a big smile, and said, "My findings are pretty self-explanatory. Any questions let me know."

"OK…thanks, Lisa." After she left, Glenn realized how stupid he must look squatting in front of his desk. Returning to his chair, he threw the folder on his desk. Rummaging through his middle desk drawer, he retrieved a pack of Camels. Lighting a cigarette and propping his feet up on his desk, he watched his exhaled stream of smoke curl towards the ceiling. He thought she was a real piece of work—not to mention a real nice piece of ass. This could get interesting…

CHAPTER 19

AFTER PICKING UP a $25K stocking PO from Nick at Alexander's, Scott figured he had enough time to drop it off with the Customer Service department at the office before he headed to the airport. Maneuvering through mid-morning Southern California traffic, he listened to Rush Limbaugh on the radio. Some of the goings-on at the White House reassured him in a cynical way that Campbell was not the only establishment without a moral compass.

His white sedan veered into the Commerce Business Park. Running up the entrance steps, Scott hurried past Lori.

She looked up and flashed a big smile. "Hi, Scott!"

"Hi, Lori—I'm in a hurry—I have a flight to catch," he said as he hurried by. Suddenly she knows my name? Why all the sudden interest in me—a lowly sales rep?

Walking quickly down the main corridor, he made a left by Regina's cubicle. "Mornin,' Regina."

"Scott? Don't you have a flight out today?"

"Yes, ma'am, I just have to drop an order off with Customer Service, then I'm on my way."

"Will you get to see your family while you're in Memphis?"

"I hope to be able to get together with them one evening."

"Well, good. And have a great trip."

"Thanks, Regina, I will."

Entering the cube farm that made up Customer Service, he made his
way to Toni Hemmings' 6x6 enclosure. Toni had responsibility for the
wholesale accounts in the South Bay territory. With her harsh, military
style haircut, multiple earrings, and extremely long, ornate fingernails,
his first impression of her turned out to be off the mark. Not an airhead
ditz, she was a hard worker, and handled customer problems professionally. He now appreciated her behind-the-scenes competence.

Toni was on the phone, but acknowledged his arrival with a wide
smile. "Glad I could help. Is there anything else I can assist you with
today? Thanks again, George—and thanks for calling Campbell."

Pushing the mike on her headset away from mouth, she asked, "OK
Scott, I'm off—what can I do for you?"

"I just picked up this stocking order from Alexander's and wanted to
get it entered ASAP," he said, handing her the purchase order.

"Great…hey, nice order. Guess you're bucking for top performer two
months in a row, huh?"

"Not really, just doing my job."

"Cute and modest—I like that in a guy!"

"Uh, OK, you'll notice the first release is clearly marked for immedi-
ate shipment, and then two more shipments each a month apart."

"Got it, no problem. I know what a stickler Mr. Lunsford can be."

"Thanks, Toni. I have to hoof it to the airport."

"Where are you heading?"

"Memphis…new employee orientation."

"Orientation?…*Dulls-ville*…drink lots of caffeine."

"OK, I will, thanks."

"I'll hold down the fort until you get back."

He knew Toni would take care of it. Nice not to have to sweat the
small things. Walking to his workstation, he picked up the phone and
checked his voicemail. No messages—good. Hit the men's room, and

I'm out of here. He glanced over at Lisa's darkened office. It looked as if she had already left.

*   *   *

PUSHING THE MEN'S ROOM DOOR open, Scott was surprised to see Glenn Stevens and Jon Cassler to his left, leaning over the counter-top between the two sinks. As they stood up, he could tell by their expressions that they were surprised to see him as well.

Glenn quickly turned around and snapped, "Get the hell out of here, Murphy!" Scott noticed the rolled-up currency in his right hand—a twenty he guessed—and several lines of a white powdery substance on the countertop.

"Sorry…I, uh, was just going to…"

"You heard him, shithead! Get the fuck out of here!" Cassler screamed at him almost hysterically.

"No problem," Scott said as he backed out of the men's room.

Jerry Fujisaka was on his way into the men's room when Scott stopped him. "I wouldn't go in there right now, pal."

"What's up?"

"Let's just say that Glenn and Jon are having a *meeting.*"

"I guess I'll use the men's room in the warehouse."

"Good call, me, too."

As they entered the drab warehouse men's room, Jerry noticed a pair of brown hush puppies under the only stall, topped with a rumpled pair of chocolate Sansabelts, with an issue of *Computer Monthly* on the floor between them. "How's it going, Marv?"

"Leave me alone, I'm concentrating," came the reply from within the stall.

"More than I need to know, Marv. So what was going on in there, Scott?"

"Man, I'm not touching that with a ten foot pole…I guess all I can say is it's business as usual at this place." Jerry looked confused.

Standing at adjacent urinals, Jerry said, "Well, I like to visit this men's room anyway—just to read the philosophy of the guys in the warehouse—listen to this one, 'Never underestimate the power of stupid people in large groups.'"

"Hmmmm…that's deep…OK, here's another, 'New Office Vocabulary: Assmosis—the process by which some people seem to absorb success and advancement by kissing up to the boss—see Jon Cassler.'"

"Wow, a sage of the warehouse, Scott chuckled. Listen to this, ' I married Miss Right. I just didn't know her first name was *Always*.' "

"Very profound."

*　　　　*　　　　*

NOW SCOTT HAD TO HURRY. Hopefully the 405 would be moving. Taking the Century Boulevard exit, he navigated his way to the long-term parking lot at LAX. Removing his ticket from the automated dispenser, the cross arm lifted, and he cruised the lot for an available slot. Parking in what appeared to be the hinterlands, he removed his Samsonite Pullman from the trunk, grabbed his briefcase, locked the car and pulled his luggage toward the terminal. He couldn't help thinking about what he had witnessed at the office. Snorting coke right out in the open. Unbelievable…

"How many bags are you checking today, sir?" asked the upbeat lady at the Northwest ticket counter.

"Just one. I have an e-ticket for a 1:05 flight to Memphis," he said as he handed his driver's license to her.

"Okay, Mr. Murphy, I show you with an aisle seat, is that okay?"

"Yes, ma'am."

"Did you pack your bag yourself?"

"Yes, I did."

"Has the bag been in your possession since you packed it?"

"Yes, it has."

"Has anyone unknown to you given you anything to carry on board?"

"They have not."

"Thank you Mr. Murphy. Northwest flight 1105, non-stop service to Memphis is on time. We have one bag checked…here is your boarding pass, seat 10-D, gate C24. Have a great flight."

"Thank you," Scott said, taking his boarding pass and heading for the C-terminal.

Arriving at the gate, Scott spotted Lisa right away. She absolutely glowed among the huddled masses. She was seated close to the gate, legs crossed and looking radiant as usual. It took him several moments to notice that Tim Newsom was seated next to her, jabbering incessantly. She showed him polite consideration, but looked uninterested in whatever subject matter he was babbling on about. Probably himself, Scott thought.

"Howdy, padnuh," a voice from behind him drawled as he felt a strong grip on his shoulder.

He turned to see Jimmy Brady's smiling face. "Hi Jimmy—I didn't know you were going to Memphis…"

"Yeah, just a little 'train-the trainer' sort of class…I'm actually lookin' forward to it. Say, what seat did Regina book for ya?"

"Uh, 10-D."

"Well, I'm sittin' in 10-E…guess we'll be neighbors."

"Great." Just then he glanced back at Lisa, and caught her looking at him.

She smiled, waved and mouthed a mute "hello." Scott waved back, as a voice came over the speaker, "Ladies and gentlemen, we will begin boarding Northwest flight 1105, non-stop service to Memphis, beginning with our first class passengers, our WorldPerks Gold and WorldPerks Preferred members, those traveling with small children, needing special assistance or unaccompanied minors. Thank you." Maybe he'd luck out and Lisa would have seat 10-C.

Scott and Jimmy approached Lisa and Tim. Jimmy asked, "Where do they have ya'll sittin'?"

"8-B," replied Tim.

"I'm in 8-C," said Lisa. "How about you guys?"

"We're purty close, they got us in the tenth row," answered Jimmy. Lisa looked genuinely disappointed.

"We are now boarding rows ten through fifteen," the voice on the speaker said. "That's us, cowboy!" Jimmy said, nudging Scott. "See ya'll on the ground." Once they reached their aisle, Scott removed a book from his briefcase before storing it in the overhead compartment. Taking his seat beside Jimmy, he fastened his seat belt. It was a pretty full flight. Jimmy turned to him and said, "Hope you don't mind, but I'm gonna try and get some shut eye."

"Go right ahead."

Scott reached up, turned on his overhead light and adjusted the air-flow nozzle. Then he saw Lisa boarding. Her eyes met his, and she smiled. He felt a shiver go down his spine. He watched her let Tim in first and then she took her seat on the aisle. From this vantage point Scott would have a great, unobstructed angle to stare at her the whole flight. Things could be worse. She crossed her shapely legs, as Tim resumed his banter. Tim glanced back, noticed Scott looking in his direction, smiled and extended his middle finger, unseen by Lisa.

CHAPTER 20

THE CAB came to a stop in front of The Peabody Hotel. Lisa, Scott and Tim collected their luggage, while Jimmy paid the fare. A doorman in a fancy gray overcoat held the door to the main entrance open for the group.

Once inside, Lisa exclaimed, "Wow! This place is beautiful! I can't wait to see my room."

After they all checked in at the front desk, they made their way over to the elevators across from the lobby. "What's the crowd all about?" asked Lisa.

"I guess it's about time for the ducks to leave the fountain," replied Scott. "Ducks? Real Ducks?" Tim asked with dismay.

"Oh, yeah," Jimmy chimed in. "The world famous Peabody Ducks— these fellers have even been on the Tonight Show—back when Johnny Carson was on, not that guy with the big chin."

Just then the recorded *"March of The Peabody Ducks"* blared through the overhead PA system. Lisa and Jimmy pushed their way through the throng to witness the green-headed male mallard lead several hens out of the ornate marble fountain, and down a red carpet spread across the lobby to the elevator. Once all the ducks were in the elevator, the carpet was rolled up, and the doors shut behind them as they headed to quarters for the evening. "They were so cute!" exclaimed Lisa. "Are they in the fountain every day?"

"Every day," said Scott.

"Good—I can't wait to see them tomorrow."

"What a bunch of hicks," said Tim to no one in particular. "Getting all excited about a herd of livestock roaming around indoors—give me a fucking break!"

Lisa and Tim got off elevator at the fourth floor. Jimmy and Scott continued on to the fifth. "You goin' to see your family tonight, Scotty?"

"Yeah, I'm meeting my sister a little later."

"Good, hope ya'll have a nice visit. I'm gonna pile up a big tab on my expense report at the Chez Phillipe—man, that's some good fancy food, I tell you what."

"Have a good time, Jimmy."

"Good night, padnuh. Hope your class isn't too boring."

Scott opened the door to his room and flipped on the light. Like Lisa, he too was curious to see what a room at The Peabody looked like. He had been in the lobby several times before, but never in a room. It was tastefully appointed, with two twin beds. He was glad he didn't have a roommate on this trip. He opened the curtains, and took a deep breath as he stared at the sun setting on the Mississippi River. It was good to be home.

*   *   *

AFTER UNPACKING, Scott left the hotel and walked west to Main Street, where he hopped on one of the trolley cars. He could have walked to Beale Street, but he decided he would like to take the trolley instead. Once on board, he paid his fifty-cents, and took a seat. There were only two other people on board—tourists, more than likely—the camera around the man's neck, and the woman's Graceland T-shirt were dead give-aways. Who knew what they were here for...the Elvis crowds made their pilgrimages in January and August, and the Tiger basketball game wasn't until Wednesday night.

"Excuse me," the man with the camera asked. "Are you from around here?"

"Yes, I am," Scott replied, trying not to stare at the man's mutton-chop sideburns, ala '70's Elvis.

"We're staying at the Holiday Inn Select, and were told we could take the trolley to B.B. King's Blues Club—what stop do we get off?"

"Next stop, Beale Street...I'm heading that way, I can show you."

"Thank you," said his female companion with a toothy grin. "You don't sound like you're from Memphis." Scott smiled weakly, reflecting on her stereotyping.

After exiting the trolley and walking up the hill, a sea of colorful neon signs came into view. Scott learned the couple was from Davenport, Iowa, and here on their second honeymoon. They were excited because they had reservations to see Jerry Lee Lewis play tonight at B.B. King's.

The couple's energy level intensified when they noticed Elvis Presley's club on their left. "Would you mind taking our picture in front of Elvis's?" the man asked, handing Scott his camera.

"No, not at all." As the two embraced under the neon sign picturing Elvis surrounded by a gold record, the sounds of the rockabilly band VooDoo Train could be heard sporadically as club patrons entered through the doors with the E.P. monogram. "Okay, smile on three...1...2...3."

Right before the camera flashed, the couple smiled, saying, "Elvis!" in unison.

Returning the camera to 'Mr. Sideburns,' Scott directed them across the street to their destination. "Right under the neon guitar...hope you guys have a good time. 'The Killer' usually puts on one heck of a show."

"Thanks, we will," said the toothy female. "And thanks so much for your help. It's true what they say about Southern hospitality—everyone has been so nice to us."

"Don't mention it. Hope you enjoy the rest of your trip."

          *   *   *

AFTER ENTERING Blues City Cafe, Scott scanned the dining area for his sister. She spotted him first, and was waving him over to the table. "Hey, Scott!" she said, giving him a big hug. She had a new haircut—short and professional. "Was your flight okay?"

"Yeah, no problem."

"And they put you up at The Peabody, huh? Not bad...That's quite a company you work for."

"I can't complain about the accommodations."

The waitress, a petite black woman in her mid-thirties, wearing a red Blues City Cafe T-shirt approached them. "Well...I see he finally made it! What can I get ya'll to drink?"

"Amstel Light," said Kathy.

"Same for me." He thought his sister looked happy.

          *   *   *

AFTER THEY both polished off a rack of ribs, Chef Bonnie Mack stopped by their table, "So how was everything?" the large black man in the white apron and chef's hat asked.

"Excellent," said Scott.

Kathy piped in, "My brother moved to California, and he's been craving some Memphis barbecue."

"Hope that hit the spot, young man."

"Yes, sir, great ribs—as always."

"Glad to hear it. Now you get home more often, ya hear? Stay out in California too long an' ya might go gettin' all strange."

"Yes, sir."

Scott paid the tab, and they walked down three steps into the section of Blues City Cafe known as the 'Band Box,' and took a table under a large framed photograph of Jerry Lee Lewis to continue their conversation. The picture made him wonder how his new friends from Iowa were doing across the street. After ordering two more Amstel Lights, Kathy asked, "Are you going to be able to see Mom & Dad while you're here?"

"I don't know…I haven't seen the schedule…it all depends on how busy they keep us."

"Well, try and make the time—Mom wants to see how you're doing; and so does Dad."

"Oh, yeah, I'm sure he does."

"C'mon Scott…in his own way he…"

"Let's change the subject, okay?"

"Fine. Whatever…"

The band was doing a sound check, as Scott asked, "I didn't get a chance to pick up a paper, who's playing tonight?"

"I don't know…" Kathy replied as she tried to get the attention of their waitress.

Walking over, the waitress asked, "What can I do for you?"

"We just wanted to know who's playing tonight?"

"Oh, the Blue Larry Blue Band from Nashville—they're real good."

"Thanks." Turning back to her brother, she said, "I've never heard of him."

"I think I've seen him before…back in college."

"Speaking of college, before I forget, here are your tickets for Wednesday night's game," she said extracting the ducats from her purse.

"Thanks, I really appreciate you picking these up for me."

"So, who are you taking to the game?"

"I don't know…I might make a few calls to some old friends, maybe a guy from work, I don't know…"

"Hi, Scott!" said a soft voice from behind him. Scott turned to see Lisa. She had changed into a sweater and jeans—both of which he thought she filled out admirably. "I hope I'm not interrupting…" Scott seemed visibly surprised to see her.

"No, not at all—and since my tongue-tied brother is too impolite to introduce me, I'm Scott's sister, Kathy."

"His sister? I'm Lisa LeDoux—I work with your brother—it's so nice to meet you."

"Same here."

Finding his vocal cords, Scott said, "I didn't know you liked the blues…"

"Scott—I'm from New Orleans, we know a thing or two about music down there, ya know."

"Won't you join us?" Kathy asked.

"No, no, this is a family get-together. I'm sure you two have a lot of catching up to do…but thanks—see you in the morning, Scott."

"OK."

"Nice meeting you, Kathy."

"You, too." Lisa walked away and perched herself on a stool at the bar that ran along the exterior wall.

Realizing he must have been staring at Lisa for an inappropriate amount of time, Scott turned to see his sister smiling mischievously at him. "What?" he asked defensively.

"She's pretty."

"I guess…if you're into that drop-dead gorgeous thing."

"You work with her?"

"Yeah, actually she just started—uh, she transferred from the home office in New Orleans."

"Have you been out with her?"

"Are you kidding? She the HR manager…that would be politically incorrect to fraternize at the office…and, uh…well, she's out of my league, anyway…"

"Your selling yourself short, big brother. She likes you—I can tell. She's looking at you right now…" Scott turned his head, as Kathy said,

"Well don't look! That was real smooth." Kathy was right; Lisa *was* looking their way.

As their eyes met, she smiled at him. Scott returned her smile, and turned back to face Kathy. "You were right…"

"About what?"

"That she was looking at me."

"I'm also right saying that she likes you."

"How can you tell?"

"Women know these things. She seemed nice. I think you should ask her out. Besides, she's got to be more your type than those *California girls.*"

"They are a little different…*so*, how's Robert doing?"

"There you go, changing the subject again…"

"Are wedding bells in the future?"

"Well, I did tell him that a ring for Christmas would be good timing…"

"Nothing like a pushy woman."

"Shut up!" she said, shoving him playfully.

"Good evening ladies and gentlemen, and welcome to Blues City Cafe," the bearded singer said into the microphone. He was tall, and bore a resemblance to St. Louis Cardinals' slugger Mark McGwire. "My name is Blue Larry Blue, and this is my band. I'd like to play a little song I wrote about Memphis—the City of Good Abode. This happens to be featured on my new CD, *Big Blue World,* which is available in the gift shop and numerous sites on the Internet." He flashed a smile at the audience, and strapped on his black, Lucille model Gibson guitar. Backing him were a bass player, keyboard man and a drummer, in front of a circular neon Blues City Cafe sign.

As Kathy was watching Blue Larry Blue tune up, Scott stole a quick glance at Lisa. She, too, was watching the guitar player. Her eyes sparkled in the dark bar. Was Kathy right? Should he ask her out? Could he ask her out? Hell, she probably had a boyfriend…but then again, nothing ventured, nothing gained…except maybe humiliating rejection from someone he would have to see at work on an everyday basis....yeah, that would be real smart. Blue Larry Blue played the opening chords on his Gibson, causing Scott to look back at the stage.

"Rain was falling—I was feeling down
So I talked myself into going down town
To catch the scene on Beale Street
A perfect night for the Blues
The man inside the club sang 'The Thrill Is Gone'
Well I've felt that way myself a little too long
Then something came over me
That's when I got the news..."

This guy is good, he thought. He observed Kathy swaying to the music. It was good to see his little sister so grown up and happy. She really seemed to have her head on straight. And he approved of Robert—he was a pretty good guy. He felt proud of her. Turning around, he noticed that Lisa seemed to be enjoying the music, too. A girl that likes the blues...not bad. She was certainly no wallflower—walking into a place like this alone, in an unfamiliar town. She was obviously very self-assured. Besides having stunning good looks, she seemed to be a genuinely nice person—very polite and polished—nothing slutty about this girl. Worldly, too. Definitely not an airhead—extremely intelligent, and classy. She came off as being very upbeat and positive. With all that going for her, how in the world could she be interested in him? The more he thought about it, he figured Kathy had to be pulling his leg.

"...I was walking in the Memphis rain
When a tear trickled from my eye
I felt the Blues wash away the pain
Her memory left behind
They say that music has the power
To reach down to your soul

I felt it that night
Walking in the Memphis rain..."

CHAPTER 21

AFTER CONSUMING a bland Continental breakfast, a chunky, moon-faced woman in a dress that looked to be two sizes too small, introduced herself. "I'm so glad you all made it in this morning to join us for our new employee orientation session. Good morning! My name is Debbie Hill, and over the next three days you'll learn why being selected to work for Campbell Industries is a real badge of honor in today's business world. Starting a new job is always exciting and challenging. We look forward to your growth in your respective positions, and with the company. We are excited about your joining the Campbell team and your participating in our quest for world leadership and customer satisfaction. We at Campbell Industries are very confident that we have the vision, the technology, and—most importantly—the people, to succeed today and into the future."

"Now I'd like to introduce you to Lisa LeDoux," Debbie said. "Lisa recently left the home office HR team, and accepted the position of Human Resources Manager for our Western Region office. Since she was already committed to helping me out this week—and I wouldn't let her out of it—Lisa will be assisting me to facilitate this class."

Lisa walked in front of the group, and Scott could hear the collective low-pitched growl from the men in the audience. "Thanks, Debbie. We at Campbell want all employees to have a clear understanding of our business environment and direction, and the contributions that each

employee makes. During your first few months on the job, you'll participate in activities—like this class—that will give you the information,
resources, and support you'll need to become a productive, important
member of the Campbell team as quickly as possible."

Lisa paused and smiled at the group. She was wearing a sharp, navy
suit, white blouse and a Hermes scarf loosely tied around her neck. The
growl from the captive men was heard again. Lisa, unfazed, continued,
"These three days at new employee orientation will offer you insight to
the heritage, objectives and strategies, and expectations of Campbell
Industries, and how you fit in. This is your class, and your participation
is required. The information discussed here will help get your career off
to a great start. It's your career—make it happen!" It sounded like fod-
der from the corporate mission statement, but Lisa sure made it sound
good, Scott thought.

"Thanks, Lisa," Debbie said, re-taking the floor. "I want you all to
remember that we will be covering a lot of information in a short time,
but you can always call me or any other member of the HR team with
any questions that might come up in the future. And before we begin,
I'd like to go over a few ground-rules: No smoking is allowed in the
meeting room here at The Peabody. You can smoke outside or in the
lobby. We will take a 15-minute break mid-morning and mid-afternoon
each day; along with a one-hour lunch break. Bio breaks can be taken at
any time. And remember, there are no stupid questions—I just can't
promise the same about my answers!" Debbie laughed alone at her joke
in front of the dazed group.

Scott noticed that quite a few guys were ogling Lisa, who had taken a
seat in the corner of the room. He felt a tinge of jealousy, and didn't
know what to make of it. He thought about asking Debbie for a defini-
tion of bio-break, but then concluded it was her politically correct way
of saying bathroom. Tim was asleep in his chair.

✶   ✶   ✶

AFTER ENDURING an hour-long film about the history of Campbell Industries, and listening to Debbie prattle on for the remainder of the morning, Scott was completely mind-numbed at lunch. It was being served in the Skyway Ballroom—buffet style. After filling his plate with his selections, he took a seat at a round table covered with a white tablecloth. A couple of weathered, admin-types sat down across from him, without acknowledging his presence. They continued their private conversation with their raspy, smoker's voices.

"Are these seats taken?" said a familiar, cheery voice.

Scott looked up to see Lisa smiling at him. He returned her smile, but quickly lost his when he noticed Tim Newsom was with her. "No, have a seat."

"Great, thanks!"

Lisa took a seat to Scott's right, and Tim followed suit, taking the seat to her right. The two admin-types looked at Lisa, scowling simultaneously. "So, what do you think so far?" Lisa asked.

"Really good...I think I'm going to get a lot out of this," Scott said, trying to sound sincere.

"It was bullshit! A total waste of my time!" blurted Tim, giving his unsolicited opinion.

"I'm sorry you feel that way, Tim. Maybe you'll find the rest of the course more beneficial."

"I can only hope. I could barely keep my eyes open...I stayed out way too late."

"Speaking of being out," Lisa said, ignoring Tim's attitude, but using his remark for a segue, "that Blues singer last night was really good."

"Yeah, he could really play guitar."

"Did you have a good visit with your sister?"

"Yeah, it was good seeing her...she seems to be doing really well."

"She seemed very nice, and pretty, too."

"She said the same...uh, never mind."

"What, Scott?"

"Yes, please share with us, Scott," Tim said mockingly.

Scott frowned at Tim; returned his attention to Lisa and said, "It was just that she said the same thing about you."

"Isn't that sweet?" Lisa said.

"Gee, Scott, is your sister some kind of a lesbo?" Tim asked mockingly.

"I'd seriously advise you not to talk about my sister," Scott said sternly.

"Oh, yeah, I forgot, given your propensity towards violence, I guess I'd better behave myself. What is it with these rednecks?" he asked Lisa.

"By rednecks, if you mean someone from the South, then I can't help you. According to your generalization, I'm a redneck, too." The two stared at Tim in silence for several moments.

Tim finally broke the quiet, by standing up and saying, "The food here tastes like crap!" and walked away. Lisa looked at Scott and they both laughed.

*   *   *

CLASS BROKE for the day, and Scott made his way to the elevator to find the carpet laid out in preparation for the ducks departure from the fountain. "Not the fucking ducks, again!" said Tim walking up behind him. I guess I better grab an elevator before Ma and Pa Kettle show up to take pictures!"

Scott was about to join him and several other classmates when he heard Lisa say, "Scott…" He turned and stepped off the elevator as she approached.

"We're not holding this for you—take the next one!" said Tim snidely. "Push four!" he demanded as the doors closed.

"What's up?" Scott asked Lisa.

"You're not going to stay and watch the ducks?"

"I can…"

"Good, you can keep me company," Lisa said, smiling the most beautiful smile he had ever seen. As they walked to the fountain, Scott looked at his watch as Lisa watched the ducks swimming in a counter-clockwise pattern.

"They should get started in about five minutes," Scott commented as the onlookers began lining up along the red carpet leading to the elevator.

"Come on—let's get a good spot," Lisa said, grabbing him by the arm and pulling him along.

Shortly, music blared through the lobby speakers. Scott observed Lisa's face as the ducks left the fountain on command and waddled toward the elevator. She seemed as if she were really enjoying the spectacle. He noticed other men in the crowd not watching the ducks, but unbeknownst to their wives and girlfriends, they were looking at Lisa, too.

"So what are you doing tonight?" she asked coyly.

"Actually I was planning to eat at the Rendezvous and catch Preston Shannon at B.B. King's…"

"Are you meeting anyone?…"

"No, not actually…"

Just then Jimmy Brady approached them through the dispersing crowd. "Doggone it, I missed the ducks!"

"They just left," Lisa said in a sympathetic tone.

"Hey, ya'll wanna go eat at Corky's tonight? Good barbeque! I've got a friend pickin' me up here at six, and ya'll are more than welcome to come along…"

"Thanks, Jimmy, but we were planning to eat at the Rendezvous tonight…right, Scott?"

"Yeah, right," Scott said with a smile, realizing Lisa was now joining him.

"That's purty good eating, too. Ya'll have fun." Jimmy left, hopping in the next available elevator.

Lisa looked at Scott. "You don't mind that I invited myself to tag along, do you?"

"No, not at all."

"Good! What time did you want to leave?"

"As soon as I change…"

"Is it casual?"

"Oh, yeah, we're talking paper plates, plastic utensils…very casual."

"Great. Let's change, and I'll meet you in the lobby in a few minutes."

"OK."

They stepped into the elevator, and Lisa got off at the fourth floor. "I'll only be a minute!"

"OK…see you in the lobby." When the doors closed, Scott slumped back against the wall of the empty elevator and let out a long breath. The doors opened at the fifth floor, he exited, walked to his room and thought about how unbelievable the last ten minutes of his life were. Was he reading this wrong? He didn't know, but he looked forward to finding out…

*   *   *

AFTER THEY CONSUMED two large racks of dry ribs and two pitchers of Michelob, Lisa paid the tab—she insisted, he didn't argue—it all goes to Campbell anyway, he figured. As they walked through the alley leading away from the Rendezvous and in front of the Days Inn, Scott couldn't believe he had eaten ribs two nights in a row. What the hell, the heartburn would be worth it. When would he get the chance to eat Memphis barbecue again in the near future?

Crossing at the light, they proceeded down Second Street. When they got to Beale Street, they turned right at Rum Boogie Cafe, and made their way up to B.B. King's Blues Club.

As they walked among the crowd, he noticed guys doing double takes as they caught sight of Lisa. She was oblivious to it all, as she took in the sights and sounds. A cop on horseback stopped by them, tipped his cap and said, "Good evenin', ma'am. "I'm Officer Thompson, and this here is Sonny."

"What a beautiful horse," she said, petting the large sorrel on the neck.

"Yes, ma'am, he's a keeper. You folks from out of town?"

"Actually, we're from California," Lisa said smiling at Scott.

"California, huh? Been there before—nice place to visit—but I wouldn't want to live there. So where are ya'll headed tonight?"

"We're headed to B.B. King's," she said enthusiastically.

"I hope you enjoy the show." The cop grinned a toothy smile at Lisa.

"Thanks, I'm sure we will." Never had a cop stop and make small talk with me before, Scott thought to himself.

As they walked up the sidewalk, Lisa was reading aloud the names of the artists listed on the brass music notes on the Beale Street Walk of Fame. "Memphis Minnie...Otis Redding...Albert King...Bobby Blue Bland...Booker T. and the MGs...Carl Perkins...The Memphis Horns...Roy Orbison...Stax Records...Sam and Dave..."

Entering through the gift shop, Scott paid the cover charge, and they found a table on the main floor, to the left of the stage. The place was filling up fast, and he was grateful they were able to get such good seats. A smiling waitress approached, "Can I get you something to drink?"

"I'll have a seven-and-seven," Lisa said.

"Jack and Coke," replied Scott.

Lisa smiled at him. "I really like Beale Street. It's a lot smaller than Bourbon Street, but it seems so much cleaner."

"I've always enjoyed it here...although back in college, the temptation to come down here made it hard to make an eight o'clock class sometimes."

"Same with Bourbon Street," she sighed in acknowledgment.

As the band members began to file on stage, a voice came over the P.A. "Good evening ladies and gentlemen, and welcome to the world's premier Blues address: B.B. King's, Memphis! Tonight we are pleased to present Rounder Records, Bullseye Blues recording artist, 'Mr. *Beale Street*' himself, Preston Shannon!" The audience responded loudly.

"If you like the blues, you're in for a treat—this guy is unbelievable!" he said to her above the crowd noise. And so are you, he thought to himself. As Preston Shannon, *guitar-god,* ripped into a scorching version of *"The Thrill Is Gone,"* he studied Lisa's smiling face, oblivious to the music.

CHAPTER 22

THE NEXT MORNING Scott was not in the meeting room—at least not mentally. His mind was reviewing the previous evening on a continuous reel in his head. He and Lisa had a great time at B.B. King's. He was sure he had never danced so much in his entire life. Lisa was a fantastic dancer; a fact that didn't go unnoticed by the men at the club. And it really made his head swell whenever some guy would ask her to dance, and she would say, "No, thanks, I'm with him." I'm with him…meaning she's with me! He was disappointed that nobody from high school or college had spotted him out with her.

To date, it was easily the most ideal evening of his life. Leaving the club, they walked back to the Peabody. He remembered Lisa asking him if he had a girlfriend. He said no, but didn't have the nerve to ask her if she was seeing anyone. He wondered if his lack of inquiry came off as casual nonchalance, or uninterested. He hoped it was nonchalance…playing it cool…holding his cards close to the vest…how could she ever imagine that he was not interested? Maybe he was playing it too cool—a defense mechanism he had acquired long ago—guaranteeing that he wouldn't let anyone get close enough to hurt him.

He also remembered how she walked close to him in the chilly fall evening. About two-thirds of the way back, she took his arm, leaned in close, looked up at him and said, "Thanks for a great evening."

As he gazed into her bright eyes, all he could stammer was, "You're welcome."

As they neared the hotel entrance, she asked him what his plans were for tonight. He told her about having two tickets to The University of Memphis vs. Tulane basketball game. "I went to Tulane!" she exclaimed.

"Really?" he intoned in mock surprise. He had read her position announcement memo, and knew full well that she was a graduate of Tulane University.

She followed up with, "Well, are you going with a friend?..."

"Actually, I was hoping you would like to go," he remembered saying with all the suavity he could muster. Her response was positive and enthusiastic. Which was why all he could think about was last night and their planned outing for this evening, and not the remainder of the long-winded orientation class.

*   *   *

ONCE THE CLASS had wrapped up, he told Lisa he would meet her in the lobby, next to the fountain, at 5:30. He hurried to his room, removed his shirt and tie, and laid out his apparel for the evening. After a quick shower and drying his hair, he pulled on a white polo shirt, Wrangler jeans and his royal blue MEMPHIS sweatshirt.

Before leaving his room, he dialed his mom's phone number. "Hello?"

"Hi, Mom, it's Scott..."

"Scott! I was wondering when you were going to get around to calling us. Are you coming over tonight?"

"No, ma'am...I'm not going to be able to...they're keeping us pretty busy here."

"So we're not going to get to see you at all this trip?"

"No ma'am, I'm afraid not..."

"Well, at least you got to see your sister…so you're leaving in the morning?"

"Yes, ma'am—an eight-thirty flight."

"You're Father will be so disappointed…"

"I'm sure."

"I'd let you speak to him, but he's out working in his shop."

"That's OK."

"I'm sorry they're working you so hard…take care, son…I love you."

"I love you too, Mom."

*   *   *

THE GOLD ELEVATOR doors opened, and his eyes zeroed in on Lisa standing by the lobby fountain. He thought she looked really cute. Instead of her corporate armor, she was wearing jeans, a white TULANE sweatshirt with green lettering, and had her hair pulled back in a ponytail. "Ready to watch us mop up the floor with the Green Wave?" he asked.

"I'm ready to watch your Tigers drown in a Green Wave!" she said boisterously. Laughing at each other's alma-mater-verbal jab, they left the hotel and made their way to the Main Street Trolley. Scott paid the fare and they climbed aboard.

"Have you ever ridden on a trolley before?" he asked.

"Have I? I'll have you know that the St. Charles Avenue Streetcars—we don't call them trolleys—run right by my parents' neighborhood."

He had asked her earlier if she wanted to get something to eat before the game, or could she handle 'stadium food.' She had laughed and said that 'stadium food' was one of the best reasons to go to a ball-game. What a girl! By the time they had consumed corn-dogs, pizza, popcorn and peanuts—washed down by a couple of sodas—the Tigers were up by four at halftime. "Would you excuse me while I go to the ladies room?"

"Sure."

"Can I bring you anything back?" she asked as she gracefully stepped over him and out into the aisle.

"No, thanks. I'm good for now." After she left, the ten-time National Champion Memphis Pom-Pom squad took the Pyramid floor and put on one of their typical high-energy, athletic routines. Being home at a basketball game made him feel grounded, and made California and Campbell Industries seem a million miles away. They were both two-thousand miles away, but unfortunately, he would be back in that world tomorrow.

*   *   *

SHE RETURNED to their seats balancing two large souvenir cups of soda. Scott stood and took the cups from her as she made her way to her seat. Once seated, he handed her a plastic cup and asked, "Went for the large ones this time, huh?"

"This will be it for me...besides, I wanted a souvenir to take home," she said, smiling, as she examined the logos plastered around her large cup.

The second half was exciting, as Memphis squandered a ten-point lead, only to come back, pull away at the end and win by five. U of M Coach John Calipari, whose constant sideline pacing had put his Armani suit through quite a workout, thrust his fist in the air at the conclusion, glad to have this Conference USA win under his belt.

*   *   *

Exiting The Pyramid, Lisa sighed, "Well, it was a close game..."

"It was a great game."

"You're not going to gloat are you?" Lisa asked.

"Me? Rub it in? Never!" Just like the night before, she took his arm as she walked beside him.

They walked out of the stainless steel monolith overlooking the *Mighty Mississippi* and down the steps to street level. Passing several horse-drawn carriages for hire, Lisa asked flirtatiously, "Wanna go back in style?"

"Sure. Why not?" Lisa selected a white carriage with a large-boned black gelding in the harness. Scott negotiated a twenty-dollar fare with the driver, and helped Lisa aboard.

Climbing up, he noticed the driver's dog—a shepherd-collie mix—staring threateningly at him. "Don't worry about Pancho," the driver said. "He ain't as mean as he looks." Turning he clucked to the horse and said, "Get up, boy!"

Staring at the backs of the driver and Pancho, the clopping sound of the black gelding's hooves could be heard in the carriage among the din of cars and buses returning to their suburban destinations. The foggy breath of the dog and horse were visible in the crisp late evening air. Scott was aware that he was seated across the padded seat from Lisa. "Are you cold?" he asked.

"A little," she said. He unfolded the navy wool blanket on the seat and offered it to her. As she pulled it up to her chin, she smiled and said, "You get under here, too."

Scott slid close to Lisa, and she wrapped the blanket around him. She snuggled close to him under the blanket, almost forcing him to put his arm around her. She looked up at him with a soft smile. Either the crowd noise had dissipated, or he just couldn't hear it as he stared at her beautiful face. Her warm expression let him think that maybe he wasn't reading something into this. Maybe a girl like this—a girl with every-thing going for her—just maybe, could be interested in a guy like him. As he held this living, breathing angel in his arms, he wished he could slip the driver his credit card…and ask him to let them ride all night.

The warmth of her body next to his under the blanket was intoxicat-ing. Her hair smelled like wildflowers. He was afraid if he said anything it would ruin the moment. Just as the magical ambiance was causing his thoughts to drift away, she said, "I've really enjoyed seeing your home-town the last few days…you're quite the tour guide."

"I've enjoyed spending the time with you."

"I'll have to return the favor, in my hometown."

"What did you have in mind?"

"Well…we have a customer satisfaction workshop scheduled at home office in a few weeks—put on by the HR department—and we'll be seeking input from all departments: Management, admin, quota-tions, and sales."

"I'm not sure if my input would have any value…I mean, I've only been on board a few months…"

"And you've already won Salesman of the Month in our top district! Don't sell yourself short! I think you have a lot of valuable insight."

"I don't know if Allen would approve…"

"Do you want to go or not?"

"Sure, I'd…"

"Well then, don't worry about…I can pull some strings."

"Great! Sounds good." He found her straightforwardness to be dis-arming and charming at the same time.

The driver pulled back on the reins and said, "Whoa, big fella," as the carriage lurched to a stop at the Union Avenue entrance of The Peabody. Scott relinquished his long hug of Lisa, and stepped down. Taking her hand, he helped her to the ground. Slipping the driver a twenty and a five dollar tip, Scott walked behind Lisa as the doorman held open the large glass door.

After they stepped into the elevator, Scott pressed the buttons for the fourth and fifth floors. As the doors closed behind them, Lisa leaned into him, and he put his arm around her. The elevator car came to a stop at the Lisa's floor. Lisa turned to face him, lifted her arms over his shoulders, and laced her fingers behind his neck. "Thanks, again," she said softly, tilting her head back.

Scott placed his hands on her slender waist, leaned over and kissed her gently on the lips. His heart was beating so fast, he thought it would explode. Lisa slowly opened her big brown eyes, smiled and said, "See you in the morning." Scott watched her walk down the hallway, her ponytail swinging side to side. Just before the doors closed, she turned and waved to him as a large smile brightened her face.

CHAPTER 23

"So what exactly are the 'International Police Games,' Andy, and why are they being held in Australia?" Glenn asked with a hint of frustration in his voice.

Clicking the chrome Zippo lighter closed, the heavy-set man with the slicked-back hair and five o'clock shadow sat back in the leather chair, exhaling a stream of smoke toward the ceiling. "Like I told you, Glenn, they're just some bullshit excuse for a bunch of cops to take a trip and get together. Some of the guys will play grab-ass, run races, and act like they're at some sort of poor man's Olympics, but for the most part it's a social event. And the wives are going, too."

"Okay...but why do you need three grand from me for your trip?"

"Look Glenn, this isn't extortion, if that's what you're implying...consider it a donation to LA's finest."

"Let me borrow your lighter." Lt. Cavanarro slid the Zippo across the large desk. Glenn retrieved a filtered Camel from his desk, lit up and deeply inhaled.

Sliding the lighter back, Glenn leaned forward and said, "I gotta tell ya Andy, I'm not sure how much longer I'm going to be a soft touch every time you're looking for some mad money."

"Gee, I'm really sorry to hear that Glenn. What? You think that I'm taking advantage of you? What a load..."

"I didn't say taking advantage..."

"Bullshit! Look pal, you're the one who called me—needing my help—remember?"

"Yes…"

"So…I come in and sweep your missing secretary problem under the rug, and now you think I'm taking advantage of you?"

"Not exactly. It's just that…"

"Not exactly? Look, Glenn…your situation was very sloppy, to say the least. Have you had any hassles since I took over the case?"

"You know that I haven't…"

"Then don't start bitching about your hardship, buddy. If you want a real problem, I can always disclose that we went to high school together—I wouldn't want it to appear I had a conflict of interest here—and turn this deal over to one of the department's hard-chargers like Mike Harris. With all the loose ends leading back to you, then you'll have a problem worth pissing and moaning about." The two men stared at each other as the cigarette smoke circled between them.

Glenn smiled at Lt. Cavanarro. "Let's not blow this out of proportion, okay?"

"Your call, buddy."

"Andy, you have to know that I do appreciate the way you've handled things here…it's made us able to keep things business as usual around here. I just didn't know you would require so much monetary compensation…"

"I know your wife's loaded. Hey, convenience comes at a cost, you know."

"Agreed…and I do value your help and friendship, Andy."

"Likewise."

"Okay, so how 'bout we hit the ATM on the way to lunch, and I'll withdraw another donation."

"Great. You know I wouldn't bug you if it wasn't for somethin' important—this trip means a lot to the wife, you know, second honeymoon kinda thing."

"I know. Are you at least going to pick up lunch?" Glenn asked in all seriousness.

"You have got to be kidding—you're the business guy—I know how this shit works. You buy, charge it to your expense account and call me a client."

*   *   *

GLENN OPENED the passenger door and Lieutenant Cavanarro plopped his considerable bulk into the Mercedes. The Lieutenant smiled up at Glenn, threw his cigarette butt past him into the parking lot, and pulled his door closed. Glenn stared at the man through the glass window. He couldn't help thinking what a mistake this sordid relationship had become. This fat, fucking pig was going to slowly drain him. The snake was already into him for over thirty-five grand. He and Pam kept separate bank accounts, and it was only a matter of time until she noticed the large deductions he had made from hers. Her money. Her family. Everything's hers—including the house. The office was his kingdom, the one place in his life she—and her father's money—couldn't mess with him.

Walking to the driver's side of the black sedan, Glenn eased himself behind the wheel, and placed the key in the ignition. "We're off to lunch," he said, trying to feign enthusiasm.

"After we hit the ATM, buddy," Lt. Cavanarro said with a cheesy grin, as he buckled his seat belt.

*   *   *

ACROSS TOWN, an elderly Hispanic woman walked into a police station house with a small, dark-headed girl in tow. As she approached the desk sergeant, she said in uncertain English, " 'Scuse me…"

"Yes, ma'am, what can I do for you?"

"My…it is my Maria…she is missing…"

"How long has she been missing, ma'am?"

"A very long time…three months…"

"And you're just now reporting this?" the desk sergeant asked incredulously.

"No…your man, Cavanarro…he try to help us."

"Lieutenant Cavanarro? He's not in at the moment, ma'am…"

"Is there a problem, Sergeant?" asked Sgt Harris, as he entered the building.

"Sergeant, this lady is looking for Lieutenant Cavanarro. Something about a missing person…"

"Maria Lopez?" he asked the woman.

"Si! Si!" she said, as the light of recognition crossed her eyes.

"OK, Fine, I'll help her, Sergeant." Turning to the woman, he smiled and said, "Please come with me."

"Si, gracias."

Sgt. Harris led the woman and the little girl to his cube. "Please, have a seat." The woman sat down and pulled the little girl up on her lap. Rummaging through his desk, he found a Happy Meal toy left by his daughter. He handed the figurine to the little girl. She accepted it with a broad smile.

"Gracias," the old woman said, also smiling. Even smiling, the woman looked very tired and sad.

"My name is Sergeant Harris."

"Harris, si," the woman responded.

"What is your name, please?"

"I am Maria's madre, Lupe Lopez."

"How can I help you, Senora Lopez?"

"Have you found my Maria, she is missing."

"No, ma'am…as far as I know, we still have no information regarding your daughter's disappearance. But, it's not my case, I'd have to check with Lieutenant Cavanarro"

"Cavanarro! He no call me back!"

"You've tried to reach him?"

"Si—many times, I leave messages—he no call me back."

Sgt. Harris looked at the frail woman for several moments. He didn't know what to say next—Cavanarro was heartless son-of-a bitch—this poor woman needed some sense of closure. "Senora, would you care for something to drink? A Coke? Coffee?"

"Si, agua."

"Yes, ma'am, anything for the girl?"

"Agua."

"Stay here please, I'll be right back." The woman's eyes followed him out of the cubicle as the girl played with the toy.

On his way to the break room, Sgt. Harris ran into Jeff Davis, team leader from the crime lab unit. "Hey, Jeff…any breaks on the Lopez missing person case—from El Segundo—that Cavanarro's handling?"

"Breaks? You've got to be kidding."

"Whaddya mean?"

"Look Mike, I'm not trying to get my ass in a sling here, but since you were taken off the case, I haven't been asked anything else about our findings. I assumed it was closed."

"You mean Cavanarro hasn't asked you about anything?"

"Like I said Mike, I'd just as soon stay out of this, you know, the political ramifications…"

"You mean bullshit!"

"OK…I agree it's a damn shame. We found some good stuff."
"Look, I'm not coming down on you. You guys did your job."

"I understand, man. If I can help, let me know."

"Yeah, I will. Thanks, Jeff."

"Hey, who's that in your cube?"

"The missing person's mother."

"You forget they have family, I mean, uh, you know…"

"I know what you mean. It's all part of the job."

"Glad it's your job," Davis said as he gripped Sgt. Harris on the shoulder, buttoned his lab coat, and proceeded to the exit.

Sgt. Harris returned to his cubicle, and handed two bottles of Arrowhead bottled water to Senora Lopez. "Gracias," she said, as she removed the twist off caps and handed a bottle to the little girl who was now playing on the floor.

The girl grabbed the bottle and took a big gulp of the water. "Thank you," she said smiling at Sgt. Harris.

"Your both very welcome. What's your name, sweetheart?"

"Rosie."

"Rosie. That's a pretty name."

"Thank you," she said sweetly. Then she looked up at Sgt. Harris with her big dark brown eyes, and asked, "Do you know where my Mommy is?"

Sgt. Harris sat down in his chair, suddenly feeling nauseous. He looked at Rosie and said softly, "I'm sorry, but we don't know where she is." Rosie looked upset and climbed back into her Grandmother's lap.

Sgt. Harris took a deep breath, and now wished that he had a drink himself—something strong. He loosened his tie, and looked at the sad, old woman holding the bright-eyed child. He glanced over at the pictures of his two kids. He knew they would be devastated if something happened to their mother. He wished Cavanarro were here to look these people in the eyes. Then again, with a hard-ass like Cavanarro, it probably wouldn't have any impact on him whatsoever.

"Ma'am, I'm sorry, but I don't have any information for you at this time. Lieutenant Cavanarro is out of the office, and it's his case…"

"When will I know something about my Maria?"

Sgt, Harris handed her a legal pad and a pen. "Senora Lopez, if you will write down your phone number for me, I will ask the Lieutenant to give you a call and update you on his findings…"

"Cavanarro! He no call me!"

"Please write your telephone number down for me, and if I learn of anything regarding your daughter, I will call you. I promise."

The elderly woman scrawled her name and phone number on the pad, and handed it back to Sgt. Harris. "Gracias," she said solemnly.

"Thank you, ma'am. And I'm so sorry that your daughter is missing." The woman's eyes softened, as she patted him on the arm. He took out a business card, flipped it over and quickly jotted down his number. "This is my card. This is the telephone number at the station." He turned the card over, and said, "And this is my home telephone number. If you learn anything about your daughter's disappearance, or if you have any questions, please call me."

"Gracias," she said, taking the card from Sgt. Harris and tucking it down her blouse.

Grabbing the child by the hand, she said, "Come Rosie, we must go."

"Here you go," Rosie said, as she handed the toy back to Sgt. Harris.

"That's okay, sweetheart, you can keep it." The girl's smile made him feel better.

"Thank you," she said in a high-pitched, chirpy voice.

"You're welcome, Rosie," he said. "I only wish I could do more," he mumbled, looking down at the floor. "Hey," he asked, "how did you get here today, ma'am?"

"We took the bus."

"Let me give you a ride home, it's the least I can do."

"No, no, we not want to be any trouble."

"No trouble at all…please, I insist."

The old woman grasped him by the forearm, and looked him in the eyes. "Gracias, Senor Harris. You are a good man."

CHAPTER 24

SCOTT HAD CALLED in sick today, just as he had on Friday. He tried to suck it up and tough it out on Thursday, but it was a losing battle. He didn't get sick often, and had no idea where he contracted this crud. Probably a combination of the lack of rest he had gotten during the trip, and the re-circulated air on the jet during his flight back to Los Angeles.

Lounging in a pair of boxer shorts, he did take care of some business, returning his phone calls. He left his pager on, and checked in with Regina periodically to monitor his voice-mail. Allen told him to stay home as long as it took to feel better. He appreciated Allen's no-hassle attitude. He felt he could probably get back to the full schedule tomorrow. At least tonight he would miss the Monday meeting, including "snack buying" duty. That responsibility would now fall to Tim Newsom—couldn't happen to a nicer guy.

After eating a bowl of chicken noodle soup for lunch, and listening to about an hour of the Rush Limbaugh radio program, he fell asleep. His intent was to rest for a couple of hours.

✗   ✗   ✗

A KNOCK at the door startled him. Rolling over, the clock on his nightstand read 6:12 PM. He couldn't believe he had slept as long as he had. Who in the hell could be at the door? Probably some kid selling

magazine subscriptions, or something. Hopefully it wasn't Kevin wanting to go bar-hopping—he knew it would be tough to convince him
that he was really sick. Pulling on his terry cloth robe, he proceeded to
see who was the source of the knocking.

He opened the door and felt as if he had just had the wind knocked
out of him. Flashing a dazzling smile, Lisa was standing across from
him. "Oooh, the 'stubble-look,' I like it," she said as she reached out and
rubbed his unshaven cheek with her soft hand. "Did I wake you up?"

"Yeah, I, uh, guess I slept a little longer than planned."

"How are you feeling?" she asked, as she quickly kissed him on the
lips, and handed him a bag of groceries.

"Better…I think," he responded, as she pushed her way past him.

"Well, good. Mind if I come in?" she asked after she was already three
steps inside.

"No, not at all…"

"Nice place. It screams bachelor."

"How did you know where I lived?"

"Scott…I am the HR manager…give me a little credit," she said, followed by a giggle.

Judging from her casual apparel, Lisa had obviously been home to
change. She was wearing a red, v-neck, cotton sweater over a white T-
shirt, with a pair of khakis and white Keds tennis shoes. Of course, she
would look beautiful in a burlap sack, fuzzy slippers and pink curlers in
her hair, he thought. She slid her purse off her shoulder, and placed it
on the kitchen counter. "You can put the groceries over here. I thought I
would make you dinner—if that's OK…"

"I wouldn't want you to go to any trouble…"

"I wouldn't do it, if I didn't want to."

"Well, if you're sure, I won't turn down a home cooked meal…"

"I'm sure."

"Uh, let me grab a quick shower, and I'll help you."

"Take a shower, and relax…you're sick, remember? I can handle myself in the kitchen just fine, thank you," she said sassily.

"I guess all New Orleans women can cook, huh?"

"You'd better believe it, honey."

Scott quickly grabbed a change of clothes, shut the bathroom door behind him, and turned on the shower. Glancing in the mirror, he thought about shaving, but decided against it. Maybe she did like the unshaven look. Hey, whatever it takes, he thought.

Stepping into the shower, he doused his head under the stream of warm water, and tried to collect his thoughts. He hadn't called Lisa since the Memphis trip, partly because he was sick, and partly because he wasn't sure if he had read her signals correctly. He was hoping that she was interested, and if not, he was in no hurry to spoil the illusion. But then again, she showed up uninvited to his place, she kissed him when he opened the door, she was in the next room cooking dinner, and hey, she even called him honey. Maybe it was time for him to stop analyzing this situation—take a chance—and let his guard down.

Toweling off, Scott ran his fingers through his damp brown hair. After applying deodorant and splashing on a little cologne, he pulled on a pair of jeans and a navy Polo shirt. Leaving the bathroom, he flopped on his bed and put on some white crew socks and laced up his Nike cross-trainers. He craned his neck to catch a glimpse of Lisa in the kitchen. She was stirring the contents of a pan on the stove, and humming along to a Jimmy Buffett CD she had loaded herself. He walked up behind her and lightly placed his hands on her waist.

Looking over her shoulder, he asked, "What's cookin'?"

"Gumbo—my mother's secret recipe—guaranteed to get you feeling better."

"It smells great. Is there anything I can do to help you?"

"Just go sit down and rest. I'll let you know when it's ready."

"Yes, ma'am."

*   *   *

IT WASN'T LONG before Lisa called out, "Come and get it!" Scott turned down the CD player, and stood behind her as she ladled the gumbo into two bowls. She had poured two glasses of red wine and set a small votive candle in the center of the table. "Do you have any matches?"

"Sure," he replied as he removed a book from a drawer and lit the candle. She turned off the overhead light and he pulled out her chair.

"Why, thank you, sir," she said, seating herself. Scott sat down across from her—he only had two chairs—and his kitchen/dining area seemed smaller than ever with two occupants.

After his first bite, she smiled, and asked, "Is it all right?"

"Excellent. I really appreciate you going to all this trouble for me."

"I hope you don't mind…"

"Mind what?"

"…I know I sort of invited myself…I hope I'm not imposing…you'd tell me if you weren't feeling up to this, wouldn't you?"

"Yeah, but it's no problem. Like I said, I appreciate you making the effort. I'm really glad you're here. I've been meaning to call you…"

"I know you've been sick…"

"Yeah, but that's no excuse…"

"Sure it is. At least we're together now…and that's what's important, right?"

"Right," he said with a big grin. He lifted his glass and said, "To the best meal and best company I've had since I've been in California—or probably ever, for that matter."

"Cheers," she said, returning his smile as she lifted her glass to clink with his.

*   *   *

AFTER THEY had eaten, and he had helped her with the dishes, she refilled the wine glasses and joined him on his small sofa, demurely curling her legs under herself. Handing him a glass, she asked, "Can I ask you something?"

"Sure. Anything."

"Murphy—is that an Irish name?"

"Yes, I believe it is."

"I'm guessing there's a good chance you're Catholic then?"

"Uh, as a matter of fact, I was raised Catholic. But I'm probably more of a lapsed Catholic now, if anything…"

"If you had kids, would you want them to be raised Catholic?"

"Yeah, if that's what my wife and I agreed to, but, I, uh, don't have a wife or kids, so where exactly is this going?" he asked, bemused.

"Well, I guess that's what I wanted to ask you—where do you think this is going—relationship-wise?

"Whoa—you are really direct, huh?"

"I come from a family that appreciates straightforwardness. I hope that doesn't bother you…it's just that, when I set my mind on something, I don't waste time."

Scott took a long drink of wine, and deeply inhaled, letting his breath out slowly. Trying to choose his words carefully, he said, "Lisa, I am very attracted to you—and would like to pursue this—and see where it might lead. You are the most intelligent, attractive woman I have ever met in my life."

Lisa gently tossed her hair, smiled and placed her hand on top of his. "I always told myself I would never date someone from work…but since I've met you, Scott…I guess my policy needs some re-thinking."

"So, you want us to date?"

"Is that what you want?"

"Yeah, that's what I want…"

"Exclusively?"

"Absolutely. Lisa, I, uh, I haven't been able to stop thinking about you…"

"Me, too."

Scott leaned over and kissed her softly.

Slowly opening her eyes, Lisa smiled and asked, "Are you the kind of guy that is totally opposed to marriage and kids?"

"No, not in theory, uh, if I met the right girl, I'm sure I would want to start a family. You don't hold back, do you?"

"Well, it's just that so many guys out there want to fool around and have fun, but are terrified of long-term commitment…they have no sense of responsibility or moral obligation. I'm not that kind of girl—and I don't want that kind of guy—I do want to find my soul mate and have a lifelong, meaningful relationship."

"That's nice. I, uh, I feel the same way…"

"I realized that about you the first time I met you. My grandmother says I'm very perceptive about judging people. She's says I get it from her." Her eyes sparkled at the thought of her strong-willed grand-mother. "And speaking of not 'holding back,' there's something else I need to discuss with you…"

Her ominous tone made Scott ask, "Sounds serious…do I need to get another glass of wine for this?"

"No, but if we're going to date—that's what you want, right?"

"Yes."

"Exclusively, right?"

"Yes."

"Then I need to tell you…I don't believe in pre-marital sex." She paused, staring at him, and then asked, "Is that going to be a problem for you?"

Mixed feelings rushed over Scott as he tried to formulate an answer for her. He wished he could tell her he had lived by the same policy, but he didn't want to lie to her. During college there was Brenda. A girl who—at the time—he thought he would marry. Until shortly after graduation, when she dumped him for a law student.

He also was a little shocked that an aggressive, stunning girl like Lisa had such high moral standards; but figured she had no reason to lie about it. "No, I don't have a problem with that...not at all. I think it's smart," he replied, hoping his disappointment was not revealed in his tone.

"I told you, I'm only interested in a serious relationship, with long term potential, and if that's going to be a problem..."

"I told you, it's not a problem for me."

Lisa could tell by his sincere look that he was not trying to con her. Her instincts about him had been correct. She smiled softly and said, "My Mother told me that the best gift you could give your husband is yourself."

"Your Mother sounds like one smart lady," Scott said as he pulled her toward him, holding her close in a gentle embrace.

Whispering into his neck, she said, "Speaking of my Mother...remember the Customer Satisfaction workshop I told you about...at home office?"

"Yeah, sure."

"Well, like I said, I can sign you up, and the meeting breaks up a couple of days before Thanksgiving...would you like to cash-in a few vacation days, and have Thanksgiving dinner with my family? Unless you already have plans..."

"No, I didn't have any plans. That would be great. I'd love to."

"Really?"

"Sure. I'd like to meet your parents—unless you think it's too soon, or, uh..."

"No, I don't think it's too soon for you to meet them," she said, kissing him softly on the lips. "I've already told them about you."

"You have?"

"Well, I'm not going to lie to them."

"What did you tell them?"

"That I had met a really nice guy."

"Thanks."

"I'm just sorry I didn't get to meet your parents last week."

"Maybe next time…"

"Although I'm glad I did get to meet your sister—Kathy—she seemed like a real sweet girl."

"She is. Hey, I don't even know, do you have any brothers or sisters?"

"Nope—I'm an only child—I guess that explains a lot," she said, giggling.

Lisa glanced at his clock and said, "It's getting late, and I have to get to work early tomorrow. Do you think you'll feel up to working tomorrow?"

"I feel pretty good right now," he replied with a grin.

"Speaking of work, I think it's best we keep our relationship private there."

"Fine with me."

"I just don't want it to create any problems…"

"Look, I'm not worried about my career at Campbell…I'll probably find another job, anyway…I don't want you to be uncomfortable at the office."

She smiled at him, appreciative of his concern, and said, "This is just a step for me on the corporate ladder; my next step will probably be back to home office in a few years. Maybe we could transfer back together?"

"In all honesty, I don't think I can last three years in this environment—but don't worry—we can work it out."

"I bet we can."

Scott helped her up and she retrieved her purse in the kitchen. Walking her outside to her car parallel parked in front of his place, he said, "So what are you doing Saturday night?"

"Oh, I'm busy," she said. "I have a date with my boyfriend."

"Okay, well maybe some other time…"

"That's you, silly," she said, playfully shoving him.

"Oh…in that case, maybe you'd like to go to dinner and a movie."

"What time do you want me to be ready?"

"How about six o'clock?"

"Great," she said, propping her arms on his shoulders and giving him a long kiss. Pulling back, she said softly, "I think I'm falling in love with you, Scott."

Scott leaned down and kissed her for what seemed like minutes. He hoped she couldn't feel his heart pounding or hear the butterflies churning in his stomach. He leaned back, looked deeply into her gorgeous, big brown eyes and said, "I think I'm falling in love with you, too."

CHAPTER 25

GLENN STEVENS returned from a late lunch and entered his office. He immediately noticed the large envelope on his desk marked personal and confidential, with Janet Carter's name in the upper left hand corner. Even before he opened it, he was pretty sure he knew the contents. He pulled out his letter opener with the Cal-Berkeley crest in gold inlaid on the wooden handle, and ripped opened the envelope. His prediction was confirmed, as a pair of high-cut, black silk panties fell out on his desk. This was a code Janet had established to let him know that she wanted to negotiate. Holding the delicate undergarment to his face, he inhaled deeply. His afternoon was looking up.

*　　　　　　　*　　　　　　　*

ALLEN CLEANED his glasses with his tie. Returning them to their perch on the bridge of his nose, he smiled at Scott. "Glad you're back in the saddle," he said cheerfully.

"Sorry, but I don't get sick often," Scott replied sitting across from Allen in his office.

"I just wanted to let you know that, once again, your numbers look great this month. Whatever you're doing, keep it up."

"Thanks. I'll do my best."

"I know you will. Okay…so here's pretty much everything you missed at last night's meeting," Allen said, handing Scott a stack of papers. "Oh, I haven't even asked you yet, how was the new employee orientation class?"

"Good. I got more out of it than I thought I would."

"Glad to hear it. I know they can really drag that thing out sometimes. Anyway, is there anything I can help you with—questions, problems, etcetera?"

"No, I think I've got a handle on everything right now, but I appreciate the offer, and if something comes up, I'll let you know."

"Keep up the good work, Scott. You're off to a great start."

Leaving Allen's office, Scott made his way over to Toni's cube in Customer Service. It looked as if her short hair was a different shade of red today, and he thought he noticed some new earrings in her multipierced lobes. "Hi there, stranger," she said smiling.

"Hi, Toni. How's it going?"

"Can't complain—and if I did—who would want to listen anyway?"

"Good point. I just wanted to drop off an order I picked up at ESD this morning."

"Nice order—you da man! I'll take care of it, chief."

Just then, Lisa opened her office door and asked, "Scott, can I see you for a moment?"

"Sure. Excuse me, Toni." Scott was surprised, and hoped Toni didn't notice his expression change when he saw Lisa.

Following Lisa into her office, Scott waited for her to make her way around her desk, and seated himself. Lisa smiled broadly, and asked, "So, how are you feeling today?"

"Great. Thanks."

"Good."

"How about you—I hope I didn't get you sick."

"No. I feel fine."

"Good. I was hoping I would get to see you today…I wanted to say thanks again for dinner last night."

"My pleasure. Hey, I know you're busy, but I forgot to give you my address and phone number," she said, handing him an envelope across the desk. "We're still on for Saturday, right?"

"Oh, yeah," he replied, "you bet."

"I'm really looking forward to it Scott."

"You know I am, too."

"Can you call me tonight?"

"Sure."

Lisa followed Scott to the door of her office. He turned, held up the envelope, smiled and said, "Thanks, again."

"You're welcome," she replied, returning his smile.

As Scott walked away, Toni stood up and stared at Lisa watching him exit. "He's real cute, huh?" she asked with a knowing smile on her face.

Blushing, and slightly embarrassed that she was being observed, Lisa smiled at Toni, and said, "Now you know it wouldn't be appropriate for me to comment on a co-worker."

"I just need to know if I have some competition?"

"What do you mean," Lisa inquired.

"I've been waiting for him to make a move, but I think he's real shy," Toni said, as she ran her thumb up and down the multiple earrings on her right ear.

"Well, I wish you luck," Lisa said sweetly, "but I would be careful with office relationships."

"Office relationships? Do you have any idea where you're working?" Toni asked as she rolled her eyes and laughed.

"You'll have to tell me all about it, sometime." Lisa smiled at Toni and returned to her desk. "She digs him," Toni said under her breath, as she sat down in front of her PC and plugged in her headset.

*   *   *

AS SCOTT PASSED through the doors leading to the lobby, he noticed Kevin parking his car in the lot. "Hi, Scott!" Lori said with a surprising amount of enthusiasm as he passed her receptionist station.

"Hey, Lori…how's it going?"

"Good! Thanks for asking, Scott." Scott nodded as Lori beamed a megawatt smile at him. Her change in attitude toward him was baffling. Pushing open the heavy glass exterior door, he spotted Kevin walking to the entrance.

"Hey, man—what's up?" Kevin asked, as he approached the front steps, juggling his car keys, briefcase and an accordion file.

"Not much, just had to meet with Allen for a minute to catch up."

"Hey, how are you feeling, man?"

"Good, good. I think the worst is over."

"That's cool."

"Did I miss anything last night?"

"Naw! Same ol' shit. Hey, I've been meaning to ask you—have you made a move on the new HR goddess, yet?"

"Uh, no…"

"Man! What in the hell is wrong with you? You had a golden opportunity in Memphis—you mean you didn't even talk to her?"

"No. We talked. She's a really nice person."

"Nice person? Dude, she is totally hot!"

Scott smiled. "She's easy on the eyes, I'll give you that."

"Look, I told you I'd give you first crack at her, bud, but if you don't quit screwing around, I'll just hafta step in and make my move."

"You're too good to me, Kev." Scott slapped Kevin on the shoulder and proceeded to his car.

"Whaddya doin' this weekend, man?" Kevin called out after him.

"I've got plans." Scott smiled as he opened his car door, and eased behind the wheel.

After he closed the door, he saw Kevin mouth the words, "What plans?" Scott honked and waved as he left the lot.

*   *   *

STANDING WITH HER SEXY silhouette framed by the doorway to Glenn's office, Janet asked in a husky voice, "You wanted to see me?"

"I thought you wanted to see me."

"You know I do, big guy." Janet closed and locked the door behind her, and sashayed over to a leather chair opposite Glenn. She observed Glenn staring at her bare, tanned legs protruding from her micro-mini skirt, as she walked. Glenn reached over and twisted his blinds closed, shooting a devious grin in her direction.

Reclining in his high-backed chair, Glenn loosened his tie. "So, you wanna *talk* first?"

"There is something I need to discuss with you."

"I'm listening…"

"Okay…since my promotion to sales…I'm not sure all the guys take me seriously."

"Really? What makes you think that, sweetheart?"

"Well, Glenn…since I left Customer Service, it seems like some of the guys, no, all of the guys think I'm not qualified for this position. I don't think I get the respect I deserve. I think a lot of it is misplaced jealousy…and maybe even a little intimidation on their part, I don't know…"

"What do you think we should do about this, Janet?"

"Wellll…I was thinking that maybe if I was awarded Top Performer this month, the guys would know I'm legit."

"Well, you know that Jon and Allen select their Top Performers each month based on sales performance."

"My performance has been pretty good...I just don't have some of the larger distributors in my territory. Couldn't you add some *subjective* criteria to the mix? I mean, after all, bottom line, it is your call, right, Glenn?"

"You know I run the show, babe."

"I know! And I want you to know how important this is to me," she purred, as she wantonly uncrossed her long legs, confirming that the panties in the envelope were the ones she wore to work this morning.

"I completely understand what you want, dear. And I can see that you understand what I want."

"You know I do." She batted her eyes seductively.

"Then consider it done," Glenn said, as he motioned her toward him.

Janet stood and slowly strutted around his large desk. Glenn pushed his chair back from the desk, and Janet straddled his lap. The two exchanged deep, sloppy kisses. Janet rubbed Glenn's hardening crotch as he caressed her breasts. Janet unzipped his trousers, slipped her hand inside and continued her massage. With her other hand she unbuckled his belt. Glenn unbuttoned her blouse, unfastened her bra and buried his face in her chest. Janet pulled his pants away, slipped his briefs down, and set him free. She knew better than to ask Glenn to wear a condom. "Turn around," Glenn said breathlessly.

Janet slid off the large man, did a dainty pirouette, and placed her hands on his desk. Glenn peeled up her short skirt and slapped her firm buttocks. "Ow! Not so hard, Glenn."

"I think all bad girls deserve a *good* spanking!" He slapped her buttocks repeatedly, each blow harder than the one before, until her soft butt cheeks turned a rosy red. He then pulled her bottom toward his face, and bit down hard.

"Dammit, Glenn! That hurts!"

"Good! It's supposed to!" He bit her a dozen more times, and then fell back hard against his chair. "Let's go," he barked.

Janet backed up and on to his lap. She reached down behind her and grabbed his rigid manhood, directing the pulsing organ to its desired destination. Easing him into her, she slowly slid down, stopping when she reached his lap. Using the armrests of his chair to support herself, she slowly pushed herself up and then back down, as if she were working on her lats and triceps on the dip station at the gym. She could feel his hot breath on her back. "Oooh, good stuff, huh?" she asked. His only response was an occasional grunting sound.

Suddenly, Glenn lurched forward, throwing her across the top of his desk. Standing upright, he flipped her skirt up and dug his fingernails into her shapely buns. Glenn began thrusting back and forth with a violent, jerky motion. Janet braced herself for his onslaught, letting out a staccato series of, "Ungh…ungh…ungh…ungh…ungh…"

"Can your husband do *this* for you? Huh, bitch? Huh? Can he?" Glenn barked in a strained growl.

"Ungh…you…ungh…know…he…ungh…can't…ungh…Glenn …you're…ungh…the best…ungh."

"I didn't think so! You like to be fucked, don't you bitch?"

"Ungh…oh, yeah…Glenn…ungh…you know…ungh…I do, baby…ungh…oh…fuck me…ungh…"

"Glenn?" came a voice over the intercom.

"Yes, Regina, what do you want?"

Regina easily surmised what was taking place in his office from what sounded like the rhythmic slapping of flesh, accented with soft grunts. "Sorry to interrupt, Glenn. Lieutenant Cavanarro is on the phone wanting to confirm your lunch date for tomorrow. Would you like to speak to him?"

"Tell him I'll meet him at…ugh…at, uh…the Crab Cooker in Newport…at…ugh…eleven-thirty."

"Will do."

"Thanks, Regina. You're a good girl."

Never altering his ongoing propulsion, the burly man pushed the off button to disconnect the intercom, and wiped the sweat from his brow. He leaned over her and with each hand grabbed a handful of Janet's short-cropped hair. She arched her back as he pulled her head up, as if he was gripping a set of handlebars. He rammed her hard with four quick bursts, let out a deep groan, and relinquished his grip on her hair. Janet slumped forward on the desk, trying to catch her breath, and wiped the tears flowing from her eyes.

Removing her panties from the envelope on his desk, Glenn wiped himself off and tossed them beside her. "Don't forget these, sweetie." He opened his desk, pulled out a cigarette, lit it and inhaled deeply. Janet slowly pushed herself up, stood, and gingerly walked around the desk. She pulled her panties up her long legs, rolled down her skirt, and told herself she wasn't going to let him see her cry. She loaded her ample breasts into her bra, and buttoned her blouse. Wiping her eyes with her index fingers, she then tried to smooth her tousled hair.

She turned, mustered a weak smile, and asked, "So we have an understanding?"

He blew a long stream of smoke in her direction, grinned and gave her a lascivious wink. "You know it, baby. Hey, I just banged the Salesman of the Month—that's a first!" She heard him laughing to himself as she unlocked the door, and slinked down the hall.

CHAPTER 26

THE PAST WEEK had been unbelievable. Scott had spoken to Lisa every night on the phone, finding that the more he learned about this woman, the more he wanted to know. She was absolutely incredible. Her lively personality and infectious laughter made his problems with Campbell Industries seemed like a distant memory. They had dinner at her place on Friday, went out to dinner and a movie on Saturday evening, and met for brunch on Sunday. Monday morning found them sitting next to each other on a flight bound for New Orleans.

After renting a car at the airport, they drove downtown and checked into their rooms at The Monteleone Hotel on Royal Street for the Customer Satisfaction workshop. The meeting droned on through Wednesday morning, with various speakers explaining the multiple elements of the customer satisfaction process, ad nauseam.

The class was lectured on the seven steps of the Quality Improvement Cycle, different ways to measure your performance with customers and how to design/define the delivery process. An elementary power-point presentation was given on the importance of taking care of both your internal and external customers.

A guest speaker from the New Orleans Saints professional football organization came in and spoke about how to determine your customer's wants and needs—apparently a winning football team must not be part of a customer's wants or needs, Scott thought, questioning the speaker's credibility.

All this was capped off on Wednesday morning with mind-numbing analysis of a series of Pareto charts, cause and effect fishbone diagrams, Histograms, scatter diagrams, run charts and a Force Field "T" graph examination of Campbell customers from various segments and market channels.

Under normal circumstances Scott knew he would have felt like jumping out in front of a moving bus rather than be subjected to an endless force feeding of such bland corporate Pablum. But Lisa's presence made this detention camp in unforgiving straight-backed chairs more than bearable. During the days, she obviously gave him something better to look at than some corporate weasel instructor scribbling furiously on a flipchart.

*   *   *

THEY STARTED the evenings after class on both Monday and Tuesday in the Carousel Bar in the lobby of The Monteleone. They both found it amusing to watch the inebriated patrons try to step off their "carousel" bar stools that rotated around the main bar. Monday's dinner destination was the Gumbo Shop on St. Peter Street for some authentic Creole cuisine.

Tuesday evening she took him to Copeland's on St. Charles Avenue for blackened redfish. They ended the evening with a walking tour of the Marketplace on the Riverwalk, followed by dessert at Cafe Beignet. Scott figured this place was relatively safe since it was located next to a police station. They returned to the hotel after midnight, and Scott remarked how fast the evening had flown by. But then he thought that any time spent alone with her went too quickly. If she had any serious personality flaws or quirks, he had yet to discover them. He found himself amazed that someone as physically beautiful as Lisa could be even more beautiful on the inside.

*   *   *

CLASS BROKE at noon on Wednesday, and not a minute too soon for Scott. He and Lisa retrieved the luggage from their rooms, and met in the opulent lobby of The Monteleone. They turned in their keys at the front desk, and made their way across the street to the parking garage. After loading the suitcases in the trunk of the rental car, Lisa asked, "Are you ready to meet my parents? No, wait, don't tell me—you were born ready, right?"

They both laughed, and Scott tried to recover from her verbal jab by answering, "That's right, how did you know?"

Heading east, crossing Canal, Royal Street turned into St. Charles Avenue. She gestured at Canal Street and said, "Saks Fifth Avenue is that way—my mother spends a lot of time there—so do I, whenever I get the chance." She laughed as Scott pondered her expensive tastes. As they drove, Scott noticed the surrounding neighborhoods changing from drab to more upscale. "See that?" Lisa said, pointing straight ahead at an oncoming trolley car. "That's one of the St. Charles Avenue Streetcars I was telling you about." She continued along the winding, oak lined avenue past Ante-bellum and Victorian mansions. Turning left on Third, she slowly maneuvered the car past houses that seemed to be getting continuously larger. She stopped in front of a monstrous white structure and turned into the driveway that had large oaks draped with Spanish moss on either side. Parking on the circular drive in front of the luxurious front doors, she noticed Scott staring at the house. "What's the matter?"

"You told me your parents had a big house…this is a mansion!"

"They've had it for about twenty years now. It was built in 1877."

Scott whistled as he got out of the sedan and took a good look at the estate. "You're sure it's okay with your folks that I stay here."

"Scott, they *insisted*."

"Well, I guess it's not like they're lacking the space."

As he pulled the luggage from the trunk, he heard Lisa say, "Hi Mother!" He turned to see Lisa embrace a very attractive, smartly dressed older version of herself.

"Hi, sweetheart. So, this must be Scott…"

Lisa interjected, "Scott, this is my mother, Judy LeDoux."

"Hi, Mrs. LeDoux, I'm Scott Murphy. Nice to meet you, ma'am," he said offering his hand.

"Welcome to our home," she said with a warm smile. "We're so glad you'll be able to join us for Thanksgiving dinner tomorrow."

"Thank you for having me."

"You two come in and get settled." Scott followed the two women around the side of the house, to the entrance across from the garage. As they walked into the bright and spacious kitchen, Mrs. LeDoux said, "Lisa, show Scott where to put your luggage, and then you two come tell me all about how your meeting went."

"Yes, ma'am. Follow me, Scott."

Scott followed Lisa through the kitchen, and into a cavernous great room, that featured a shiny, black baby grand piano near a large brick masonry fireplace. Making a left, she led him to the base of a circular staircase in the main entry. Their heels clicked on the charcoal gray marble floor. At the top of the stairs, Lisa headed left and then turned into the first room on the left. "This is my room." Scott left his bag in the hallway and carried hers into the large room. His eyes were drawn upward to the cathedral ceiling trimmed with gold-leaf crown molding, that had what appeared to be an antique chandelier hanging from the center. A large canopy bed was to the right. It was draped with frilly white linens that had a pink embroidered floral design pattern. To the left was a large mahogany chest with a matching dressing table and nightstand. The hardwood floor had an inlaid pattern running along its edge. "I know you're probably thinking this looks like a little girl's room…"

"No, it's very nice."

"This furniture was first my Grandmother's, then my Mother's, then mine…I hope I can pass it along to my daughter, someday."

Leaving her room, she pointed to the left at a closed door at the end of the hallway. "That's my parent's room. Yours will be over here." She turned right, and led him down the hall, back across the staircase to the second room on the right. This room had a much more masculine feel. A double bed with a hunter green bedspread was against the back wall with an oak nightstand on each side. What looked like a pirate's treasure chest was at the foot of the bed. An oak chest of drawers was to the left. An oak framed oval mirror was hanging on the wall above it. A large ceiling fan with five lamps hung from a brass rod in the center of the cathedral ceiling. She pushed open what he thought was a closet to reveal a spacious bathroom. The floor had white ceramic tile with a green tile border. Hunter green towels were hung on a brass tree next to a white claw-foot tub. A white pedestal sink was against the wall, with an oak framed medicine cabinet/mirror above it. She then opened a set of French doors that led to a small balcony with wrought iron railing, overlooking the front yard. "I think you'll have everything you need, here."

"Wow," was all he could say.

They descended the stairs and rejoined her mother in the kitchen. "Have ya'll already eaten lunch?" she asked.

"Not yet, mother—and I'm starving!"

"Would the two of you mind if I joined you? I've been cooking so much, I'd like to get out of the house for a little while."

"Sure, mother…where did you want to go?"

"How about the Caribbean Room?"

"Sounds good to me…you up for more Creole food, Scott?"

"Sure."

*   *   *

THE AMBIANCE of the restaurant was very elegant. The Caribbean Room featured a rich navy and gold color scheme. "This place has been in business for over forty years," Mrs. LeDoux informed Scott. He was trying hard not let on how blown away he was by all the extravagant trappings of Lisa's lifestyle. Her upbringing did not negatively affect her. She didn't appear to have a snobby bone in her body. They ordered their menu selections from the attentive waiter, and made a little small talk as they sipped their iced tea. Mrs. LeDoux excused herself before the entrees arrived.

Lisa leaned over and gave Scott a soft kiss. "Thanks for coming. I'm glad you're here." Her smile convinced him.

During the meal, Mrs. LeDoux said, "Now Scott, I'm not going to bother you with a lot of questions right now, just to have Donald ask you the same things all over again later tonight." Scott returned her smile. She was a classy lady, Scott thought. Very poised and polished. It was obvious to him where Lisa learned to be so refined.

The waiter eased the bill under Scott's left arm. He picked up the check, and heard Mrs. LeDoux say, "Don't you even think about paying, Scott. You kids got me out of the house. This is my treat."

"It's no problem. I insist," Scott replied as he handed the waiter the check along with his credit card.

"Well, I certainly didn't mean for you to pay for me. But, thank you very much."

"It's my pleasure." Mrs. LeDoux smiled at Lisa and they both smiled warmly at Scott. He was hoping they couldn't detect the look of shock on his face after he saw the tab for the meal—which totaled $92.00 with tip—for lunch! He was even more depressed when he realized he was now officially on vacation, and couldn't turn this in on his expense report.

✳   ✳   ✳

AFTER RETURNING to the house, Lisa informed her mother that she wanted to take Scott on a walking tour of the neighborhood. As they were leaving her mother called out to remind them that her father would be home soon and that they had dinner reservations at six. "Dinner? I've eaten more in the past three days than I have in the past three years," Scott remarked.

"You're a big guy—you can handle it," Lisa replied as she patted him on the stomach.

✳   ✳   ✳

"THIS PART OF TOWN is known as the 'Garden District.' All these homes are standing on what was once part of the plantation that was owned by the family that founded New Orleans," Lisa told him, as they walked down the tree lined street between the large homes.

"I can see why it's called the 'Garden District,'" Scott said, noticing the cultivated flowerbeds surrounding the houses. A Gray Line tour bus lurched past them.

"Tourists. They drop them off for walking tours," Lisa explained. Scott reached for her hand as they turned right on Coliseum Street. "I think my Mother really likes you," she said gleefully.

"What makes you think that?"

"Believe me, she would have let me know, ever so subtly, if she didn't. She always has." Passing a large house on the right, Lisa pointed to it and said, "That's the Short-Moran House. It's even older than ours. That fence is called a 'cornstalk fence.' I believe it was cast in Italy."

"Interesting…"

"Would you like to see the Lafayette Cemetery? My grandfather is buried there."

"Can't honestly say a cemetery was on my top ten list of things to see…"

"They're different here. New Orleans is below sea level, so people have to buried above ground." She led him through a tall wrought iron archway connected to two open gates.

As they walked through the tombs, Scott said, "This looks like a scale model city." As they passed through the myriad of vaults, monuments and obelisks hand-in-hand, it dawned on him how much he really enjoyed her company—even in a cemetery.

*　　　　*　　　　*

THEY RETURNED to her house and Scott noticed that the garage door was up, revealing two shiny Mercedes. Walking through the side entrance, a large man scooped up Lisa in a bear hug and said, "Come here, peanut!"

"Hi, Daddy!" She kissed him on the cheek, pulled away and said, "Daddy, this is Scott. Scott, this is my father, Donald LeDoux." He was tall and stocky, with steely, dark brown eyes. His face was framed with a well-trimmed gray beard. His hair was just a shade darker, thick and cropped short. He was wearing a starched white, pinpoint oxford shirt, a lavender silk tie with black leather braces attached to his Cambridge gray wool trousers. He stuck out a giant bear-like paw for Scott to shake.

"I'm Scott Murphy. Nice to meet you, Judge LeDoux."

"Nice to meet you, Scott. Welcome to New Orleans, 'the City That Care Forgot.'" He had a sincere smile. No B.S. here—this guy was a straight shooter. Scott liked that. Lisa may have gotten her delicate features from her mother, but her dark, intense eyes were the same as her father's. "Excuse me for just a minute—I have a couple of phone calls to make—and then we can all go to dinner."

*   *   *

LISA AND SCOTT sat in the back seat of the large Mercedes as Judge LeDoux navigated through traffic. Scott was trying to determine if this was the same model as Glenn Stevens' car. This was the first time he had ever ridden in a Mercedes Benz. Mrs. LeDoux asked, "What did you think of the Garden District, Scott?"

"It's a very beautiful neighborhood, ma'am. I really found the cemetery interesting."

"You went to *Lafayette?* Lisa! That's a dangerous place! All sorts of muggings—and even worse—have taken place there…"

"Mother, I was with Scott…I felt perfectly safe."

"But, darling…"

Judge LeDoux interjected, "Judy, they made it back, didn't they?"

They valet parked the car and walked into the Commander's Palace. They were greeted by the maitre d'. "Good evening, Judge LeDoux—and Mrs. LeDoux. We're so glad to have ya'll with us again this evening."

"Good to see you too, Joe," replied Judge LeDoux.

Joe the maitre d' showed them to a table upstairs. "Marty Falgout will be your waiter tonight, sir." When Marty appeared, Judge LeDoux greeted him by name, and ordered a bottle of wine and spinach and broccoli dip with deep-fried bow-tie pasta appetizer, before they placed their dinner orders.

"So tell me, how do you like working for Campbell Industries, son?" Judge LeDoux asked.

"It's been challenging—I've only been on board for three months…"

"And he has already won a Salesman of the Month award," Lisa chirped.

"So where'd you go to college?"

"The University of Memphis."

"Well, I believe they're in the same athletic conference as Tulane."

"Yes, sir, Conference USA."

"Ol' Tommy Bowden really turned our football team around. I'll never forget our undefeated season in '98. So, how do you like California, son?"

"It *too* has been challenging. It's taken some adjustment."

"I can imagine. Where did you work at before Campbell?"

"I was a sales rep at Mid-American Electric in Memphis."

"That's a good outfit. Do you know Paul DeBartello? He's on their Board of Directors—we went to law school together."

Scott shrugged and said, "No, sir. I can honestly say I never met anyone on the Board of Directors." Judge LeDoux gave Scott a knowing grin.

Mrs. LeDoux broke the momentary silence. "Do your parents live in Memphis, Scott?"

He sensed by her tone that the grilling was about to begin. "Yes, ma'am."

"And may I ask, what does your father do for a living?"

"He works for the railroad."

"Isn't that interesting. Does he work in a management or sales capacity?"

"No ma'am, he's a brakeman."

"So he *drives* the train?"

"Not exactly…he's an assistant to the conductor."

"Oh, I see. Well, I'm sure it's fascinating work. And does your mother work outside the home?"

"No, ma'am."

"Well, good for her. I believe the wife should stay home and raise the children. Especially if your father had to travel a lot with his job. Do you have any brothers or sisters?"

"Yes, ma'am, one younger sister."

Lisa interrupted, "Her name is Kathy—I've met her—she's really nice." Lisa smiled at Scott as if to let him know that this was routine, and all was going well. He wasn't so sure.

"And is she still in school?"

"No ma'am, she graduated from the University of Tennessee-Martin."

"The Tennessee Volunteers?"

"No ma'am, actually, the Skyhawks. It's part of the UT system, a satellite school."

"I see…and what does she do?"

"She has a marketing position with the Memphis Redbirds."

"The Memphis *Redbirds?*"

"Yes, dear," Judge LeDoux stepped in. "It's a triple-A baseball team Judy, like the New Orleans Zephyrs, you know."

"Oh, I understand." Judge LeDoux cast a quick wink in Scott's direction as Mrs. LeDoux was silently processing all the information she had acquired. Lisa smiled lovingly at him as Marty and Joe arrived with two trays of food. Scott smiled back at her and then slowly exhaled, hoping he had passed her mother's inquisition.

CHAPTER 27

THE LONG mahogany claw-footed table in the LeDoux family dining room was set with Thanksgiving-themed Spode china, Waterford stemware and Reed & Barton sterling silver flatware. A magnificent crystal chandelier hung overhead.

Scott was watching television in the den. Lisa was scurrying back and forth, helping her mother with the final details. Judge LeDoux walked through the kitchen entrance, having returned home from Metairie, after picking up his mother. Lisa greeted her grandmother with a big hug. "Grandmother! It's so good to see you!"

"Hello, angel. We're glad you made it home for Thanksgiving. Now, where is that young man your father was telling me about?"

"Follow me," Lisa said with a big smile.

Scott stood when he saw Lisa walk into the den holding the hand of a genteel, elderly woman. "Grandmother, this is Scott Murphy."

"Nice to meet you, Mrs. LeDoux," Scott said extending his hand. She grasped his hand and held it with both of hers.

"You are a good lookin' boy, Scott." She smoothed her pulled-back white hair with her right hand. "So, you met my Granddaughter in California?"

"Yes, ma'am."

"Judging from your manners, I would have to guess that you're not originally from California?"

"That's right, my family's from Memphis."

"You don't sound like you're from Memphis, but…I'm glad Lisa found herself a Southern boy out there." She smiled at Lisa, who was looking at Scott with admiration. "Can I have a word alone with you, young man?"

He had no idea what this could be all about, but Lisa's reassuring smile let him know there was no need to worry. "Certainly, ma'am."

He followed the woman down the hall and into the Judge's study. She sat on a tufted wingback chair, and motioned Scott to take a seat on the tapestry sofa across from her. As she cleared her throat, Scott noticed her fiery eyes were the same as Lisa's. "Mr. Murphy, can I assume that your intentions with my Granddaughter are honorable?"

"Yes, ma'am. I have a great deal of respect for Lisa. She's a very special person."

"I want you to know that Lisa is a good girl. I'm sure you know what I mean by that." Scott nodded, solemnly. "Lisa is a beautiful and brilliant girl. She has a bright future ahead of her. I want your word, as a gentleman, that you will respect and look out for Lisa while she's out there in California."

Squaring his shoulders, he looked her right in the eye and said, "You have my word, ma'am."

"I'm going to hold you to it, son," she replied, as a warm smile spread across her weathered face. "I can tell you make her happy." Standing, she said, "Let's go join the others." Scott stood, and as they were leaving the study, she took his arm, gently clasping her right hand around his left arm.

*   *   *

THANKSGIVING DINNER went off without a hitch. Scott and Lisa sat beside each other, across from her grandmother. Her parents sat at both ends of the table. Scott followed Judge LeDoux's lead on which utensil and glass to use with the assorted food groups. The fried turkey—Scott's first encounter with the Louisiana delicacy—was delicious.

The conversation was lively and pleasant. Judge LeDoux told a "local" joke to the group: "Ol' Man Thibedoux called 9-1-1 and said, 'Hey, lady, 'dis be Joe Thibedoux, and my wife is hurt real bad, and we need us an ambulance, right away.' The 9-1-1 operator asked, 'What street do you live on, Mr. Thibedoux?' 'We live on Tchoupitoulas Street.' 'Can you spell that for me, sir?' 'Uh, hold on, just a minute,' he said. Several moments passed, and the operator was becoming concerned. Just then his voice came back over the line, 'Okay,' he said breathlessly, 'I dragged her over to Oak Street. O-A-K.' "

✴   ✴   ✴

AFTER DINNER, Judge LeDoux and Scott went in the den to watch football, but soon fell fast asleep in front of the television. Since the maid had the weekend off, Lisa helped her mother and grandmother with the dishes in the kitchen. "So, what do you think of Scott, Grandmother?"

"He seems like a very nice young man, dear." They exchanged smiles, as Lisa's mother looked on, trying to choose her words carefully.

"I just don't want you to rush into anything," she said in a pernicious tone. "I think your different backgrounds could be a problem in the long run."

"What do you mean, different backgrounds, Judy?" her mother-in-law queried. "He's Catholic, isn't he?"

"Yes, Grandmother," Lisa interjected.

Mrs. LeDoux continued, "Don't misunderstand me—I think he's a perfect gentleman—it's just that his family apparently doesn't come from any *real* money..."

"Oh, Mother," Lisa sighed and rolled her eyes.

"Real money?" the widow LeDoux exclaimed. "Goodness gracious, Judy. My Donald didn't come from any real money either—as a matter of fact, we were dirt poor—and apparently the two of you have managed pretty well…"

"Mother LeDoux, that's different…"

"Is it?" her mother-in-law asked with a knowing smile.

Flustered and outnumbered, Mrs. LeDoux said, "You're right. You both are. I just want the best for my little girl."

"Mom, I wouldn't settle for anything but the best—you taught me that—you married Daddy."

Mother and daughter embraced. Mrs. LeDoux whispered to Lisa, "I'm sorry, sweetheart. You know I want you to be happy. Just don't rush into anything…"

Lisa stepped back and looked her mother in the eye. "Mother, he makes me very happy. He's a good person. I won't make any rash decisions…"

Her grandmother squawked, "Well, don't take too long to make up your mind—I'm not going to be around forever, you know—and I want some great-grand-babies." The three women smiled and laughed as they joined in a group hug.

*   *   *

LATER THAT EVENING, alone in his bedroom, Scott pulled his calling card from his wallet. He dialed the 800-number, his mother's telephone number and entered his PIN code. He was grateful that his mother answered. They exchanged their respective versions of Thanksgiving dinner. His mother still seemed a little upset that he didn't make it home, but seemed glad he was enjoying his time with Lisa's family. His sister was spending the evening with her boyfriend's family, and his dad was already asleep. Not having to participate in a stress-filled, long-distance dialogue with his father was something to be truly thankful for.

*   *   *

THE REMAINDER of the weekend flew by quickly. Lisa continued her role as tour guide, showing Scott the sights and sounds of her hometown. Friday morning found them on a shuttle bus meandering through Cajun country. Lisa had made reservations for them with Jean Lafitte's Swamp Tours. The green bus with a large alligator profile painted on each side dropped them off at a rustic boat dock. They waited for their swamp boat at a ramshackle structure called the Cypress Dugout. Scott thought it was appropriate that the strains of music he heard coming from the gift shop was John Fogerty singing, *Born on the Bayou.*

Boarding a mid-sized watercraft with about a dozen other tourists, they followed the directions of the Captain and slipped on life vests. The boat's engine roared loudly as they churned through the thick, brown water. The dock was soon out of sight, and Scott had never felt more in the middle of nowhere in his entire life. Banking hard to the right, the boat quickly threaded its way through a group of moss-draped Cypress trees. Startled by the oncoming boat, two large, white egrets took flight. The boat's speed decreased as the cluster of trees grew thicker. Entering an inlet, the shoreline was visible on both sides. Upstream, bait fish jumped out of the water, apparently trying to escape an unseen predator.

Over the P.A. system, the Captain's voice crackled, "Now lookey der, a big un is right over der off da port side of da boat." The boat leaned against the weight of the tourists making their way to the left side of the craft for a glimpse of what the Captain was alluding to. A twelve-foot alligator slithered from the shore and into the water, with surprisingly fluid movement.

"Have you ever seen such a big, slimy reptile before?" Lisa asked excitedly, grabbing his arm.

"Other than Glenn Stevens? No, can't say that I have," he answered sarcastically.

*   *   *

AFTER DINNER with her parents at the nearby Little Tokyo Japanese restaurant, Lisa informed him that they had reservations at The House of Blues that evening. Scott was really excited when he learned that none other than legendary Chicago blues man, Buddy Guy, was the featured performer. Halfway through Buddy's set, Scott was mesmerized by the indelible impression of Lisa's candle lit profile.

Lisa felt as if it had been a real date when they returned home, parked in the circle drive and walked to the front door. Scott put his arms around her and they exchanged a long, passionate kiss.

*   *   *

ON SATURDAY they joined her parents and grandmother for brunch at the Home Furnishings Cafe, near the Prytania Park hotel. They spent the afternoon at The Aquarium of the Americas, where they watched a diver hand feed sharks in a large tank, and Scott saw the aquarium's much hyped white alligator. "I didn't know there was such a thing," he remarked. Lisa smiled up at him warmly.

*   *   *

THEIR LAST evening was spent having dinner at home with her parents. They decided to take it easy tonight, because in the morning they would have to pack and head out for the airport. Scott was feeling much more comfortable around her family and his burgeoning relationship with Lisa.

Judge LeDoux invited Scott to join him in his study, after dinner. Pouring two snifters of brandy, the judge handed one to Scott. He then opened his humidor and selected two cigars. "Cubans," he said, "not the Dominican knock-offs." Scott studied the yellow and black Cohiba ring as Judge LeDoux cut the end off his cigar. He handed Scott the heavy, brass cutter, and he did likewise. After they lit up, Judge LeDoux snickered. "This is the only room in the house Judy will allow me to do this. She wouldn't even let me smoke in here until I got those," he said, gesturing to two Honeywell air cleaners on each side of the room.

"We've really enjoyed getting to know you over the past few days, son," he said as he sent a stream of smoke in the direction of an air cleaner.

"I've really enjoyed myself, and appreciate you having me, sir," Scott replied earnestly.

"Lisa tells me you're not thrilled with some of the management at Campbell."

"Uh, well, she's right. They don't exactly exemplify the level of professionalism I'd like to be associated with."

"Do you think you would ever like to work in New Orleans?"

"I certainly wouldn't rule it out—you know, for the right opportunity."

"Well, New Orleans is really a 'big' small town. By that I mean, everybody knows everybody. It's tough to get a break if you're not connected, understand?" he asked, stroking his beard thoughtfully.

"Sure."

"What I'm getting at is…if you and Lisa continue to see each other, and things move along—you know Lisa is not going to be in Los Angeles for long—I just want you to know if you decide you would like to pursue a job in New Orleans, I want you to let me know. I think I can be of some assistance."

"I really appreciate the offer."

"I'm serious son, don't let pride keep you from asking."

"I won't."

After several minutes of silence and puffing, Judge LeDoux straightened in his chair and stated, "Last thing…I'm counting on you to treat my daughter right."

"You can count on me."

"I believe I can, son." The judge reached over and slapped Scott on the knee.

*   *   *

AFTER EXTINGUISHING the cigars, the two men joined the ladies in the bright kitchen. Mrs. LeDoux smiled warmly and said, "Scott, I want you to know how much we've enjoyed having you stay with us this weekend."

"Thank you for all your hospitality. This is the best Thanksgiving I've ever had."

"Well maybe we'll get to do it again next year," she said cheerfully. Lisa smiled knowingly at her mother. "Well then, Donald and I will say goodnight now—I know you both have to pack and leave early in the morning."

"Goodnight, Mother," Lisa said, as she hugged her mother and kissed her on the cheek. "Goodnight, Daddy," she said embracing her father and kissing his bearded face.

"Goodnight, son," Judge LeDoux said, offering his hand to Scott.

"Goodnight, sir. Thanks for everything."

Judge LeDoux gave him a quick wink. Mrs. LeDoux seemed a little uncomfortable and stepped slowly forward. Scott offered his hand for her to shake, but she stepped inside of it and gave him hug. "Take care of my little girl," she said softly.

"I will."

As she stepped back, he noticed tears forming at the corners of her eyes. "Goodnight," she said as she quickly turned around. Her husband put his arm around her and they made their way to the staircase.

Lisa stepped forward and put her arms around Scott's neck. Scott put his arms around her as he leaned back against the counter. "I'm sorry if my parents—and grandmother—came off as being overprotective of me. It's just that…"

"They just want what's best for you," Scott interjected. "You don't have to apologize for them. I'm glad you invited me, and that I got to meet them all. You have a great family. They love you very much, Lisa. And so do I." She stood on her tiptoes and kissed him on the lips. He noticed her eyes were beginning to well up with tears.

CHAPTER 28

MARVIN BEADLES stared through his Coke bottle glasses at the attractive woman across from him. She looked at her watch as he droned on incessantly about his 401K and pension plan options, along with the selection of the best medical plan option for him. "My wife works at Boeing, you know…"

"Yes, you've *mentioned* that."

"…and her benefit package is absolutely stellar," he said, sending spittle airborne as he pronounced the word stellar. Marvin grinned a geeky grin, adjusted his polyester tie and stood, extending a sweaty hand for her to shake. "Thanks so much for your time, Lisa. Some of your insights have proven to be quite valuable."

"You're certainly welcome, Marvin. That's what I'm here for."

Marvin removed a red bandanna handkerchief from his back pocket and blew his nose loudly. Returning the freshly loaded handkerchief to his pocket, he grinned at her again. "Well, I'm glad you're here. Thanks again."

"Don't mention it," Lisa said, trying to mask her disgust with this greasy, nerdy little man. She knew all in all he was perfectly harmless, and she couldn't let her personal feelings or perceptions cloud her professional outlook when it came to dealing with co-workers. A basic tenet of the Human Resources function, she thought.

After his exit from her office, Lisa dialed Scott's voicemail extension. As she waited for the tone after the completion of his recorded message, her thoughts turned to the upcoming Christmas holiday. She wanted to get him something really special. Perhaps a watch; maybe a nice shirt and tie. She hadn't decided, but knew she would have to make up her mind very soon.

A shrill beep interrupted her thoughts. Speaking softly into the phone, she said, "Hi, Scott, it's me. I just wanted to let you know that I was thinking about you, and hoping you are having a great day! Thanks again for having Thanksgiving in New Orleans with my family—it meant a lot to me. Anyway, I know you'll be busy tonight with your Monday night sales meeting and all, so I was hoping we could get together for dinner tomorrow night. Let me know if that works for you. Bye!"

She hung up and thought about her decision not to say, "I love you" at the conclusion of her message. Would he read anything into it? Things were happening so fast and she was filled with so many thoughts and emotions. New job, new boyfriend, and starting her graduate school classes next month—it was a lot to process. She rationalized that he knew how she felt, and that they had agreed to keep it strictly professional at work. She would make sure to tell him next time they were alone together.

Three quick knocks, followed by her door swinging open revealed Glenn's leering face. "Are you in the middle of anything?"

"No, come in."

"Good. I had a few minutes, and just wanted to stop by for a quick pulse check." He made a big production of shutting the door behind him. "How are things going for you?" His eyes narrowed as a cheesy grin spread across his face.

"Great. Everyone has been very helpful."

Glenn flopped into a chair and crossed his legs in a cavalier manner. "How about that Customer Satisfaction Workshop at home office—was that worthwhile?"

"Yes, I thought so. I think it's critical for every company not to lose sight of the importance of the customers. I also feel it's imperative that…"

"Yeah, yeah, yeah," he interrupted with obvious boredom. "Would you like to have some time set aside at an upcoming meeting to discuss what we can do here in the Western Region?"

"Absolutely, Glenn. The purpose of the workshop was to come back to our respective offices, and establish a systematic method of identifying, measuring, managing, and monitoring customer needs and satisfaction."

"Whatever you say, gorgeous…I think it's all a lot of fucked up corporate bullshit…"

Lisa tried to compose herself and respond to this crass man in a calm and professional manner. "It's a vital process that every successful organization must undertake to improve profitability and beat the competition. And, my name's not gorgeous—I prefer Lisa."

Glenn eased himself down on the corner of her desk. "Don't be so touchy! You need to loosen up. You are way too good looking to be one of those femi-nazi bitches."

"Mr. Stevens, my looks have nothing to do with my ability to perform my job. Your implication that I'm some kind of radical liberal feminist is as misguided as it is inaccurate. And I would appreciate it if you would kindly refrain from using vulgar language in my presence."

"Look, *princess,* I don't know what kind of sheltered background you come from, but this is the real world, baby. Big business. You're gonna have to get with the fucking program." He smugly smirked at her, as she avoided making eye contact. He reached down and gently lifted her head by the chin, and said in condescending baby talk, "Aw, what da matter, wittle Weesa?"

Lisa quickly jumped to her feet, and walked to the far corner of her office. Her face took on a serious look. "Mr. Stevens..."

"It's Glenn."

"Mr. Stevens, I do not appreciate your tone. I am a professional and expect to be treated as such."

Glenn sauntered over to where she was standing, and invaded her personal space. He quickly flung both arms against the wall to brace himself, caging Lisa between them. "Believe me, I've had my eye on you. You definitely have all the right tools. I want to treat you like a *professional,* baby," he hissed in her ear.

"Mr. Stevens, this is totally inappropriate!" His heavy cologne was stifling.

"Look, you can be very successful...if you know how to play the game..."

Lisa ducked under one of his arms, and marched quickly to the door. Pulling it open, she turned and said with all the composure she could muster, "I think you'd better leave, Mr. Stevens."

"Fine. Whatever. I'll leave—this time. You're just a little naive, but you'll come around. You just have a little growing up to do. You'll soon learn that I *always* get what I want. And I told you, call me Glenn."

"Good-bye, Mr. Stevens," she said, not looking at him as he slithered toward the door. As he drew along side her, he suddenly grabbed her buttocks with his right hand and squeezed hard. "Mr. Stevens!" she exclaimed as she recoiled from his grip. Her hand slapped across his face with blinding speed.

"Ouch!" he said, grinning with a mocking tone. He rubbed the side of his face, where the red imprint of her hand was beginning to develop. "I can't believe you got that one by me. I never saw it coming. You're quick—I'll have to remember that." He stepped through the doorway, looked over his shoulder, raised his left eyebrow and muttered, " By the way, primo ass, LeDoux," giving her a thumbs-up signal.

Lisa closed the door behind him and marched solemnly back to her desk. She felt sickened by the encounter that had just taken place. She tried to collect her thoughts and plan her next step. What was he thinking? How could he possibly think he could get away with such outlandish behavior? Just when she thought things were going so well, he had to pull a stunt like that. She was so angry she wanted to quit. She tried to remind herself that this assignment was just a means to an end. She unconsciously drummed her fingers on the desk.

Should she call Scott? No, probably not good to get him involved—he would probably want to beat the hell out of Stevens. Should she call her father? No, she didn't want to appear like a little girl who couldn't take care of herself. This was her fight. Her mother? She could never comprehend an assault like what had just taken place. Her father had seen to it that she was never exposed to the dark side of life. That sort of protected existence suddenly seemed appealing.

How about her mentor at home office, Pam Kinney? No, Pam showed a great deal of confidence in her by pushing her for this assignment. She didn't want to shake Pam's faith in her. She had been well trained, and was supposed to be able to counsel employees through situations like this. Taking a deep breath, she pulled out her day planner. She began to document exactly what had just transpired, while it was fresh in her mind. She regained her composure, knowing full well that she had the ability and the intestinal fortitude to structure an ironclad sexual harassment case against that creep. She steeled herself to take the initiative to do this by the book, focus on the situation—not Glenn—and thus resolve this matter quickly and professionally.

CHAPTER 29

SCOTT NOTICED Lisa staring out the window at the evening traffic moving up and down Beach Boulevard. She had seemed distracted all evening. She poked at her salad, and had yet to touch her plate of angel hair pasta. "Is there something on your mind, Lisa?"

"What? Uh, no...I mean, nothing other than work stuff."

"Anything I can help with?"

"Nothing I can't handle myself. But I appreciate the offer."

"No problem..."

Scott decided not to push it. He could certainly empathize with how crazy working for Campbell Industries could be. Lisa was sharp, and he was confident she could handle whatever situation was on her mind. He also hoped that she knew if she really needed him, he would be there for her. He finished off his lasagna, and asked, "Are you going to feel like dessert?"

"Maybe something light...I think I'll ask for a box and take the rest of this home."

After they each consumed a scoop of chocolate ice cream covered with strawberry puree, Scott paid the tab and they got up to leave. Lisa's mood seemed to have improved over the last course. They walked out of the Pacific Pasta & Pizza Company and into the cool evening air of Huntington Beach. "It's starting to feel like winter," she said snuggling up to him, as he put his arm around her.

"Winter? You've got to be kidding?"

"Well, you have to remember it doesn't get that cold in New Orleans, either."

"It'll be weird being able to wear a T-shirt and shorts during December."

"It beats having to bundle up and trudge through snow."

"I guess…but it sure won't feel like Christmas."

Lisa smiled up at him. "I'm looking forward to it. I think this is going to be a great Christmas."

Scott opened her car door. "Even though you won't be spending it with your family?"

"True, it'll be my first Christmas away from home…but, it'll be my first Christmas with you." The fiery sparkle returned to her eyes for the first time all evening.

Scott smiled and put his arms around her. He felt very warm inside. He lowered his head and kissed her. "I guess that means I'll have to get you a present, huh?"

"If you know what's good for you," she said as she playfully shoved him. They kissed again, and Lisa eased into the passenger seat of his car. As Scott closed the door, he couldn't help noticing her dazzling smile behind the glass. Whatever she had on her mind during dinner didn't seem to be bothering her now, he thought.

Seating himself behind the leather-clad steering wheel, Scott put the key into the ignition. He reached for the stick between them, and before he could shift into reverse, Lisa softly placed her hand on top of his. He looked over at her as she gave his hand a gentle squeeze. "I love you, Scott. I really do." She said the words with more confidence than ever before, as the reflection of the passing headlights danced in her eyes.

Scott smiled at her reassuringly. "I love you, too. I've never been more sure of anything in my life." He leaned over and kissed her softly. "You're the best thing that's ever happened to me." He couldn't help but admire her beautiful face.

"Scott, I have never felt this strongly before. I really want this to work."

"Isn't that up to us?" he said, smiling.

"True, but it's not going to be easy."

"Is anything worthwhile ever easy?"

"You're right, but you've got to know I'm not the easiest person in the world to get along with. I'm far from perfect…"

"I think you're perfect for me. And I'm sure you'll discover many annoying habits of mine."

She laughed and said, "I think you're perfect!"

"Can I get that in writing? I might need it later." They both laughed as he steered the car Southbound on Beach Boulevard.

*   *   *

SCOTT pulled into the main entrance of the Oakwood Apartments, and made his way to Lisa's unit, parking in front, adjacent to her car. He shut off the engine and looked over at her. Her smile was radiant and she was absolutely glowing. Her full brown hair cascaded down, framing her delicate features. She looked angelic.

Clearing his throat, Scott said, "I just want you to know that whatever was bothering you at dinner…if I can ever help with anything…"

"I know," she said softly.

"Your problems are my problems, okay?"

"Thanks." After a long pause, she said, "You want to come in and watch some TV? I can make popcorn."

"Sure. Sounds great." Scott walked around and opened her door. He took her hand and helped her from the car. She clutched the Styrofoam container holding her leftover pasta in her other hand. When they reached the door, she handed him the container and fished her keys from her purse.

Once inside, Scott turned on the television, and took a seat on the couch. It was covered in soft cotton sheeting, with a rich tan and taupe awning stripe design. Her place was much more nicely furnished than his. It was obvious Lisa's decorating tastes were strongly influenced by her mother.

Lisa poured two glasses of chardonnay and placed them on a wicker-serving tray. Three quick beeps signaled Lisa to remove a bag of freshly popped microwave popcorn. She poured its contents into a stainless steel bowl, and placed it on the tray. She placed the tray on the coffee table in front of Scott, and joined him on the couch. She handed him a glass of wine as she folded her legs under herself. Scott retrieved the bowl of popcorn from the tray, and held it in his lap.

"Not much on tonight," he said, as he surfed the channels.

"I don't care. I'm just glad you're here."

"No place I'd rather be."

"Scott?"

"Yes?"

"I think I should tell you…I'm feeling kind of vulnerable right now…I've never been in this kind of relationship, never felt this way about anyone. I'm scared about how I feel about you…you could really hurt me…"

"Lisa, I never want to hurt you. I'm in the same situation you are. You could rip my heart out…"

"Scott!"

"…but you've got to know that I'm in this for the long haul. I'm not going anywhere. I've never wanted something to work so much in my life. Don't be scared…just be happy we found each other."

"You make me very happy. I love you so much, Scott." She pulled him close and nuzzled her face in his chest.

He put his arms around her, and held her tightly. "I love you." He had never been more sure of any statement in his life. He thought it was an interesting twist of fate that only a month ago he was ready to throw in the towel with Campbell *and* California. If he hadn't stuck it out he would never have found himself with this angel in his arms. His mom always told him that all things work out for a reason. He reflected on her wisdom, and cherished the beautiful woman he was holding. She looked up at him with a warm smile and misty eyes. He gently kissed her. He had never been happier, and the future had never seemed brighter. All was right with his world.

CHAPTER 30

THURSDAY MORNING found Scott walking across the Second Street Bridge that connected Naples Island to Belmont Shore. Floating Christmas trees dotted the water, positioned between the two shorelines. A sign on a light post announced the date and time of the upcoming annual Christmas boat parade.

Crossing at the light, he pulled open the door to the Diamond Depot. He perused the jewelry-filled glass cases that lined the walls of the small showroom. The overhead track lighting made the gemstones sparkle. A pleasant looking woman emerged from the back room and greeted him with a smile. "Is there anything I can help you with?"

Scott returned her smile, and hesitated as he felt like he was blushing. There was no turning back now. He had thought long and hard about this, and was sure he had made the right decision. "I, uh, I'd like to see a ring...a, uh, engagement ring."

"Congratulations! Did you have a particular style in mind?"

"Well, uh, something very traditional and conservative."

"Okay...how about a Tiffany setting?"

"You'll have to show me...I don't know much about jewelry."

"That's what I'm here for. By the way, my name is Paula."

"Hi, I'm Scott."

232

She pulled a simple gold band from a drawer below the case in front of her. It had six empty prongs where a diamond could be mounted. "This is a very traditional setting. What color jewelry does she wear?"

"Gold and silver, I guess."

"Well, a platinum setting is very traditional, and a gold setting is a little more modern, but still conservative."

Scott racked his brain trying to think about the color of Lisa's jewelry. She didn't wear much, but what she did struck him as very tasteful. He also tried to think about what kind of jewelry her mother wore. "Uh, I guess platinum," he stammered.

"Has she told you what shape stone she would like?"

"Actually, she has no idea I'm doing this…"

"Living on the edge, huh?" She smiled at him warmly. "Based on what you said about being conservative earlier, I would probably suggest a round stone. Do you know about the four C's used to judge a diamond's quality?'

"Can't say that I do."

"It has to do with the carat size, cut, color and clarity of the stone. The grade and quality determines the cost. Did you have a price in mind?"

Scott really hadn't thought too much about what this would cost. Reflecting on Lisa's background and upbringing, he knew he didn't want to embarrass her with a cheap ring. "Maybe you can show me a few and let me know what they cost…"

"No problem. I can tell you that a lot of people consider six weeks to six months salary a good range on what to spend."

Half a year's salary, he thought to himself. Ouch! But then he remembered this was a once in a lifetime purchase, and he remembered whom he was getting it for. "Okay, let's see what you've got, Paula."

*　　　　　*　　　　　*

SCOTT LEFT THE STORE after selecting a two-carat round diamond, and felt as if his credit card was smoking in his wallet. He began to walk back across the bridge to his apartment Fifteen grand, he thought. Oh, well, amortized over a lifetime, that came out to pennies a day. At least that's what he tried to convince himself. But all in all, it was a painless experience. Paula was very friendly and helpful. Apparently her husband was the jeweler, and he would mount the stone he selected, and he could pick it up this afternoon. He was glad he had dealt with a small family-owned business, and not ventured into a glitzy store in a mall with its overhead.

Several months ago he would have laughed at the notion that he was ready, or even old enough to get married. But that was before Lisa. It made his head spin to think how quickly his life had changed. But he was sure it was all for the better. He decided that he wouldn't ask her until Valentine's Day. That would give him time to arrange a return trip to New Orleans to ask her parents' permission, and insure them his intentions were honorable. He would try to schedule it after the first of the year, unbeknownst to Lisa. On several occasions he had walked over this bridge in the evenings and had seen couples propelled slowly along in a gondola, piloted by a gondolier dressed in pseudo Italian garb. Maybe that would be a good setting to pop the question, he thought.

He had decided that he did not want to put Lisa's career at Campbell in jeopardy, and knew he would have to secure employment elsewhere before he proposed. His first call this morning was at Alexander's Electric Supply. He figured that with the rapport he had built with Nick Lunsford, he could probably get a job as an outside salesman there. If not, he figured he could always contact Kerry Balfour at RecruitersWest and see if she had any sales opportunities with her West coast client base. He felt extremely confident all the details to his plan would fall easily into place.

*   *   *

THURSDAY AFTERNOON was winding to a close. Lisa looked at the brass clock on her desk and noticed that it was almost five. She began to straighten her desk and gather her belongings. She planned to go home, put in thirty minutes on the stair-climber, shower, change, and meet Scott for dinner at eight o'clock. The anticipation of seeing Scott had her excited.

Her thoughts were interrupted by the ringing telephone. She noticed from the phone's display that this was an internal call. "Hi, this is Lisa."

"Well now you've really gone and done it, haven't you," the voice in the other end hissed through the receiver.

She had actually been expecting this call earlier, since she had e-mailed her claim to Pam Kinney at home office yesterday afternoon. "To whom am I speaking, please?" she asked innocently.

"You know good and damn well who this is, you prissy bitch! I want to see you in my office…now!"

"Mr. Stevens, if you're wanting to discuss my sexual harassment claim, I think it would be more appropriate if this meeting was conducted in the presence of somebody from home office, and my attorney."

"Yeah, right. We can have the *official* discussions any way you want. Just get in here before you leave for the day. This won't take long."

"Okay, I'll stop by. But I only have a minute…I have plans this evening."

"No problem. So do I."

*   *   *

IT WAS a little after five when Lisa left her office. The customer service cubicles had already been abandoned. The offices of Allen and Jon were both dark. Darrin Johnson and Jerry Fujisaka were wrapping up a discussion with Regina Rogers when Lisa approached them. Regina noticed Lisa had a look of concern on her face. "Lisa, is everything okay?" she asked in a knowing tone.

"Just going to meet with Glenn for a minute."

"I'm not so sure that's a good idea…I've heard through the corporate grapevine…"

"You heard correctly. I can handle myself with his type. I'm sure he just wants to blow off some steam."

"I'm not sure you realize what kind of temper Glenn has…"

"Thanks, Regina, but I can handle it. He has a serious problem and he might be about to make it even worse. I'll document anything inappropriate."

Darrin and Jerry stood in silence trying to interpret what the two women were talking about. Any bad news about Glenn was good news as far as Jerry was concerned. Regina turned off her PC and retrieved her purse from the bottom drawer of her desk. "Just be careful dear. Goodnight."

"I will. Goodnight, Regina."

Darrin and Jerry said goodnight to Lisa in unison.

"Goodnight, guys. See you tomorrow," Lisa chirped.

The two men escorted Regina toward the exit, past the open doorway to Glenn's office. As Lisa walked tentatively to his office, she noticed that Lori had vacated her post at the receptionist's station.

She entered the office and was met with a glowering expression from Glenn, seated behind his desk. "Shut the door," he said bitterly.

"If it's all the same to you, I'd prefer to leave it open."

"Suit yourself." Glenn stared at her menacingly. After a long pause he practically spit out the words, "Who in the hell do you think you are?"

"I'm the Human Resources Manager for the Western…"

"Don't give me your damn job title! Who do you think you are…to think you can fuck with me?" he snarled.

"Mr. Stevens, as I told you before, I think any discussion between us now is inappropriate. Any situation you find yourself in now is one of your own making. If you have any questions, I suggest you direct them to Pam Kinney in human resources at home office." She turned to leave. "Goodnight, Mr. Stevens."

Stevens leapt over his desk with surprising grace for a man his size. He grabbed Lisa's hair and jerked her backwards off her feet. Lisa screamed in pain, as he shouted over her, "You're not going anywhere, you little bitch!" He shoved her roughly to the floor, stepped over her and slammed the door shut.

Looking up at him through eyes beginning to fill with tears, Lisa said, "You're way out of line here, Glenn."

"He stepped forward, towering over her and boomed, "I make the fucking rules here! This is my outfit, and *nobody's* gonna come in here and tell me what I can and can't do." He reached down and grabbed a handful of her hair. "Got it? Everybody here plays by my rules, and you're not gonna be any exception." Lisa tried to stand, and he shoved her back to the floor. "Sit down!"

Trying to sound as forceful and authoritative as she could, Lisa said, "Glenn, you're not helping yourself at all with this kind of behavior…"

"You just don't get it, do you? I am the boss! What I say goes! You have no control, no authority here! All the people here understand that, *especially* the women. I get whatever I want, whenever I want it. Those are the rules! You should be smart enough to understand that, huh? It's not too late to get along—you can still withdraw your claim…"

"You've got to be kidding," Lisa interjected.

"Okay so you're not as smart as I thought you were. But I'll tell you one thing…you've got to be the best looking piece of ass that's ever walked through these doors. Seriously, the first time I saw you I thought you were good looking enough to be a porn star."

"Gee, I'm flattered."

"Now, there's something I've been wanting to do for a long time. I'd like you to take off your clothes…"

"I don't think so…"

"Look, you make this easy on yourself or do it kicking and screaming. Actually, I'd kind of like to see you kicking and screaming." He
grabbed her hair with one hand and pulled her to her feet. With his
other hand he grabbed her blouse by the collar and ripped downward.

She couldn't believe what was happening. She steeled herself and
drove her knee firmly into groin.

He backed up and doubled over in pain. "You fucking bitch!" She
then swung the corner of her briefcase into the side of his head. The
blow made him wince.

She walked around the slumped and groaning man. "Why don't you
wait right here, while I call the police. You better hope they get here
before Scott Murphy, because he will probably kill you."

"Murphy? You've been fucking *Murphy*? I don't believe this. You
could've had filet mignon and you were eating hamburger?" Just as she
reached the door, he forcefully jumped on her, tackling her with his
body weight. He flipped her over on her back and tried to pin her arms
with his legs. She tried to slap his face, but he caught it with his large
hand. "You're quick," he growled, "but you're not going to get me twice."
Successfully pinning down her arms, he began to fondle her breasts.
"Unbelievable. Are these real?"

She felt repulsed as she glared at the despicable man straddling her.
"You have gone way to far. It's all over for you!"

"Over for me? Missy, it's over for you." He began laughing maniacally as his hands left her breasts and made their way to her slender
neck. Lisa tried to move, but couldn't budge the large man's frame. His
hands squeezed her throat tightly. Lisa struggled to inhale. Glenn's
shark black eyes were riveted on her. Beads of perspiration dripped
from his face, and she could taste his salty sweat that entered her open,
gasping mouth. Glenn was growling something at her, but she couldn't
make out what he was saying. Her last thoughts were of her mother,
father and grandmother. And Scott. Her last sight was the hulking

man's staring face. She closed her eyes to avoid looking at him, and began saying the "Hail Mary" prayer to herself. Red. Black. Red. Black.

Glenn struggled to his feet and walked away from the limp body on the floor. He walked out of his office and down the hallway to the vacant warehouse. He was relieved that everyone had left for the evening. He found a box of large, black Hefty bags, and extracted two from their container. He returned to his office and slipped one over her torso and put her legs in the other. She was bigger than Maria Lopez, he thought, as he squatted and slung her over his shoulder. He walked through the lobby, down the steps and over to his parked car. He pulled out his keys with his free hand and opened the trunk. He slowly lowered the baggage into the opening. Closing the trunk, he returned to his office and looked around for any possible evidence from their struggle. He picked up her purse and briefcase, turned off the lights, set the alarm, and locked the front doors. He knew the drill.

*   *   *

THURSDAY EVENING Scott parallel parked in front the Bay Bridge Cottage Apartments. He had always thought the name was a deceptive description of his tiny, one bedroom dwelling. Getting out of the car, he noticed he was parked behind a Mercedes that looked a lot like Glenn's. He checked his watch and noted the time was 6:45 PM. He was supposed to pick Lisa up at eight. He figured he had enough time to walk over to the Diamond Depot. He crossed the bridge and noticed that the floating Christmas trees were now illuminated and rocked cheerily in the water.

He entered the shop and was greeted by Paula. "Hello, Scott. I was hoping you'd make it before we closed. He's finished and I think it turned out really nice." She disappeared into the back room, and returned with a friendly-looking, bearded man behind her. "Scott, this is my husband, Roman."

"Nice to meet you," Scott said, offering his hand.

"Good to meet you," Roman said smiling. After shaking hands, he handed Scott a jeweler's loupe. "Sit over here, the light is better," he said, directing him to a stool against the corner of the glass cases. Scott took a seat as Roman placed the solitaire on a piece of black felt. "Look through there, and I'll tell you what you're looking at." Scott did as he was told, and examined the magnified view of the diamond. "Your color is good, I've noted that here in your appraisal," Roman said gesturing toward a folded piece of paper. "There were two small inclusions, but I've hid them behind the posts. Can you see them?"

"No, I can't."

"That's because I do good work."

"What do you think?" Paula asked, excitedly.

"Looks good to me."

"I think she'll love it! Now remember, we give you a lifetime warranty and we'll clean it anytime she wants, no charge. Also, she should probably come in about once a year and let Roman examine it to make sure the stone is secure, again, no charge."

"Okay. Great."

"When are you going to ask her?"

"I was thinking about Valentine's Day."

"How romantic!"

"You should get a rider on your homeowner's insurance," Roman suggested.

"I rent…"

"Renter's insurance, whatever. They'll need this appraisal."

"Thanks. I really appreciate all your help."

"Well, thank you very much," Paula chimed in. "And congratulations! She's a very lucky girl."

"Thank you. But, I'm the lucky one," Scott said smiling, as he walked toward the door.

Roman locked up behind him and he retraced his steps over the Second Street Bridge. The ring box bulged from the front pocket of his slacks. Hopefully, he thought, no one noticed him leave the jewelry store and would try to mug him on the way home. He picked up his pace, not wanting to be late to see Lisa. He hummed happily to himself as he studied the festive Christmas decorations on the lampposts along the way.

Reaching the cluster of apartments, he turned left down the narrow walkway, making his way to his unit at the end. He noticed that he had a lot of mail protruding from his small mailbox mounted next to his door. His eyes then moved to the window screen on the ground under his window. Did his window look to be opened more than he had left it? He typically left the window cracked for a little circulation—there was no air conditioning—and figured a strong wind must have knocked the ancient screen off the window. He pulled the mail from the overstuffed container, as he located his keys with his other hand. He inserted the key into the dead-bolt lock, and opened the door. He was overcome with a wave of nausea, as he confronted the sight of Lisa's lifeless, naked body sprawled across his bed. His heart pounded against his rib cage and he felt his knees wobble intensely. "Murphy, what in the hell have you done?" he heard a gruff voice say from the kitchen. He turned just in time to see Glenn Stevens forcefully swinging a golf club baseball-style at his head.

CHAPTER 31

A QUIET, nasal sounding voice could be heard talking in hushed, but urgent tones. It took him several moments until he could understand with clarity what the situation was. He was sitting slumped in the passenger seat of his own moving car. He decided it would be best to continue the illusion of being unconscious until he knew exactly what was going on. He felt something digging into his right leg, and realized it was the box containing Lisa's engagement ring. The thought of Lisa almost made him cry out. The anguish he felt was overpowering. His head was throbbing fiercely.

Without opening his eyes, he was able to determine the voice he heard was that of Jon Cassler, apparently speaking to someone on a cell phone. Probably with Glenn Stevens, he thought. He had no idea how long he had been out, or where Cassler was taking him. He couldn't risk glancing at his watch.

The terrain seemed to get increasingly rougher. It felt like the car had been taken off-road. Scott could now feel and hear the car slowly ascend a bumpy incline. Several minutes later the car eased to a stop, and he felt Cassler shift into park. Moments later a second car could be heard approaching, and then stopping next to them. Cassler opened the door and stepped outside. Scott could hear Glenn's low voice mumble something or other to Cassler. Jon sounded extremely nervous.

A minute or so passed, and Scott could no longer hear the voices. He thought about making a break for it, but then heard the passenger door open, and felt the interior dome light illuminate the cabin. Glenn's long arms wrapped around his upper body, and pulled him from the car. Scott continued to play possum and let Glenn drag him from the car. He came to a stop at the driver's side. Glenn lifted him up with a jerking motion and thrust him into the bucket seat on the driver's side. "He's a heavy son-of-bitch," Glenn grunted. Glenn placed Scott's legs under the steering wheel, reached around the column for the ignition key and re-started the car. "Give me the fucking note," he barked at Cassler. Glenn tossed the piece of paper across Scott and onto the front passenger's seat.

The large man straightened and wiped the sweat from his brow. "Okay, it's show-time," he said with a slight snicker. He leaned over, grabbed the stick and shifted the running car into drive. Scott could feel the transmission engage as Glenn stepped back and closed the door on him. Scott cracked his eyes and could see what appeared to be twinkling lights ahead of him. Opening wider, he realized that he was looking down through the darkness on the lights of a city below him. He quickly surmised that this was supposed to look like an accident or a suicide plunge.

Glenn walked over and joined Cassler, who was leaning against his black Mercedes. Glenn methodically lit a cigarette and blew a stream of smoke in the direction of the City of Brea's skyline. The only sounds the men could hear were Glenn's heavy breathing, traffic from a distant freeway, and the crunching sound of the earth under Scott's slowly moving car. "Mission accomplished," Glenn sighed contentedly.

Suddenly, the men noticed the body in the car lurch upright behind the wheel. They saw the brake lights of the sedan illuminate the wooded area with a bright red glow, followed by two white lights as Scott grinded the transmission into reverse. Looking through the windshield, Scott realized he had stopped the front-wheel drive vehicle just inches before the precipice. After backing up ten feet, he slammed the car into drive and cut the wheel sharply to the right. He mashed the accelerator to the floorboard, sending clouds of dust in the direction of his panic-stricken observers.

He was roughly jostled as the car careened down the craggy slope. He wasn't even sure where he was, or where he was going. Pure adrenaline was powering his get-away. Glenn tossed away his cigarette and ran around to the driver's side of his car. He jumped in quickly as Cassler fell into the front passenger seat. Glenn smoothly shifted the big Mercedes into drive, turned quickly right and accelerated after the bouncing taillights ahead of them. "Fuck!" Cassler whined. "I thought he was out cold. What if he gets away?"

"He won't," Glenn replied in a cocksure manner. "Once we hit the road, my car will eat his up."

"But, what if…"

"Shut up, Jon!"

"Okay…but this was *your* plan! And now I'm a fucking accomplice! Do you know what kind of trouble…"

"Shut the fuck up!" Glenn scowled at Cassler.

The steel-belted radials gripped the asphalt and pulled Scott's car on to the road. The steering wheel momentarily whipped out of his hands, and the car lurched across the remote two-lane street. Regaining control, he released the over-drive button and stomped on the accelerator. The tires chirped as the engine revved.

Scott looked frantically for street signs or any familiar landmarks. So far, nothing looked familiar. In his rear view mirror, through the dust, he saw Glenn's headlights jump on the black top behind him. IMPER-IAL HWY was printed on a sign ahead. Scott cut the wheel hard to the left and headed west. He couldn't reach his Thomas Guide, but was pretty sure Imperial would take him all the way into LA, and dump him out somewhere around LAX, he thought. He figured he just had to stay ahead of Glenn until they hit a more populated area, and then he could lose him.

Glenn turned off the air conditioner, as he watched the speedometer crack 100 miles per hour. "What did you do that for? I'm hot."

"Shut up, you pussy. The car can go faster without the A/C draining its power."

Glenn was aware that the gap between the vehicles was beginning to close. He watched Scott pass an eighteen-wheeler up ahead. Glenn prepared to execute the same maneuver, when he heard the high-pitched wail of a siren. Blue lights flashed in his rear-view mirror. He craned his head around to see a motorcycle cop behind him. "We're fucked! We are so fucked!" Cassler moaned.

"I'm not going to tell you again, you better shut up before I beat you to death." Cassler pondered the possibility of Glenn's threat as the Mercedes slowed down and pulled over to the shoulder.

The motorcycle cop zipped up behind them and slid to a stop. He stepped off the bike, and walked purposely toward the driver's side of the car. The roadside gravel crunched beneath his boots. Glenn lowered the electrically powered window. "Evening, Officer."

"What's the hurry, sir?"

"I don't think I was the fastest car on the road. Did you notice that white car ahead of me? He was *really* moving."

"Yeah, but I caught you. Tough break, pal. I need to see your license and registration."

"Uh, sure, Officer. You wouldn't happen to know Lieutenant Andy Cavanarro would you?"

"Let me guess, he's your brother?"

Glenn handed his driver's license and auto registration form to the motorcycle cop. "No, just a good friend. A real good friend."

The cop read the license and pulled out his metal clipboard and began to fill out the information required on the ticket form.

"Had anything to drink tonight, Mr. Stevens."

"No, sir, Officer. Do I need to get out of the car?"

The cop stared into his clear eyes. "That won't be necessary. Mr. Stevens, I'm writing you a ticket for speeding—I clocked you doing one-hundred in a fifty five-zone—maybe your good friend the Lieutenant will fix this for you. I think he'll agree with me that I was just doing my job." He handed the clipboard through the window to Glenn. "Sign by the X, sir. You can pay your fine by check; just send it to the address on the back. If you decide to appeal, you can call the number on the front to schedule a court date. Any questions?"

Glenn hurriedly scribbled his name. "No sir, Officer."

"Top copy's yours. You keep the speed down and keep it on the road, okay?"

"Sure. Thank you," Glenn said sarcastically, as he returned the cop's clipboard.

"We are so *screwed*," Cassler whimpered. Glenn glared at him in a threatening manner. Cassler looked away as Glenn pulled back on to Imperial Highway.

*   *   *

SCOTT FOLLOWED the signs to LAX. He parked in short-term parking and entered the terminal. He walked into the men's room, looked in the mirror and noticed the dried blood on the side of his head. He turned the sink on and ripped off a paper towel from the dispenser. He soaked the towel and gently removed the blood from his scalp. He splashed water on his face and ran his wet fingers through his hair. He noticed a small Asian man with a camera around his neck behind him, apparently waiting for his turn at the sink. "All yours, buddy," Scott said, as he threw the damp towel in the trashcan.

Out in the terminal, he made his way over to a bank of pay phones. His head was throbbing as he leaned into a vacant telephone stall. He recalled seeing the cop pull over Glenn's Mercedes behind him. That was the only break he'd gotten all night. He opened the folded sheet of laser printer paper he had found in his car. It was a suicide note, composed by Glenn he supposed, stating that he had killed Lisa and was now going to kill himself. Their plan would have worked if he hadn't regained consciousness when he did. Probably a good thing the cop didn't pull him over, cruising around with this note and a dead girlfriend back at his apartment. The absurdity of it all made his head pound even worse.

He removed his wallet, and fingered through the various slots and compartments until he found a card with the LAPD logo. He didn't have any change on him, so he pulled out his Campbell Industries calling card and dialed the telephone number beneath Lieutenant Andrew Cavanarro's name.

CHAPTER 32

STEVENS AND CASSLER sat in a red vinyl booth overlooking the traffic and strange Hollyweird pedestrians along Sunset Boulevard. A heavy-set waitress delivered two cups of coffee. She asked if she could get them anything else, but was shooed away by Glenn. They had resumed their pursuit of Murphy to no avail, and sat in silence, pondering their next move. Cassler wanted to complain about their predicament, but thought better of it as he observed Glenn's intense, steely-eyed expression. He slowly sipped his coffee, while Glenn rhythmically mixed in artificial creamer with a spoon.

The chirping ring of Glenn's cell phone broke the silence. The two men stared at each other, both wondering if Glenn should answer. After the third ring, he pulled the phone from the inside pocket of his suit jacket and flipped it open. "Hello?"

"The eagle has landed."

"Who is this?"

"Glenn, it's Andy. I understand you have a problem."

"What are you talking about?"

"Oh, I thought you might be looking for one of your employees…Scott Murphy?"

"Uh, maybe."

"Well, *he* seems to think so. He just called me…"

Glenn covered the phone with his hand and said to Cassler, "Murphy called Lieutenant Cavanarro."

"…he thinks you killed his girlfriend, and that you tried to frame him for her murder. You can imagine my surprise…"

"Where is he now?"

"Oh, we've arranged to meet shortly. Turns out he wasn't kidding about his girlfriend…I contacted the Long Beach PD and they sent a car over to his apartment, and sure enough, dead girlfriend. They tell me it looks like she was strangled. They said she was quite a looker, too. What a shame."

"And you think I had something to do with it?"

"Hey, I'm not a judge, pal. I'm just passing along some info I thought you might find *valuable,* if you know what I mean."

"Can you tell me where you're going to meet him?"

"That depends…"

"Depends on what?"

"If you brought your checkbook, my friend. I figure that being the solid citizen you are, that you would like to steer way clear of this mess, and avoid any unnecessary grief or confusion."

"You're right, Andy. I would hate to be considered guilty by association."

"I knew you would."

"Would fifty grand make this go away?"

"*Fifty grand!*" Cassler blurted. Glenn scowled at him, as an elderly black man in the adjacent booth turned to see who was talking about such a large sum of money. Glenn's menacing grimace shifted in his direction, and he quickly turned around.

"Well, you know I consider you to be a friend, Glenn…"

"I know you do, Andy."

"…and I guess that sounds like a nice round number."

"Okay Andy, but I obviously don't have it on me. I can get it for you tomorrow. I'll have to make a withdrawal from my 401K."

"Guess you wouldn't want Pam finding out. Hey, whatever it takes. I know you're good for it, pal. Tell you what…Murphy is going to meet me at eleven o'clock at the sports bar in the LAX Marriott on Century. I'm in my car and headed there now. But let's not meet there, it's too public."

"Where then?" Glenn asked, as Cassler looked on anxiously, trying to fill in the gaps of the one-sided conversation he was listening to.

"Do you know where that triple-X adult bookstore is on Century?"

"Sure. Big sign, real eyesore, can't miss it."

"That's the one. Why don't you meet me there at 11:30, and I'll hand him over to you—nice and gift wrapped."

*   *   *

A SPARSE CROWD patronized the Champions Sports Bar this Thursday night. Assorted team pennants and sports memorabilia was displayed on every available inch of wall space. Top-40 music was playing on the sound system. Scott was seated on a stool at the end of the bar, facing the entrance. He looked at his watch and noted that it was now five past eleven. He would give Lt. Cavanarro another ten minutes. The bartender with the name badge declaring, *"Hi! I'm Ted,"* refilled his glass without asking. Scott quickly threw back his third Jack Daniel's on the rocks.

He looked up to notice Lt. Cavanarro walk through the entrance with the swagger of a bully sizing up the schoolyard. He descended down the ramp leading to the bar and stopped as he tapped a cigarette against the face of his watch to pack the tobacco. The heavy-set man studied the bar's inhabitants. Scott had never personally met the Lieutenant, but had seen him when he came and spoke to the Campbell employees about the Maria Lopez case. Scott stood and waved his hand, catching Lt. Cavanarro's eye. The policeman nodded in acknowledgment, and lit his cigarette.

The multi-colored overhead lights reflected off Lt. Cavanarro's slickly gelled hair as he approached Scott. "I figured you were Murphy. Only guy in the bar wearing a tie." Scott had forgotten that he was still wearing his work clothes. Given the day's events, he obviously had not had a chance to change into something more casual.

Lt. Cavanarro straddled the stool next to Scott. "Sounds like you've had one helluva night." Scott nodded in agreement to his stating of the obvious. "You did the right thing calling me. Did you call anyone else?" he asked, as smoke streamed from his nostrils.

"No."

"Good. Your story checks out. We found your girlfriend. I'm sorry."

"What about Glenn Stevens? Have you found *him?*"

"Not yet, but I've issued an APB. I'll tell ya, he doesn't seem the type to pull something like this."

"I guess you don't know him too well." Scott stared at the burly man, and noticed he wouldn't make eye contact with him.

"You're right, I don't." He held up his hand to get the attention of Ted the bartender. "How 'bout a martini over here, dry with two onions. What are you drinking?"

"Jack Daniel's. I didn't think you guys were supposed to drink on duty."

"I'm not on duty. Hey, and a Jack Black for my friend."

"Excuse me sir, but there's no smoking inside, it's the state law," Ted the bartender apologetically explained.

Lt. Cavanarro opened his suit jacket to reveal his badge clipped to the inside pocket. "Call a cop, numb nuts," he told Ted with a shit eating-grin. Ted shrugged his shoulders and began to prepare the Lieutenant's drink order.

The drinks were placed before the two men, and Scott quickly downed his. He watched Lt. Cavanarro slowly sip his drink. His expensive tie, starched, pinpoint shirt and Rolex looked out of place on a cop. Scott remembered having the same thought when the Lieutenant addressed the employees at the office.

"You said something about a note?" Cavanarro asked Scott without looking at him.

"Yeah, check this out," Scott replied as he pulled the crumpled, folded paper from his shirt pocket. "It's my confession *and* suicide letter."

"Hmmmmm," the Lieutenant said as he scanned the note, rubbing his chin with his hand. "Pretty damning stuff, huh?"

"They had everything planned out—except for me escaping." Lt. Cavanarro didn't comment, re-read the note, folded it and stuck it in his shirt pocket.

The burly cop finished his drink, and slid the baby pearl onions off the swizzle stick and into his mouth with his teeth. He smiled at a passing waitress wearing a short denim skirt. Glancing down at his diamond-crusted time piece, he said, "Well, we better get you to the station. You'll be safe there—but you won't get much rest—there are a lot of questions to answer."

"I couldn't sleep if I wanted to."

"Let's go," Lt. Cavanarro said, as he stubbed out his cigarette in his empty glass and threw a twenty-dollar bill on the bar. As he sauntered toward the exit, Scott stepped down off his bar stool and followed.

Out in the parking lot, Lt. Cavanarro stopped and turned to face Scott once they had reached his unmarked cruiser. "Oh, uh, you'll have to ride in the back, and, uh, since you're technically a suspect, I'm gonna have to cuff you. Standard procedure, you know."

Scott noticed that the Lieutenant still would not make eye contact with him. Warily, he said, "Okay," and extended his arms, palms up. Lt. Cavanarro closed a stainless steel bracelet on his right wrist, and walked the arm behind Scott's back. He reached around, pulled back his left arm and snapped the connected handcuff to his left wrist. Scott heard several metallic clicks, as the Lieutenant tightened the restraints.

Cavanarro slapped his paw of a hand on Scott's head, and his thick gold ring band stung Scott's scalp. "Watch your head," he said as he pushed him below the doorframe, and Scott lowered himself into the back seat.

The unmarked Ford bolted left out of the Marriott's parking lot and crossed the oncoming traffic. The stout man aligned the vehicle in the inside lane as he accelerated. "What station are you taking me to?" Scott asked to the back of Lt. Cavanarro's head. No answer followed, but Scott looked in the rear-view mirror and for the first time tonight, made eye contact with the cop. The glance was fleeting, but there was no mistaking the sinister look in his eyes. Warning bells were ringing in Scott's head. He'd try again. "Maybe you didn't hear me, I asked you..."

They hadn't gone far when the car braked hard, sending Scott hurtling into the rigid wire mesh between them. The car turned sharply left into a parking lot under a huge illuminated sign advertising adult books, videos and novelties. When they reached the back of the lot, Lt. Cavanarro turned the car hard to the right, accelerated, and quickly slammed on the brakes. Once again, the cold, hard wire barrier greeted Scott's face.

As Scott awkwardly slid back into his seat, Lt. Cavanarro threw the vehicle into park, turned off the headlights, and shut off the engine. A car parked about thirty yards in front of them flashed their headlights. Lt. Cavanarro answered by pulling back on his turn signal lever, flashing his high beams twice. He then opened his door and gripped the steering wheel to pull himself out of the driver's seat. Opening the rear door next to Scott, he gruffly said, "Get out." Scott looked up at him, but he was looking in the direction of the car parked in front of them. "C'mon, let's go!" he barked as he grabbed Scott by the left arm and pulled him from the back seat.

Scott couldn't see them in the darkness, but he heard the sounds of two car doors opening and closing, followed by what sounded like two pairs of footsteps. Lt. Cavanarro reached behind the driver's seat and removed a black, wooden nightstick. Before Scott realized what was happening, he was struck sharply across the shins. The searing pain dropped him to his knees. A second blow was delivered sharply to the back of his head.

Scott tried to stay conscious, as his head was brutally throbbing. Trying to focus, he noticed what appeared to be a familiar pair of highly polished, black, cap-toed oxfords and a pair of cordovan loafers in front of him. He could make out Lt. Cavanarro asking, "Why did you bring him?"

A familiar voice answered, "He's okay. He works for me."

Lt. Cavanarro opened the trunk of his car and removed a bundle of nylon rope. "Tie him up," he heard Lt. Cavanarro order the new arrivals. Scott felt rope being laced around his legs and across his torso. Two sets of strong arms lifted him from the ground, pulled him for a short distance, and threw him into the back seat of a car. He woozily held his head up and blinked hard, trying to clear his blurred vision. He couldn't make out whom the two men were walking away with the Lieutenant, but he did make out the Mercedes star embossed on the steering wheel of the car.

Stevens and Cassler followed Lt. Cavanarro back to his government issued sedan. He leaned into the trunk, shuffled its contents for a moment, and emerged with a small leather pouch. He unzipped the pouch and produced a small handgun with a chrome slide and mother-of-pearl handgrips. "This is untraceable, Glenn. Took it off some gang-bangers in Compton. It's a twenty-five caliber—a Saturday Night Special. I suggest you take him up to the mountains, and make it look like a suicide. This note would be a nice touch," he said as he handed the confession note back to its author.

"We've got it covered, Andy," Glenn said with a sincere tone of grati-tude. "Let's meet for lunch tomorrow to settle up."

"The Formosa in Hollywood, eleven-thirty."

"I'll see you then."

Lt. Cavanarro pulled a small, silver key from his front pocket and tossed it to Glenn. "Take the cuffs off him, and bring them back to me tomorrow." He shook a cigarette out of a pack of Lucky Strikes, tapped it on his watch face, lit it with his Zippo and took a long drag. Exhaling in the direction of Cassler, he offered one to Stevens, who accepted and lit his with the borrowed lighter. "Fuck this up, Glenn, and I can't help you."

"No problem, Andy. I can handle it."

CHAPTER 33

GLENN STEVENS PILOTED the powerful Mercedes through the winding isolated road called Highway 395. His headlights pierced the dark wilderness. The only other light came from the headlights of the car trailing him, driven by Jon Cassler. His restrained passenger was going in and out of consciousness in the back seat. Glenn monitored him closely in the rear view mirror. A small roadside marker indicated they were passing a historic site that was once a camp used to house Japanese-American P.O.W.s. A lone billboard with peeling paint stated that one should not miss Santa's Village on one's next visit to Arrowhead. He remembered reading that Santa's Village had closed a couple of years ago. It was being razed to accommodate the hordes of urban dwellers wishing to own a weekend retreat in the great outdoors. Glenn pondered the conflicting ideals of a former P.O.W. camp and Santa's Village co-existing in such close proximity to one another.

He figured there was no need to drive all the way to Mammoth. Bishop was closer and probably even more isolated. Typically a haven for trout fishermen, December should find the remote area very secluded. There would be no witnesses, and no mistakes *this* time. His confidence in the successful execution of his plan grew with every passing mile, but suddenly wavered as he passed a sign indicating that the Boron Federal Penitentiary was out in the darkness, on the right. No way in hell he'd ever spend a single day in a place like that. He was too smart, he assured himself.

The speed limit dropped to thirty-five as they cruised through the commercial district of Bishop, California. It was now 2:15 AM, and all the small shops were shut down for the evening. He motored by Brock's Sporting Goods, a bait and tackle shop, a gas station, a drive-in burger joint and a small white building with the word ANTIQUES painted in red across a large window. He flipped on his turn signal for Cassler's benefit, and turned right on the first paved road. There were no streetlights or directional signs, but to the best of his recollection he was headed toward the Owens River. He clicked on his high beams and continued on as the main highway disappeared from his view.

Moments later, he felt like he had gotten his bearings when he recognized an ancient stone and wood water well on the left hand side of the road. He turned left off the road past the well, and slowly proceeded along the grassy terrain. Cassler also pulled off the road and followed the taillights of the Mercedes through the billowing dust. About two hundred yards later, Glenn parked his car and killed the engine and the lights. Cassler pulled along side him and did the same.

By this time, Scott was fairly coherent and fully aware of his predicament. "Where in the hell are you taking me?" he blurted out.

Glenn glanced up at his rear view mirror and observed the younger man glaring menacingly at him from the back seat. "You'll find out soon enough," he answered smugly. "Have a nice nap?" Scott did not respond. He strained against the handcuffs and the nylon rope cutting into his ankles. More rope was wound so tightly around his chest it made breathing difficult. He was still in shock over Lt. Cavanarro's betrayal. He wished he had called Kevin…Allen…Nick Lunsford, or even Judge LeDoux, instead. The more he thought about it, he guessed that maybe calling Sgt. Mike Harris would have been a better move—he certainly didn't seem to be cut from the same cloth as Cavanarro.

Cassler took out his handkerchief and wiped down the interior of Scott's Maxima. He left the keys in the ignition, and placed the confession/suicide note on the dashboard. He then stepped out closed the door and wiped off the handle. He walked over to where Glenn was standing, guided by the amber glow of a freshly lit cigarette. He noticed movement from the shadow in the rear of the Mercedes. "Is he awake?" he inquired tentatively.

"Yeah, came to a little while ago. Mad as a wet hornet, too."

"So, what's the plan?"

Glenn took a slow drag of the Camel. His eyes locked on Cassler's. "We'll do it here." He filled his lungs with smoke and nicotine one last time, and flipped the butt into the wooded area behind him. "Help me pull him out of the car." Glenn opened the left rear door and grabbed two handfuls of the rope tied around Scott. Placing his foot against the doorframe for leverage, he jerked Scott up and off the seat. Cassler knelt down on one knee under Glenn, and reached in to get a hold of Scott's legs. He heard Glenn suck in a deep breath, and together they pulled their victim from the sedan. Glenn held Scott upright momentarily, just long enough for Scott to spit in his face. Glenn threw him roughly to the ground. "You little bastard!" he said, wiping the expectorate from his face.

"Go to hell!" Scott screamed as he rolled over to face his abductors.

"You'll be there holding the door for me, Murphy," Glenn said snidely. "I tell you what, Jon, I think I'm gonna enjoy killing this punk as much as I did Lisa."

"Why did you kill her, Stevens?" Scott demanded.

"*Why?* Because I could. Because I can do any fucking thing I want to."

"Did you rape her, you son-of-a bitch?" Scott asked with a raspy voice.

Glenn laughed softly and said, "No, I wanted to fuck her, I mean *really* fuck her brains out, but unfortunately, I had to kill her first. She put up a good fight, I can tell you that. She was a feisty little bitch. But, I must confess," he said in a cynical tone, "I did think about it afterwards.

Now, I'm no necrophiliac, but if I ever was going to fuck a corpse, her hot little body would have been a prime candidate."

"You're one sick son-of-a bitch, Stevens."

Cassler interrupted their dialogue, "Why don't you ask me if I fucked her?"

"Why would I do that, Jon? You're a homosexual."

"I am *not!*"

"Jon, everybody knows you're a homosexual—hey, but to each his own," Scott said, watching the nervous, overweight man look at Glenn as if he were waiting for him to jump in and correct this statement.

"Glenn! You know I'm not gay!"

"Frankly Jon, I could really care less, you're too good a whipping boy."

"I'm *not* your whipping boy! And I'm not gay! I'm married! Glenn, you know my wife!"

Scott interjected, "It's a known fact, Jon, that a large percentage of homosexual men are married and have kids. It's their cover—their way of trying to blend in—but I guess you'd know more about that than me."

Cassler kicked Scott sharply in the ribs. "Shut the fuck up! I ought to kick your ass!"

"Like you did at Calamity Jane's?"

"You sucker punched me!" Cassler had now worked himself into a full-fledged frenzy.

"Okay. Let's make it fair. Untie me, you little weasel, and I'll let you take the first shot." Scott's eyes narrowed defiantly.

Cassler kicked him in the ribs again. "I'll untie you after you're dead, you arrogant prick!"

Scott grimaced from the blow. "Gee, don't get so upset Jon—I won't tell anyone you're gay. I won't even tell about all the times I passed you in the hallway, only to turn around and catch you looking at my ass. Your little secret's safe with me."

Cassler began to stomp around in small circles, absolutely furious that he had been unexpectedly outed. Glenn's laughter broke through his seething trance.

"What is so fucking funny? Huh?" Cassler snapped at Glenn.

"He's right."

"Right about what? That I'm gay?"

"I told you I don't give a shit about that. He's right about your secret being safe." He waved the pistol at Cassler. "Dead men tell no tales, Jon."

Cassler stared at the gun for several moments without making a sound. He finally took his eyes off the weapon and looked at Glenn. "You never said I had to do it."

"C'mon Jon, you *owe* this son-of-a bitch. Remember? He humiliated you in front of the entire sales team. Remember your bloody nose? I still hear the guys talking about it. It's pay-back time."

Glenn noticed the lenses of Cassler's thick glasses were beginning to fog up in the cool night air. He could see perspiration beading up on his forehead in the moonlight. Cassler stammered, "Yeah, but…Glenn, I, uh…I know, why don't you untie him, I'll kick his ass, then *you* can finish him off."

"Because, if I untie him, he'll kick *your* ass. C'mon, take the gun. You're in this as deep as I am, pal."

"But, I…"

"Take the fucking gun and put a bullet in his brain, you little pansy, before I put one in you!" Glenn said ominously. He leveled the gun at Cassler, then slowly turned it around and offered him the handle. "Take it!"

From his vantage point, Scott observed Cassler's shaking hands take the gun from Glenn. Glenn smiled at his nervous subordinate and said, "Just aim for the head, and pull the trigger. It's easy."

Jon nodded as if he were in agreement, and pointed the twenty-five-caliber firearm at Scott's temple. His right hand was shaking violently, and he clasped his left hand around it to steady his aim. Leaning over, he looked back at Glenn. His mentor nodded in approval. "You want to beg for mercy, asshole?" Cassler asked with a high-pitched, cracking voice. Lying on his back, Scott stared up directly into the beady eyes of the trembling man and clenched his jaws in response. Cassler squeezed the trigger two times in rapid succession. The sounds of the gunfire echoed across the still wilderness. His hands were still shaking as Glenn removed the Saturday Night Special from his sweaty grip. The standing men observed a small pool of dark liquid forming against the earth under Scott's head in the darkness.

"Why in the hell did you shoot him twice? This was supposed to look like a suicide!" Glenn muttered as he wiped off the pistol with his handkerchief.

"I didn't know what to expect—I've never fired a gun before, asshole!"

Laying the pistol on the ground next to Scott's motionless face, he ordered Cassler to help him untie him. Cassler tried to regain his composure, and obliged Glenn's request. Once they had removed the nylon cord, Glenn gently turned Scott on his side and unlocked the handcuffs. Stashing the cuffs and the key his rear pocket, he eased the lifeless body over, and positioned the right arm as if he was waving hello. Using his handkerchief, he picked up the pistol and placed it in the palm of Scott's hand. Using a handful of the nylon rope, he brushed the ground around the body, as he walked several concentric circles, shuffling backwards.

He stopped beside Cassler who was taking in the scene. His face was expressionless. "I'm gonna start the car and back up about a hundred feet," he said, as he handed Cassler the bundle of nylon rope. "You follow me and brush over the tire tracks, and be sure to turn around and brush away your footprints as you go."

Cassler took the rope and stared at Glenn with a look of concern. "You're not thinking about leaving me out here are you?"

"Not until you just brought it up. Sounds like a helluva idea." Glenn laughed out loud at Cassler's troubled expression. "I'm just bullshitting you, man. C'mon, we're partners! Just do as I said so we can wrap this up and get the hell out of Dodge." He slapped Cassler on the shoulder, trying to instill a sense of confidence in the worried little man.

Glenn started the car and began to slowly back up. Cassler did as instructed, looking up frequently to make sure the Mercedes was still in front of him. After they conducted this exercise for about one hundred feet, Glenn wheeled the car in a half-circle and stopped. He leaned over the driver's seat, and watched Cassler brush across the tracks of the car and his footsteps with a bent over, crab-like gait. Once finished, he scurried to the car, opened the heavy door and plopped into the front passenger seat. Not saying a word, he cranked the air-conditioner full blast, and proceeded to direct all the dashboard vents in his direction.

"I guess that about does it," Glenn said to the visibly shaken man. "Let's get back to LA."

As the black car sped off in the direction of the two-lane highway, leaving a dusty trail in its wake, a stout man stepped out from behind a large oak tree. Once he was sure the occupants of the fleeing vehicle could not see him, he quickly jogged in the direction of the fallen man.

CHAPTER 34

THE WESTERN REGION OFFICE of Campbell Industries was buzzing with unusual electricity for a Friday morning. A Detective from the Long Beach Police Department greeted Regina at 8:00 AM. A representative of the LAPD soon joined him. Word of Lisa LeDoux's horrific demise at Scott Murphy's apartment spread quickly among the work force by all modern means of electronic communication available. E-mails, voicemails and pagers were working overtime as the office grapevine was in full gear.

Kevin Forrester and Jimmy Brady were in the small conference room, meeting with the Long Beach Detective. Kevin looked like he was in shock, while Jimmy looked down at the table, leaning forward on his elbows. "I just can't fathom that Scott is in any way responsible for this tragedy. I just don't think he had it in him." He sighed deeply, and shook his head slowly from side to side. "What a tragedy. What an unbelievable tragedy."

"So it's your opinion that Mr. Murphy was incapable of committing such a heinous act?" the Detective asked with a clipped delivery.

"That's right. You can put me down for no way, there's just *no* way."

"I have to agree with Jimmy," Kevin added. "Look, Scott's a straight-arrow, man. Not an evil bone in his body. We became pretty good friends over the last few months, and I think I got to know him pretty well. He's a real stand-up guy. I'd trust him with my own sister. I think somebody's trying to pin this on him, man."

The Detective flipped back to a page in his legal pad. He quickly read his notes, and stated, "It's my understanding that Mr. Murphy assaulted one of your Sales Managers, Mr. Cassler, in a public place."

Visibly agitated, Kevin snapped, "Did Cassler tell you that? That's a crock, ask Allen Goldman. He was in the men's room when it happened. Scott was acting strictly in self-defense. That worm Cassler wouldn't get out of his face."

The Detective scribbled a few notes, removed two business cards and placed one in front of each man. "You've both been very helpful. I appreciate your candor. If you think of anything else that might be relevant, call me at this number."

Kevin and Jimmy left the conference room and were greeted by Allen and Tim Newsom. "We're next in the box," Allen said, trying to inject some levity. "How'd it go in there?"

"We told him that we don't think Scott could be involved with this in any way," Jimmy answered.

"Yeah, I don't believe Scott had it in him, man. This reeks of a set-up," Kevin added.

"I wouldn't be so sure, you know that *Southern gentleman* routine, what a bunch of bullshit," Tim said sarcastically.

"Got a problem with the South, you little pencil-neck?" Jimmy asked in a threatening tone as he squared up against the shorter man.

"No, it's just that…"

"You better watch what you say next, Tim, a good ass-kicking could be riding on it, dude," Kevin said, stabbing a finger in Tim's sternum.

Allen stepped in front of Tim, facing Jimmy and Kevin. "Okay guys, everyone's nerves are a little frayed right now…"

"Don't defend this punk, Allen," Kevin blurted, no longer wishing to conceal his mounting anger. "He's never been a real team member, I don't care *how* much he sells! He belongs on Cassler's team with all the other snakes!" Tim was squirming behind Allen, now his human shield.

"Let's just cool it, guys. We're going to go in there and see if we can be of any help. Jimmy, why don't you take Kevin out for some fresh air and buy him a cup of coffee? I want to take everybody on the team to lunch so we can discuss this later, okay?"

"Sure, Allen. We'll see ya'll back here in a little while. C'mon, Kev," Jimmy said as he placed an arm around Kevin's tense shoulder. Allen nodded, as if asking Kevin to take his advice. Kevin studied Allen's gray-flecked beard framing his sincere face. He turned, took a couple of steps with Jimmy, looked back over his shoulder and stared at Tim as if he could burn holes through him with his eyes. Tim smiled weakly, all his cocky, self-assured confidence drained. The Detective opened the conference room door, exchanged introductions with Allen and Tim as they followed him inside. Kevin glanced back one last time to see the door close shut.

They passed Regina Rogers, who looked as if she'd been crying. Toni Hemmings stood next to Regina's workstation, visibly shaken. Jimmy spoke to the sad women, "We're gonna grab a cup of coffee. Can we bring ya'll anything, Regina? Toni?"

Regina smiled the best she could. "No thanks, guys. But I appreciate it." Toni looked up at them briefly with glassy eyes, but didn't respond.

"Take it easy," Kevin said as they walked on.

They passed the closed door of Glenn Stevens' office. They could see the lights on through the slits in the Venetian blinds covering the rectangular window. In the lobby, Lori Johnson was leaning over her receptionist's desk, headset on, with her mouthpiece tilted up and away from her mouth as she spoke with Janet Carter. "Morning, ladies," Jimmy greeted them.

"Hi, guys," the two young women said in unison. Janet's face was clouded with a look of real concern as she queried, "I guess you both heard about Lisa, huh?"

"Just finished talking to a cop from Long Beach," Kevin answered.

Lori asked sheepishly, "I, uh, I heard they found her at Scott Murphy's apartment."

"Rumor has it," Jimmy said quietly.

Lori continued, "He was so cute and polite. He was the only gut that ever stood up to Glenn—ever. I'll never forget that. He seemed like such a decent guy."

"He *is* a decent guy," Kevin corrected her.

"Has anybody heard from him this morning?" Janet asked the group. They all somberly shook their heads in the negative. "I wonder where he is?"

Lori softly said, "I know Regina has tried his apartment, cell phone and pager. No answer yet."

"He'll turn up, and I'm sure he'll be just as shocked and outraged about this as we all are," Jimmy stated as if he were hoping saying it out loud would make the thought more convincing. His Alabama twang was no longer apparent in his seriousness.

"I hope so," Kevin said, shuffling to the door. "I would hate to think that Lisa's murderer has already killed Scott, too." The two men left and the two women resumed their verbal speculation.

*   *   *

THE FORMOSA WAS PACKED for lunch. Glenn couldn't figure out why anyone would want to eat here. He thought the place was a total dump. Standing in the small foyer next to a cigarette machine, he peered around the establishment, but saw no sign of Lt. Cavanarro. A sleep deprived looking waitress holding a stack of menus against her hip stepped forward to greet him. "Welcome to the Formosa," she said as if she were reading the line. "Are you here for lunch?"

"Yes, I'm meeting someone."

"Two for lunch? We have about a fifteen to twenty minute wait, but you can sit in the bar now if you want. You can order sandwiches there."

"That'll work."

"Right over there," she said pointing to the long bar on her right, and then looked past him to greet the patrons behind him, letting him know that she would not be leading him to his seat at the bar. He proceeded to the bar, and stepped up on a red Naugahyde covered bar stool. He ordered a scotch and water, single malt, from the bartender and checked his watch. It read 11:35 AM. He had spoken to Andy earlier this morning, and re-confirmed the time. The movement along the bar of a long, dark brown cockroach grabbed his attention. He watched the insect methodically weave in and out of the glasses stacked at the end of the bar.

A large hand slapped him firmly on the back. "Punctual as always, Glenn. One of your better traits, huh?" Lt. Cavanarro stepped around him and mounted the stool to his right.

Glenn smiled and said unconvincingly, "Good to see you, Andy."

The bartender delivered Glenn's drink, and asked if Cavanarro wanted anything. "I'll have a dry martini…and bring me a Rueben sandwich and some chips. You eating, Glenn?"

"No, just drinking," he answered, casting a quick look in the direction of the cockroach. He took a large gulp of the scotch and water. "You wouldn't believe the cops crawling all over the office this morning."

"Why wouldn't I? You have one employee found dead—in the apartment of a fellow employee—and two employees that turn up missing in the last three months. I'd say the boys have probable cause to poke around a little."

"What do you mean, *two* missing?" Glenn asked as he tried to decipher the Lieutenant's statement.

"First, did you bring something for me?" The greedy look in his eyes confirmed what he was really interested in. Glenn produced the borrowed stainless steel handcuffs and slid them across the bar. He then removed the key from his pocket and placed it on top of the cuffs. "Yeah, okay, thanks…but I was thinking something more monetary in nature, if you get my drift," the cop said, raising an eyebrow.

"Yeah, just picked it up from the credit union." Glenn glanced nervously over both shoulders. The crowded restaurant seemed oblivious to them. He reached inside his jacket, and removed two thickly stuffed envelopes. He placed the envelopes nonchalantly on the bar in front of them and slid it in front of Lt. Cavanarro. "There ya go, Andy. You won't need to count it here."

The dirty cop laughed out loud at Glenn's statement and at the ease of collecting his biggest score ever. "I'm not worried, pal. I know where you live." He greedily tucked the envelopes in a small briefcase he had brought along just for this purpose. His drink arrived, and he lifted his martini glass and gestured to Glenn, who in turn clinked his tumbler against Andy's glass. "Pleasure doin' business with ya, pal."

"Sure. Now tell me what you meant when you said *two* employees are missing?"

"Like I said, missing. No sign of Mr. Murphy in Bishop."

"What?" Glenn blurted out loudly, and noticed that he now had the attention of several people in the crowded restaurant. "Did you go where I told you, first right off the main drag and left at the well?"

"I didn't go personally…"

"Don't tell me you called the local yokels!"

"We did call the Inyo County Sheriff's Department, but only to meet one of my guys when he got there. You know, common courtesy, to let someone know when you're gonna be nosing around their backyard. Don't worry, I sent a good man. Told him he was checking out an anonymous tip I'd received. He didn't mind too much, either. I told him to bring his gear and take the rest of the day off and try his luck fishing." Andy's sandwich was delivered, and he wrapped his hands around it and picked up the sloppy creation.

Before it reached his mouth, Glenn grabbed the Lieutenant around the wrist, squeezing the links of the Rolex's bracelet into his flesh. "It warms my heart that you're such a compassionate boss, but how could your fuck-up miss a dead body? With directions, no less."

Lt. Cavanarro looked Glenn in the eyes, and then at the hand holding his arm. "I would seriously suggest you let go of my arm, pal." Glenn did as he was instructed, realizing after the fact what an iron grip he'd had on the man's wrist. Andy took a big bite of his sandwich, and chewed it slowly, fully aware of the imploring look riveted on the face of his companion. He swallowed and took a sip of his martini. Out of the corner of his eye, he looked at Glenn and said, "We didn't find a body. But we did find some evidence. Your directions were fine, the success of your execution is what seems to lacking."

"What kind of evidence?"

"My man went just where you told me to go. He did find some blood, a couple of shell casings from a twenty-five caliber pistol, some footprints, tire tracks, and the imprint of what appeared to be a scuffle, or somebody being dragged into the brush. But no corpse. Why would he find two shells?"

"Two shots were fired. It was an accident."

"Two shots for a suicide?"

"Never mind that! What about Murphy's car?"

"No car."

"No car? Where in the hell did he go?"

"How should I know? We called the local hospital—no Scott Murphy or John Doe has been admitted. One guy was admitted for a gunshot wound…Beachum, something or other. Hunting accident—my man said it checked out. At first I thought maybe a bear or a mountain lion had dragged Murphy off, but then I couldn't figure out why they'd wanna take the car and the pistol. And you can't rule out alien abduction…"

"Get serious."

"I don't know, anytime I've ever shot someone, I didn't have to worry about them going anywhere." Andy chuckled, clearly enjoying Glenn's predicament.

"He *was* shot. I saw it with my own two eyes," Glenn mumbled low. "He was dead as a doornail." He went over what had taken place in his mind as he absent-mindedly swirled the ice cubes in is glass. Andy continued to eat his lunch.

Glenn turned and scowled accusingly at the Lieutenant. "So what are you guys going do to about him? If he's not dead, you've got to find him, right? He's still your number one suspect, isn't he?"

Andy wiped his mouth with his napkin. He took another swig of his drink and cleared his throat. He looked at Glenn and said calmly, "Yes, he's still a suspect, and yes, I've put out an APB for his arrest. I did fail to mention to the department that they should be looking for a *dead* guy." Glenn was not amused. "I tell ya what, pal, if we find him, you'll be the first person I call." Lt. Cavanarro got up to leave. And since you got me messed up in this bullshit, if we *don't* find him, you'll still be the first person I call."

"What should I do?"

"Watch your back, pal."

CHAPTER 35

HE OPENED his eyes, but couldn't focus. Blinking repeatedly didn't improve his blurred vision. His body ached and he became acutely aware of a stabbing pain in his head. After what seemed like several minutes had passed, he began to be able to make out some of his surroundings. He first noticed a triangular bar made of tubular steel that was hanging above his head. His body was covered with a white sheet and a white cotton blanket; his head propped on a thin, foam pillow. He tried to clear his throat, and found himself choking on a large plastic tube that ran down his dry throat and was taped to his mouth. He could hear the repetitive beeping sounds of a heartbeat monitor.

As the fog began to clear, he saw a plastic bag hanging from a chrome IV pole. A tube extended from the bag and was attached somewhere on his body, he assumed. He painfully clenched both hands into a fist. He strained to see his feet move at the end of the bed beneath the covers. A wave of relief swept over him as the fear of paralysis subsided.

A solitary window with the shades closed was centered on the wall to his left. There was a worn, brown vinyl couch against the wall, beneath the window. A matching recliner sat next to it. A television mounted on a stand hung on the wall directly in front of him.

Looking to his right, he noticed the wood-grain door swing open, followed by a plump woman with short bottle-dyed, red hair. She was wearing a white smock, and as she approached the end of his bed, he could make out the words Bishop Community Hospital embroidered in cursive on it. She picked up the chart secured to the bed frame, looked at her wristwatch and jotted a few notes. She looked up from the chart with a startled expression, as she noticed that he was conscious and looking at her. "Mr. Beachum—you're awake! That's great! Now you wait right here, and I'll go get Dr. Williams and let him know. Oh, and I'll try to find your uncle…I think I saw him in the waiting room earlier. He's been real worried about you." She had a pleasant smile, and left not waiting for a reply, not that he could if he wanted to, he thought.

A picture with a rustic, wood frame was hung on the wall to his right. He studied the print of a lone fly fisherman in waders and casting into a winding river. He became aware of the adhesive bandages that crowned his head. The painful throbbing in his head intensified. The tube in his mouth was choking him, and he wished he could spit it out. He closed his eyes and tried to put together the series of events that led to him being a patient in this hospital.

The plump nurse burst back through the door with a frantic look on her face. "Omigosh! I forgot your dosage of painkiller! I was so excited to see that you were conscious…but I'll take care of it right away." She stepped over next to the IV pole and turned her back to him. She hummed cheerfully and was working on something unseen by him. She turned around and said soothingly, "There. That should fix you up in no time flat." She had warm, caring eyes and a pleasant smile. It seemed to him that nursing was a very suitable vocation for someone with her demeanor.

*   *   *

WHATEVER PAINKILLER she had administered began to take effect, much to his relief. A tall, thin elderly man in a white lab coat walked through the door. He had small, black-framed glasses perched on his long, thin nose. His snowy-white hair was combed straight back.

"Well, Mr. Beachum, Nurse McDaniel tells me that you're back among the living." He smiled in a grandfatherly way as he sat on the edge of the bed. "I'm Dr. Williams. Let me have a look at you, young man." He clicked on a penlight, and said, "Look straight ahead, please." He could feel the doctor's steady breath against his cheek as the man looked closely into his eyes. "Okay, now I want you to follow my finger, without moving your head." He followed the doctor's finger left and right; up and down. "Excellent," he said in a reassuring way. "You're very lucky, Mr. Beachum. A couple of days ago things were a little touchy, but you've made a lot of progress. Being young and strong certainly didn't hurt you. Now, it's important that you try to rest and not over exert yourself. The initial prognosis looks good, but it's important that you follow all of our directions. We'll need you to help us help you, son. Sound like deal?"

He tried to smile at the doctor, but realized that was impossible with the hollow plastic cylinder in his mouth. Dr. Williams squeezed him on the shoulder, looked in his eyes and smiled confidently. The doctor stood, walked to the foot of the bed and reviewed the chart. He added some notes of his own and nodded at Nurse McDaniel. "Your uncle is waiting outside. I'm going to let him see you for a short visit, how's that sound?" His blue eyes twinkled from behind his glasses, as he smiled at his patient, and walked briskly from the room.

Moments after Dr. Williams left, a man walked purposefully into the room. He was stocky and barrel-chested, about 5'9' or 5'10". He wore circular wire frame glasses with tinted lenses. He was bald on top, with short-cropped gray hair that encircled his round head. He had a thick, bushy mustache that gave him a walrus-like appearance. He looked in the direction of Nurse McDaniel, who was cracking the blinds open. She turned and said, "Oh, hello, Mr. Beachum. Your nephew is doing *much* better, I'm happy to say." As she walked past him she patted him on his burly shoulder. "I'll leave the two of you alone," she said, smiling sweetly.

"Thank you, ma'am," replied Beachum, as he watched her leave the room.

Beachum walked over to the brown recliner, and pulled it over next to the hospital bed. He sat on the edge of the chair and said, "How ya doing, Scott?"

Scott let out a gagging sound, and raised his eyebrows in acknowledgment.

"Under the circumstances, I thought it would be best if I checked you in as my nephew, Scott *Beachum* I have your ID, wallet, clothes, car and everything."

The man shifted in his seat and said, "Let's make this quick, in case the nurse comes in and makes me leave. First, I should tell you that you've been in here for a week." He paused and rubbed his hand over his mustache. "I figure you're wondering how you got here. Well, I was doing a little night fishin' on the Owens River. I heard some voices, and made my way over to see who was making all the ruckus. I crouched below a drop-off and that's where I saw two guys in suits standing over you. You were all tied up and lying on the ground. Before I could do anything, one of them puts two bullets in your head. They untied you, tried to cover their tracks and left in a big, black Mercedes. You remember any of this?"

Scott stared intently at Beachum and nodded slightly in the affirmative.

"I put you in your car—I know it's your car because I read the Tennessee registration—and got you here as fast as I could. I also found the suicide note those two planted in the car—I'm *assuming* they planted it, because with you being all tied up, it sure as hell didn't look like a suicide. The note also said you killed somebody named Lisa LeDoux. Did you?"

Scott's eyes began to well with tears at the thought of Lisa. This was the first recollection of her he'd had since he'd been conscious. He slowly shook his head no.

"I didn't think so," Beachum said sincerely. "Anyway, like I said, I got you here as fast as I could. I checked you in under my name, said you were my nephew, and that you got hit with stray bullets from what I guessed to be somebody illegally hunting at night—I don't know—it was all I could think of on such short notice. Pretty weak, huh?" he said with a slight laugh. "Especially since I brought you in here in a bloody shirt and tie. Doctors haven't really questioned it so far...bullet wounds are not exactly the specialty of these folks up here. I just figured it would be best if I made something up and concealed your name, just in case those two men found out, and wanted to finish what they botched up. Real lucky they were using such a small caliber pistol. And that he was such a lousy shot. Doc told me that one bullet entered and exited along the top of your skull. Doesn't look like it did any serious damage. The other one grazed you above your left ear." He smiled at Scott. "I'm sure it doesn't feel real good right now, but it could've been a lot worse."

Nurse McDaniel entered the room and gestured to her watch. "We'd better let him get some rest, Mr. Beachum."

"Yes, ma'am." He stood and placed a strong hand on Scott's arm. "You hang tough, Scotty. I'll come back and check on you in the morning." The stout man walked past the nurse without looking back. Nurse McDaniel flashed Scott a smile and gave him a little wave as she left the room and pulled the door closed behind her.

The dosage of painkiller had eased the pounding in his skull. The sound of the heart monitor seemed to echo in the quiet room. He noticed through the slightly opened blinds that it was getting dark outside. The weight of his predicament began to settle in. Closing his eyes, he tried to process the information that Beachum had supplied him. He felt like Beachum was a trustworthy man. Not that he would get any awards for shrewd judgment after turning himself in to Lt. Cavanarro. He wondered if the Lieutenant, Stevens and Cassler had any idea he was alive.

CHAPTER 36

"YOUR MOTOR SKILLS seem intact," Dr. Williams said after putting Scott through his paces. For the past week and a half the doctor, assisted by Nurse McDaniel, had monitored Scott as they directed him through a series of physical therapy sessions. Scott learned that there was not a Physical Therapist on the staff at Bishop Community Hospital. "We'll be letting you go home today, son. But I'd like you to schedule a follow-up appointment after the holidays so I can monitor your progress. Okay?"

"Yes, sir," Scott said. "And thanks so much for all that you've done for me, Dr. Williams."

"Just doin' my job. I have to tell you, I like it when they go as well as things have with you, Scott." He smiled, patted Scott on the back, and flashed a thumbs-up sign as he left the room.

Scott was feeling stronger with each day that passed. He noticed in a mirror when Nurse McDaniel was changing his bandages that his head had been completely shaved. He also had two and half weeks worth of beard growth. The nurse had offered to shave his face, but he thought better of it, thinking this new look might assist him in concealing his true identity.

*   *   *

LANGSTON T. BEACHUM had been to the hospital everyday to see how Scott's recovery was coming along. Scott had learned that his first name was Langston, but it was obvious the man preferred to be called *Mister* Beachum. Scott had interrogated the man as to whether or not he knew Glenn Stevens or Lt. Cavanarro. His earnest answers convinced Scott that Beachum didn't know either of them. He was indebted to Beachum for saving his life, and had come to the conclusion that he could trust this man. Not that he had a lot of choice at this point. Beachum had offered to let him stay at his place while he determined what his next move should be. Since no one else had offered to put him up, and he was pretty sure he just couldn't waltz into the office tomorrow or fly home to Memphis, it seemed like the only logical option.

Beachum had even brought him a new pair of jogging shoes, new blue jeans, two packs each of Hanes T-shirts and underwear, a six-pack of white cotton socks, and a couple of sweatshirts. One was maroon with a silk-screened mallard duck in flight pictured on it; and the other was forest green with the portrait of a whitetail buck.

"I know somebody who's going to be home in time for Christmas," Nurse McDaniel said in a cheery tone as she entered his room. She was wearing a Christmas tree pin on her lapel, two dangling snowman earrings, and a round, gold bell on a red cord around her neck that jingled as she walked. Scott had completely forgotten about Christmas. He wondered how his family would be celebrating this year. He then thought of the LeDoux family in New Orleans. How were they coping with the loss of their daughter? How was he going to cope?

Nurse McDaniel noticed Scott's melancholy expression. "I know this has been traumatic, but you're going to put this behind you, and get on with your life dear," she said with a touch of genuine concern. "Believe me, there's no worse place to spend Christmas, than a hospital."

"I'm okay," he said. "I am glad to get out of here."

"I know your uncle will be glad to take you home today."

"Thanks for helping me, Nurse McDaniel. You've made this whole deal bearable for me. You're a real professional, a very talented nurse, and a genuinely nice person."

Nurse McDaniel smiled and blushed. "That's the nicest thing a patient has ever said to me."

Three quick knocks at the door were heard, followed by Beachum swinging the door open. "Ready to go home, Scotty?" He tossed a small nylon duffel bag on the bed.

"You bet," Scott replied as he picked up the bag and quickly loaded his meager belongings.

"Okay, you need to get these prescriptions filled right away, and follow all the directions," Nurse McDaniel said as she handed Scott three slips of paper. "And if you have any questions, promise you'll call me."

"I will. Thanks, again." Scott quickly embraced her. "Merry Christmas."

She hugged him back, "Merry Christmas to you, too Scott." She stepped back and wiped a tear from her eye. She smiled broadly, and said, "And, Merry Christmas to you, too, Mr. Beachum. I'm sure taking your nephew home is the best present you could receive."

"Yes, ma'am," he said tipping an invisible hat. "We've been truly blessed this year. Merry Christmas to you and your family." He smiled at her, and put his arm around Scott's shoulder, and walked him out of the hospital room.

*　　　　　*　　　　　*

THEY DROVE ALONG the deserted roads in Beachum's old Jeep Cherokee. Along the way, Beachum peppered Scott with questions, now that they could privately converse for the first time. Scott covered all essential background: His family, his upbringing, his first job out of college, the lure of working for an industry giant like Campbell Industries that brought him to Southern California, his relationship with Lisa, and finally, all the dirt on Campbell Industries, finding Lisa's body in his apartment, how he was ambushed, how he ended up hog-tied in the wilderness, Lt. Cavanarro, Glenn Stevens, and Jon Cassler, he of the shaky aim.

The Jeep pulled off-road and on to a gravel drive. The ground below the SUV dipped sharply, and then began to incline slightly. Through a grove of trees, Scott spied a log cabin with a tin roof, sitting in a clearing. Beachum parked the vehicle in front of the cabin, and jumped down out of the truck. Scott stepped out and noticed the earth covered with pine needles, leaves and pine cones. A chilly breeze swept across them. It felt good to be out of the hospital and in the fresh air.

He followed Beachum up four wooden steps and through the front door. The interior was dark, and very rustic, as one would expect. The front door opened into a great room with a large, stone fireplace that was adjacent to the kitchen and dining area. Beachum flipped on a light switch and motioned for Scott to follow him down the hallway. A bathroom was at the end of the short hallway, with a door on either side. "This is my room," Beachum said knocking on the wooden door to the right. "You can bunk in here," he said, opening the door on his left. Inside, Scott threw the duffel bag on a queen-sized, Shaker style bed. There was a matching nightstand between the bed and the wall. To the right, a rectangular window on the wall that overlooked the surrounding woods. A small chest of drawers was positioned directly across from the bed. Next to it was a small closet. Its door was partially open, revealing a cedar lining, and Scott's dry-cleaned dress shirt, slacks and tie hanging in plastic bags. His freshly shined dress shoes were on the floor of the closet, with his clean socks rolled-up inside them. The serendipity of the circumstances that brought him here was not lost on Scott. "Okay..." Beachum said, clapping his hands, the word trailing off as he marched resolutely out of the room and back down the hallway.

Scott followed, and the burly man stopped at the dining room table. He looked up at Scott, and looked as if he was trying to choose his words carefully. "I'm going to run into town and get these prescriptions filled ASAP." He walked to the far corner of the table and stopped in front of a large stack of newspapers. Rapping his knuckles on the papers, he said, "Look, I saved these so you can catch up on what's been said, and maybe try and piece together what happened, and where things stand today—only if you feel up to it—stop if your head starts hurting." He gave Scott a stiff upper lip expression. "Make yourself at home, Scotty. There's food in the refrigerator. I'll be back shortly."

"Thanks, Mr. Beachum."

Beachum marched out of the cabin. His footsteps could be heard descending the steps outside. Scott heard the door to the Jeep open and close, the engine turn over and then the tires crunching through the leaves and pine cones along the drive. Before he sat down to read the papers, a few items clustered on the interior wall of the log cabin's den caught his eye.

He walked over to a framed certificate, indicating that Langston T. Beachum had graduated from Jump School in Fort Benning. Next to it, in the shape of a shield, was a wooden Army Airborne Ranger School plaque. There was also a framed black-and-white platoon photo. The men were decked out in full combat gear. An inscription in felt-tip pen at the bottom of the photo stated: LRRP—Vietnam—'67. Next to that was a framed Certificate of Meritorious Achievement, awarded to Sergeant 1st Class Langston T. Beachum, US Army, Long Range Reconnaissance Patrol, *The Headhunters*. There was also a certificate indicating that Beachum had received the Purple Heart, so he obviously knew a thing or to about recovering from a gunshot wound, Scott thought. The largest frame on the wall contained a document that read: The United States of America, To all who shall see these presents, Greeting: This is to certify that the President of the United States of America authorized by act of Congress, July 2, 1926 has awarded THE SILVER STAR to Sergeant 1st Class, Langston T. Beachum, E-7, United States Army, for heroism and valorous acts in combat in the Republic of

Vietnam on 10 March 1967. It was stamped at the bottom with the seal of The United States of America War Office, and signed by J.H. Hay, Commanding Major General, USA, and the signature of the Secretary of the Army, a Stanley R. something or other, he couldn't make out. This guy was a certified war hero. Scott was impressed.

He was about to return to the stack of papers on the dining room table, when he noticed a framed 8x10 picture on an end table next to a comfortable looking leather recliner. The woman in the picture had dark hair, green eyes and a nice smile. She was attractive, and judging from her clothing, Scott guessed the photo was taken in the early Seventies. He turned and noticed a large pair of what he guessed to be moose antlers mounted above the fireplace.

His hands began to tremble when he noticed Lisa's picture on the cover of the newspaper that was on top of the large stack. He scanned the article and quickly learned that he was indeed the number one suspect, he was still missing, and no comment from Campbell Industries or his family in Memphis. The Long Beach Coroner's report indicated strangulation was her cause of death. The next paragraph seized him with pain, as he read how Judge LeDoux stated he had recently met Scott for the first time, and had never been more wrong about an individual in his life. He also said that he wanted justice for his daughter's murder, hoped the legal system in California had enough backbone to enforce the death penalty, and that his family would never get over the tragic loss of Lisa. He was surprised and mildly disappointed that he was not getting any benefit of the doubt from the Judge. He also found himself empathizing with the man, not only for the loss of his daughter, but figuring he had been on the receiving end of multiple "I told you so's" from his wife, concerning the suitability of Scott Murphy dating their daughter.

Beachum had arranged the papers chronologically. Campbell Industries had been kind enough to give the press the photo from his employee ID card. The same picture appeared over and over again, as

Scott's whereabouts and motives where analyzed. He did find an article quoting his Sales Manager at Campbell Industries, Allen Goldman, as saying that he did not believe Scott Murphy was capable of such a heinous crime. Good old Allen. He then found the work of one industrious reporter, under the headline, *Foul Play at Campbell in Commerce,* who brought up the Maria Lopez missing person case, indicating that Ms. Lopez was missing before both Murphy and LeDoux went to work for the Western Region office of Campbell Industries. Scott felt sickened when he noticed that Lt. Cavanarro was quoted, and listed as the *Officer in Charge* of both the Lopez missing person case and the LeDoux murder case.

Scott read snippets about himself and Lisa, biographical information that was often false or embellished, and a bunch of psycho-babble from various experts, concerning theories as to why he may have snapped, and the pressure in today's workplace, road-rage, and all sorts of violence and harassment angles perpetrated against women. The injustice and lunacy of the situation made his head spin. He had no idea how long he had been reading the papers, when he heard the Jeep stop and Beachum apply the parking brake. Beachum tromped up the stairs and opened the door. He took one look at Scott and noticed immediately that he looked white as a ghost. "You better stop reading that stuff for a while and get some rest," he said with noticeable concern. "Here, it's probably time to take some medicine," he said, handing Scott three stapled together paper bags from the pharmacy.

CHAPTER 37

OVER THE NEXT TWO DAYS, Scott and Beachum got to know each other better. Beachum quizzed Scott with numerous questions about Campbell Industries, Glenn Stevens and Jon Cassler. He also had a lot of questions about Lt. Cavanarro.

Scott tried his best to express the depths of his gratitude for all that Beachum had done for him. He found out that Beachum paid all his hospital bills in cash. Scott let him know that he was good for the money and would reimburse him. Beachum didn't seem concerned about it—but strongly cautioned Scott about trying to make any withdrawals from his bank accounts or use his credit cards—he figured the police were monitoring them for any activity that might lead them to his whereabouts.

Scott also learned that Beachum lived alone in the cabin, and that the attractive brunette in the picture was his wife, Pat. She was originally from Columbus, Georgia, and they had met when he was stationed at Fort Benning. It was obvious from the reverential tone he used speaking about her that he had loved her very much. Beachum explained with pained recollection of how she was killed by a drunk driver in a head-on collision in 1975, one year after he left the service. He said the driver walked away from the wreck and did six-months in jail. Beachum also said with a hint of regret that they did not have any children.

Beachum shared that he was originally from Bowling Green, Kentucky. "They make Corvettes there now," he noted with pride. He went on to explain that after his stint in the Army, he accepted an engineering position with McDonnell-Douglas, and that's what brought him and Pat to California. He also exposed his dislike for the tactics of big business when he went into great detail about his layoff in 1991. It seemed the Southern California economy had hit rock bottom, and businesses were fleeing in droves to find more tax-friendly states to set up shop. The military bases and aerospace industry were especially hard hit by the recession. Big companies slashed jobs and moved production work to Mexico, as corporate executives reaped monetary windfalls in previously unheard of amounts.

He told Scott that once he got over feeling angry and betrayed, he figured it was a good time to assess what was important and how he wanted to spend the rest of his life. He said his father, a carpenter, had once told him that if you can make a living doing something you enjoy, you'll never work a day in your life. Beachum knew several rocket scientists who left the industry to design titanium golf clubs in Carlsbad, and never looked back. He went on to say that woodworking had always been his favorite hobby, and that he decided to make it his new job. His older brother had retired and moved to Bishop with his wife and daughter in 1989 and opened a bait and tackle shop. Beachum decided to follow them to Bishop, to get away from the rat race, and be close to his only family. He set up shop, and said he had had some success selling custom, hand-made furniture to the locals and the tourists. Leaning back in his recliner in front of the fire, he admitted it wasn't McDonnell-Douglass money, but it was hard to put a price on peace of mind, and being your own boss.

Scott was also impressed to discover that Beachum had built his log cabin himself. He said that he first bought the property, put a trailer on it, and worked on the house in his spare time, with some help from his brother. It took him two years to complete the project. The painstaking craftsmanship was evident throughout the structure.

When he wasn't mourning over Lisa, or thinking about how to avenge her death, Scott found himself reflecting on Beachum's insights about big business. His own anger and betrayal stemmed from a much different set of circumstances than Beachum's. Maybe Scott's early thoughts about climbing the corporate ladder and grabbing the brass ring would never hold the happiness he originally thought they would. He knew if and when his predicament was resolved, that he too, would have to spend some introspective time assessing his future goals and what was really important. His thoughts often included the words of wisdom his own father had tried to impart to him about life, work and death—words he had previously given little credence—but they now somehow resounded with much more intelligence and common sense. Maybe he should have listened to the old man more when he had the chance. He told himself that if he got through this dilemma that he would work hard to establish a fresh start with his dad.

The time he spent with Beachum was enjoyable, and helped take his mind off what happened to Lisa, and how he ended up here in the first place. He had managed to read through the entire stack of newspapers, and began some initial strategy discussions with Beachum. He consistently assured Scott that there would be time enough for that after the first of the year, and after he had completely recovered. He felt his strength returning, but still seemed to be sleeping about half the day. He didn't know if the fatigue was due to his injury or the medication he was taking.

Out of curiosity, Scott had asked Beachum several questions about Army life, and his stint in Vietnam. Scott backed off this line of questioning when he realized this was not a comfortable subject matter for Beachum. He did learn that Beachum earned what he called his Ranger tab, and seemed to take a certain amount of pride in that accomplishment. He also learned that his job specialty was that of an infantryman, also known as 11-BRAVO. As far as his tour of duty in Vietnam, Beachum either didn't respond to the questions asked, or subtly changed the subject matter. Scott couldn't even imagine what kind of horrific experiences could render a tough guy like Beachum mute.

*   *   *

LATE THAT AFTERNOON, Scott stirred from his mid-day nap, glanced at his watch, and proceeded to the kitchen for his next round of pills. He noticed Beachum sitting at the dining table, putting the finishing touches on several boxes wrapped in Christmas paper. He looked up at Scott and asked, "How ya feelin'?"

"Not too bad."

"Good. I don't know if you know it or not, but it's Christmas Eve."

"Yeah, I noticed the header on this morning's paper."

"Wrapping was never my specialty, that was more Pat's department," he said, holding up a package for close inspection. "Well, I've sort of got a family commitment—recent tradition, I guess—I spend Christmas Eve at my brother's house. I'd invite you along, but…"

"No, don't worry about me."

"What I was going to say, is that I'd invite you to come along, but I haven't told them, or anyone about you. It's not that I don't trust my own family—I just figure the fewer that know, the better. You know the saying, 'loose lips sink ships.'"

"I understand. I'd like to call my family, but I know it's not the right time. You go and have a good time. I'll be fine."

"I intend to," he said as he stuffed the packages into a large canvas bag. "There's some chili in the 'fridge. Just heat it up on the stove." He stood and walked over and handed Scott a small, square shaped felt box. "I held on to this for you, son."

Scott opened the box, already aware of its contents. Lisa's engagement ring sparkled in the low light of the room. "Thanks."

"They gave it to me at the hospital. I figured it was for Lisa. I knew then the papers had it all wrong about you. Never heard of a guy buying an engagement ring for a girl he was going to…you know."

"I appreciate it. I appreciate everything you've done for me."

"Aw, I haven't done anything, son."

After studying the ring for several moments, Scott snapped the lid closed. "This might come in handy someday if I'm strapped for cash…"

"Don't talk like that! You should save that for the girl you eventually marry."

"I don't think I'll ever find someone like Lisa…I don't even want to think about it. Hell, look at what happened to her…I don't deserve to get married."

"You're right, I'm sure Lisa was very special and one of a kind. But you're so young, Scott. Don't shut yourself off to the possibility. I did, and it's probably the biggest mistake I ever made. I know now that Pat would have wanted me to get on with my life; and I'm sure Lisa would want you to do the same. She loved you, right? Why would she want you to punish yourself for something that wasn't your fault?"

Beachum's words hung in the air for a few minutes as the two men stared off at the flames in the fireplace. Beachum broke the silence. "Life is for the living, Scotty. It took me a long time to learn that," he said softly. "Too long. I know it's too soon to be discussing this, but don't close yourself off to the possibility someday." He loudly cleared his throat. "Well, I better shove off before they start wondering what happened to me." He slung the canvas sack over his shoulder and Scott thought he resembled St. Nicholas himself, as he lumbered toward the front door. "I should be back around ten or eleven. Oh, uh, there's a little something for you on the table. I figure you've earned it, son," he mumbled, not looking back as he slammed the cabin door shut.

Scott popped his prescribed medication into his mouth and washed it down with a glass of water. He gently rubbed his bandaged head as he left the kitchen and approached the small wrapped package Beachum had left for him. He seated himself at the head of the dining table in front of the small, flat box. He pulled off the green and red ribbon and carefully removed the white wrapping paper. The paper had a white-on-white imprint of evergreen trees staggered across it. It had concealed a slim, black box. The edge along the opening of the box was trimmed in brass. He opened the spring-loaded lid, and for a moment felt as if the wind had been knocked out of him. His throat tightened and tears burned his eyes as he looked at Beachum's Purple Heart medal.

CHAPTER 38

CHRISTMAS DAY was quiet in Beachum's log cabin. The two men were silent for the most part, reflecting on their individual thoughts and memories. Either man never mentioned it, but they each seemed grateful for the company of the other. Beachum didn't have a Christmas tree, but the roaring fire accompanied by various Christmas albums playing on the ancient record player made for a tranquil setting.

Scott had fallen asleep before Beachum returned the night before. In the morning, over a breakfast of buttermilk pancakes topped with authentic Vermont syrup, Scott tried to return the medal to Beachum, explaining that he couldn't accept such a generous gift, but truly appreciated the sentiment. Scott felt strongly that a Purple Heart was reserved for those wounded in combat. Beachum wouldn't hear of it, and told Scott that it was important to him that he keep the medal. He reiterated that Scott had indeed earned it, as he was an unfortunate witness to the fact.

*   *   *

OVER THE NEXT FEW DAYS, Scott felt his strength returning. He also felt a slight case of cabin fever. Beachum decided to take him to his shop, so he could get a change of scenery. They both figured with Scott's shaggy beard and a baseball cap hiding the bandages, he would be virtually unrecognizable to anyone that might be looking for him. Beachum thought the prospect of that was unlikely, and that they probably wouldn't even see any customers at this time of the year.

Beachum's Wood Working was located in Bishop on Pleasant Valley Road, situated on one end of a strip of small shops. Book-ending the nondescript mall was his brother's shop, Beachum's Bait and Tackle. The Jeep Cherokee was parked in front of his store in the deserted parking lot.

Beachum unlocked the door and a cowbell rang to announce their entry. The front of the store served a showroom. It contained several table and chair combos, an assortment of rocking chairs, serving hutches, china cabinets, desks, chests and even a section devoted to custom made cigar humidors. As they walked past the ornate humidors, Scott couldn't help thinking about Judge LeDoux.

The back wall of the shop looked a lot like the interior walls of Beachum's log cabin. "Scraps," he said, knocking on the wall, as he opened and walked through a door with a mirror on the upper half. "This is where it all happens," he said as led Scott into his workshop. As they entered the adjoining room, Scott noticed that the mirror was two-way, and enabled Beachum to see anyone walking into the store. The room smelled of sawdust and was arranged in several workstations. A Delta table saw stood next to a large drafting table. There were four worktables that had a variety of miter saws, routers, sanders, and drills scattered on them.

Scott noted that some of the man's power tools were stamped with the Porter-Cable trademark. "Did you know that Porter-Cable tools are made in Jackson, Tennessee, about an hour east of Memphis?" Scott asked.

"Yep, I knew that. Did you know that they're the best tools on the market? Can't stand to use any of that import crap," he said with the voice of experience. He walked over to one of the tables and tapped a rectangular shaped piece of oak. "This is a project I'm working on for

Mrs. Leatherwood—she's a local—it's gonna be a bookshelf," he said, as if amused by the possibility. His rough, callused right hand gripped a palm held sander. He turned the unit on and methodically passed up and down the wood for several minutes. Turning off the sander, he looked up at Scott observing his work. "I also find it to be therapeutic. I'm able to get a lot of thinking done. Wanna give it a shot?"

"Sure, why not…"

"First, put these on." Scott slipped on the protective goggles he was handed. He then took the sander from Beachum and imitated the motion he saw the older man use with the power tool. "Not bad, for a rookie," he heard Beachum snort from over his shoulder.

The two men spent the afternoon undisturbed by any patrons, as Beachum's prognostication turned out to be correct. He was also correct that Scott would find it easier to think more clearly, losing himself in his thoughts as he carried out the repetitive tasks assigned to him.

*　　　　　*　　　　　*

AS THE DAYS PASSED, Scott spent more time in the shop assisting Beachum. Occasionally a customer would ring the front door's cowbell, and require Beachum's attention. These were the only time Scott was left unsupervised with the tools. He took great care not to screw anything up. He didn't want to disappoint the old guy. One morning Beachum's brother, Silas, stopped in for a cup of coffee, and it was explained to him that Scott was some new, part-time help he had decided to take on. Turned out Silas was also ex-military, a Marine. Scott noticed Silas exhibited many of the same mannerisms as his brother.

*　　　　　*　　　　　*

NEW YEAR'S EVE was spent alone in the log cabin, since Beachum was celebrating with his family. He told Scott that it would probably be okay if he came along, but Scott replied that it might even look more suspicious if Beachum invited his new part-time grunt. Beachum laughed out loud. Scott watched the New Year's Eve telecast from Times Square on a small TV set. A combination of exhaustion and pain medication prevented him from making it to the end of the broadcast. He was excited about tomorrow—not because it was the first day of a new year—but because Beachum's shop was closed, and he had promised that they would discuss their ideas on how to get Scott out of the mess he was in. He was eager to hear Beachum's thoughts on the matter.

CHAPTER 39

JON CASSLER sat on his sofa in a cocaine-induced stupor. He was holding his Campbell Industries Corporate AMEX card in one hand, and a tightly rolled-up twenty-dollar bill in the other. The flickering glow of the un-watched television reflected off the pale, pudgy man, who was only wearing a pair of red bikini briefs. His wife of convenience slept soundly in her bedroom.

The past few weeks had been nerve-racking. Cops were crawling all over the office; asking questions about Lisa LeDoux's murder and the coinciding disappearance of Scott Murphy. Employees were even starting to whisper about the long-missing Maria Lopez. The office atmosphere was morose.

Glenn had repeatedly tried to reassure him that there was no way they would be caught. Murphy's missing body was the main reason his thoughts were tortured about his own fate. Cassler was no weapons expert, and prior to that memorable evening in Bishop, had never fired a gun in his life. But he still couldn't fully grasp what had happened. How could a person get up and walk away with two bullets in his head? He replayed the scene over and over again in his mind. Every time, he heard the sound of the gun exploding, followed by the sickening sound of the bullet entering flesh.

Two times.

Over and over.

The only rational explanation he could come up with, was that Murphy's car was probably found and stolen sometime that morning. As for the body, there was no reason for a car thief to take it. Glenn told him that Murphy was probably breakfast for some of the local wildlife. But even then, Cassler thought, it seemed like an article of clothing would have turned up. But nothing did. Not a damn thing.

How did he let Glenn bully him into this situation in the first place? He could have stood up to him, a first, but in hindsight, it would have been a good time to take a stand. He had always relished his assigned role as Glenn's hatchet man over the years. Termination, lay-offs, putting an employee on short-term objectives, threats, intimidation and ball busting were what he absolutely *loved* about his job. He knew he was an asshole, and took pride in being the best asshole he could be. He was hated by all in the office, feared by some, and basked in the resentment. As much as he got off on all the dirty work, he never figured Glenn would make cold-blooded murderer part of his job description.

The Campbell Industries office Christmas party had been a lackluster affair. Attendance was way off, and the usual sexual escapades, drunkenness and drug consumption was not present, either. A cloud of grief hung over the event. Cassler found himself trying to read between the lines of casual conversation, and analyzed every handshake, every gesture, every glance. If Murphy had figured out he was gay, and had only worked there a few months, how many others knew, or suspected his sexual preference? It caused him a good deal of heartburn, because, over the years, he had gone to great lengths to painstakingly create the facade of normalcy. He was acutely aware that a homosexual would find it tough, if not impossible, to climb the corporate ladder in their good ol' boy industry, with a company headquartered in the South. But maybe Murphy was just guessing. Or bluffing. Hell, he was tied up, facing certain execution. He was probably just venting his anger, trying to get under his skin. Maybe no one else suspected. Maybe no living, breathing Murphy would ever turn up. He clung to those thoughts as if they were a life preserver inscribed with the word: REALITY.

*   *   *

TIM NEWSOM unlocked and opened the door to room number 126 at the Barstow Motel 6. Pamela Stevens giddily followed the younger man into the familiar setting. Tim had convinced his wife that he had to entertain a client on New Year's Eve. Pamela convinced her husband that she was going to some frou-frou spa in Palm Springs—and that would take place—tomorrow.

Tonight they were unofficially celebrating the one-year anniversary of their tawdry relationship. Tim's wife was too ill to attend last year's company Christmas party, and he had decided that he had to make an appearance; for political reasons, and to pick up his Salesman of the Year award. Nothing like basking in the envy of your colleagues.

After dinner and the presentation of awards, Glenn Stevens was ignoring his wife, as usual, and spent his time rotating Lori, Janet and Sheila as his dancing partners. Tim had bumped into Pamela at the bar, and struck up a conversation. Twenty minutes later, he was banging the wife of his boss's boss, in the reclined front seat of his BMW. She was a sex-starved animal. It was pretty awesome.

From that point on, they began seeing each other several times a month. Tim had decided on Barstow as the optimum destination for them to meet for a couple of reasons. First, no one was likely to see them in this remote area. Second, he had an actual customer out here, and thought it was really humorous to be able to take Pamela out to a nice dinner, rent a room for the evening, ride her like a rented mule, and turn in the receipts on his expense report for Glenn's approval and reimbursement.

Pamela was an attractive brunette, an older trophy wife, from even older money. She had stood by Glenn as he advanced through the ranks at Campbell, putting up with his long hours and surly demeanor. She justified this because the elite social circles she ran in required that she had to have a presentable—and reasonably successful—husband. Not working and spending money were two of her favorite past-times. And now that she had a young stud on retainer—one that was employed by her husband—well, that was just the icing on the cake.

Tim thought about trying to end it with Pamela several times, but always thought better of it. He was making some serious coin at Campbell—and didn't want to risk it on the chance Pamela would blow the whistle on him to her husband—the old, *hell hath no fury,* angle. Since the birth of his children, his wife had absolutely no interest in sex. Being young and virile—and totally lacking morals or a conscience— Pamela provided a good release for his pent-up sexual frustration. And it didn't hurt that she was suffering from the same affliction. Tim found it perversely gratifying when she shared with him the details of Glenn's long battle with impotence. Since he received this information, he now viewed Glenn's cocky swagger around the office as more dysfunctional than macho.

Pamela quickly stripped down to a flattering, black teddy. The hours with her personal trainer, and at the tanning bed were well spent, Tim thought, admiring her body. She jumped on the bed and ripped off the cheap comforter and thin blanket. She sexily slithered across the cotton-poly blend sheets, motioning him to join her. He kicked off his shoes, pulled his shirt off over his head, and walked to the side of the bed.

She gave him a deliciously slutty smile as she unbuckled his belt. She quickly undid his pants, reached in and forcefully freed him from his confinement. She pulled him down beside her on the lumpy mattress. Pamela had a flair for the dramatic, and Tim liked that a lot. She was into role-playing and spankings. She liked to tell him with a pouty face what a bad girl she had been. He always let her take the lead, and followed willingly. This seedy environment always seemed to put this country club girl into a kinky mindset. Over the past few months, she had added a twist that Tim really found to be a turn on—and hoped she repeated tonight—when she would scream out in the height of orgasmic ecstasy, "Fuck me like Glenn never could! Fuck me like Glenn never could!"

Chapter 40

THE NEW YEAR began over a breakfast of buckwheat pancakes, straw-berries, orange juice and coffee. Beachum always had a hearty appetite, and breakfast seemed to be his favorite meal of the day. He was con-stantly telling Scott he had to put some meat on his bones. Scott figured he had lost about twenty pounds during his hospital stay.

After the pancakes were consumed, the paper read and the dishes put away, the two men retreated to the den of the log cabin for the long awaited strategy session on Scott's future. Scott was wearing jeans and a sweatshirt; Beachum was still in his pajamas, terry cloth robe and deer-skin moccasins. He slowly sipped a fresh cup of coffee.

"I don't know," Scott started. "My thoughts have been all over the place. One minute I think I should call a lawyer, turn myself in and take my chances—especially since I have you as a witness to my attempted execution. Then, I think I'd just like to walk into the office—unan-nounced—and beat Stevens and Cassler to death for what they did to Lisa…"

"I don't know if taking the law into your own hands is the best approach," Beachum said calmly.

"Yeah, but, say I turn myself in, and Stevens and Cassler are found guilty of murdering Lisa—and attempted murder on me—these crazy, liberal California juries wouldn't even convict O.J.! Hell, Charles Manson is still alive! Why should I take a chance of those two going to trial and getting off? I'm not sure I can take that chance—Stevens would probably charm the socks of a jury—he could probably convince them to pin it all on me. I owe it to Lisa—and her family—to see that justice is served."

Beachum took a sip of coffee and reflected on what the young man had said. Scott sat in silence, leaning forward, waiting to hear what words of wisdom the older man might impart.

Beachum cleared his throat and ran his hand over his thick mustache several times. He then removed his eyeglasses, held them up to the light, and squinted to locate the offending particle. He fogged the lenses with his breath, and methodically cleaned the glasses using the sleeve of his cotton robe.

Several moments passed in silence before Beachum decided to speak. "You make a good point about the prospect of standing trial in front of an LA jury. Our whole criminal justice system seems to be geared toward protecting the rights of criminals; no real consideration given to the victims or their families."

"You're right—and that's what scares me to death—that Stevens and Cassler might get off with only a hand slap."

"That would be a terrible miscarriage of justice. I'm not sure it's a risk you should take, or can afford." Beachum cleared his throat. "You familiar with the concept of *leverage*, son?"

"What do you mean by leverage?"

"Leverage in hand-to-hand combat. It's where you use your opponent's own weight against them. Have them working with you to accomplish your goal."

"So you're thinking I should just show up and kick some ass."

"Not exactly, although I'm sure it would be therapeutic for you. If you did do something like that, their lawyers could probably spin it to make it look like you returned to kill again."

"Hmmmmmm. You could be right."

Beachum took on the tone of an instructor. "You see, what we have here are three cowards: Stevens, Cassler and Cavanarro. And the only thing you can ever count on a coward to do is try to save his own hide, no matter what the circumstances are. If it can benefit a coward to turn on you—even if you're his friend—to save his own sorry self, well, you can bank on it. That's what he'll do. It's not all that complicated to figure out how a chicken-shit thinks. Strip away morals, integrity, character, conscience and courage—and it all boils down to basic instinct—self-preservation."

"Okay, so that's how a coward thinks and acts, but how does that help me?"

"We've established that we know how a coward thinks and acts. We're dealing with three gutless wonders. That's where leverage comes in, son. By knowing how they will think and behave, we can manipulate a coward to do exactly what we want him to do."

Beachum shuffled into the kitchen to refill his coffee cup. Scott tried to absorb what the man had just explained to him. After a few moments, he spoke. "So what's my first step?"

Beachum returned to his seat on the couch. "First, you are going to keep your appointment with Dr. Williams in two days for your checkup. Once we get a clean bill of health on you, we'll proceed with Plan A."

"What's Plan A?"

"Well, the way I see it, your Lt. Cavanarro would be a logical candidate to help us to get the ball rolling."

"How so?"

"Well, I figure if he's convinced that the other two cowards are conspiring against him—being a cowardly man of the law—he will use his power against them to save his skin. We can take out two birds with the proverbial one stone."

"And how exactly do we get the cowardly Lieutenant to act on our behalf?"

"Well, first we'll have to kidnap him…"

"What? Kidnap a cop? How do you figure we can pull that off?" Scott asked, suddenly not liking the direction of Beachum's proposed plan.

"We'll have to physically grab him, and then…"

"Physically grab him? With all due respect Mr. Beachum, Cavanarro does carry a gun. I've seen it. I'm not sure he'll come along peacefully, just because we ask nice."

"I didn't say it would be easy…and I don't plan on asking him."

"I just don't see how you think we can…"

"Son, you're talking to an Airborne Ranger, two tours in 'Nam…I think I can handle a cop."

"But don't they get training in how to fight and defend themselves…apprehend criminals, you know, at the Police Academy?"

"Police Academy? You ever see that movie? Probably pretty close to real life, if you ask me. You probably couldn't find a handful of men on the LAPD who could earn their Ranger tab, son." The older man's eyes narrowed defiantly.

"Okay, I'm sure you're right…I don't have a damn thing to lose. So how do we implement your plan? Am I supposed to walk up to him on the street and startle him while you whack him in the head with a bat?"

"Something like that. But we don't want him to see you…just in case something goes wrong, I don't want him to have a clue that you're involved." Beachum reached over and patted him on the knee. "It'll be all right. You've got to trust me."

"I do trust you. Probably more than anyone I've ever met. So, tell me how you think we should go about getting Cavanarro to use as leverage?"

Beachum smiled warmly. "You ever heard of interrupting the body's meridians? Dim Mak point striking? Shock points? Pressure points? Nerve points? Short-out points?"

Scott continuously shook his head no to all of the terminology Beachum was rattling off. "No, sir. I have no idea what any of that is."

"Well, I do," Beachum said with a toothy grin. "And it's some wicked shit."

CHAPTER 41

DR. WILLIAMS clicked off the penlight that had been shining in Scott's eyes. He had earlier removed the bandages on Scott's scalp; and was wrapping up the examination. "Everything looks good," the doctor exclaimed. "But I still want you to take it easy. I'm going to renew your prescription for the painkiller, but I don't think you'll need the anti-inflammatory any longer." He scribbled some notes in Scott's file. "The entry wounds have healed nicely. You'll want to continue to use some Neosporin for another week, or so." Scott nodded at Dr. Williams' instructions. Beachum was leaning against the wall of the examination room, his brawny arms folded across his chest.

"And I'll want to see you again in a month. Any questions?"

"No, sir."

"Mr. Beachum?

"Nope. Thanks for everything, Doc."

"Yes, thank you," Scott said sincerely.

"You're both very welcome. I'm just glad everything has worked out as well as it has. I don't even want to think about how bad things could have been."

*   *   *

SCOTT LEFT THE BARBERSHOP later that afternoon. The shop was located in the same strip mall as Beachum's Wood Working. Scott used some of the cash he had left in his wallet to pay for the haircut. Now that the bandages were off, and his hair was growing back, he had looked pretty scruffy. He now had a short crew cut and a neatly trimmed beard. He was pleased with how well his beard filled in. He wondered if his own mother would recognize him?

He walked back to Beachum's shop and noticed through the window that Beachum was conversing with his brother in the showroom. He entered the store and was greeted by Silas Beachum. "First time I've seen you without a cap on, Scott. With that flat-top and beard, you look like a Navy man."

"Thanks."

"That's not a compliment," the former Marine replied, as he shared a belly laugh with his brother. "I'm just messing with you."

"Don't worry about it."

"Boy's got a thick skin," Beachum interjected.

"Good to know. Well, I better get back to my counter. Take it easy, Scott. See you later, L.T."

"See ya, Silas," Beachum said, as he turned and walked back to his workshop.

"Bye," Scott said, following Beachum, as the cowbell clanged behind Silas.

Scott watched Beachum disconnect the power cords to several tools. He grabbed his keys off a bench, and pulled on a cotton fishing hat. "Wanna go for a ride?"

"Where are we going?

"Thought we'd do a little *research* today."

∗   ∗   ∗

THE JEEP CHEROKEE motored south on Highway 395. They passed a sign that indicated they were now in Lone Pine. "You ever heard of Lone Pine?" Beachum asked.

"No, can't say that I have."

"You ever watch any John Wayne movies?"

"Yeah, sure."

"Well, a lot of the Duke's movies were filmed out there in what are called the Alabama Hills. I'll show 'em to you, sometime."

They passed through towns called Big Pine, Independence and a town called Randsburg. Beachum told him Randsburg was a ghost town, but is making a small resurgence as a mining town. "If they really wanted some traffic, just let the Indians open up another casino there— like the new one in Bishop," he said, shaking his head. He also told Scott that if he was ever in the mood to get in a fight, there was a bar in Randsburg called the White House. All you had to do was walk in, order a drink, and wait for a fight to break out, which usually happened about every ten minutes. Scott noticed Beachum examining the knuckles of his right hand as he commented on what a rough place it was.

The traffic picked up as they got closer to Los Angeles. Beachum pulled his Thomas Guide map out of the glove compartment. He alternated his attention between the map and the road in front of him.

"Do you need me to look something up?" Scott asked.

"No thanks, just had to refresh my memory," Beachum replied with a wink.

*   *   *

TWENTY MINUTES later, Beachum parallel parked the SUV across the street from a parking lot full of marked LAPD patrol cars. There were several unmarked Ford Crown Vics parked in front of the precinct house. It was now 1:15 PM. "What are we doing here?" Scott asked tentatively.

"Made a few calls. Turns out your Lt. Cavanarro works out of this station."

"So what's the plan?"

"We're just observing today. Remember? I said we were going to do a little research."

"What kind of research?"

"I wanna get a feel for his routine."

"What can I do?"

"Let me know when you see the son-of-a-bitch," Beachum replied as he settled in his seat, pushed back his hat and opened a *Field & Stream* magazine.

It didn't take very long. Scott nudged Beachum's arm when he saw Lt. Cavanarro drive his unmarked cruiser into the parking lot. He parked in front of the building, and walked inside, with what appeared to be a spring in his step.

"Okay," Beachum said. "Let me know when he comes out," and returned his attention to an article about the complexity of fly-fishing.

Lt. Cavanarro exited the precinct building at 3:30 PM. He roughly slammed his car into reverse, then pulled it into drive as he stomped on the accelerator. Scott alerted Beachum that he was on the move. "Gotta love how he treats government property," Beachum observed as he started his Jeep.

They followed the Lieutenant to a residence in Santa Monica. The cop parked his car in the driveway. Beachum cruised past him, circled the block and parked across the street from the house. He pulled out his binoculars, and examined the dwelling across from him. The cop was already inside. "Says CAVANARRO on the mail box," he said gruffly. "Guess he's knocking off early. We'll hang out for a little while."

*   *   *

IT WAS almost four when Lt. Cavanarro opened the front door to the house. He had changed clothes, and was now wearing a T-shirt, a pair of shorts and carrying a gym bag. He jumped in the Ford and repeated the rough shifting of the transmission as he sped away from the house. "Let's saddle up," Beachum said with a grin, as he fell in behind the cop, cautious not to get too close.

The Jeep followed the Crown Vic into the parking lot of the LA Sports Club. They watched Lt. Cavanarro park his car and enter the large building. The Jeep was parked at the edge of the parking lot, but the engine was left idling. Beachum looked at his watch, and picked up his map. After making a few notes on his Thomas Guide, he reached over and slapped Scott on the knee. "Okay, that's enough for today. Traffic is going to be a bitch."

They crawled through the LA rush hour congestion, until they hit Highway 395. They followed the same route back to Bishop, but instead of turning off to go to the cabin, Beachum kept heading North, toward Mammoth Mountain. They drove about fifteen miles, and then pulled into the parking lot of an establishment called Tom's Place. Beachum parked the Cherokee and shut off the lights and engine.

Tom's Place had a general store on the right hand side of the building, and a cafe on the left. The lettering over the door stated they had been in business since 1917. A huge rack of antlers was mounted to a brick chimney next to the cafe.

They seated themselves inside the cafe, and were greeted by a friendly, middle-aged waitress who acted like she recognized Beachum. She wore a white apron with the Tom's Place logo silk-screened in brown print on it. She left menus and two glasses of water. She returned shortly, and took their dinner orders. Beachum took a long drink of water, and then used his paper napkin to wipe the droplets off his mustache. Beachum seemed to be in deep thought all afternoon, and Scott was growing a little impatient by his detached silence. "So, did we accomplish anything today?"

"Yes, we did."

"What's our next move?"

"Same thing tomorrow—only an earlier start—we'll be outside his house when he starts his day."

"Then what?"

"Same as today, just doing research."

"And what about day after tomorrow?"

"More of the same. Gotta establish his routine." He laughed at Scott's anxious expression. "I'm sorry, I'm not laughing at you. This'll take a little patience if we want to do it right. Trust me."

Scott grinned and nodded knowingly as the waitress arrived with their meals. "All right—soup's on!" Beachum declared. "This surveillance business really works up an appetite." He winked at Scott and the two men dug into their steaming entrees.

CHAPTER 42

LT. CAVANARRO parked his unmarked cruiser in the parking lot of the LA Sports Club. He retrieved his duffel bag from the back seat, checked his slicked back hair in the side view mirror, and proceeded to the club's entrance. He stepped over the curb and up on the sidewalk beside the cavernous structure. Walking along the sidewalk, he approached a stocky man wearing a sweatshirt, gym shorts and what appeared to be a fishing hat, who was apparently leaving the club. He too, was carrying a tote bag. The stocky man tipped his hat and said, "Afternoon."

"Yeah, hi," Cavanarro replied as he passed the man, in a tone that indicated the hurry he was in.

"Oh, excuse me sir," the man said from behind him. "I believe you dropped a twenty-dollar bill."

Lt. Cavanarro wheeled around to see the older man pointing at a twenty on the sidewalk. "Oh, thanks," Cavanarro said with a sheepish smile. He knew it wasn't his, but couldn't justify passing up found money. "Guess it fell out of my shorts."

From his vantage point inside the cargo section of the Jeep Cherokee, Scott saw Beachum approach Lt. Cavanarro, and toss a twenty-dollar bill on the ground behind him. Apparently he must have said something to Cavanarro, because he was walking back to pick up the bill on the sidewalk. Beachum's initial instructions to Scott had been to lift the rear hatch and whistle if anyone approached them.

As Cavanarro leaned over to collect the money, Scott saw Beachum deliver a swift knee into the cop's tailbone. He then adroitly stepped beside the hunched over man and kicked him sharply on the side of his knee, with practiced precision. Scott watched in amazement as this move took out Cavanarro's leg like a kickstand propping a bicycle. Beachum then took one step back, grabbed the Lieutenant's head with both hands, and drove his knee into the fallen cop's face.

Lt. Cavanarro slumped forward as if he'd been shot. Beachum picked up the cop's gym bag as he unzipped his own, and pulled it over Cavanarro's head. Beachum then locked his arms around Cavanarro's chest and half carried, half dragged the man to the Jeep. Scott pulled a knit ski mask over his face, and popped open the hatch, as was the plan. He helped pull Cavanarro's bulky frame into the back of the Cherokee. Once he was completely inside, Beachum unzipped the Lieutenant's bag, and removed a pair of handcuffs, and nimbly cuffed the man's hands behind his back. Scott quickly tied Cavanarro's feet together. Beachum took a piece of rope and tied the man's feet to the handcuffs behind his back, leaving the gym bag over his head. Beachum slammed the tailgate shut as Scott clambered out of the cargo area and over the center seat. Before he left, he noticed the cop had pissed his pants.

Beachum jumped into the driver's seat, started the SUV, and calmly left the parking lot and merged into traffic. Scott left his ski mask on, per Beachum's earlier instructions, just in case Cavanarro managed to slip his head out of the bag. He slid low in his seat, so as not to draw attention to himself, and stared at Beachum with admiration of what he had just witnessed. Beachum had to have at least fifteen to twenty years on Cavanarro, yet the older man handled him like a rag doll. The swiftness with which he dispensed with a trained law enforcement officer boggled Scott's mind.

He wanted to ask Beachum a dozen questions, but he had been instructed not to speak—only grunt when spoken to—just so Cavanarro wouldn't recognize his voice. Scott looked back at the lifeless body from

time to time, as it would suddenly launch into a grotesque spasm, followed by a painful groaning sound. He remembered that this was the
man who handed him over to Stevens for execution.

As they drove, Beachum tossed Cavanarro's gym bag on to Scott's lap.
"Take out his gun…and his wallet. Make sure you have his badge, too."

Scott nodded, and removed the articles.

Beachum methodically drove to their pre-determined destination.
Within moments, he parallel parked the Jeep beside what appeared to
be an abandoned building. They took a moment to check the street for
cars and pedestrian traffic. Feeling confident the coast was clear, the
two men stepped out of the vehicle and walked back to the rear lift-
gate. Beachum lifted the hatch, dropped the tailgate, and pulled the
hog-tied cop out of the cargo area. Scott couldn't help noticing the
rope-thick veins protruding from Beachum's massive forearms. It was
apparent that Cavanarro was beginning to come out of shock, but was
in no condition to walk due to his restraints.

They pulled the beaten cop into the alley that ran between the abandoned building an another large building that had been converted into
a night club called, APOCALYPSE, that would not see any activity until
much later that evening. Beachum propped the Lieutenant against the
wall, behind a smelly garbage dumpster. Beachum slipped on a ski
mask and removed his gym bag from Cavanarro's head. Scott was surprised to see that his eyes were badly swollen and already turning a
purplish black. His nose appeared to be broken, and had bled a large
quantity of blood into the bag. It was now streaming down his chest,
quickly adding a crimson stripe down the center of his white T-shirt.

Cavanarro's eyes were open, but clearly not focused. Beachum
removed a bottle of Avian from the cop's bag, and poured the water
over the man's head and down his bruised face. He then threw the gym
bag on the ground, next to the Lieutenant. He motioned for Scott to
untie the man's legs. When Beachum made sure the beaten man was
coherent enough to understand him, he began to recite his lines from

the script they had composed the night before. "Okay. Stevens wants us to cap him with this little peashooter. Says it'll look like a gang-banger did it." He waved the gun around Cavanarro's face for dramatic effect; and to make sure the cop recognized it as the.25 he had given Stevens to kill Scott with. Beachum leaned over and looked into the Lieutenant's disoriented eyes. He had once seen a coyote caught in a spring trap that had the same mixture of confusion, anger and fear in its eyes. He had shot that poor animal to put it out of its misery. He wanted the animal before him to suffer much longer. "Sorry man, just following the boss's orders. You know, dead men tell no tales, that sort of thing. Stevens says you know way too much, and doesn't feel like he can trust you any longer, or risk having you around. After he murdered Lisa LeDoux and Scott Murphy, you're just another dispensable player. I believe that's how he said it. Nothing personal."

He leveled the unloaded twenty-five-caliber weapon right between Cavanarro's puffy eyes. Beachum held it there for several moments, letting the Lieutenant verify that the pistol was indeed the aforementioned weapon. "See you in hell," Beachum growled as he pulled the trigger. The click of the hammer striking the empty chamber echoed through the vacant alley. Scott heard a squishing sound, and then realized that Cavanarro had just shit in his pants. The Lieutenant's body was involuntarily shaking as the brown stain spread across the back of his white shorts. "Damn it!" Beachum blurted in mock anger. "This piece of shit jammed on me! That's what I get for trusting Stevens. What in the hell does he know about guns, anyway?" He sighed, and continued. "You watch him while I go back to the car for my.44." He began walking out of the alley, and said over his shoulder, "Naw, maybe I should use his cop.38—Stevens wants them to be able to recognize the body, for some reason." Within a few seconds, Beachum had left the alley.

Scott was now alone, and standing in front of the man who tried to assist Stevens to murder him. He looked down at the kneeling, blood-covered, sweaty man; who was trying desperately to keep his weight off his shattered knee. He looked up at Scott with severely blood-shot eyes and hoarsely croaked, "You're about to really fuck up." Scott wanted to respond, but remembered Beachum's instructions to remain mute. Instead, he took a step back, and kicked Cavanarro in the groin as if he were kicking a field goal. The Lieutenant slumped over and made a pathetic groaning sound.

Scott thought about kicking him again, just as Beachum shouted from the street, "Hey, Buster! C'mere for a minute—I need a hand." Scott slowly walked down the alley, leaving the hunched over man, who was still gasping for air.

He turned the corner, and noticed Beachum had removed his mask, and had the motor running. "I saw you nail him, Scott…"

"Well, I had to get in at least one good shot."

"I'd say that was a pretty good shot, son. Hopefully it wasn't too good. We still want him to be able to crawl away, remember?"

"I know."

Lt. Cavanarro struggled to his feet and peered down the alley in the direction his abductors had walked. With his hands still cuffed behind his back, he crouched down to pick up his gym bag, and limped in the opposite direction as fast as he could go. The sickening smell of his own excrement filled his nostrils. His body was racked with pain, and felt as if he'd been hit by a truck. The rage he felt for the men who had assaulted him, and the need to extract revenge on Stevens fueled his tortured walk. Once he cleared the alley, he hobbled in the direction of a small Chinese restaurant that had bars over the door and windows.

Beachum walked over to the edge of the abandoned building, and looked around the corner, into the alley. "He's gone. I wasn't sure if he was going to make it out of here or not," he said with a chuckle. Scott removed his ski mask and jumped in the passenger seat of the idling Jeep. Beachum got in, closed his door and gunned the accelerator.

As they began the long drive back to Bishop, Scott examined Lt. Cavanarro's pistol. He then flipped open the man's wallet, and examined his LAPD badge. "So why did we need to take these?" Scott asked.

"The gun was just to humiliate him—if he has the balls to report it missing—an officer never relinquishes his weapon," Beachum said with authority. "I thought for a moment that walking the streets of LA handcuffed with a bloody shirt, a big urine stain on his pants, and shitty underwear might embarrass him, but then again, that's probably not an unusual sight down here." The two men laughed at the mental image of Cavanarro's journey. "The badge? I figure we can use that down the road when we go about getting your name cleared. No way you could have that in your possession if Cavanarro wasn't involved."

Beachum grinned as he drove. "I'll tell ya, son...I haven't felt an adrenaline rush like that in about thirty years." It was obvious he felt a sense of personal satisfaction at accomplishing their mission plan.

"The way you handled him in the parking lot of the gym—I mean just took him out—that was pretty incredible!"

"I told you not to doubt a Ranger, boy," he said, giving Scott a wink. "But seriously, I'm glad I didn't kill him...I'm a little rusty, and...you don't execute one of those blows correctly, or apply too much force, it's light's out, if you know what I mean."

"He apparently had just enough left to get out of there."

"No thanks to you kicking him in the balls!" Beachum said, enjoying the moment.

"Sorry, I couldn't help myself," Scott shrugged with a grin. "So what's our next move?"

"We don't have to move next. Remember what I said about using leverage to accomplish what we want. Well, we've just dispatched a coward who will—if I've got this figured out—make the next move for us."

CHAPTER 43

AFTER A PHONE CALL to his ex-partner, enduring the incredulous looks of the employees and patrons of the Dragon Palace Chinese restaurant, and a lot of explaining during the car ride, Lieutenant Andy Cavanarro finally made it home. His ex-partner, Howard Price, had unlocked the handcuffs with a master key, and supplied Andy with a cigarette. The nicotine did nothing to quell the pain shooting through his battered body.

Price tried in vain to extract details from Cavanarro about what had happened to him. He also offered to take Andy to the emergency room, but the Lieutenant wanted to go home and clean up first. He assured Howard that he would get his wife to take him. Price helped Cavanarro from his car and to the front door of his house. He rummaged through Andy's gym bag, found his keys, and opened the door.

He then helped Cavanarro through the door and into the living room. "Marie?" he yelled out. "Marie? Are you home?"

"She's probably still out," Andy grunted, hobbling alongside Howard. "Just help me back to the bathroom." Once they reached the master bedroom, Cavanarro told Price he could leave, and implored him not to mention a word of this to their colleagues. He told him that he would be fine, and that Marie would take him to the hospital to get checked out. Howard Price nodded soberly, and promised to check on him later.

        *   *   *

    MARIE CAVANARRO entered her home through the garage and walked into the kitchen. She dumped a handful of mail on the counter next to the sink, and poured herself a glass of water. A noise coming from the back of the house startled her. Andy's car was not in the garage, but she called out his name anyway, "Andy?"

    A barely audible voice responded. "It's me, Marie. I need your help."

    She walked quickly to the master bedroom. She was taken aback by the trail of bloody clothes leading to the bathroom. Slowly following the stained garments, she then screamed at what she saw next, inadvertently dropping her glass and sending pieces of the shattered glass across the tile floor. Andy was naked, sitting slumped on the closed toilet seat, leaning against the wall. His nose was horribly swollen and his eyes were bruised and blood-shot. His right knee was aligned at a grotesque angle, and appeared to be about the size of a basketball. She was now shaking uncontrollably and tears were running down her cheeks.

    "Don't cry, Marie. I need you to take me to the emergency room."

    "Have you been shot?" she whispered through quivering lips.

    "No, no. Just banged up a little. I'm okay…I just need to go…now, please." Kicking aside the shards of glass on the floor, she slowly approached her husband and leaned over to help him stand. He put his arm around her for support. In the bedroom, she helped him into a pair of underwear and a nylon-jogging suit. She removed a pair of flip-flops from the closet and slid them on his feet. She cautiously assisted the beaten man from the house and into her car. Marie then focused all her energies on staying calm and driving to the emergency room as fast as she could.

        *   *   *

WITH A CANE in one hand, and a brown paper grocery sack in the other, Lieutenant Cavanarro slowly made his way up the front steps of Campbell Industries. The attractive, blonde receptionist greeted him with a perfect smile. "Good afternoon, Lieutenant." She acted unaware of the condition of his face.

"Hello, Lori," he replied, after a quick glance at the nameplate on her desk.

"Are you here to see Mr. Stevens?"

"Yes, I am."

"Do you have an appointment?"

"No, but this won't take long. Just ask him if I can have a minute of his time."

After conferring with Glenn through her headset, she smiled and said, "He'll see you now. You can go right in."

"Thank you."

Glenn Stevens walked across the great expanse of his luxurious office and met Lt. Cavanarro at the door. He quickly noticed the blackened, puffy red eyes, the cast on the man's right leg, and the cane he was using to support himself. Unseen were his testicles, now swollen the size of baseballs. "Good Lord, Andy! What in the hell happened to you?"

"Gee, Glenn, you seem genuinely surprised to see me."

"In *that* condition, yes I am."

"Your concern touches me, pal. Mind if I have a seat?"

"No, not at all," Glenn said, directing the Lieutenant to a seat in front of his desk. He then walked around his desk, and took his seat. He couldn't help but notice the tight grip Cavanarro had on the paper sack. "So tell me, what happened to you?"

"Well, I spent the majority of last evening in the emergency room getting this cast put on my leg. Seems my knee is shattered and I have severe ligament damage. I also have a broken nose, which they can't do anything about until the swelling goes down. I was able to get some rest only because of the codeine the doctor gave me. You can imagine how upset Marie is. Fun stuff, huh?"

"Wow…were you involved in breaking up a robbery or something?"

"Good one, Glenn. You almost sound believable. I bet you are surprised to see me, though. I was going to be a smart-ass, and say something like, don't send boys to do a man's job, but your men were good, especially the old one. I didn't know you knew people like that, pal."

"My men? I don't know what you're talking about."

"You mean they didn't even call you to tell you they fucked up and I got away?"

"This isn't funny, Andy. If you think I had something to do with this…"

"Shut up! Do you think I'm stupid? They had the gun I gave you, dumb-ass." Lt. Cavanarro glanced at his watch. It was almost five o'clock. "When do all these slackers clear out of this place?"

"Around five…why? And what do you mean, 'they had the gun?'"

"You can cut the innocent crap! Is your little gay buddy, fat-boy still here?"

"Fat-boy? Uh, do you mean Jon Cassler?"

"Cassler—that's it."

"Yeah, he should still be in…"

"Call him. Tell him to get his fat ass in your office. I have something I need to discuss with both of you." Glenn did as he was told, and after a little whining about the hour, Cassler agreed to come to Glenn's office.

Cassler opened the door, looked at Lt. Cavanarro, and asked in a smart aleck manner, "You get hit by a bus?"

"Shut the door, shithead! And close the blinds to all the windows." Cassler looked at Stevens, wondering what to make of this greeting. Glenn nodded his head, assuring Jon it was all right to follow the Lieutenant's instructions. Once he completed his assignment, he almost took the seat next to Cavanarro, thought better of it, and walked behind Glenn's desk and stood next to him.

"I tell you one thing, Glenn," Cavanarro snarled. "You have more balls than I ever gave you credit for, pal."

"Andy, seriously, I don't know…"

"Shut up! I'll tell you when to speak." Cassler looked at Stevens nervously, as Cavanarro removed a hand-held tape recorder from his paper bag. "I want you to say you killed Maria Lopez, after I turn this thing on."

"What? You killed Maria Lopez?" Cassler blurted.

"Shut up, Jon!" He turned and looked imploringly at the Lieutenant. "What's this all about Andy?"

Cavanarro then removed a pistol from the bag, slowly pulled back the hammer and aimed it directly at Stevens. "Don't piss me off, dickhead! When you hear this thing click on, you say what I told you."

Cold sweat was running down under Glenn's arms as he watched the cop fumble with the recorder. In his peripheral vision, he noticed the heavy perspiration forming on Cassler's forehead and upper lip. "Andy, if this is about money, I can…"

"You do exactly as I say, or I'm gonna blow your fuckin' head off. Are we clear?"

"Crystal," Stevens replied anxiously. Cavanarro turned on the recorder and waved it threateningly at Glenn. He held the pistol steady with the other hand. Stevens cleared his throat and said, "I killed Maria Lopez."

The Lieutenant tuned off the unit and barked, "How did you kill her, and what did you do with the body? Say it in the recorder!"

Glenn heard the clicking sound and saw the red RECORD L.E.D. illuminate. "I strangled Maria. I, uh…then I put her in the warehouse dumpster. Pacific Sanitation takes all our uh, waste to an incinerator. That's about it."

Cavanarro clicked off the recorder and smiled ominously. "Good job, asshole. Now I want you to confess to the murder of Miss LeDoux and the frame-up of Murphy."

Andy turned the tape recorder back on and held it in front of Stevens. "I also murdered Lisa LeDoux…strangulation, again. I then…I took her body to Scott Murphy's apartment…left it there…trying to frame him for her murder."

Cavanarro turned the hand-held recorder off and walked over to Glenn's bar. "You're doing excellent work, pal. Mind if I fix myself a drink?"

"No, by all means, Andy." Stevens looked at Cassler, who was obviously gravely concerned at the proceedings.

Regina's voice on the intercom broke in, "Glenn? This is Regina. I'm on my way out—you and Jon are the last guys in the office. Do you want me to lock you in?"

Stevens looked at Cavanarro, who shook his head no. "No, that's okay Regina. We'll be leaving soon. See you in the morning."

"Goodnight," she replied. Seconds later they heard her heels click past his door as she left the building.

Stevens watched Cavanarro return to his seat with his Wild Turkey on the rocks. He took a deep breath, and tried to speak calmly. "Okay, Andy, I don't know what happened to you, or why you're so angry with me, but I…"

"Did I ask you a question?" Andy barked.

"No…"

"Then shut the fuck up! Okay, sweetheart, you're up."

"Who? Me?" Cassler asked, pointing to himself.

"Yes, you, you limp-wristed, fat sack of shit!"

"Lieutenant," Cassler protested, "I don't know where you get your information, but you couldn't be any more wrong…"

"Just shut up, princess, and say what I tell you to. Okay?" Cassler looked at Stevens for direction, but Glenn wouldn't make eye contact. "Now, I want you to explain how you witnessed Glenn shoot Murphy."

"Okay," Cassler began, "we drove up to…"

"When I turn on the recorder, you dip-shit!"

Cavanarro clicked on the tape, and Cassler nervously said, "I, uh…I, I followed Glenn out to some remote area—I don't even know where in the hell we were—it was on Highway 395, that's all I know…like I said, I was following him. I was driving Murphy's car—same kind of car my *wife* has, for your information—and I…f-followed him, Glenn Stevens, and uh…" Lt. Cavanarro waved the pistol in a circular motion and scowled at Cassler, pleading him to get to the point. "Okay…so, um…we parked and got Murphy out of the car and, uh, we removed the handcuffs you gave us…"

"Son of a bitch!" Cavanarro yelled as he shut off the recorder. "You don't mention *anything* about me! Got it?" He glared at the two men as he re-wound the tape, listened to it, erased the portion he wanted deleted, listened to it again for verification and turned off the unit. He took another long drink of Wild Turkey as he reached in his shirt pocket, fumbling for his pain medication. He opened the plastic, amber container with his teeth, shook a couple of pills into his mouth, replaced the cap and returned it to his pocket. He washed down the pills with another swig of the bourbon. "Okay where were we? You removed Murphy from the car, and, action!"

The recorder was turned on as Cassler continued. "Murphy was on the ground—tied up—and Glenn had the gun…" Cavanarro frowned at him as if to remind him not to mention the source of the pistol "…Glenn had the g-gun, and…" Now Glenn was staring at Cassler in threatening manner. "…and, uh, he…he gave it to me. I shot him Murphy—in the head. Twice."

Cavanarro turned off the hand-held tape player and set it on desk. *You shot him? I guess you couldn't do it, huh, Glenn? Killing girls is more your specialty, huh pal? Well, anyway, good job, you little ass-wipe." He then dictated a note, at gunpoint, for type on his PC and print out on his printer.

"Oh, c'mon, Andy. You've got to be kidding," Stevens said i typing the words he was told to. "Is this really necessary?"

"Hey, you upped the ante, pal. Now just do what I tell you, unless you want me to pop you right now."

"What guarantees do I have that you won't *pop* me later, anyway?" Glenn inquired with a trace of anxiety in his voice.

"The way my fucking leg is throbbing right now? Absolutely none."

Lt. Cavanarro picked up the brown, paper grocery sack and threw it at Stevens. Glenn flinched as the bag hit him, but then quickly realized it must be empty. "Look Andy, I think you're terribly mistaken about something," Glenn pleaded. "If there's a problem, I'm confident we can make some arrangement to work it out." Glenn gave Andy his most trusting look.

"So am I," Cavanarro said mockingly, finishing the glass of Wild Turkey. "Now, I want you boys to strip down—buck naked—I've got a little surprise for you. And Cassler, you're gonna *love* this."

*   *   *

MARIE CAVANARRO looked on in dismay as her husband hobbled through the door that evening. "I can't believe you went to work today! Remember what the doctor said…"

"Yeah, yeah, yeah. I just had a few loose ends I had to tie up, babe." He limped past her leaning on his cane. "I'm gonna hit the rack. I'm beat."

"What about dinner?"

"I'm good. I grabbed a bite."

"Do you need any help getting undressed?"

"I don't think so," he said from the bedroom. "But I'll let you know."

"Honey, I know you'll think this is strange of me to ask," she said following him to the back of the house. "I did laundry today—your clothes from yesterday were such a mess—and when I was putting it away, I noticed some of my lingerie was missing…"

"Last time I had it on, I put it back where I got it," he said humorously.

Marie laughed, and said, "Oh, who knows, I'm sure it'll turn up. Did you take your medicine, Andy?"

"Yes, Mother."

CHAPTER 44

REGINA ROGERS thought she would be the first at the office, but was surprised to see Glenn's Mercedes and Jon's SUV already in the parking lot of Campbell Industries. She parked and hurried up the steps, figuring those two would be screaming for coffee.

The front doors were still locked, so she let herself in with her key. She often would lock the door behind herself if she was all alone in the building; but thought it strange that Glenn and Jon would do the same first thing in the morning. Walking past Glenn's office, she noticed the light was on, but the door and the window blinds were closed. She flipped on the hallway light, dropped her purse off at her workstation, and headed for the break room to get the coffee started.

An hour and a half had passed since she arrived, and the office was now humming with activity. Glenn's boss, Mr. Schillace in New Orleans, was on the phone, and urgently wanted to speak with him. Regina tried his intercom twice, but received no answer. She apologized to Mr. Schillace, put him on hold, and headed down the corridor to Glenn's office. She knocked on the door, and didn't hear anything. Knowing Glenn might explode at her interrupting, she decided to stick her head in the door anyway, knowing an apology from him would be forthcoming when he realized Mr. Schillace was on the phone. Just doing my job, she thought.

Regina knocked again, and opened the door slowly. "Glenn, I'm so sorry to disturb you, but Mr. Schil..." Regina momentarily froze, and was overcome with conflicting thoughts of passing out or throwing up. She was completely shocked by the sight before her. Glenn Stevens and Jon Cassler were both lying motionless on the floor of the office, each with a halo of thick, dark liquid surrounding their heads. Glenn was holding a pistol in his claw-like hand. She then realized her initial sense of shock was not from seeing the two men dead on the floor, but from finding them both decked out in nothing but women's lingerie!

She noticed a small cassette recorder on Glenn's desk, next to a sheet of paper. She walked along the wall, leaving as much space between herself and the bodies as possible. Careful not to touch anything, she leaned over the desk, and scanned the note. It outlined Glenn's confession of the murders of Maria Lopez, Lisa LeDoux, and Cassler's admission to murdering Scott Murphy. It then concluded with the sentiment that the guilt was too much for the two of them to bear, along with their refusal to go on living a lie, and not being able to express their long-standing homosexual love affair openly to a cruel and judgmental corporate world that would not understand their tormented love, or their desire to express themselves as they truly were. It then stated that Maria, Lisa and Scott had to be killed, because they had discovered the two men's secret, and had threatened to expose them, jeopardizing their careers and families. So, apparently Glenn killed Jon in a previously agreed upon murder-suicide pact.

Regina carefully left the office, closed the door, and returned to her desk. She immediately phoned 9-1-1, and gave the operator the details and their address. She noticed the hold light flashing, and picked up an irritated Mr. Schillace at home office. She diplomatically explained to him that a tragic accident had taken place—involving Glenn Stevens and Jon Cassler—and that she had just called 9-1-1 for assistance. She also suggested that it would be prudent for him to catch the next flight to LA. Hanging up the phone, she picked up her card file, and flipped to

L, for LAPD. Lieutenant Cavanarro's card was on top. She looked at it for a moment, thought better of it, and then flipped it over to reveal the card of Sergeant Mike Harris. She dialed the number, and was immediately connected to Sgt. Harris.

*   *   *

SGT. HARRIS arrived, along with Jeff Davis and his Crime Lab Unit. The paramedics were already in the room, and informed the Sergeant that both men were dead, and awaited instructions. He told them to hang out for a little while, grab a cup of coffee, and he would let them know when they could move the bodies. Stepping behind Glenn's desk, he pulled on a pair of latex gloves. He read the letter and listened to the taped confession of the two men. When he thought Davis wasn't looking, Harris pulled a Ziploc bag from his coat and emptied a chrome plated, car cigarette lighter into the middle desk drawer. He looked up, and noticed Regina standing in the doorway, observing his actions. Harris smiled at her, stepped from behind the desk, and joined her in the hallway, closing the door behind them. "You're probably wondering what you saw me put in his desk?"

"I was curious, yes."

"Well, that was the cigarette lighter from Maria Lopez's car. It had some human skin on it—DNA—I figure it'll match Glenn Stevens. So if you think I'm planting evidence, well, see, Lieutenant Cavanarro wouldn't listen to me and all the facts I had surrounding the Lopez case—it was like he was covering for Stevens—so, I just thought I'd leave that behind and let the boys in the Crime Lab Unit take a sample from Stevens, and then we'll know for sure…"

"It's all right," Regina said, trying to reassure the Sergeant. "I'm on your side." She handed him a folded tissue. He opened it to find a woman's gold-plated clip-on earring. "It was Maria's. I found it in Glenn's office the morning after she disappeared. Don't ask me why I didn't mention it sooner, I was scared, or stupid, or both. Anyway, I thought it might help your case if you were to *find* it in his office. I can testify that I've seen Maria wear it.

"Thanks, Ms. Rogers."

"Don't thank me, I'm just glad that this nightmare is over."

"Yes, ma'am. I'm just curious about one other thing…"

"What's that?"

"On the phone you said you decided to call me and not Lt. Cavanarro. Why?"

"I think he's involved in all this too, but I'll let you figure that one out. I can tell you that he was in Glenn's office last night—with Jon Cassler—*after* all the employees had left for the day."

"Isn't that interesting. Thanks, Ms. Rogers."

"If I can help with anything else, please let me know."

"If you can keep the employees away from this office—maybe make them use the rear entrance to the building—that would help a lot."

"Will do." Regina smiled knowingly at the Sergeant, and walked down the hall as if a huge burden had been lifted from her shoulders. It had.

*   *   *

TWO DAYS AFTER the bodies of Glenn Stevens and Jon Cassler were found at Campbell Industries in Commerce, Scott Murphy sat at the dining table in Beachum's log cabin, reading the newspapers before him, over and over again. Beachum was stretched out in his recliner, in front of a roaring fire, listening to an old Patsy Cline album. Scott looked over at the relaxed man with great respect. He had told Scott to have a little patience, stick to the plan, and everything would fall into place. He admired how Beachum was able to separate emotion from logic, and piece together a way to clear Scott's name. The old guy was something else.

The articles in the papers went into great detail about the crime scene, the taped and written confessions, even the apparent sexual preference of the two men found at the office. Beachum told Scott it was the obvious work of Lt. Cavanarro—they had simply leveraged the predictable acts of a coward—and that there was no way those two dressed up in bras and panties and ended it on their own.

Scott noticed that Sgt. Harris was quoted extensively in the coverage. He was confident they had solved the Maria Lopez murder—with Glenn's taped and written confession. He disclosed that an earring was found in Glenn's desk, and confirmed by none other than Regina Rogers as one she had seen Maria last wear on the day of her disappearance. Sgt. Harris also cited several witnesses placing Glenn at a convenience store across the street from Lopez's apartment on the night she disappeared. A Coastal cab driver had picked up a man there that night, matching Glenn's description, and delivered him to the Commerce Business Park. The last bit of damning evidence was Glenn's DNA matching skin found on the cigarette lighter from Maria's car—apparently he had hidden it in his desk all this time. Scott vaguely remembered seeing what could have been a burn mark caused by a car's cigarette lighter, on Glenn's neck, back during his first week at work.

Glenn's DNA also matched tissue that was found under Lisa's fingernails. Both Judge LeDoux and Mrs. LeDoux were quoted as saying how relieved they were that the true identity of their daughter's killer had been solved. They also expressed great remorse at the murder of Scott Murphy, were greatly upset at the LAPD for ever listing him as a suspect, were apologetic that they ever suspected him capable of such a heinous act, talked about what a fine young man he was, and sent their condolences to Scott's family. They truly were good people, Scott thought, and had to be suffering enormously, dealing with the loss of their only child.

Scott also took great pleasure in reading that Lt. Cavanarro was being held as an accessory to murder, for helping Stevens cover up the Lopez and the LeDoux murders. It seemed that Sgt. Harris discovered several large withdrawals from one of Glenn's bank accounts, and matching deposits—on the same days—into Cavanarro's accounts. Bribery with a capital 'B.' Scott figured he could add to the Lieutenant's list of charges.

So the only remaining mystery in this bizarre case was the location of Scott Murphy's body. The confessions left in Glenn's office were not specific about location, only that it was somewhere in the wilderness, and that he'd been shot twice in the head. Scott read and re-read the comments that were said about him, in sort of a memorial tribute. His co-workers at Campbell Industries: Allen Goldman, Regina Rogers, Kevin Forrester, Jimmy Brady, Darrin Johnson, Jerry Fujisaka, Toni Hemmings—even Tim Newsom, Janet Carter, Marvin Beadles and Lori Johnson—had nothing but exemplary things to say about him.

Michael Schillace, President and CEO, issued a brief, sanitized statement offering the condolences of Campbell Industries to all the victim's families that read as if it had the approval of the legal department. He also stated that Campbell Industries was in the process of setting up a college fund for Rosie Lopez, Maria's daughter. Scott hoped that the little girl had a good lawyer to get more than just her college covered. After all, she had lost her mother, and Campbell had deep pockets.

He choked up reading everything his mother and sister had said, about losing a son and a brother. But his father's comments were the most surprising. First of all, he was shocked that his old man would even talk to reporters, but the pride with which he spoke about his son's accomplishments and the kind of man he had turned out to be, made him sob uncontrollably the first few times he read it. During these outbursts, Beachum would nonchalantly go outside, as if he suddenly had to check on something.

Later that evening, after confirming with Beachum that the time was right, Scott sat next to the telephone and opened his wallet. Locating the business card of Sgt. Mike Harris, he turned it over and dialed the handwritten number on the back.

CHAPTER 45

THE NEXT MORNING, Sgt. Mike Harris made the long drive up 395 to Bishop. Following Scott's directions, he found Beachum's secluded log cabin. He admired the craftsmanship of the structure as he approached the front door.

He was greeted by Scott, who introduced him to Mr. Langston Beachum. Beachum gave Harris a firm handshake and invited him to come inside.

Seated at the dining room table, Sgt. Harris listened intently and took voluminous notes as Scott told him about finding Lisa dead in his apartment and being ambushed by Glenn Stevens. As Beachum looked on, Scott went into detail about escaping from Stevens and Jon Cassler when they tried to stage a suicide in his car; and how he contacted Lt. Cavanarro. Sgt. Harris was writing furiously as Scott explained how Cavanarro cuffed him and turned him over to Stevens and Cassler. He then described how Cassler shot him—under duress from Stevens—with a gun provided by Cavanarro.

Beachum now spoke, and told Harris how he witnessed the attempted execution of Scott. He went into vivid detail about pulling a still breathing, but unconscious Scott into his car, and checking him into the hospital under his name.

Scott jumped in and breathlessly enumerated Beachum's plan to nab Cavanarro, making it appear as if they were acting on direct orders from

Stevens. During this part of the discussion, Beachum retrieved the .25-caliber pistol that Cassler had shot Scott with, as Scott explained how they threatened Cavanarro with the same gun. It was unloaded, and Harris looked at it with awe as he pieced together the story the two men were sharing with him. He was then presented with the Lieutenant's badge and .38.

Harris scribbled a few more notes, put down his pen, and reviewed his text—making sure he had not omitted any pertinent information.

"So you're telling me that when Cavanarro thought Stevens had turned on him—ordering his murder—he, Cavanarro, went and took them out, staging a murder-suicide scenario at the office?"

Beachum nodded solemnly. "That's what happened...a little exercise in 'thinning the herd.' But you'd probably have a hell of a time proving it. Cavanarro's a pro, and I'm betting he did a good job covering his tracks. Personally, I thought the taped confessions was a nice touch."

"You're probably right, sir. But we already have him nailed as a willing accomplice, obstructing the investigations of the Lopez and LeDoux murders. And now, we have him as an accessory to Scott's attempted murder."

"I'd say if you boys dot the I's and cross the T's, you've probably got enough to put him away for quite a while," Beachum said with an air of authority. "Just make damn sure he goes to prison—they *love* cops in prison."

Sgt. Harris concluded the meeting by telling Scott that it was okay, if he was ready, to re-enter society. That wasn't good enough for Beachum, who demanded the sergeant's word that Scott was cleared and no longer a suspect. Harris gave him his word, and the two men shook hands again.

Scott thought about this for a moment, and told them he'd probably call his parents first; then contact Lisa's parents. His next call would be to Allen Goldman at Campbell Industries, to let him know he was alive and well. Scott then said that he'd like to fly to Memphis and New

Orleans. Beachum remarked that he would bet Campbell Industries would be more than happy to pick up his tab. Harris offered to go along—if it would help to have him explain what had happened—from an "official" perspective.

*   *   *

THE WESTERN REGION OFFICE of Campbell Industries was the setting for Scott's first back from the dead appearance. He entered the building, thinking that at one point he never expected to see this place again. At the front desk, he had to tell Lori who he was—she didn't recognize him with a crew cut and beard—and she rushed around the receptionist's station and gave him a long hug. When she pulled away, Scott was surprised at the volume of tears streaming down her pretty face.

He passed Glenn's sealed office, and momentarily felt nauseous at the thought of the man. Halfway down the hall he saw Regina, who rushed forward and greeted him with a heartfelt hug. As she stepped back, Scott noticed Allen standing next to them. He slapped Scott on the back and shook his hand vigorously. He put his arm around Scott and led him down the quiet hallway.

Inside Allen's office, he apologized profusely to Scott for everything he had been through, because of his association with this company. After Scott assured Allen several times that he didn't hold him responsible, Allen caught him up on the latest at Campbell. First of all, Allen had been promoted to Regional VP. Scott was genuinely happy for him, feeling it would take someone with Allen's even-handed leadership style to salvage the operation. He then informed Scott that Mr. Schillace had approved his request to fly to New Orleans and Memphis, and that Scott was still considered a valuable employee of Campbell Industries. When in New Orleans, Mr. Schillace would like to meet with him personally, he was told.

Allen told Scott he was putting his new team together, and would like him to be his new Sales Manager for the LA County territory. Scott was flattered, but told Allen he'd have to think about it. Allen told him to take all the time he needed.

Leaving Allen's office, he heard a voice from behind inquire, *"Scott? Dude, is that you?"*

Scott turned around to see his friend Kevin Forrester staring at him as if he'd seen a ghost. "It's me, Kev."

"Man, you look like friggin' Grizzly Adams."

"My new look."

"How are you holding up?"

"The best I can."

"All this shit is so unbelievable! Oh, and man, I'm sorry about Lisa."

"Thanks. Me, too."

"You comin' back to work?"

"I don't know yet." He extended his hand to Kevin, but it was ignored as Kevin embraced him and slapped him on the back several times.

Now Kevin was becoming misty-eyed. "If there's anything I can do for you, just let me know."

"I appreciate it. I will."

              *   *   *

THE NORTHWEST FLIGHT from LAX to Memphis went smoothly. During the flight, Mike Harris shared the news that he had been promoted to Detective. Scott congratulated him, and told him he was really deserving.

They rented a car on Campbell's dime, took I-240 to the Perkins Road exit and proceeded to Scott's parent's house. They were absolutely stunned when he phoned them three nights ago. It took some persuading to prove to his mom it wasn't some kind of a sick joke. Once they all got over their shock, they seemed relieved and excited to learn that he was coming home.

The rented Chrysler Cirrus rolled to a stop in front of the Murphy house. His mother burst from the front door, ran across the small Bermuda grass lawn, and jumped in his arms. She was laughing and crying simultaneously. She was followed by his sister, who repeated the same greeting. Scott introduced them to Det. Mike Harris, who was also greeted with hugs and tears. As the three walked arm-in-arm to the house, Scott's mother couldn't resist letting him know much she disliked his beard.

Scott noticed his father standing in the doorway. He said hello to his father as he approached, but his dad didn't respond. When he entered the house and came face to face with the man, he noticed that he was too choked up to speak, and had tears forming in his eyes. He hugged his father for the first time in over twenty years.

Over the next three hours, Scott and Det. Harris fielded questions while filling them in on everything that had happened to Scott. His sister, Kathy, expressed sincere sympathy for Lisa and her family. And for her brother's loss.

Mrs. Murphy insisted Det. Harris join them for dinner and spend the night, but he politely declined, explaining that he had already committed to spending the night with his cousin, in Collierville.

*   *   *

IN THE MORNING, as he was preparing to leave, Scott's father leaned against the doorframe of his room.

"So, you think you'll be moving back home, son?"

"I don't think so, Dad."

"You're not seriously thinking about going back to work for that bunch of corrupt bastards in LA are you?"

"No, sir."

"Then why don't you move back home?"

"I've decided to take your advice, and learn a trade."

"What? And give up the suit and tie?"

"Seriously, Dad…I think I've had my fill of big business—I'm gonna try my hand at wood-working—custom furniture, that sort of thing. I told you about Mr. Beachum…"

"Yes."

"Well, he's offered me a chance to go to work for him—up in Bishop—*not* LA."

"Wood-working, huh?"

"I've picked up a little already, but I've got a lot to learn. Anyway, whaddaya think?" Scott shot a sincere look at his father, wanting to receive his approval.

"Sounds like you've thought this out."

"I've even decided what my first project will be—I'm going to make you a rocking chair—for your retirement."

"But that's ten years away!"

"Obviously, you've forgotten how good I am with tools. It'll probably take me that long to get it finished."

The two men laughed together for a moment, and then stood in silence. His father put a hand on his shoulder and looked him in the eyes. "If I can ever help, let me know. I'm really proud of you, son."

"Thanks, Dad. That means a lot to me."

They embraced briefly for the second time in two days. "Be sure and write and visit when you get the chance…it means a lot to your Mother."

"I will, Dad. I promise."

*   *   *

THE RENTED BUICK cruised through the shady streets of the Garden District. Scott could tell Det. Harris was impressed with the stately homes. He felt a confusing mix of emotions as he pulled into the LeDoux's circular driveway.

The maid answered the door, and led the two men into the great room. Judge LeDoux greeted Scott warmly, followed by his wife and mother. He introduced the family to Detective Mike Harris. Judge & Mrs. LeDoux apologized to Scott for everything they had said about him to the press; and anything they might have thought about him. Scott assured them both that no apology was necessary, and if he'd been in their shoes, he would have reacted the same way. After all, the case against him appeared to be pretty solid, he told them. The widow LeDoux stated emphatically that she *never* believed Scott had anything to do with Lisa's murder. Scott gave Lisa's grandmother a hug.

Scott found it hard to look at Mrs. LeDoux because of her striking resemblance to Lisa. She looked tired, and was obviously still grieving from the loss of her daughter. Det. Harris offered his condolences, and explained, refraining from graphic detail, about how Lisa's murder had taken place. Judge LeDoux listened solemnly, patting his wife on the hand to comfort her. Mrs. LeDoux dabbed at her eyes with a tissue.

*   *   *

JUDGE LeDOUX'S MERCEDES drove slowly through the wrought iron gates of Lafayette Cemetery. He parked on the right hand side, and walked around to open his wife's door. Scott let himself out of the back seat.

They walked a short distance, and Scott spotted the large crypt with the LeDOUX name engraved in the stone. Judge LeDoux's father, Donald, Sr., was buried here along with Lisa. The large tomb obviously had enough room for the remaining family members.

They walked to the back of the above ground structure, so Scott could read the engraved words: LISA LeDOUX, LOVING DAUGHTER. HEAVEN NEEDED ANOTHER ANGEL. Instead of being overcome with grief, sadness, or anger; Scott felt a strange sense of calmness wash over him, as he rubbed his hand across the letters inscribed on the stone.

*　　　　　　　*　　　　　　　*

AS THEIR VISIT was ending, the LeDoux family told both Scott and Det. Harris that they were welcome to return any time. Mrs. LeDoux presented Scott with a lovely framed picture of Lisa. He thanked her, and shared with them his intentions of proposing to Lisa on St. Valentine's Day. He told them how much he loved and respected their daughter, and what a special person she was. Judge LeDoux smiled, and knowingly told Scott that Lisa would have said yes. And how proud they would have been to have him as a son-in-law.

Mrs. LeDoux sobbed softly, as her husband wrapped a large arm around her small shoulders. She told Scott, that as far as she was concerned, he would always be part of their family. She then asked him for a favor—that if he were to ever marry and have children, if it would be possible for she and her husband to be surrogate grandparents? Scott choked up when he heard this—told her he had no intentions of getting married—and couldn't imagine ever feeling again the way he felt about her daughter. She told him not to close himself off to miracles. He smiled, and replied that he had been the recipient of similar advice, not long ago.

CHAPTER 46

THE NEXT MORNING Scott entered the corporate office of Campbell Industries, escorted by Det. Mike Harris. Scott was clean-shaven, and wearing a suit for the first time since his abduction. It didn't feel right.

Michael Schillace, President and CEO, greeted him as if he were a conquering war hero, returning home from battle. After praising Scott and Det. Harris for all their courage and bravery, he began to apologize to Scott on behalf of his organization. He also wanted to know if Scott had given serious consideration to Allen Goldman's offer to stay on as his LA Sales Manager. Scott told him that Allen was a good man, and that he'd made a wise choice in promoting him. He also informed him that he was not accepting the promotion officer, and would be submitting his resignation to Allen when he returned to California.

Schillace pleaded with Scott not to be hasty; and to take all the time he needs. He then slid a typed document in front of Scott, and requested his signature at the bottom. RELEASE OF ALL CLAIMS was printed boldly at the top. The legalese stated that Scott would hereby release, acquit and forever discharge Campbell Industries of and from any and all actions, causes of action, claims, demands, damages, costs, loss of services, expenses and compensation, on account of, or in any way growing out of, any and all known and unknown personal injuries and property damage resulting or to result from accident that occurred at or near Bishop, California, while in the employment of Campbell

Industries, Inc., of New Orleans, LA. This agreement is for and in consideration of the payment at this time of the sum of TWO MILLION, FIVE HUNDRED THOUSAND AND XX/100—Dollars ($2,500,000.00) PAYABLE TO SCOTT MURPHY, resident of Long Beach, CA.

Scott read the document twice, and handed it to Det. Harris. Harris read it, and suggested Scott contact an attorney. Schillace interrupted, and pointed out that an attorney would take at least a third of the settlement offer. He then stated coldly, that this offer was null and void after twenty-four hours, and that he was prepared to give Scott a cashier's check immediately.

Scott thought about his proposal for several moments, and rubbed the scar tissue on his scalp as he read the settlement document one more time. He, nodded at Harris, moved to the edge of his seat, squared his shoulders and stared at Schillace for a full minute without saying a word. He took a deep breath, and finally said, "Cut the check."

*   *   *

AFTER COLLECTING their luggage from the LAX baggage claim carousal, Scott followed Det. Harris to his car. Scott asked Harris to stop at his bank, promising not to be long. He gladly agreed, and waited in the car while Scott went inside. He caused quite a commotion among the bank employees as he deposited the $2.5 million dollar cashier's check into his savings account, and requested the withdrawal of one hundred thousand dollars. After thirty minutes involving numerous questions, requests for ID, phone calls and slobbery thanks from several bank VPs, the transaction was completed.

*   *   *

DETECTIVE HARRIS made a quick call to directory assistance on his cell phone, trying to locate the nearest Jeep dealership. Once there, he offered to wait, but Scott assured him that he would be able to secure a ride back to Bishop. He thanked Mike for all his help and going to the trouble of making this trip with him. They both promised to keep in touch.

Scott walked up and down a row of gleaming Jeep Grand Cherokees. He liked the new body style. He stopped in front of a champagne colored model and reviewed the sticker on the window. It was loaded to the gills. A salesman approached, and tried unsuccessfully to make small talk. Scott offered him thirty-thousand for the Jeep. The salesman laughed, and pointed out that the sticker price was thirty-eight and change. Scott pulled out thirty thousand dollars in bundles of one hundred dollar bills and laid them on the hood. He suggested the salesman go see his sales manager, and let him know that this offer would only be good for ten minutes. The car salesman anxiously sprinted across the lot and into the showroom. Three minutes later, he returned, followed by the smiling General Manager. The GM handed Scott the keys as the salesman collected the stacks of currency off the vehicle.

*   *   *

THE DRIVE TO BISHOP went quickly, as Scott experimented with the Jeep's sound system, intoxicated by the new car smell. He saw Beachum on a stepladder, working in front of his shop, as he parked the shiny SUV. He quickly noticed that the project Beachum was undertaking was hanging a new shingle in front of the store that read: BEACHUM & MURPHY WOOD WORKING.

"I see you shaved off the beard."

"Yeah, my Mom didn't think too much of it."

"How's the family?"

"Good. Lisa's too."

"Good. I'm sure they were all relieved to see you alive and well."

"It was a good trip."

"You didn't have to rent a car," Beachum said as he stepped down off the ladder. "I would've picked you up."

"I didn't rent it. I bought it," Scott said with a grin.

"You bought it? What do you need with another car?"

"It's not for me," Scott said as he tossed the keys to the old man.

"What? You've got to be kidding. Scott, I can't accept this."

"Hey, don't ruin this for me. Giving away a car makes me feel like Elvis."

"Maybe I didn't make it clear enough, but you're not going to have this kind of money to throw around if you set up shop with me."

"The money isn't an issue," Scott said, handing Beachum a copy of the Settlement Document from Campbell Industries. "Typical corporate move, throwing money at their problems." Beachum brushed his hand across his bushy mustache as he perused the contents of the letter. "Look, this is my way of saying thanks for everything you've done for me. Besides, your old bucket of bolts is on its last leg."

"Nah, there's a lot of life left in that old girl. But it looks like you've got yourself a pretty nice nest egg. I'm happy for you. And seriously Scott, you don't owe me anything"

"That's where you're wrong," Scott said as he handed Beachum a handful of bank envelopes. "Don't be mad, but I found the receipts for my medical bills in one of your kitchen drawers—just over $65,000 dollars—how did you come up with that kind of money?"

"You know, I've put away a little for retirement…"

"Well, there's seventy grand in those envelopes, debt repaid with gratitude and interest."

"All this really isn't necessary right now."

"My Dad told me long time ago, that 'the borrower is slave to the lender.' Now you don't want me to feel like your slave do you?"

"No, I guess not. You're father's a smart man." Beachum gave Scott a quick pat on the back. "Thanks. And I'm glad you decided to come back."

"Glad to be back."

"Come inside the shop. There's somebody I want you to meet," Beachum said with a wink. They walked through the door, and triggered the cowbell. Sitting in one of Beachum's custom made rocking chairs was a very attractive blonde woman. Her legs were crossed and she was reading a magazine. When she noticed them, she stood and flashed a lovely smile. She was wearing a pink jacket over a white turtleneck, and clingy black leggings tucked into hiking boots. A black headband held her long hair back. "This is my niece—Amy—Silas's daughter."

"Nice to meet you, Scott," she said demurely.

"Nice to meet you." He turned to Beachum and said, "You didn't tell me you had a niece."

"You didn't ask. Anyway, I just wanted you to meet Amy, and I have a little surprise for you," he said, handing Scott an envelope. It had the red and blue logo of a woolly mammoth on snow skis. "You see…Amy here is a ski instructor up at Mammoth Mountain. The season's coming to an end, but I bought you a gift certificate for some lessons. Thought you might enjoy it. Might help you clear your mind, with all that you've been through."

"Have you ever been skiing before, Scott?" she asked in a perky tone.

"No, not snow skiing, just water skiing."

"It's a little different on the powder. I think you'll enjoy it, though. It's lots of fun." She smiled at the two men. "Just call me—the number's on the gift certificate—when you're ready to get started."

Okay, I will," Scott said, returning her smile. He had never seen eyes as blue as hers.

"I've got to run. It was nice meeting you, Scott. Bye Uncle L.T.," she said, giving Beachum a peck on the cheek. The cowbell clanged loudly as she walked out of the shop.

"Uncle *L.T.?*"

"Yes—that's what she calls me—always has."

"She's a very pretty girl. The two of you sure don't look like you're related."

"I'll have you know the Beachum women are very delicate creatures…and fortunately for her, she looks like her mother."

The two men shared a laugh. Scott spoke first, "Look, I appreciate what you're trying to do, but I think it's to soon for me to start thinking about dating…"

"Dating? Who said anything about dating? I didn't hear you ask her out. I was just talking about ski lessons. Then we'll see where it might lead." Beachum smiled and his eyes twinkled behind his tinted glasses. "Amy's a good girl, and I wouldn't introduce her to just anybody."

"I'm sure you wouldn't. And I appreciate it."

"If the two of you did happen to hit it off—somewhere down the road—I can't say I'd be disappointed. But enough about that for now…you want to rest up after your trip, or are you ready to get to work?"

"Actually, I am ready to get to work. I've been doing a lot of thinking about the business, and how you go to market…"

"Uh-huh," Beachum said in a dubious tone, waiting for what would follow.

"…and I've got some ideas about starting a website—with an online catalog—why limit ourselves geographically? I'd also like to load all our customer information on a database, so we could send out flyers for promotions, that sort of thing. Then, I thought we could network with shops similar to ours all across the nation and form a buying group, so we could increase our buying power and lower material costs. We could also target furniture distributors, who could sell our product…"

"Whoa, whoa, whoa, cowboy," Beachum pleaded, raising his hands to shield himself from the young man's barrage of ideas.

"What's the matter?" Scott asked, puzzled.

"You would think that after all you've been through...you'd be the last person in the world trying to 'corporatize' us."

ABOUT THE AUTHOR

photo by Tom Scott, Collierville Photography

Tom McCrory is a graduate of The University of Memphis, and has worked in various sales capacities for several FORTUNE 100 companies over the past 15-years. He is a member of the Writer's Roundtable, the Southern Writers Guild and Wicked Company Mystery Writers Group. Currently residing in Memphis with his wife and two children, he is working on his next novel, due out in 2001.

www.TomMcCrory.com